a
daughter's
secret

D0231409

Eleanor Moran is an executive producer for TV Drama. She's worked on shows ranging from *Rome* to *Being Human*, as well as being behind a number of biopics such as *Enid and Shirley* during a long career at the BBC. Eleanor grew up in North London, where she still lives. This is her fifth novel.

Also by Eleanor Moran

Stick or Twist
Mr Almost Right
Breakfast in Bed
The Last Time I Saw You

ELEANOR
MORAN
a
daughter's
secret

SIMON &
SCHUSTER

London · New York · Sydney · Toronto · New Delhi

A CBS COMPANY

First published in Great Britain in 2015 by Simon & Schuster UK Ltd.
A CBS COMPANY

Copyright © 2015 by Eleanor Moran

This book is copyright under the Berne Convention.
No reproduction without permission.
All rights reserved.

The right of Eleanor Moran to be identified as the author of this
work has been asserted by her in accordance with sections 77 and 78
of the Copyright, Designs and Patents Act, 1988.

1 3 5 7 9 10 8 6 4 2

Simon & Schuster UK Ltd
1st Floor
222 Gray's Inn Road
London
WC1X 8HB

www.simonandschuster.co.uk

Simon & Schuster Australia, Sydney
Simon & Schuster India, New Delhi

A CIP catalogue copy for this book is available
from the British Library.

Paperback ISBN: 978-1-4711-4169-0
Trade Paperback ISBN: 978-1-4711-4170-6
eBook ISBN: 978-1-4711-4171-3

This book is a work of fiction. Names, characters, places and incidents are either a
product of the author's imagination or are used fictitiously. Any resemblance
to actual people, living or dead, events or locales, is entirely coincidental.

Typeset by Hewer Text UK Ltd, Edinburgh
Printed and bound in Great Britain by CPI Group (UK) Ltd, Croydon, CR0 4YY

To my Aunt Claudia, with love

Shock cleaves me. As my eyes strip their way across the glowing screen of my phone, each of my senses separates out, develops a mind of its own. The stench of hospital-strength disinfectant almost overpowers me, my free hand shooting out to grasp hold of the frame of his hospital bed, clammy against the cold metal. I dip my head down: I can't afford to let him see this.

He's speaking now, but the blood is pounding too hard in my ears for the words to reach me. The beep, beep, beep of the ward's machines sounds like a symphony – electronic caretakers, the difference between life and death.

I force myself to look up, blindsided yet again by the sight of him. The livid bruises, his right arm suspended and band-aged. I make my voice bright and sterile. In this moment, truth is not to be trusted.

'Nothing. It's nothing for you to worry about.' I give him a flash of a smile. 'Just my mum.'

I didn't lie to you, Mia. It's the truth!! I need your help. Gemma xxx

Delete. Delete, delete, delete.

MARCH

(two months earlier)

Chapter One

It's chrome, the oven. Chrome so gleaming and polished I can see every last crack and crevice of my face. I peer critically at my nose, the tiny train track of a scar that skitters down the centre a lifelong testament to my dubious skills at riding a two-wheeler. Just for a second, I wonder how I could erase it.

Marcus looms up behind me, filling the frame. I spin on my heels, caught out. This is the fourteenth flat: my nose is really not the point. Everything about Marcus is big; his broad shoulders, his expanse of chest bursting out of his well-cut suit like a superhero with an office job. He's fifty-four, nearly twenty years my senior, and he looks like he's juiced every one of them, but somehow it adds to his appeal. He doesn't hide his greys under a sneaky rinse of Just For Men, he lets them add to his handsome authority. He wears his narrow-framed black glasses, they don't wear him. For Marcus, life does exactly what you tell it to do.

'Sorry, darling, I'm an unpunctual dick,' he says, powering across the acreage of dark-wood floor and kissing me extravagantly, oblivious to Lucy, the timid blonde estate agent who is trapped in the doorway. I'm convinced it's her first week, the way she keeps anxiously scrabbling through her too-new handbag for her phone like it's an animal that she needs to keep fed. I can't help liking her for her awkwardness: she lacks the bullet-proof determination of her brethren, all of whom behave as if renting us a home would be up there with single-handedly brokering world peace. Her skirt and jacket pretend to match, but they don't, not really, they're different shades of black, and she's wearing a long-sleeved T-shirt underneath, as if a crisp white shirt would be too galling a surrender. It's March. I bet she graduated last summer, started out dreaming of a miraculous opening on a broadsheet or slaving away at a TV company for just her tube fares and a foot on the ladder. She thought she was too good for this job, but now she's starting to wonder if it's the other way round. I spy on her over Marcus's shoulder, her teeth worrying away at her cuticles.

'Finally!' I say, rolling my eyes at her, conspiratorial, cringing inwardly the second I've done it. Spoilt bitch, she's probably thinking. I'm off duty. I need to focus.

'So could you be mistress of all of this?' says Marcus, oblivious, swinging an expansive arm into the flat's cavernous kitchen. It's like it's his already, like it's him deigning to give Lucy a look-around – I could love him or hate him for it.

I force myself to engage, feel how the space feels, stop obsessing about what it is I've got to do today. It makes me light-headed. You could pretty much fit my whole flat into this kitchen. There's a tea towel hanging over the oven handle: I neaten the edges, move it until it sits, perfectly flush, in the centre.

'Let's do the tour,' I say, slipping my hand into Marcus's large paw, and deftly leading him away from the question.

I'm late now. I'm half running once I get off the tube, trying to avoid barrelling into the milling crowds of tourists, their worldly goods humped on their backs like they're camera-wielding tortoises. Every time I reach this door, tucked away behind Baker Street, I have to metaphorically pinch myself. It's navy blue, the paint worn, with a round brass bell to the left, an instant target for your finger. It's a tall, thin Victorian building, a maiden aunt who's fallen on hard times.

Brendan – our part-time receptionist, part-time Hollywood star in training – is bustling around the waiting room, putting out flowers and dispatching hastily abandoned coffee mugs. He's handsome, Brendan, properly handsome, twenty-six years old, with those kind of well-turned, angular features that look great on camera and make mere mortals like me feel utterly pudding-faced. He's dark-haired and olive-skinned, with soulful green-grey eyes that can make you feel like you're the only thing that matters in the entire world, when all he's asking is if you want a Very Berry smoothie from Pret. Despite all that, I don't find him in the slightest bit attractive. For me he's like an incredibly sweet and efficient work of art.

'Morning, gorgeous,' he says, jiggling a mug at me quizzically. 'Judith should still have twenty minutes, if you go straight through. Pink tea?'

I appreciate the compliment, even if I don't entirely deserve it. I'm not gorgeous per se, but I do work hard with the raw materials. My face is a bit too much of an upside-down triangle, which I offset with my masterful use of bronzer, and my long dark hair lacks the luscious bounce of a Pantene advert. I blow-dry it painstakingly, slather it with unguents, and I know how to dress in such a way that looks deceptively expensive (trust me, therapists only earn the big bucks in Beverly Hills).

'Perfect. Did you hear . . .?' I tail off, seeing his crestfallen smile. How does he stand it – all those baby-faced directors demanding he stand on one leg and mime being a tree, then sniffily telling him he 'didn't quite sell spring' to them. 'They're fools, Brendan!' I say, hurrying towards Judith's office. 'Nothing but fools!'

Judith's my supervisor, which basically makes her Yoda to my Luke. All therapists have one – a senior figure who monitors the progress of our cases, and makes sure we're following the ethical guidelines. I've known Judith since I was in training, and she'd come to give the occasional awe-inspiring lecture. I was thrilled enough when she agreed to supervise me , but when one of her therapists left London last year, and she asked me to join the practice, I was ecstatic. For me, it was like that call from Spielberg that Brendan's waiting for, and I've been doing everything I can to justify her faith in me. The fact she's assigned me today's case, when she could have assumed it demanded her level of seniority, is making me feel just a tiny bit triumphant.

Judith's got a large corner office, graced with a sweeping view over Regent's Park. No herbal tea for her: she's sipping from a tiny china cup of espresso that I know will be strong enough to stand a spoon up in. She's wearing a red-velvet shirt over some cropped green trousers: she should look as though she's auditioning for Dick Whittington, but instead she seems vivid and unapologetic. She's late fifties at least with the wrinkles to prove it, but she still oozes sex and vivacity. I think about that famous poem, the one about growing old disgracefully wearing purple and munching sausages, and hope I'll have the balls for it.

'Mia,' she says, bright eyes taking me in. 'What's the panic?'

I throw myself down on her sofa, pulling Gemma Vine's notes out of my bag at the same time. I don't just see the 'worried well' – the slightly anxious but essentially sorted people who use therapy to give them the sense of calm they need to survive an increasingly chaotic world. I also specialize in treating children, particularly those who've experienced serious trauma. You might find me kneeling in my sand tray, working with a six-year-old who hasn't got the words to express his grief over his mummy dying, but can build it for you once you hand him a plastic spade.

'I've been going back over Gemma's notes . . .'

Gemma's too old for the sand tray. She's thirteen, the last person to see her dad before he disappeared off the face of the earth three weeks ago. Her father owns a large accountancy firm, whose clients include a tycoon named Stephen Wright. Wright claims his multimillion-pound business is whiter than white, but the police are convinced that waste disposal and property are cover for a whole host of nefarious activities, from money laundering to people trafficking to large-scale fraud. His assets have been frozen, leaving thousands of investors – who thought they'd poured their savings into a legitimate business – desperate and angry. Meanwhile his trial, which was due to start this Monday, is on hold for seven weeks whilst the police search for their key witness: Gemma's dad.

'Of course you have . . .' says Judith, a wry smile on her face. 'Till midnight, I imagine?'

'I'm a swot, what can I say?'

The manhunt's been all over the papers, but I've been trying to avoid the lurid headlines so I can meet her fresh. I've still found myself worrying about her all weekend, pulling the facts I do have in all directions, like dough I'm still deciding how to shape. How must it feel to have her dad disappear in a puff of smoke, only to have him reappear plastered across the front of the *Daily Mail*?

'How can he not have known – Gemma's dad? That's what he said, isn't it? That he didn't know Stephen Wright was a criminal.'

'Wright's definitely a criminal,' says Judith drily. 'It's just that he's clever enough and ruthless enough to have prevented the police from building a case until now. One particularly charming anecdote I was told is that he slashed the face of someone who had the temerity to disagree with him in a business meeting. Imaginative way to make it clear who's boss.' I shudder involuntarily. 'Don't look so worried, Mia. I'm not planning on stealing any management tips from him.'

'Yes, so Christopher Vine must have known? And if he knew – surely the whole family must've known. Gemma even?' Judith looks at me, face neutral, spoon gently clinking against the bone china cup. 'I just want to go into this session ready for whatever could come out of her mouth.'

'Mia, it's not for us to speculate. I told you that. You're just here to provide a safe space for Gemma.'

'But . . .'

'Besides, all this information is only just coming out in the press. Stephen Wright might have deliberately kept Vine away from the underground part of the business. Having a squeaky clean accountancy firm was a great way to give himself a veneer of respectability.'

'So if Vine didn't know anything, why go on the run? He's abandoned his family. He's left his own daughter to be interrogated by the police . . .'

Judith shrugs, deliberately non-committal.

'The police will have put pressure on him by telling him the horror stories. If Stephen Wright's idea of a friendly greeting is a knife to the throat, you wouldn't want to risk taking the stand at his trial, even if you were going to do nothing more than recite nursery rhymes.'

'But if she did say anything about his whereabouts . . . I'd have to tell the investigation, wouldn't I?'

'In principle, yes, but I don't think that's a real concern. Her mum wouldn't be bringing her here if there was any danger she knows anything. She's a mixed-up kid from a mixed-up family, who desperately needs our support.'

'And it's her mum asked for the appointment?'

'Yes, I know a friend of hers socially. It's too close for me to see Gemma, but I absolutely think you're ready for it.' Judith wriggles her shoulders, shaking it off, and takes another slug of coffee. 'Besides, I think you'll have real emotional insight into her situation.'

Judith's a very instinctive therapist: one of her most deeply held convictions is that we get the clients we need for our own healing. I stand up a little too abruptly, smile a smile that shines extra bright.

'OK, that's really helpful. Wish me luck!'

'You won't need it. You'll be great.'

Gemma's twenty minutes late. I sit in my room, painstakingly rereading her notes, trying not to feel a sense of anticlimax. It's a full half-hour after our appointment time before Brendan buzzes to say she's finally arrived. I walk through to the waiting room, a tiny tremor of nervous anticipation running through me. I still get it on a first session, even as I'm outwardly projecting the smooth glide of a swan. There's an intimacy to doing this work well, a locking together that has to happen.

Gemma's jammed into the furthest corner of the grey sofa, hugged as close as a clam to its arm. She looks young for thirteen, like the endless billboards and MTV videos of girls dancing in just their teeny-tiny pants have somehow passed her by. She's wearing a baggy unzipped hoodie and loose jeans, her small thin body lost in the swathes of fabric. Her dead gaze is fixed on an empty point in the distance, her sharp chin jutting forwards. Thin blonde hair, shaggy and unstyled, falls over her shoulders. A smattering of freckles punctuates her pale skin, playing across her small nose. There's an innocence about those freckles that slightly breaks my heart: they speak of carefree summers playing outside, roaming around with a gaggle of friends – or perhaps that's only in some storybook version of childhood. The thing that's puncturing me is the way she embodies the fact that once innocence is lost it cannot be regained.

Next to Gemma sits a woman who must be her mum. She's mid-forties, I think; her impeccable highlights and caramel skin making it hard to tell, a fidgety nervousness pulsing through her. Her fingers worry at her iPhone, her tongue darts out and moistens her lipsticked mouth. She's faux casual – second-mortgage skinny jeans and a silk peasant blouse – a million miles from Gemma's aggressively unkempt style. She jumps to her feet as I arrive, thrusts a hand towards me.

'I'm Annie, Gemma's mum,' she says, the vowels slightly

extending, a Northerner who's lived South too long. 'I'm SO sorry we've wasted your time.'

Her eyes blaze as she looks down at Gemma, but her gaze simply boomerangs back, no acknowledgement.

'Please don't worry,' I say, shaking her hand, feeling its tremor. I turn my gaze to Gemma. 'But we'd better make the most of what's left. Do you want to follow me?'

My words simply hang there in the ether, unclaimed. Slowly, deliberately, Gemma turns to look at her mum. I wouldn't want to receive that look: anger's clean, but this is something else, harder and colder. Annie forces a smile as Gemma reluctantly prises herself from the sofa and stalks after me towards my treatment room.

'Where would you . . .'

I've tried to make my room as welcoming and unthreatening as I can. There's a dark red sofa scattered with big squishy cushions, and a box of tissues planted within easy reach. It's light, too, with a big window with a view nearly as good as Judith's – it's very different from the little grey cage, deep in the bowels of an NHS clinic, where I first went, too desperate to carry on pretending I could keep it together. I was going to ask Gemma where she'd like to sit, but she's already sprawled herself across my sofa like she's got squatter's rights. I sit down squarely, right opposite her.

'I'm Mia,' I say. 'Mia Cosgrove. I'm a psychotherapist, and I can tell you more about what that means if you'd like me to.'

'You're a doctor. A head doctor.'

'I'm not a doctor, no. But I do have qualifications. The idea is that I can help with the head stuff.' Gemma's eyes slide towards the big picture window – cars stream down the Marylebone Road, a haze of exhaust fumes throwing a gauzy grey blanket over the top. 'We're here to talk about whatever you'd like to talk about. This is your space. I won't be telling your mum, or telling your teacher. You can use it however you like.'

'Ooh, sounds like fun,' she says, then snaps back to silence.

I let it run for a minute or so before I try again. I'm not one of those therapists who let the silence go on forever, pooling and deepening, waiting for the client to swim to shore. You can both end up drowning out there.

'It feels to me like there's quite a lot of tension in the room. Do you think that's true?'

Sometimes it works, naming the big old elephant rampaging round the room; sometimes it doesn't.

'Maybe for you,' she says, shoulders shrugging under her baggy hoodie. 'I'm fine.'

'That's good,' I say, managing to hold her gaze for a few seconds. 'I just wanted to check in with how you were feeling. So you're in Year Nine?'

She nods, almost imperceptibly. With the family's assets frozen, Gemma's been yanked out of her expensive private school and sent to the local comp.

'And you've just moved schools?' I pause, waiting to see if she'll volunteer anything. 'You've had a lot of changes

15

happening all at once.' Gemma shrugs, pale face effortfully rigid, like she's putting everything she's got into keeping me out. I keep inching forward. 'Has it been hard for you, Gemma?'

'No. It's been like one big birthday party,' she spits.

'And Christmas?' I say, cocking my head. It's a risk. 'Just one non-stop celebration?'

'And Easter,' she says, a tiny smile on her face. 'Loads of chocolate.'

'Hanukkah? No, you're not Jewish.' She's softened, her body not quite so much of a fortress. 'What *has* it been like, Gemma?'

'What, at Shitsville Academy?'

'Mmm, unusual name.'

Another tiny smile.

'It's shit. It's a shit-hole, stuffed full of losers. Can I go now, or do I have to keep talking to you?'

'Of course you can, if that's what you want. I haven't bolted the door.'

We look at each other, gazes finally locking. *Stay*: I send it out into the silence. Perhaps she hears it. Her shoulders slide downwards, the tension finally starting to lift. 'Is there *anyone* you'd like to talk to, Gemma?'

I keep my voice gentle, watch for her instinctive reaction rather than the likely verbal missile. She folds a cushion into her belly, hugging it close. Her gaze drops to a point on the woven green rug that my best friend Lysette gave me when I started here, her eyes filling. This time I let the silence linger. Her eyes meet mine for a second, something close to desperation there, and then drop back to the rug. It's round, with thick white stitching that spirals inwards, chasing itself round and round in an eternal circle. It's either the perfect accessory for my work, or the absolute opposite.

'If you want to ask about my dad, just say it. We both know why I'm here.'

The air feels taut again the moment she mentions him. No, 'mention' is far too feeble a word. It's more like a bomb she drops.

'Do we? I meant what I said when we started, Gemma. It's your time. You're the boss. We can talk about him, or we can talk about – I don't know, Harry Styles' lamentable use of hair gel. It's up to you.'

'I'm not a kid, Mia,' she spits, as if there could be no worse insult. 'Don't patronize me. One Direction are a bunch of twats.'

'They're not really the point.' I wait for her to look at me, keep my expression soft. 'What I mean is, I want you to feel safe here.'

Safe: seems comical now. My naivety.

'Dad knows where all the speed cameras are,' she says, suddenly animated. 'When we go to Westfield, he drives really fast on the Westway and he plays his music – not crap like One Direction – so loud the car shakes. It's lucky we never get stopped.'

'So what does he shake the car with?'

'Old stuff. Blur and Radiohead. You know. Proper music.'

She's grinning as she says it, eyes shining, like she's there on the Westway right now, the music pumping, a hint of danger laced under the racing of her heart. *Proper music.* I play with the phrase in my head.

'So his music is proper music? Do you like the same things as him, or do you like your own stuff too?'

'What do you mean?' she says, quick as a flash.

'I'm just interested. Do you have your own version of proper music? You might like things he doesn't.'

'Don't start thinking you can slag him off because he's not here.'

She's his guard dog: ferocious, quick to bare her teeth.

'I'm sorry if it sounded like I was slagging him off. I was actually trying to find out more about you.'

'Step away, Mia. There's nothing to see.'

That's when she starts to push up the ballooning grey cotton of her sleeves. It's so very gradual, the way she does it, like a game of Grandmother's Footsteps.

'I'm not sure about that, Gemma. I think you might be selling yourself short.' That spitting anger – it smacks of self-hatred that's turned itself outward. Perfectly honed, forcing the outside world to keep confirming her darkest feelings about herself. And now, the one person who makes her believe differently has abandoned her – I bet, however illogical it is, it feels inside like it's the casting vote. 'There are lots of things I'd like to find out about you.'

'Shame!' She deliberately rolls her eyes towards the clock, the session almost ticked away. Then she gives her left sleeve a last, triumphant tweak. 'We're all out of time.' That's when I see them, deep, bloody scratches criss-crossing the tender flesh of her wrists. I try to control the shock in my face. 'Gemma, have *you* done that? Have you been hurting yourself?'

She whips down her sleeves, busies herself with her scruffy rucksack.

'Don't be nosy. You think you're so *qualified*, don't you? You think you can just know all about us from some crap I've spun you, like you're Sherlock or something. Well you're not. My dad would never make me come here.'

I feel a surge of anger, not at her but at him. They merge and meld in her mind, like she doesn't know where she starts and he ends.

'I'm worried about you, Gemma. I think what you're dealing with is incredibly painful and hard. Of course you don't have to come here, but if you want to see me again, I'll be here for you.'

She stands up, grabs the straps of the rucksack; her fury so palpable it feels violent. She won't look at me.

'He's going to hate this,' she hisses, her eyes suddenly finding their focus. 'He's going to hate you when I tell him.'

'Gemma, why don't you sit down? Take a few minutes to get calm before you go out there.'

'Don't tell me what to do,' she says, the door flung open so violently that the handle crashes against the plaster.

I want to give her a minute before I follow her out, respect her desire to get as far away from me as possible, but as I stand up to shut the swinging door, I realize it's not just her who needs a minute. Did I go in too hard? I don't think I did. Those livid scars, thin trails of dried blood.

When I brave the waiting room there's no sign of Gemma, just Annie, looking even more flustered and anxious than when she arrived. I feel a burst of frustration. That session wasn't for Gemma, it was for her.

'What the hell happened in there?' she says.

'It was – not easy. But a first session often isn't,' I say.

'She's waiting outside. I told her I had to talk to you.' She grabs, suddenly, for my arm, her fingers digging into my flesh. I don't like the way her grip handcuffs me, but I try not to react. 'What did she say to you?'

'I'm sorry Annie, what's said in there has to stay confidential. She's obviously in a lot of pain, and there's a lot of anger coming up. But you're her mum, I'm sure you know that.'

It's delicate dealing with parents; you don't want them to think you're stepping on their turf. Truth be told, I'm not sure it's Annie's turf either. She stares at me, as helpless as a fish on a slab, and I feel a rush of sympathy for Gemma. There's no certainty here, no one who knows the answers.

'Is that it?'

'I definitely think we need a follow-up phone call, tomorrow preferably, but I think that's the last time I'll be seeing Gemma. A client has to *want* to come and see me.'

Annie's painted red mouth twists into a smile that never translates. She yanks on a smart beige trench coat and jams on a pair of bug-eyed sunglasses, her knuckles white.

'Thanks,' she says, turning on her heel, refusing to look at me.

'Annie . . .' I start, but by now I'm talking to thin air.

He's going to hate you when I tell him. I could be wrong, but it didn't feel hypothetical. It felt like present tense.

24 December 1984 (six years old)

I'm not sure I like the idea of Father Christmas. A man with a big, puffy cloud of a beard pouring himself down the chimney and sneaking into my bedroom while Mum and Lorcan snore away next door. Mum promised me – crossed her heart and hoped to die – that there was nothing to be scared of. I wanted to hang up one of Lorcan's stripy cotton socks, but she pointed out the holes in the toes, told me it had to be a stocking so it could fit all the presents. She'd bought one specially, and now it's pinned to the end of my bed, all woolly and hopeful. I hope he really is coming. But also I hope he's not.

Lorcan doesn't really like Christmas. He keeps going on about the 'comm-er-shall-ization', which means that Moneybags Men have stolen the idea and turned it into something else, and saying he doesn't want any presents. I made him a card at school, with stick-on stars and a flock of cotton-ball sheep: Miss Harper couldn't understand me putting 'Lorcan' in glitter pen, not 'Dad', but she doesn't understand about stuff like 'comm-er-shall-ization' and why you have to keep watching out for it. I did try to explain it to her. I was a bit scared of giving my card to him, but his face lit up like the pilot light in our noisy boiler. 'Thank you, petal,' he said, scooping me onto his knee and squeezing me against him so hard I could feel his skeleton. It made me feel full of happy, like a balloon blown so big it pops.

To fox the Moneybags Men we're having a Continental Christmas, which means that instead of boring old lunch tomorrow we're having dinner tonight, and I'm allowed to stay up until at least nine, which is ages past my bedtime. Mum's downstairs roasting a chicken, the radio blaring out the kind of carols that are sung by posh boys with high-pitched voices, her lovely, tuneless voice trying and failing to hit the high notes along with theirs. Lorcan can't be home yet. He can sing for real, it's his job, and if he was here, he'd tease her enough to make her gradually turn herself down to silent, like turning off the radio when *The Archers* has finished. I stop staring at my stocking, imagining how fat it might become, and run down the narrow corridor to find her.

She's pulling the glossy brown chicken out of the oven, her pretty face all flushed and shiny. I think she's prettier than other people's mums, even though she doesn't bother with lipstick. When I'm a grown-up I'm going to wear make-up every single day, even if I'm ill in bed. She's wearing a flowery red dress instead of her normal jeans, and her hair is pinned up on the back of her head, with little bits trailing downwards like vines that princes climb up to rescue fair maidens.

'There you are!' she says. 'Why don't you get out three knives and forks, and start laying the table?'

'Is it suppertime?'

'Yes,' she says, even though she's making a big tin-foil tent for the chicken and turning the oven down low enough to push him back in.

'When Lorcan gets home?'

'Yes,' she says again, not looking round. Her 'Yes' makes a flat sound, like something heavy being dropped. The posh boys are starting on their next carol: I want her to sound happy and sing-y again.

'What's this one, Mum? I heard you singing "Oh Come All Ye Faithful" with them.'

'Could you hear me upstairs?' she says, a smile back in her voice. 'Did I sound like a cat being strangled?'

That's what Lorcan always says.

'No!'

'Is that a big fat lie, Mia?'

And then we hear his key in the lock. I can't help looking at where the little hand is on our kitchen clock: it's well past eight, and I wonder if Mum will be cross, but she rushes across the room and throws her arms around his neck.

'Hello, sex bomb,' he says, kissing her on the lips for ages. She pulls away in the end, and he comes over to me, my hands still full of knives and forks. He picks me up by my waist, swings me around, and the knives and forks go flying like confetti but it doesn't make him stop.

'Hello, petal,' he says, loudly kissing each of my cheeks. I'm squealing, feeling sick and happy all at once, and Mum's telling him to put me down right now, but she's laughing too much to make the words come out properly. He sets me down, looks at the scattered cutlery, and drops to his knees.

'Quick, it's a treasure hunt,' he says, crawling under the table and pulling the cloth across his face, peeking out at me. I crawl straight after him, but he's already hidden the knives and forks. Every time I find one, he sings, 'We are the champions,' and when I find the final knife he tickles me so hard I think I'll explode.

'Come on now, supper,' says Mum, voice firm, and Lorcan makes his naughty face, but he does crawl out from our hidey-hole, his hand extending back to me. I perch on a chair, my legs swinging beneath my dress, just watching him.

'Are you getting excited about Father Christmas?' he asks me.

Mum gives him a look I can't quite decode, even though I'm so good at codes I could be in the Famous Five – I'd solve far more clues than useless Anne. Perhaps Mum's thinking I'll get scared again.

'Yes!' I say, in an extra-excited voice, so they won't worry. 'I've asked him for the Famous Five omnibus and a glitter pen.'

'That guy is quite a dude!' says Lorcan, and Mum gives him another funny look. I don't know what a 'dude' is, but

I nod slowly like I do when I'm pretending I understand. Meanwhile Mum pulls the chicken out, telling Lorcan to make the gravy, and Lorcan produces a bottle of champagne from his rucksack even though I'm sure we can't afford it. It's what posh people – like Lord Snooty in the *Beano* – drink. Lorcan is very good at singing but people don't appreciate him enough and it means that we don't have many new things. Most of my clothes have been worn by other children, apart from when my grandparents decide they need to dress me ('Like rags!' said Granny, yanking at my blue corduroy pinafore, and my cheeks felt like sunburn), and my toys come from jumble sales. I don't really like toys anyway; they're for babies. I like books. My reading age is eight even though I'm six. I heard Miss Harper saying to Mum that I'm very 'mature', which means I'm like a grown-up trapped up in a child's body.

Mum produces a box of crackers, bright green foil ones, and puts one next to each plate with a flourish. Lorcan looks at his for a few silent seconds, then asks me to pull it with him. He pretends it's very, very hard – like we're having a tug of war – then falls off his chair as the cracker springs in my direction. Inside there's a red plastic ring, a shiny pretend diamond stuck to the front. I screw up my face to show that I know it's a bit yucky, but Lorcan picks it up.

'Princess Mia,' he says in a Lord Snooty voice, dropping suddenly to his knees. 'May I kiss your ring?'

I nod, giggling, a bit scared, and he gives it an extravagant smack of the lips, pushing it onto my middle finger. I look at it, glittering there: now it seems like the most beautiful thing I've ever seen. I don't take it off once, all Christmas holidays, even when I'm in the bath or in bed. Every time I see it, it reminds me how big and puffy I got with happiness.

Chapter Two

'You're being very hard on yourself.' Judith smiles at me, teasing. 'Just for a change.' I don't smile back.

It's 7.30 a.m., the sun almost tentative as it filters through Judith's impressive windows. The tube was half empty, the other passengers sleep-dazed casualties of a too early start. Lucky them: I barely slept a wink.

'This isn't me being self-obsessed or . . . or neurotic,' I say, trying to keep my voice from reaching a neurotic fever pitch. 'I know I did my best. But it wasn't good enough.'

'Did I call you neurotic?'

'She needs help. I wish I could've got her to see that I could be someone for her to talk to.'

'You had half an hour. She's furious, traumatized. And you've got no idea how much help you've already been. You telling her mum she's been self-harming might be a huge gift to them all.'

'Yeah . . .' I say, trying not to sound dismissive. 'It's not just about the self-harm. That's just a symptom.'

'What do you mean?'

'It wasn't just what she said, it was the way she said it.' I've gone over and over this already with her. 'It really felt like she was going to go straight home and tell him every single detail.'

Judith pauses, carefully picking out her words.

'That's where I think you could be veering off course. Mia, fathers and daughters, it's going to be very triggering for you. Perhaps she even sensed that . . .' Judith waves her elegant, ring-laden hands, aware it sounds a little woo woo. 'On some level. Of course she doesn't want to think Dad's gone. Present tense makes the prospect of never seeing him again a bit less real.'

Judith must think I'm an idiot, following a trail of breadcrumbs right into a teenage girl's fairy story. I should have worked this through myself, not exposed the multicoloured chaos of my thoughts.

'Thank you. And thanks for coming in so early.' My first client is at eight, a corporate lawyer who likes an hour before real life begins to work on the dream life he swears he can't afford to live. Judith smiles.

'Sometimes there's a limit to what we can do. Knowing that fact is a big part of the job.'

'I know.'

'Let me know how the call goes. Oh and Mia, Maria from the ACA called about your application. She was still a bit sniffy about whether someone in their mid-thirties could be experienced enough, but they were very impressed with the paper you wrote.' The ACA is a specialist organization who work with child bereavement. There's a spot that's come up on their board, and I want it. Even more now she's said that.

'Is there anything else I can do to prove what a wise old crone I can be?'

'We'll keep gently nudging the door. I'm sure it'll swing open.'

'Thanks again,' I say, smiling my gratitude.

I try Annie twice between patients, but she doesn't pick up. Come lunchtime, I decide it's a sushi kind of day, virtuously sipping on a miso soup in the window of the Japanese place on the corner, before ruining it at a stroke with a hastily grabbed bar of Green & Black's en route to the office. I'm passing the tiny green handkerchief of park round the corner when I see her name flash up. I duck into the park, drop onto a bench and accept the call.

'Annie. Thanks for calling me back.'

'Can you talk?'

'That's why I picked up. I'm really glad you called.'

'Not that you *can* talk to me. That's what you said.'

Are they all this aggressive, the Vines?

'I can't talk about things that are covered under patient confidentiality, but there is something I need to raise with you as Gemma's parent.'

God, I sound pompous. I'm glad she can't hear how hard

my heart is hammering in my chest. I look around, anchor myself. I shouldn't be this rattled. A little girl is sitting in a swing, the kind for tiny kids with bars to hold them safe, begging to be pushed higher and higher, hair flying back behind her like a magic carpet, her face alight with exhilaration.

'Yeah, and I was calling to book another appointment.'

'Another appointment?' I can't keep the shock out of my voice. 'Does Gemma really want to come back? She seemed pretty adamant she didn't.'

'You don't know Gemma,' says Annie, her voice like lead.

'That's true.' I pause, choosing my words carefully. 'But she needs to want to come for herself, not to please anyone else.'

'Yeah, I get it. Don't worry, she hasn't got a gun to her head.' She's pissing me off now. 'You obviously got somewhere with her,' she says, wheedling, like she's detected my mood in my breathing. 'She wants to see you as soon as you can fit her in.'

I feel a tiny nudge of self-satisfaction. I squash it down.

'Annie, what I'm concerned about is self-harm. Have you seen her wrists? There are cuts all over them, which I assume she did herself.'

Annie pauses. I hear the flick of metal, a sharp breath inwards, smoke going down into her lungs. I wait. Should I have been more gentle? Insisted we meet face to face?

'I've seen it,' she says, voice catching. 'I'm not being harsh, but it looks worse than it is. She did it with a compass, just scratched away at herself. She's never done it before.' She waits. 'We need you. You can see that, can't you?'

I think for a split second, then hold the phone away from me, page through my calendar. She's minimizing what Gemma's done, protecting herself.

'Let's book one more in, and then we can talk again.'

'Thanks,' she says, relief warming her up. 'Thanks so much.'

I thrust the phone back into the darkness of my bag, chart a course towards the office. For once, I'm trying not to think.

He's standing next to the sofa in the unmanned reception area, wary-looking, like he's contemplated sitting on it but decided it's a trap. He's toweringly tall, but it doesn't make him seem manly to me, far from it. It's a gangly kind of height, made more so by the way his suit fits him, like a school uniform that's been unwisely awarded an extra year. His dark red hair is thick and abundant, falling against pale skin the colour of full-fat milk. He should be freckled, but somehow he isn't. I try to work out how old he is, but it's beyond me; he could be my age, but only in human years. Thinking he's another therapist's patient I try to slither past as unobtrusively as I can, like the flash of green as a grass snake streaks across a lawn.

'Hello. Are you Mia Cosgrove?'

I turn to him. His large brown eyes should be soft, but they aren't, not the way they're tracking me.

'I am. I don't believe you've made an appointment.'

I hate the haughtiness I can hear in my voice, like it's the 1940s and he's addressed me improperly, but then I notice how he's sizing me up, his sterile smile on a time delay.

'I don't need one. I'm acting for the police.'

I try to control my face, avoid a wave of shock jumbling my features.

'What's it concerning?' As if I didn't know.

'Gemma Vine.'

'There's really nothing I can help you with, but if you'd like to follow me.'

'Oh, I think you might be underestimating yourself.' His words are aimed at my retreating back, and I ball my fingers up, crunching down my anger.

In my room he makes for the sofa, and sits up straight, large hands dangling between his suited knees, bog-standard black office shoes planted firmly on my rug.

'I'm sorry, I didn't mean to ambush you,' he says, his apology failing to soak the dry, paper-thin words with any meaning. 'I'm Patrick O'Leary.' Irish, but not. A plastic paddy, second generation. His voice is neutral, professional, but the odd London vowel creeps in unawares. 'I'm a lawyer with the SFO, overseeing the Stephen Wright case. Are you aware of the details?'

'I've read the headlines. I'm aware it's a large-scale trial, and that his accountant's disappeared, but I don't know much more than that.'

'Seems unlikely, considering you're seeing our friend Christopher Vine's daughter.'

'Yes, and my job is to provide her with emotional support. I don't want to have my judgement clouded by spurious press stories.'

'You're a therapist. People confide in you. You realize she was the last person to see him before he disappeared?'

'I do.'

'So you understand how vital her input could be to our finding him?'

'Have you ever had therapy?' He snorts, then tries to turn it into a cough. I know I should calm down, haughty was way better than this, but it's beyond me. 'I'll take that as a no. The most important thing is that the client trusts the therapist. Even if I knew anything – which I don't – it would be a complete betrayal. Don't you think she's been through enough?'

'How about all those pensioners who've lost their life savings? Do you think maybe they've been through enough? I'm sure they'd love to come to your fancy office and pay you a small fortune to cry about it, but guess what, they can't afford it. Or how about the women he's trafficked? I'm sure they'd be really grateful if you handed them a Kleenex.'

'Where do you get off being this hostile?'

I feel colour flooding my cheeks, my breath suddenly twisting up high and tight in my chest. I hate everything that's coming out of his mouth, not least the implication that what I do is nothing more than an expensive aspirin, a temporary treatment that masks the pain. He leans back, opening large hands up into a more believable kind of apology, but it just makes it worse. I'm scorched with humiliation, the humiliation of him seeing how much he's riled me.

'I'm sorry. I shouldn't have come tramping into your place of work in my size twelves, I should have made an appointment, but I'm like you.' I narrow my eyes, waiting for the follow-up. 'I'm one of the good guys,' he says, smiling self-deprecatingly. 'I want to help. Stephen's victims are desperate: if it turns out there's a way you can help them, I'm sure you'd want to take it.'

I stand up, put out a hand.

'It was a pleasure to meet you, Mr O'Leary, but my next patient is due any minute. I'm afraid you're wasting your time as well as mine. I've only had one session with Gemma, nothing of which revealed any information about her dad's whereabouts.'

He gets to his feet, his body taut and rigid.

'I can take a hint. But just so you know, if we end up needing more information from you, we can use formal channels to obtain it. The authorities are in no mood to let men like Christopher Vine, who give vicious criminals a fake respectability, get away with it. I'm asking myself how come they've got the cash to splash sending their daughter here, when their assets are frozen.'

'I do know my legal responsibilities. If she told me something I thought was vital to your investigation I'd pass it on, but that's not going to happen. I'm trying to provide some comfort for a traumatized child: if she brings in any bank statements for the Cayman Islands I promise you'll be the first to know.'

'You do that, Miss Cosgrove,' he says, yanking a card out of his wallet. I snatch it from him. 'This isn't going away.'

'I'll put you on speed dial. And it's Ms.' I hate that word, it sounds like a speech impediment. I hold the door open before I can make any more of a fool of myself. He moves towards it, but then he turns back, his face flooded with anger.

'Trust me, you've no idea what you're dealing with, getting involved with the Vines. I wouldn't lose that card if I were you. Something tells me you're going to end up needing me more than I need you.'

I hold his gaze a second too long, my eyes betraying me. *He's going to hate you when I tell him*. I push it all away. I'm there to support her, nothing more. She's a child who needs a safe haven, far away from all the power play.

The open door reveals my next client, patiently waiting. I smile at her, then try to smile at Patrick, regain some control over the situation. He barely registers it. He scissors his way across reception on his lanky legs, Brendan widening his eyes at me.

'Hilary,' I say, above a thumping heart. Annie flashes across my mind. Her expensive suntan, her designer shades. 'So sorry to keep you waiting. Would you like to come through?'

I went in search of Judith as soon as my last appointment had ended. I felt like I'd used up my panic chips: I wanted to seem like I was the kind of cast-iron professional who could be trusted with a case involving a criminal trial without breaking a sweat.

'What do *you* want to do, Mia?' she'd asked, searching my face with her blackberry eyes. 'I know how worried you were this morning that she might know more than she's let on. If the responsibility feels too much, you should step down. There's no shame in that.'

Too much. Step down. Neither of those were phrases I liked. They felt like a cattle prod applied to my overachieving backside.

'I want to help her.' Patrick's smug face floated into my mind, the infuriating way he'd set up camp on the moral high ground. I thought of his passing shot, his warning about the Vines, but then I remembered Gemma's pale smudge of a face, her sliced-into flesh. There was something small and fragile about her underneath it all. She'd found something she needed in me: who was he to snatch that away from her? The truth was, he wouldn't just be taking it away from her; the idea of us failing to meet again made me feel strangely deflated. 'I want to give her a refuge.'

Judith considered me, then nodded.

'OK, you sound clear, but if I think there's any danger to you, either emotionally or professionally, I will step in. That's my job, as your supervisor.'

I thanked her, grateful to feel a little bit mothered in the midst of it all, then went to call Annie.

'Just goes to show how desperate they're getting,' she said, defiant. It rattled me, the 'they', made me question myself, but I pushed the feeling away, told myself not to be so grandiose about my role. I wasn't throwing my lot in with a bunch of criminals, I was supporting Gemma.

'You don't have to decide now. You can cancel in the morning if you want to. No charge.'

'Thanks, but I know what's best for my little girl. We're coming back. We'll be there tomorrow, on the dot this time.'

'If you're sure. I just wanted you to understand my legal obligation.'

'Do you have kids?' she demanded. I wished I didn't hate that question as much as I do.

'No,' I said, hoping I didn't sound too clipped, too brittle.

'But you were a teenager.' She laughed, without warmth. 'She just wants to bitch to someone who isn't her mum. The only thing Chris would have talked to her about when he dropped her off was whether or not she'd done her French homework. And knowing my darling daughter she'd have lied her head off.'

'Fine, as long as you're . . .' I was going to say happy, but luckily it got stuck in my throat.

'Honestly, Mia, from the way she's acting at home, with her brothers, you could be a godsend—'

I cut across her.

'I don't want to dismiss what you're saying but, if she's coming back, it's best I talk to *her* about how she's acting.'

'Yeah, thanks, I've got the drill. See you then,' she said, ending the call before I could respond.

I sat there for a moment. The last twenty-four hours had been like arriving at an unfamiliar house in the dead of night, dark shapes looming and bumping against you, sofas like sea monsters until you flood the space with light.

Marcus is holding court when I arrive. I slip into my seat next to him, and, still in mid-flow, he grabs my hand under the table, squeezing hard enough for me to feel my bones. I wrap my fingers tightly around his, the angst of the day abating as he pours me a glass of white wine with his other hand.

The restaurant is a typical Marcus find: an incredibly chichi new Chinese, tucked away underground somewhere deep in Belgravia. The colours are soft and muted, the lighting dusky and atmospheric. Impeccably dressed waiting staff glide around in a perfectly choreographed dance: I spy our waiter looking positively devastated at having missed the moment I needed a drink poured. I sink into the banquette and take a proper gulp of it. Marcus's eyes track me: I'm not, ordinarily, a gulper of wine – I can tell he's enjoying it. His daughter Juliet smiles at me across the table, and I swiftly rest my glass, smiling back. She's twenty-nine, newly engaged, her adoring fiancé Robert, a terribly proper Army officer, surgically attached to her. There's no sign of Christian, Marcus's son: I try to pretend to myself it's not a relief. I let the conversation wash over me, my mind elsewhere.

'You can't just throw up a building. "Throw up" is the word. If you end up covering London, which is the most beautiful city in the world, bar none—'

'Er, Rome, Dad?' says Juliet, laughing. 'Paris?'

I watch how she reaches out to him, exasperation and admiration perfectly balanced. When she questions him or challenges him, it's only ever a gentle joust: his authority is absolute. She's grown up without any financial worries thanks to Marcus's entrepreneurship. He started out as an architect, then moved into developing his own properties, buying low and selling high when it was still possible to pick up a bargain. What I love about him is that he's still an artist, despite all that commercial success. He's like a physician with buildings, the way he can look at them and instinctively know what will bring them back to full health. Sometimes I'll watch him sketching something out, utterly consumed by what he's doing, and it gives me the shivers.

'You obviously haven't been to St Paul's recently. Of course we need affordable housing, but it can't be any old shit. That's my point.'

It's all so hypothetical for them, no more than a rousing debate. My eyes flick guiltily around the room. Mum would hate it here, with its £7 bottles of water and insistence that you leave a tip in a silver salver if you want a pee. I suddenly long to see her, our weekend meeting too far away, even though for both of us the anticipation is often sweeter than the reality. I take another slug of my wine. It's honeyed and expensive, a waterfall cascading down my throat.

'But there should be proper council housing,' I say, my voice sounding a little too loud and forthright to my own ears. 'They should never have sold it all off. People need a safety net.'

'You're right,' Marcus says. 'In France, people rent all their lives, no problem. The government stops landlords bleeding them dry.'

I'm being unfair; he does think about things properly. I couldn't bear him if he was just a horrible old moneybags Tory, but he isn't. He still teaches architecture, and his business sponsors a broke architecture student every year.

'How's your house hunting going?' asks Robert, and my eyes flick quickly to Juliet, catching the splash of pain that she quickly conceals. Marcus and Lila's divorce – bitter and expensive – is only two years old. I suspect it's the hardest thing that's ever befallen her.

Marcus misses it, perhaps because he wants to. He's looking at me, wobbling his head mockingly, his eyes dancing. I grin back, despite myself.

'She's like Goldilocks,' he says, hands waving girlishly. 'Too big, too small, too noisy, too quiet.'

Juliet's playing with her napkin now, eyes sliding away. My laughter slides away too. I feel for her, I really do. Intermittently we get on well – we meet for a hurried coffee or discuss going to a film – but it's a spluttering, second-hand car of a relationship, never quite making it onto the road. A tableful of sharing platters arrives, providing a welcome distraction.

'You need a top-up,' says Marcus, still oblivious.

He turned round one day and simply said that he'd fallen

out of love with Lila, that he thought they'd both lost that loving feeling, truth be told, and that life was too short for them to stay together. There's a lovely innocence about him – the bit that dreams and creates – and he thought that perhaps she'd be relieved it was out in the open. Surprise, surprise she wasn't.

My friend Zoe fixed us up a few months later at a dinner party: in my more paranoid moments I wonder if his kids think that the window of time is no more than PR bullshit and I was always waiting in the wings.

'How come we're not finding you a place?' asks Juliet, her voice tight. She works for the firm now, Daddy's right-hand woman. She's bright, a Cambridge graduate who could work anywhere, but chooses to stay close to home.

'Cue the explosion,' says a laughing Marcus, covering his ears.

'No explosion! I want it to be . . .' I pause, suddenly snatched away by the past. I think about some of the limpets who clung to my father, the elaborate pantomime of pretending to care about me. The last thing she wants is a visceral sense of us. 'I want it to be somewhere that's mine too.'

My flat's a loft conversion, the ceilings low and perilous, the upstairs a raised platform – I'm more Heidi than Goldilocks.

'I think we need more greens,' says Juliet, picking up the menu, long blonde hair shielding her face.

'Good idea,' I say, grabbing the menu next to me, suddenly determined to be more than an aggravating, painful reminder of her mum's absence. 'What shall we have?'

'Um, maybe these, with the oyster sauce?'

'Let's do it, they sound yummy!' God, I sound like Brown Owl. Worse, the kind of Brown Owl who has a nip of whisky in the gym cupboard before Brownies starts.

'So,' I say, turning towards Robert, realizing as I do that I haven't actually constructed an end to this sentence. 'How's the world of war craft treating you?'

Sharing plates, let alone in a place like this, are invariably a disaster. I feel like I've eaten about one portion of my five a day plus a couple of shrimps, and yet the bill still tops £300. The whole process is painful. First Marcus offers to pay it all, then Robert insists on paying half and then I insist on paying half. 'Don't,' says Marcus, his hand trapping mine as I reach into my purse.

'No,' I say, prising his hand off. 'You paid on Sunday.'

'So?'

'I'm paying,' I say, aware that Juliet's silently enjoying the tennis match, no doubt recording the highlights for her mum. I want to sound generous and bountiful, but instead I sound petulant and stroppy: why can't Marcus ever book somewhere ordinary? There's no way I'm going to be able to pay my credit card this month without dipping into my savings.

'Fine,' he says, his hand retreating to his glass. 'Thank you.'

Finally we emerge, mole-like, into the sodium glow of the

street lights. The wide, hushed road stretches ahead of us, lined with the kind of high-end furniture shops with nothing but a flash of gilt in the window and a double-barrelled name over the door. As Robert starts casting around for a cab, we say our goodbyes. I can feel myself hugging Juliet a bit too hard, her gym-taut body refusing to yield. Still I won't quit.

'Let's do that night out. I mean, if you want to. We could go to one of those cinemas with sofas.'

Stop talking.

'Yeah, no, we should.'

'Not if you don't fancy it, but—'

'Absolutely,' she says, looking relieved as a cab pulls up. 'Bye, Dad,' she says, arms flung upwards to loop around his neck.

'Bye, sweetheart.' Marcus turns back to me as they drive off. He grins, a bit wolfish. 'That was fun.'

'Sort of,' I say. I feel like newly sprayed crops, covered by a thin, invisible layer of humiliation. I take Marcus's hand, a little unsteady on my high heels. 'Do you think Juliet hates me? You know, wax dolls, pins?'

He stops, swinging round theatrically and encircling my waist.

'Come on, let's walk a bit. Don't be so bloody stupid. How could *anyone* hate you?'

The road feels very empty all of a sudden, eerily quiet. Something makes me dart a look behind me, even though the only things to see are overpriced armoires trapped behind plate glass. I hold on a little more tightly to Marcus, wishing

I could let the contents of today tumble straight out of me, like water from a jug. Of course I can't.

'Even if she doesn't hate me, she hates the idea of me. Not as much as Christian, but you know . . .'

I watch his face as he runs my hypothesis through the computer.

'Tell you what I do know. Life's short, and the sooner she realizes that, the happier she'll be. What would you say? I'm *modelling* it for her.'

He sets off again, a problem solved. He's sneaky, the way his quick brain swallows the jargon and vomits it up, reconstituted in a way that suits him. I lag behind him, trying to drag his urgent feet into step with mine.

'Do you miss her?'

'Who?'

'Li-la,' I sing-song.

'Not after the last couple of years. I didn't know what a vindictive bitch she could be.' I feel myself recoil at the venom. He senses it, I think. 'I don't have to, do I?' he adds more softly. 'Once you've got kids with someone, they're never really out of your life.'

'Is that what commitment is? Children?'

'It's the only one that's permanent, isn't it? Rest of them are written on paper. That one's made of flesh and blood.'

'Sometimes,' I say, my voice catching, but too slightly for him to notice. He could remember, but I know he won't. I should do what I'd sagely advise any of my patients to: speak up, rather than silently resent him for not being Mystic Meg;

but I don't. I never do. I only show him the manicured lawns, never the compost heap. Does he do the same? I look at his profile, the jut of his hawk-like nose, his angular cheekbone. It's a slick package.

'Is it not enough commitment for you? Is that it?' says Marcus, stopping suddenly. 'Do you want something sparkly on your finger before you live with me but you're too postmodern to admit it?'

My flat flashes into my mind, the way the door clunks shut after me. The way I can flick the deadlock for an extra bit of security.

'No. It's not that.'

'Then what is it? You trying to suss me out with all these questions about Lila? Work out whether I'm worth putting all your chips on red for?'

'No!' I say, hating how inarticulate I am tonight. 'It's just, it's huge, isn't it?' I grab his hands between mine, stiff to my touch. 'We're not kids. We know what can happen.'

Sometimes I do feel like a child – a weird, supersized one, responsible and hopelessly irresponsible all at once. It's so long since I lived with someone – Jamie, my twenty-something boyfriend – and the truth is, I wasn't very nice to him. Marcus stares at me, his eyes burning.

'Bit of positive thinking might come in handy right now, don't you think? In your professional opinion?'

'If we move in . . .' I look at him, continue more quietly. 'I don't want to have to move back out.'

His face softens. We're under a street light, the lines and

crevices of his face smoothed out by its sympathetic yellowish hue.

'I'm not going to skip out on you.'

'I hate it when people make those kind of promises,' I snap, before I can edit myself. 'You can't say that.'

'Well guess what, I just did,' he says, grinning, refusing to rise to it. His certainty in his own certainty makes me feel safe. I slip my arms around him, pull myself against his bulky chest. I'm cold now.

'Let's go back to yours,' I say.

'Let's go home,' he says, hand already hailing a cab.

April 1987 (eight years old)

Lorcan's fingers are caressing the neck of his guitar, back and forth, so long and thin and white as to be almost girlish. Everything about him has that elongated quality, his cheekbones high and fine, his brown curly hair straggling around the collar of his stripy flannel shirt. I know how the fabric will feel when my cheek presses against it, but right now I'm sitting at his feet, my gaze zigzagging up and down, chasing the chords he's picking out. I daren't look away. If I look away he might be gone, but if I concentrate hard enough I can keep him ensnared in my web. I'm a big, fat spider and he is my prey. You must never tell your prey that they're your prey, in case they make a run for it.

'Is that your song?' I ask, as he lays the guitar down on the battered floral sofa we got from Molly's mum and dad when her family moved house. He laughs, his face a Polaroid of the stupidity of my remark, and I search desperately for something better. 'Is it The Beatles?'

'No, darling, it's classical guitar. Can't you hear it?' He picks out a refrain again, his blue eyes – almost as dark blue as my new, scratchy, uncomfortable school uniform – tracking my face. Can he see I'm more grown-up now? I try to make my listening face reflect how mature I've become in the months he's been gone. I drink tea with breakfast, like Mum, and I read *Smash Hits*.

'It's beautiful,' I say. 'Did you play it on tour?'

'*You're* beautiful,' he says, laughing at the grown-up description, this laugh very different from the knife-slice laugh from before. I look at him, counting all the bits that make him a whole person. He's younger than other people's dads, his skin smoother, his shaggy hair untroubled by grey. 'My beautiful, beautiful baby. I missed you so much while I was away.'

'I missed you more!' I cry, risking springing up onto the sofa, my hot cheek pressed on the exact point of his chest I was eyeing from the floor. I can hear his heart beating through the soft fabric. It makes me more sure he's really here, more than a mirage that I've conjured up with the sheer force of my longing. 'I missed you every single day.'

'Shall we make some supper?' he says, standing up, long denim-clad legs unfolding from underneath him like a pair of stilts, my cheek left hot and bare. I wonder if I've been too 'mushy'. He hates mushy. I dig my nail into my palm to remind myself, hard enough for it to really hurt.

The kitchen is NOT big, in fact it is very small, with a very old oven and a fridge that rumbles like a hungry dragon and sometimes keeps me awake. Mum says if my friends say anything I should tell them it's 'vintage' but the way our flat is makes me not especially want to invite people over. I don't think they especially want to come anyway, not the girls I've met at my new school. I'm glad I've got Molly. She's got a fridge with an ice maker, but she doesn't care that I haven't.

He's pushing a bloody bag out from the recesses of the fridge, triumphantly thumping it down on the rough wood of the ancient table that we got from his mum and dad. Everything at their house is valuable, which is different from expensive, and can mean it smells very old and doggy. We don't go there very often, but I don't really mind. I sent them a letter to thank them for paying for my new school, because Mum said it was polite, but they didn't write back.

'Steak!' he says. 'You can try it medium rare now you're nearly nine.'

The clocks went forward last week, and as I watched Mum stand on a chair and swivel the arms on the plastic kitchen wall-clock I wished that she would turn round and swivel me. Nine, ten, eleven, twelve, thirteen . . . then I'd be a teenager and I would be properly mature, and we could all go on tour together. I'm only eight and a half but maybe six months is 'nearly' in Lorcan's head.

The meat glistens on the counter, a red slick of blood oozing from its marbled flesh. I don't remember the last time we had a meal like this. We have boiled eggs and soldiers, pasta and pesto. I eye it nervously.

'Chef Mia,' says my dad, producing a strange little hammer

from his rucksack, silver with a mottled surface. He bows, passes it to me with a flourish. 'Over to you.' And he throws a handful of herbs over the steaks, then shows me how to flatten them, his fingers as tight as a tourniquet around my forearm.

'Harder!' he shouts, as we hammer harder, although by now I'm giggling too much to be any use. Perhaps I don't want to gain my chef stripes: it feels safe here, his grip strong enough for me to believe that the moment will never end. '*Magnifique!*' he says, unclasping me so he can put a tape in the ancient player next to the sink. Next he produces a bottle of red from his seemingly bottomless rucksack, opening it with the same sense of ceremony he's giving everything. He fills a glass to the brim, then grabs a beaker from the cupboard.

'In Italy the *bambinos* drink wine from when they're toddlers. You can just have a taste.'

He dribbles some into the glass, then puts it under the tap until it's Ribena-coloured, different from the potent ruby red of his. I take a tiny sip, trying not to recoil from the bitter mustiness of it.

'Now you have to say cheers,' he says, and taps my glass with his.

'Cheers!' I shout, and we shout it back and forth, knocking our glasses together, harder each time. He drinks deeply, and I try to do the same, but it goes up my nose and then we both laugh some more.

★　　★　　★

Mum doesn't even try to get home for supper. The clock hands have got to quarter to ten when she comes back, and we've listened to both sides of the tape of *Dark Side of the Moon* three times. She looks a bit like she's been in a storm. Her hair – which is blonde, the best colour for a girl – is quite messy, and she isn't wearing any lipstick.

'Mia, why are you still up? You know bedtime is eight.'

She's looking at my dad when she says it, and he's looking at me. He smiles a naughty sort of smile, the kind I reckon Mr Toad would have when he gets to drive his car, and I smile back.

'I'm not tired,' I say, even though secretly I am, and the wine and water has given me a headache and I don't want to listen to Pink Floyd any more, even if they are musical geniuses. I prefer Wham! but if I ever told my dad that he might not even like me any more.

'Go upstairs and brush your teeth,' she says, in a voice that is all bossiness and not love, and which is not her usual voice.

Lorcan chinks his glass against mine. Luckily mine's empty so she can't prove there was wine in it, but she eyes it suspiciously. He's still grinning, and now he looks sort of soft around the edges.

'We've been having a fine old time. Mia's been telling me about school and what she and Milly have been getting up to.'

'Molly,' I say, before I can help it.

'That's really wonderful,' says Mum, in a voice that says different, 'but she's got to be up for school at 7.30.'

Mum has to be up at 7.30 too. She works in a café now, because it means she can pick me up from school, but in another life she was going to be a lawyer.

'She's far too clever for school. School of life is all this one needs. How about we go on an adventure tomorrow?'

I turn my head to look at Mum, but not quickly enough. Her face is already saying no. Now I turn my face into the ugliest thing I can make it. She smiles at me like she wants to make up, but I don't want to. Suddenly I am really, really angry. The dragon is inside my chest, not inside the fridge. I make my feet stomp on the stairs when I go up them so everyone will know, but I don't think they're really listening. Mum's turned her horrible cross voice on my dad, which is so stupid. He's only just come home: he's never going to want to stay here when she sounds like a wicked witch. I shouldn't have stamped my feet either.

When I'm in bed she comes to tuck me in, but I turn my face away because I want to have an adventure with my dad and now I can't.

'Night night, sleep tight, don't let the bed bugs bite,' she sing-songs, stroking my hair, which is brown, not at all the right colour for a girl. Normally I like it when she does that, but not tonight. I keep my head very still so she won't feel like she's forgiven.

It's much later when my dad comes in. I'm asleep, but I wake up when I feel the weight of him pressing down the mattress. He's sitting on the end of the bed, and he smells the way he smells late at night. Roll-ups and something sweeter.

If it's wine, then perhaps I smell of it too. My mouth is dry, and I drink from the tooth mug of water on my bedside table.

'Hello,' I say, reaching out my fingers so they wrap around his.

'Shsh,' he hisses, very loudly, putting his other fingers up to his lips, holding on tight. 'I came to say goodnight. And to tell you something.'

I'm wide awake now: I sit up straight. 'What?' I whisper.

'It's all a game of tennis. Of mad tennis.' He stands up, mimes swiping at a ball with a racket. 'Don't ever let them tell you it's you who's the mad one. It's always them.'

I giggle, because he looks so silly and funny. I don't really know much about tennis. He suddenly swipes at me, instead of the imaginary ball, gathering me up close to him. I snuggle in. It's the best place in the world, here against his chest. He is so thin that I can feel the ladder of his ribs.

'Night, D—' I wish I could call him 'Dad', or 'Daddy', but he hates it. He says 'Daddy' in a horrible voice which tells me I must never say it unless it's to make a joke about other people and how silly they are. 'Night, Lorcan,' I whisper quite loudly.

'Goodnight, my angel,' he says, and walks out of the room, his silhouette long and tall, like a skyscraper.

I won't see him again until the lack of him is like a boulder inside my chest that I can't roll away.

Chapter Three

She's already there when I arrive, patiently standing on the street, a still sliver amongst the teeming mass of commuters who casually push past her. I hurriedly shove *The Times* deep into my handbag: I shouldn't have looked, but Marcus had left it lying open on the kitchen table and my eyes couldn't help but skim a couple of paragraphs. It was a broadsheet, I reasoned, not a gossip rag. **Sources close to the Stephen Wright case are claiming that important break-throughs have been made in recent days. With the deadline for the trial approaching, the authorities are under mounting pressure to ensure Wright does not go free, but are reliant on the evidence of key witnesses.** It sounded nebulous to me, particularly when I thought of the desperation in that pushy lawyer's demeanour, but I forced myself to stop speculating.

'Gemma! We're starting at 8.30. It's only eight. Your mum did tell you that, didn't she?'

'We'll be there' is what she said, but there's no sign of her. I take in Gemma's outfit: it's like Annie's parcelled her up in shiny paper and sent her to me. She looks like she's going to her first ever job interview. She's wearing a black skirt — falling loosely over her skinny, boyish hips — paired with a dark blue top, sleeves long, a silver cross hanging at the point where her cleavage will eventually spring up to meet it. I see a lot of grown-up skinny women who live in a permanent state of ravenous hunger for all kinds of complicated reasons, but teenage skinny is a very different thing. Looking at her slight form I wonder if she's even started her periods.

'I was late last time.'

'I noticed.'

'And I left early.'

I unlock the door. No one's here yet, not even Brendan: is she trying to catch me off guard? She looks towards my room.

'That's not how it works. We'll be starting at 8.30, as planned.' I smile at her, trying to take any sting out of my words. I don't want to add to any sense of rejection. 'Shall I get you some water?'

'It's all right. I'm gonna go and get myself a coffee.' Her accent trips around, I notice: London one minute, then somersaulting back to the private-day-school girl she was until a couple of weeks ago. Is that how it feels inside too, like she's chasing after a sense of herself, now the gaze that so defined her has been turned away? 'I'm coming back though!' she adds, a certain cheekiness to it.

'I believe you!'

She's as good as her word. This time we follow protocol, with Brendan buzzing through, and me emerging, like a royal personage, to lead her into my lair. She perches on my sofa, no trace of the sprawling insolence of the last session. She's holding her knees together, chewed fingers nervously smoothing down the plain black cotton skirt.

'It's good to see you again, Gemma. I'm glad you came back.'

'Yeah, I wanted to.'

Has she been drilled to say that? I pause, feeling it out.

'And what made you want to?' She turns her gaze upwards, looks at me.

'Cos you're ama–zing!'

'Well thank you. I'm glad it's so patently obvious,' I say, smiling. 'But it's a real question, Gemma.'

'Dunno.'

'I know your mum's told you about the police coming to see me,' I say, watching her face, turned to look intently at the floor. I have to acknowledge it early, not least so I know that she's not here under false pretences. 'I wasn't sure if that would put you off. They still want to know if you've told them everything, and it is possible they'll insist on hearing what you say to me.'

Her head jerks up, cheeks splashed red.

'They don't get to tell me what to do. They think they know about Dad but they don't.' That phrase again. Contempt for people's assumptions. 'They can't make me say anything.' She looks straight at me, her gaze unwavering. 'You can't either.'

'Is that what you think? That I want to make you say things?'

'That's basically what your job is, isn't it?' she says, words tumbling out of her. 'If you were like, a lorry driver, you couldn't just stay in the car park smoking fags and watching porn.'

I go to reply, but then I stop to unknot what it is she's saying. Is that how men seem to her, base and corrupted, or is it just designed to shock?

'You're right. If I sat here all day and no one ever opened up to me, I'd probably be a pretty useless therapist. But they talk because they're parting with their hard-earned money to explore issues that are hurting them, not because I'm interrogating them. Anyway, I'd make a terrible lorry driver. No sense of direction.'

'Vee have vays of making you talk?' she says in a silly voice, but when I search her face there's no silliness there. There's something false about the way she says it too, like she's borrowed the clunky-sounding phrase. She looks back at me, vulnerable for a second, and I risk a leap.

'Is that how it felt with the police?'

'I . . .'

She pauses, looks out of the window. She's marooned on that sofa, so alone. If we'd had more sessions I might have gone and sat down next to her, but I won't risk it yet.

'I think I'd find it pretty frightening.'

I didn't plan to land here straight away. Perhaps there's some part of me protecting us both. I'm sure Judith's right, that it's no more than a fantasy, but if there's any chance she's come back to tell me what she couldn't tell the police, it's better we go straight to the heart of it.

'They're not *really* like the Nazis,' she says contemptuously.

'I know that. But it's a big deal, to be formally interviewed. And it was about your dad. I know from how you talked last time how much he means to you.' She bites her bottom lip, a tear escaping down her left cheek. She scrubs at it angrily with a knuckle, like it's betrayed her, hard enough to leave a red welt on her translucent skin. I feel a sudden twinge inside me, a memory that twists my gut. Hurting yourself to stop the hurt, like one will overwhelm the other and give you back control. Long sleeves in a heatwave: I try not to stare at her wrists. We'll get there gradually.

'If Dad was here, he'd be asking *you* the questions.'

I stared at the grainy picture of him in *The Times* this morning, trying to get a fix on him. It was from some charity benefit, him in a dinner jacket, no warmth or charity visible in his coldly handsome face. He's got the same sharp, jutting chin that Gemma has, better on a man. I couldn't find much in his eyes: if they're a window on the soul, I'm not sure he has one.

'What do you think he'd ask me?'

'He'd wanna know what makes *you* so qualified,' she says scathingly. 'Why's it you asking us?'

Us.

'What's your favourite thing about your dad?'

She pauses, eyes dancing. She's trying to grab something, like a baby extending a chubby hand to a spinning mobile.

'You can't guess what he's gonna do. Like, one time he came to school and just – he kidnapped me!' That aliveness in her face, like an addict in easy reach of a fix. 'It was Monday morning, break time, and he texted me and got me to meet him out the front. And he'd stolen my passport from Mum's special documents drawer, and used his air miles, and he just took me to New York with him on his business trip!'

'Did you worry, Gemma? Did you worry about school, and your mum, and if you'd be in trouble?'

'You only live twice. Mum doesn't get it.'

These phrases she keeps coming out with, awkward in her mouth. I can feel a heat building up in me, an anger that's maybe not about today. I damp it down, feel my feet on the fringes of the rug.

'Can you see why she might've been worried? He "kidnapped" you. He "stole" your passport. They're quite big, scary words you're picking there. You make it sound like a John Grisham book, not a holiday.'

She shrugs the bony peaks of her shoulders, affecting a nonchalance I don't buy.

'They're just stupid words. I can miss a bit of maths. I could've had chicken pox, same difference. Mum knows that, she was just getting her knickers in a twist.'

'Was she?'

'He even took me to his business dinners. I had oysters.' She pauses for a second, a trace of guilt in her voice now. 'We got her some jeans. They were like, $300.'

'Did she like them?' I say neutrally.

'Dad said they made her bum look really nice.'

'Do you think *she* thought they made her bum look nice?'

'Yeah, well, they did. She should've said thank you.' This time I let it stay silent. Gemma watches me, her eyes criss-crossing my face like she's waiting for me to break. Eventually she continues. 'It's no wonder he got so mad.'

'Mad?'

'She pushed him and pushed him.'

'What, and then he got angry?' She nods. 'What's it like when he's angry, Gemma?'

'He just goes,' she says, her voice low. She looks down at the floor. 'Thing is' – the challenge is back in her voice – 'even if I told you about my dad all day, you wouldn't really understand. He's not the same as other people.'

'You're dead right. But that's true for everyone, isn't it? You're not like anyone else either. There's only one Gemma Vine.'

You're important is what I'm trying to say to her. You're

61

not a glove puppet that he takes out of the toy cupboard on a whim: you live and breathe without his animation. There's that tightness in my chest again, that anger that I want to be rid of. It's getting bigger, not smaller.

'Yeah, no, you don't get it.'

'So help me. When you say he just goes, how does he go?'

She gives a smile that's not a smile at all, just a taut piece of string stretched tight across her face.

'He tells you about yourself. Every single tiny thing that's wrong. Then you've got . . . you've got the chance to make yourself way better than you were. Tough love.'

A memory, a fragment of the past that streaks across my consciousness. Lorcan – drunk, high, out of control. His face pushed up close to mine, in the middle of that packed night-club, me rooted to the spot. 'You stupid bitch,' he hissed, his spittle sprinkling my cheek. Even now I can feel the shame spreading through my body, the absolute certainty I wasn't the daughter he deserved. I think of those tender wrists, the pain on the inside painted on the outside.

'There's nothing wrong with you!' I say. 'None of us are perfect. We're human beings, not machines that need tuning up. You don't have to make yourself worthy of his love: it's your birthright.'

'I'm moody,' she says, her voice small. 'I answer back, even when his people come round. I don't work hard at school.' She looks at me intensely. 'You wouldn't like me if I let you really know what I'm like. I'm not – I'm not *nice*.'

'Nice' – the world's most anodyne word – is anything but

in her mouth. It sounds like a bullet of self-hatred shot from a gun. My hand reaches across the space between us and hovers. She gives a tiny nod, and I let it cover her small white one. I wonder if she'll turn it upwards, expose the flesh again, but she doesn't.

'I think I would like you. I like you now.'

'Why?'

I think about it. I don't want to come up with something that sounds like it's filched from a newsagent greeting card.

'You're funny. You're good company. You think about things in an interesting way.' She examines my face, scanning it for truth. We sit there a moment. 'I was very concerned about you when I saw the cuts on your wrists. What made you want to do that?'

'I just – I dunno, I just did it,' she says, her voice high and thin, like a top note from a badly played flute. 'I was bored. Won't do it again, cross my heart, hope to die.'

Hope to die.

'You were bored.' I cock my head, but she doesn't give me anything back. 'What else were you feeling, Gemma?'

'Dunno. I don't always have, like . . .' She mimes taking something out, examining it. 'A FEELING!'

'Or you have a feeling, but there isn't a word for it? It's just a feeling?'

She nods, a spark of recognition in her eyes.

'How about we look for some clues.' I make my voice gentle. 'Where were you when you did that?'

'School. My real school.'

As soon as the words leave her mouth, her face switches, a Venus's flytrap snapping shut. School: the last place she saw her dad.

'You must have found somewhere very private.'

Anger flashes in her grey-blue eyes.

'Yeah, private. Have you heard of that?'

She moves her gaze away, stares steadily out of the window, her eyes tracking the humming stream of traffic. I try to quell my frustration. I can't push too hard; there's enough push coming from outside without me adding to it. I look up at the clock: our time's almost gone now.

'We're going to need to stop soon,' I tell her, half expecting her to spring up, but she's still sitting there, gaze far away.

She jerks her body round, eyes bright and damp.

'You don't understand what he's dealing with,' she says, her voice rising, distorted with emotion. 'People don't understand why he had to leave us, but I do. I *know* him, Mia.'

It makes my heart hurt for her. It's not just the words, it's the depth of feeling that soaks through them.

'Do you want to come back and talk about it some more?' She nods. I continue, trying to rein in my words. 'None of this is your responsibility, OK? Loving him doesn't mean you have to defend him, whatever people are saying right now.'

She looks up at me again, a small smile on her face. Is she smiling at the sheer stupidity of my remark? The very idea that she could stop her vigilance? She nods mechanically as if she's pacifying me, her eyes somewhere else again.

'Thanks, Doc,' she says, standing up.

'You know I'm not a doctor, Gemma.'

'Yeah, no, I was just saying,' she says, grabbing her rucksack.

'Bye, Gemma,' I say to her retreating back. 'You did some good work today.'

I don't know if she even heard me.

January 1990 (eleven years old)

I've thought for ages and ages about his present. I've saved up all my babysitting money from looking after Katy next door, and spent the whole lot in one triumphant splurge. It's a red-leather song book, his name embossed on the front in gold. Mum, who will scrape a bubbly layer of mould off a piece of cheese rather than throw it away, would be disgusted with me, but I don't care. Before we set off for the station, I wedged it deep inside my rucksack where she wouldn't see it. She cries when she puts me on the train, but in a Mum-ish sort of way, only letting a few tears escape and rubbing at them angrily with the woolly arm of her striped cardigan. I wonder if I should cry too, but I'm too excited. It's eighteen months since I've seen him. Eighteen months since he last came home, and left again. Eighteen months since it definitely stopped being his home and became just ours. It feels like our house has faded to black and white, some crackly old TV programme that I don't want to watch, like he was the thing that made it colour.

I'm going care of the guard, even though the guard doesn't seem remotely interested in my welfare. I feel terribly grown-up, like I'm going to a business meeting in *Howard's Way*. I buy a cup of tea and a KitKat from the buffet, and ask how long it is until we get to Bristol, all nonchalance.

I heave open the door when the train pulls into the station, then stand on the freezing-cold platform looking left to right for Lorcan. I don't feel like I'm going to a business meeting any more – I feel like a girl who misses her mum, and who should have listened when she told me to wear a vest. I'm just starting to think I should pick someone out of the bustle and ask for help when he comes loping up the platform and folds me into a hug. A sob rises in my throat.

'There you are, petal. I've been searching for the platform.'

'You found me though.'

'Of course I found you!'

Lorcan grabs my hand on the way out of the station, swinging it high up in the air as we walk down the busy road. I wonder if I'm too old for hand-holding, but I don't want to make him realize how long it's been since he's seen me in case it makes him sad. Besides, I like it, even if I am too old. I swing even higher, and he laughs.

We stop for fish and chips on the way, the chips so hot they almost take the skin off my fingers, the steam rising off them and mingling with my cloudy breath. We walk for ages, toiling our way up a long, steep hill until eventually, right at the end of a terrace, we find Lorcan's flat.

It isn't really a flat. It's a floor of a house, with a big room for him, and a tiny kitchen area in the corner of the sitting room where I'm going to sleep. I've never slept next to a microwave before. The bathroom is on the floor below, a handful of brushes splaying out of a tooth mug like a bouquet of ugly plastic flowers. I can hear someone shuffling about upstairs, a snatch of bass booming out when they open their door. Lorcan says no one owns the house, it's a collective, but Jackie, the woman we met in the kitchen, acted as if it was hers. She looked at me as if she was deciding whether or not to welcome me, sneaking glances from behind her straggly curls as she scrabbled around the kitchen drawers for a bottle opener. I hoped Lorcan wouldn't have a glass of her wine, but he did. He clinked his glass against hers, and I tried to analyse what their eyes said to each other. I'm getting good at that, now I've realized that people don't say everything they mean with actual words. Lorcan's eyes had a laugh in them, but they often do, even when he's just paying for chips. That's why everyone likes him so much. I won't tell Mum about Jackie, but in my mind I will tell her that she's got froggy eyes, always bulging out with all the staring she can't stop doing. 'Frog Features', that's what we'd call her. Lorcan always thinks of the rudest, funniest nicknames, and Mum pretends to be horrified, but she can't help laughing.

'So, do you approve?' says Lorcan, curling out his hand theatrically.

'It's nice,' I say uncertainly, sitting on the edge of his bed. The sight of his bedspread, that familiar parade of faded Indian elephants that I would snuggle under until I was told it was high time I went to my own room, makes my heart wobble and shrink in my chest.

'*Nice*?' says Lorcan, in the voice he uses when I should know better. 'Give me a proper word.'

I pause, hating the tears that are threatening. Of course it's not nice.

'It's different. It's not our house,' I say, my voice rising up high to betray me.

Lorcan puts out his hand to cover mine, and smiles at me, his dark blue eyes searching my face.

'What's Claire been saying to you?'

She's said lots of things, but they've just been dry heaps of words. Endless stuff about them both loving me very much, about how adult relationships are hard to understand. It's like she disappeared for a while, even though I could see her in front of me doing all the normal things, like packing my lunches and driving me to school. She seemed to think it was kinder to pretend to be someone else – a made-up mother I'd never met before, who didn't shout at me to clear up my room but also didn't hug me like she really meant it. Lorcan listens intently as I describe it, then leaps up. He sticks his long, skinny arms out, dead straight, and lumbers forward, eyes glazed.

'Revenge of the Killer Mother!' he says, and I giggle, even though it means I'm two-faced and horrible. 'Sounds like a zombie film. It's not like you're a kid any more. You'll be a teenager next year!' I nod slowly, maturely. Like a person who takes an Intercity train and buys a cup of tea, not a Coke, with their own money. It's not a year really, I wish it was. It's twenty-one whole months away, but it does just squeeze into 1991. 'You understand what's going on.' He sits back down again, the springs of the spongy mattress groaning in protest. 'Ask me anything.'

A hot starburst of excitement explodes inside me: I can almost feel myself expanding on the spot like Alice does when she drinks the potion, taller and taller, until I'm big enough to deserve his belief in me. He stares at me like he's excited too, but when I go to speak, nothing comes. 'I . . .' I can feel my cheeks glowing a hot crimson, but Lorcan's crossed the room, is rootling in the pockets of his corduroy jacket for his tobacco tin. Or maybe he's going to put it on, and 'pop round the corner'. He'll be swallowed up whole, claimed by the darkness.

'Does Mum love you more than you love her?' I say, the words a desperate jumble. As soon as they've flown from my mouth, I want to hoover them back up again. I am so stupid. Right now I can believe that this is a blip, a temporary suspension of normal service, but if he says yes . . . Lorcan turns towards me, the half-rolled cigarette trapped between his long fingers ready for him to lick. I dig my sharp fingernails into my palm, glad I haven't cut them, keep my eyes glued to the elephants.

'Don't believe in the kind of love they sing about on the

radio,' he says. '"Especially for you . . ."' he croons, high-pitched, his hatred for 'manufactured crap' poisoning the words. He must NEVER know I've got the Kylie album.

'What about your songs?'

If we can talk about the album he's been recording, his new manager, we can swerve away from this stupid, awful swamp I've waded into. Although I'm worried: his house isn't very nice, no one can be paying him very much for the album. If only people knew how talented he is: unique.

'Especially my songs!' he says. 'Lust gets you through the beginning, but it's a bonfire. It burns itself out.' I try to keep my face in the right position, like I'm considering the point. One of my friends lent me her dog-eared copy of *Forever*, and I read it, guiltily, out of the house, knowing how much Mum would disapprove. I told Cara I loved it: that's what you have to say about *Forever*, but it frightened me a bit. 'It was like that with us. Couldn't stop. And then, year on, guess what, a baby.'

'I was a surprise?'

'You were *definitely* a surprise, my darling.'

'Did you think I was a boy?'

'I didn't know *what* you were,' he says, his voice coming from somewhere else. 'I was a kid myself. We didn't even know if we were going to keep you.'

My heart is thumping in my chest, so hard I think he might hear it. I put my hand over it to muffle the sound.

'Didn't you?'

'No. My beloved parents nearly keeled over when we told

them. We really thought we might have to . . . not have you. Or have you adopted.' He cocks his head, grins. 'You might have liked that. Mr and Mrs Average, in leafy Surbiton. "Dad–dy, my pony ate all the apples."'

I reach up, fling my arms around his neck, bury my head in the bony hollow beneath his shoulder.

'I would never have wanted that! Never!'

'You sure?'

'Sure as sure.' I'm crying, but I'm crying like Mum does, sneaky tears she thinks I don't see.

'Good. Because I'm so glad we kept you,' he says, rocking me against him. 'Precious girl. There's no one in the world who loves me like you do.'

Chapter Four

Lysette's invariably late – three children will do that to a person. I try and do what I'd counsel a patient to do, shift my mindset and change a problem into an opportunity. At first I find my advice intensely irritating, but gradually I start to relax into it. It's a hotel bar, this – superficially elegant, with its oatmeal sofas and slinkily dressed waitresses, but its proximity to King's Cross Station gives it an undercurrent. Commuters waiting for the delayed 7.15 to Nowheresville shun the overpriced Chablis in favour of swilled-back pints of Guinness; a besuited couple surreptitiously hold hands under a table, treasuring their last stolen moments before they head home to their other halves. Do they kiss in the photocopying room at work, I wonder, my eyes following her bare fingers as they caress his meaty digits, wedding ring firmly jammed on?

Lysette appears from behind me, squeezing me into a hug so tight I can barely breathe, her chin tucked into the crook of my neck. She nuzzles in and kisses my cheek, smelling of rose oil and something else I can't identify: does motherhood have a musk of its own, a hormonal mix of unconditional love and exhaustion that seeps from your very pores? I twist round, and hug her fiercely back, batting away the inevitable stream of apologies. We always promise each other we'll meet more often, but yet again it's been a gaping two-month hole. There aren't many people who join up my past, my present and my future: she's a string of fairy lights strewn across my history. I signal for the barman.

'Wine?' she says, twisting up her small, neat nose at my nearly full glass. It's funny watching someone age in front of you, a living embodiment of the passage of time. She's still the girl I knew – constantly smiling, her face pixie-ish and mischievous – but her hazel eyes are ringed by a subtle network of lines, her forehead similarly decorated when her fringe is swept aside. She still looks lovely, but it sort of denies me the luxury of denial. When we were sixteen, thirty-six would've seemed positively ancient.

'Only proper booze hounds drink Martinis on their own.'

'A Martini!' Her enthusiasm fades as she darts an anxious glance at the drinks list.

'Don't worry, I'm buying,' I whisper, quietly enough to be out of earshot of the barman. 'I invited you on a date.' Her face relaxes, and I feel instantly guilty for the momentary stress I caused her. I thought it would be easy for her, near to where her train comes in. Since when did I get so spoilt?

'Gin, on the rocks, with a twist. Hang on, that doesn't

work, does it?' The barman's laughing at her, immediately drawn in by her warm chaos. She smiles at him, her light brown curls tangling down her shoulders, benignly flirting. She somehow manages to make the simplest of outfits look sexy. Today it's a stripy Breton shirt over rolled-up boy-friend jeans, little black mules jammed on as an afterthought. I would agonize over my outfits when we were teenagers, saving up for literally years for a black dress from the kind of Knightsbridge store with a security guard, and she'd still out-class me with something from a charity shop: it's being comfortable in her own skin that does it. 'Whatever you think, as long as it's not vodka. Two?' she says, looking to me, and wiggling her eyebrows.

'I'm fine for now.' She stares meaningfully at my nearly full glass, and I take a large gulp to reassure her that I'm no party pooper. 'Ooh, Saffron made you this,' she says, pulling a crumpled piece of cardboard out of her overflowing cotton shopping bag and slapping it down on the bar. It's a wobbly outline of something – a woman perhaps – with some clum-sily crayoned-on eyes and a clump of shiny green nylon feathers.

'It's lovely! Is it meant to be me?'

'I think you need to take a better look in the mirror. Or get some glasses. It's a chicken, a slightly hideous one.' I look more closely. Saffron's my god–daughter, three years old and wilful, possessed by an unwavering devotion to me and *Peppa Pig*. 'I hope you're not analysing it for psychopathic tendencies.'

'No, I'm just admiring it,' I say, smoothing it down, trying to eradicate the wrinkles. 'I might even frame it.'

'Are you *insane*? I mean bless, but . . .'

She's watching me watching it, and I look away, self-conscious.

'How's Ged?' I say quickly. Ged's father to her two youngest children, a carpenter who seems to communicate mainly from inside a billowing cloud of spliff smoke.

'Lovely,' she says, grinning, the very thought of him lighting her up. 'Slightly flatulent. Bit short on actual work at the moment. Seems to be mainly doing people favours. I so want a proper week away at Easter, not a rainy week of purgatory trying to entertain three kids under an arsing piece of tarpaulin in a Welsh field, but I can't see it happening. Are you going on another mini break somewhere unbelievably hot and glamorous?'

I know she doesn't mean it, but I can't help detecting a certain spikiness in her comment. The truth is, I probably earn about the same as Ged pro rata, what with all the time I spend writing up my case notes and giving low-cost sessions to people who haven't got a bean, but I know the addition of Marcus to the mix makes my life look luxurious. And I'd be lying if I said I didn't enjoy the perks.

But the edginess is not about money, not really. It's about the fact that we no longer understand each other's lives the way we used to, like a blind person reading Braille, fingers running across, the meaning instantly apparent. We'd always been different, but our differences hadn't rolled out into real life and become something tangible and unarguable with. I want your life too, I feel like saying, but it's not quite true. Sometimes I want bits of it, even *long* for bits of it, but other times it terrifies me, the thought of playing endless games of pat-a-cake with sick down my front and no money of my own for shoes. I don't like myself for it. The fact there's no pressure from Marcus is both a blessing and a curse.

'Marcus has got a big redevelopment deal, so I'm not sure. And I'm . . .' I think of how Gemma looked at the end of the session, eyes glazed, our intimacy dissolved so entirely I could've been making it up. 'There's this girl I'm seeing. She's only thirteen, and her life's gone up in flames. I want to be around for her.'

'What, 24/7?'

I take a deliberate sip of my wine, playing for time. Confidentiality is the absolute cornerstone of my work – it's why we have supervision – but I suddenly desperately want to share something of it.

'It feels like she hasn't got anyone else. She needs me, Lys.'

I wriggle my shoulders, the grandiose words echoing around my head. I sound just like she does. I need to go and see Judith, work out why this case is wrapping itself around me like bindweed, but some part of me doesn't want to go anywhere near the answers.

'I honestly don't know how you do your job. I couldn't handle it. I'd last like . . . three hours. I'd tell someone they really *were* fat and have to resign.'

I think of Saffron's angelic face, chubby little fingers all too eager to seek out plug sockets and scalding-hot taps. I wish I *knew* I wanted it, like so many of my patients do, their ovaries shouting at them like militant peace protesters.

'Trust me, I couldn't do yours,' I say, the wine starting to make half truths feel truer. 'I get fifty minutes with a person. You're full-time.'

Lysette rolls her eyes, dismissive. It infuriates me sometimes, the bipolarity of being a woman. Both of us are failing at it, in our own unique way, and yet neither of us are.

'Just – you don't need to conquer the world single-handed. You're brilliant. You've already proved it.'

She gave me this birthday card last year with an annoyingly profound quote on it, something about how the reason we're cracked is to let the light come in. I'm sure she's right. In principle.

'I'm not doing it for that,' I say too fast. 'I love my job.'

'I know you do,' she says. I can hear the exasperation in her voice, but it's not meant meanly. 'Anyway, I've almost managed to train my third human to poo in the actual toilet, so I don't want you to go thinking you're the only one achieving professional greatness.'

'What can I say? Any god-child of mine is sure to be embarrassingly gifted.'

Lysette signals the barman for another Martini, and I drain my glass. I hope I didn't sound trite.

'She's starting full-time nursery in September. I was desperate to make it through the baby bit, but now it feels like it's disappeared in a puff of smoke.'

'You're really talented! There's loads of things you could do.'

She rolls her eyes, wrinkles her nose.

'You say that . . . even if there was an amazing job I could do between 9 a.m. and 3.30, I don't have a proper CV. Honestly, Mia, there was an advert for the Army on telly the other day, and I actually felt angry about the fact I'm too old to be a squaddie.'

The thought of Lysette in a hard hat, a rifle tucked jauntily under her left arm, is too funny an image. Once we've recovered from the giggles, I grab her hand.

'Look, if I can help . . . if you wanna brainstorm it, or we have a go at your CV together . . .'

She waves a dismissive hand, takes a determined slug of her Martini. I hope she doesn't think I lack the imagination to understand.

'You were looking at the five millionth flat this week, weren't you? Did it wow you?'

'Sort of,' I say. 'It's gorgeous.' She fixes me with a penetrating stare, waits for a postscript I'd rather wriggle out of giving. 'It was like an enormous Smeg fridge. I'd have felt like a petit pois rattling around at the bottom of the freezer.'

'Why don't you just move into his?' she asks, laughing.

'Because . . .' I know she's deeply suspicious of our slowness to commit, but I can't treat life the way she does, like it's one long bungee jump. She was pregnant within three months of meeting Ged, only a few months out of a marriage that was born out of youthful twenty-something certainty.

She doesn't seem to care if there's no safety harness. I love that about her, her spontaneity like a current of electricity that I can plug myself into for a boost, but it's not something I covet for myself. 'It's not my house. It's his house. His stupid great coffee machine. His ex-wife's bed. His porn stash, if I ever actually track it down.' She's looking at me. 'What?'

'You sound – I dunno, really cross.'

'Look, I know you don't like him,' I snap, hating my wasp-ishness. I wouldn't have picked a beardy stoner for you, is what I'm thinking, but I don't judge you for it. 'Sorry, ignore me. I think this new client is really getting to me, and—'

'It's not that I don't like him,' she says, interrupting. 'I just want you to . . . I want you to fall for someone so badly you can't even think about silly old clients. So you miss ashtanga yoga, and stuff yourself with muffins and swill back tequila shots, and text him all the time, even if it makes you look totally needy.'

My irritation melts, dissolved by the truth that fertilizes those words. Words, schmords. What she's really saying is, I know you, I know you all the way down to the roots, and I love all of it. I squeeze her hand, my fingers dipping between the hollows of hers. Her nails are painted a sea-green colour that I can't tear my eyes away from.

'I do love him, Lys. He looks after me.'

'You need muffin love, that's all I'm saying.'

'I'll bear my muffin quota in mind.'

★   ★   ★

We're standing on the platform by the last train, eking out the five minutes before the doors slam shut. There's a motley crew on board: a mixture of briefcase-wielding commuters and last-train casualties clutching cans of lager. I'm worrying about the tenner I've sneaked into my coat pocket, wondering if it's too patronizing to press it on her for a cab at the other end. It's only a short walk, and I know she'll think nothing of trotting through the dark on her clip-clopping mules, but I can't help worrying about what could loom out of the shadows.

'I should climb aboard, don't you think?' she says, hugging me. 'It was so lovely. Sooner next time. And take a sodding break if you want one!'

'You too! Why can't you go to your mum's, anyway? Ibiza's always hot, isn't it?'

When they were finally forced to sell their rambling family home, Gloria piled the little money that was left into a tiny Ibizan villa, deep in an olive grove. She supplements her measly pension by doing B&B and giving massages. I've never been there, but I like to imagine it's some kind of shabby-chic slice of heaven.

'Wasn't quick enough,' she says.

'How so?' I say, even though I know I shouldn't.

'Jim got Easter,' she says, trying to throw it away.

'*En famille*?' I ask, knowing it will hurt. There's a certain satisfaction in the hurt, like pushing at a wobbly milk tooth with your tongue.

'Yup,' she says, eyes tracking me, each of us silently

agreeing not to go there. Besides, the guard's shooing people off the platform.

'Take this,' I say, pressing the tenner into her hand. 'Thanks, Mia,' she says, naked gratitude in her eyes, and I delve deep into my bag for my purse. 'Take this too,' I say, thrusting another twenty at her. The fact she doesn't even protest makes me wonder just how broke she really is. She jumps on the train. 'Love you,' she mouths as the carriage spirits her away from me.

March 1994 (fifteen years old)

Mum is properly terrible at painting her nails. The red varnish smears itself over her cuticles, making it look like she's got her hand caught in a Victorian loom and is slowly bleeding to death. She's sitting at the kitchen table right now, wobbly right hand waving over the left, swearing under her breath. I watch her from the kitchen door, sneakily pulling down my black tube miniskirt and sliding behind the table so that, when she looks up, she can't see how short it is.

'Me and Lysette are going to the cinema,' I say, as casually as I can muster. 'I'll be back by 10.30.'

'Hang on,' she says, head jerking up, a globule of varnish landing on the battered kitchen table. 'Shit! Don't you know we're having family supper tonight?'

'Do you *see* Lorcan?' I say, in my 'whatever' voice. Big mistake. She hates that.

'No Mia, I don't. I'm not blind. But we agreed it, so I'm

sure he'll be walking through the door any minute. He's bringing fish and chips,' she adds, like it clinches it.

She's scraping at the splodge on the table with a tissue, oblivious to the fact she's turned a tiny spot of red into a full-scale crime scene. She's only started all this – painting her nails, using mascara – since Lorcan came back. She's always been a natural beauty, her long wavy hair and delicate features giving her the look of a Pre-Raphaelite portrait. I hate watching her trying to be something else. Besides, it feels like she's stealing my moment, the time in my life when I'm meant to be casting off into the exotic ocean of womanhood.

'I'm not hungry, anyway.'

'You have to eat. You're a growing girl: it's vital for your brain. Have you got much homework this weekend?'

I've done it all already. I stayed up until one last night doing my maths, and I wrote my *Jane Eyre* essay in the library after school, but something won't let me tell her that.

'Yeah, loads,' I say.

'Then you need an early night. If you're going to the cinema, I'd much rather you went to the early screening. Or not at all, tonight.'

'Lysette's waiting for me!'

Mum's hazel eyes flash with anger.

'That's not my problem. You made an agreement . . .'

'A sort of agreement,' I snarl back, taking a theatrical look around the messy, Lorcan-free kitchen. Her face crumples, and I come close to crumpling along with it. I nearly stand up, miniskirt and all, and rush round to the other side of the table to hug her, but then I remember that I'm almost there, almost out. The whiff of freedom is too seductive. 'If he's not back in half an hour, then can I go?' I can taste how much I hate myself. It's bitter, like the dregs at the bottom of the coffee pot.

When I get to the Odeon, there's a queue snaking right round the block. I rang Lysette's house to say I'd be late, but I could only do it after the allotted half an hour, or I'd have had to straight off cancel. I knew Lorcan wasn't coming, even if Mum didn't. He's recording his new album in the bowels of a Soho recording studio, and every Friday night is cause for a celebration. He'll be in the Coach and Horses or the Ship with the rest of the band: if Mum really wanted to see him she should have invited herself along. I know why she didn't though.

I was right about Frog Features: she was Lorcan's girl-friend for a while, but eventually that bonfire burnt itself out too, just as Mum was starting to take some timid steps out into the big bad world of dating. At first she made him sleep in the spare room, but it didn't last more than a month or so. I think she should've kept up the act a bit longer – all queenly and regal, going out for drinks without telling him who with. These days she's needy, which he hates, with a side salad of angry, which he also hates. Is it any wonder I'm spending all my time with Lysette? She joined my class last September – she'd left a state school in West London – and we've been best friends ever since.

'There you are!' she says. She's smoking a roll-up, which she throws to the ground and grinds out with the heel of her Doc Marten. 'I'm freezing my sweet arse off here.'

She's not really angry, which is what's lovely about her. She doesn't worry about stuff. Her whole family are like that. Her mum is super relaxed, even if I stay over in Lysette's bedroom all weekend.

'Sorry!' I say, hugging her. 'Are we in time?'

'Let's quit this joint,' says Lysette. 'I've got a cunning plan.'

I've heard about Jim, but I've not yet met him. He's Lysette's half-brother, two years older, and in the lower sixth at a private boarding school somewhere in Sussex. His Easter holidays are longer than ours, and he's just got back.

'He NEVER invites me to stuff,' says an excited Lysette, showing me a crumpled photocopied invitation, an address in Hampstead running across the bottom. **Eight till late**, it says. **Bring a bottle**. The bottle's a challenge, and so is the **till late.** 'Just tell your mum you're staying at mine,' says Lysette as we peel away from the cinema queue. If Mum knew how I felt – guilt washing up like a wave every time I lie to her or snap at her – she'd be dumbfounded. 'Where have you gone, Mia?' she says when my insolence reaches new heights, and sometimes I want to tell her that I'm still here, trapped like Rapunzel in a tower I made myself, but I never do.

We take two buses, the second one snaking up the hill of

Hampstead High Street, past the chichi shops and elegant restaurants. I look down the length of my body, my cheap high street Lycra suddenly seeming like the wrong disguise.

'We'll just ask for Benjie on the door,' says Lysette.

'Not Jim?'

'He might need a bit of time to get used to the idea.'

'Lysette . . .'

'It'll be fine! They'll be hordes of people there. Hordes!'

The house is up yet another steep hill, round the back of the High Street. It's a huge Victorian pile, lights blazing, hip hop blaring out. Lysette marches up to the grand front door and buzzes, whilst I lurk at the bottom of the wide stone steps. After a brief conversation with a bushy-haired boy in a Cure T-shirt, she beckons urgently. 'Come on!'

The smell of spliff is overpowering as we fight our way through the crowded hallway to the kitchen. You can tell it's not just a rich crowd but also a sophisticated one. Our school is suburban, safe – a bit Pony Club. The girls here are not only older than us, they're wiser too. Their hair is expertly straightened, their clothes – even when they look a bit like Madonna wannabes – have an effortless coherence. I pull down my miniskirt, and grab the plastic cup of cranberry juice Lysette hands me. As soon as it hits the back of my throat I taste the vicious splash of vodka. I splutter and choke, earning a few eye rolls from nearby guests. 'Stop it, Mia,' hisses Lysette, bashing me on the back. I've never drunk spirits before, only wine, and for a second I feel as if the earth is opening up beneath me. I can't do this: I need to make my excuses and leave. But then the second sip of vodka strips its way down my dry throat, and the edges start to blur.

'This is Boris,' says Lysette, and I try not to giggle at his ridiculous name. He's spotty, a back-to-front baseball cap worn, I suspect, to cover the acne's worst ravages. Spotty or not, he's friendly, and falls for Lysette's line about knowing Benjie, the host, from the pub. Lysette looks older than fifteen. She's got real breasts, soft mounds which give her clothes a lovely hang, and perfect skin, which make-up glides onto. She's sexy, even though she hasn't come close to having sex yet. Soon Boris's friends are drawn into our circle of three, and, with the vodka whistling through my bloodstream, I'm laughing and joking like I'm in my element.

It's half an hour later when Jim discovers us. He blows his way into the kitchen, laughing at something a blonde girl's saying to him, then is stopped in his tracks by the sight of us. I can't explain it, but there's something about the way he is that makes it feel like it's as much his party as it is Benjie's. He owns the kitchen, and the blonde gripping his arm looks like she wants him to own her too. He's darker than Lysette, with high cheekbones that point skywards. His mouth is full and reddish-pink, his skin smooth. There's something both girlish and incredibly masculine about him. I can't stop looking at him, even though his arrival might just kill our evening stone dead.

'Stay there,' he says to the girl, squeezing her waist. I feel a hot stab of illogical hatred for her. 'What are you doing here?' he demands, his face up close to Lysette's.

'I thought you said I could come.'

'I told you where I was going. Not the same thing.'

'Sorry, you know me. Shit for brains.' She grins at him. 'I wanted to see my big brother. Is that a crime?'

He stares her down, his beautiful face immobile. Then, finally, he grins back.

'I've got tequila.'

Jim pours a measure into a glass, then cascades lemonade over the top of it. 'Hides the taste,' he says, slamming the glass on the kitchen counter and swilling it back in one. He shakes his head from side to side, growling. 'Bracing,' he says. He looks at me, for what feels like the first time. I can feel heat building up, ready to stain me red. 'You next?' I incline my head towards Lysette, not quite trusting myself to speak.

'Oh Jim, this is Mia. She's made St Mary's almost bearable.'

'Mia?' he says, putting out his hand. There's a leather string around his wrist and a silver ring on his pinkie finger. He's wearing a white shirt, made of a heavy sort of cheese-cloth, flung over a pair of washed-out black jeans. 'Thanks for putting up with her.'

I can see the blonde out of the corner of my eye, hovering near the door. I look away, not wanting to draw Jim's eye in her direction.

'It's not a problem,' I say, hating how stiff I sound. 'I'm really glad she came.'

Jim's mixing another drink. He looks up, hands it to me.

'Enough small talk. Get that down you.'

I look at it swirling around in the glass, the bubbles erupting up at me. I think about Lorcan, even though I don't want to right now. I think about how he comes back from the pub a bit slurry, full of truths that are truer for him than for anyone else. I raise the glass to my lips and take a tiny sip.

'Down it!' says Jim. 'Slam it, down it!'

'Down it!' shrieks Lysette, a wild brightness in her eyes.

So I do. It's instant: the room begins to spin, the colours blurring and melding. I put my hand on the counter, and lower myself onto a stool, hoping I haven't gone green. Then Jim grabs me, kisses the side of my face, and it all feels worth it.

'Good girl,' he says, then turns to Lysette. 'You next.'

I don't really know what drunk feels like, but I'm pretty sure it's not like this: this is more like high. Jim drags us into the main room, the blonde trailing self-consciously behind, and we all dance to the hip hop that's booming out of the stereo. Normally I feel stupid dancing, but now my feet feel like cheetah's paws, unstoppable and quick. Jim grabs me round the waist sometimes, but I can't read too much into it. He grabs Lysette too, and I see him drag the blonde off for a kiss in the corner at one, excruciating, moment.

'You having fun?' shouts Lysette over the thumping bass.

'No,' I say, turning my mouth downwards, and then we

burst into giggles, hugging each other so tight I can feel her heart beating.

'My brother's the most fun ever, isn't he?' she says directly into my ear. I nod, not trusting myself to formulate a reply.

It's the police, not Jim, who end our evening, turning up on the doorstep after a noise complaint. The music stops abruptly, the lights go up, and we blink and shudder with shock. Jim disappeared a while ago, but suddenly he's there at our elbow. 'Let's go and hail a cab,' he says, which seems like the height of sophistication to a night-bus devotee like me. The blonde's still a bit part, mascara-clumped cow eyes tracking him from the other side of the room. He goes over and kisses her, right there with the lights up. I see a shocking, pink flash of their tongues before he pulls away, impervious to the way her spindly fingers are laced between the buttons of his shirt. 'I'll call you,' he says, smiling, green eyes narrowed.

And then we're out of the door and down the hill, the cold air blowing away the last traces of tequila. And as it seeps away, the guilt seeps back in. I called Mum from a phone box, hearing the resignation in her voice as I told her I was staying at Lysette's, yet again. 'Love you,' I muttered at the end of the call, but it was like a scrap of fish thrown to a seal. I push the dark thoughts away and, as I do, I feel Jim's arm around my shoulder. His other one's around Lysette, but I don't care. I've never had a boy put his arm around me, let alone a boy who looks like him. Lysette snuggles in, but I'm not bold enough for that. When the glowing yellow light of a cab appears I'm secretly hoping it will just speed past, but Jim untangles himself and sticks his hand out. We clamber in, Jim confidently giving the driver the address. He flings his arms out again, pulling us into a huddle, swaying his body extravagantly as we take the bends, like it's a fairground ride. It is: it's a big dipper, my heart soaring with every lurch.

Me and Lysette always share a toothbrush, even though the dentist says it's nothing but a short cut to gum disease. 'Spit sisters,' she says, loudly rinsing out and handing it over. She leaves me at the sink, a baggy Sonic Youth T-shirt thrown onto the toilet seat. I brush, looking into my eyes, trying to work out if I look drunk: there's something different about me, I'm sure of it. I pull on the T-shirt, twisting my body to see if my breasts have any effect on its baggy outline, but naked there's nothing, only secret Kleenex stuffed down my bra induce any kind of womanliness.

He's right outside the bathroom door, clad only in a pair of red-striped boxer shorts. I try and smile, but my mouth clamps halfway.

'It's you!' he says. 'I'm bursting for a piss.'

'S-sorry.'

'It's OK,' he says, laughter in his eyes. 'I'll live.'

'It's all yours,' I say, stepping aside.

'Thanks,' he says, his eyes surfing my bare legs. I wish I had my Kleenex boobs on – I must look so shrimpish and white to him. He holds my gaze. 'I'm glad you crashed. Even though it was very, very bad behaviour.'

'Was it?' I say, my eyes never leaving his face, my voice a squeak.

'Yes,' he says, his fingers lightly brushing my face, his nails grazing my lips. 'It was.' He leans towards me just for a second, but then he's through the bathroom door, the lock snapping loudly into place.

I stand there for a minute, my palm resting against the wood. Then I climb into the camp bed on Lysette's floor, my body shrieking its feelings so loudly I'm worried it won't just be me who doesn't sleep a wink.

Chapter Five

Friday. Was three days too short a gap? Gemma's wearing her school uniform today: a grey skirt, its newness visible in the stiff pleats, a white shirt messily tucked in. It's one of those schizophrenic spring days, summery for an hour, then so blue and chilly you'd swear you'd hallucinated the whole thing. Maybe that's why her blazer's stuffed haphazardly into her rucksack – no, angrily – into her rucksack, the fabric erupting out of the top. I'd be angry if I'd been yanked out of school the way she's been, thrown into the comp down the road, people nudging and staring and whispering behind my back. The *Mail* did a double-page spread this week, which I just about managed to stop myself devouring. It was a prime piece of Middle England outrage: how could this respectable husband and father now appear to have been window dressing for a ruthless crime boss? I couldn't bear the thought of Gemma sucking it up, the words burning their way into her consciousness, her shame mushrooming.

She said she wanted to come back. Now we're here, she's more like the silent scowler of week one, my gentle probing eliciting replies as cold and plain as day-old rice pudding. So much for what I told Lysette: judging by Gemma's cool indifference, I could probably hitchhike my way across the Outback without her even noticing I'd gone. I glance up at the clock: we're halfway through the session already. Tiptoeing around her trauma isn't doing her any favours.

'I thought about you a lot after our last session.'

'Did you?' she says, raising her eyebrows. 'Your life must be dull as, then.'

I smile, refusing to be stung. She wants a reaction. She wants me to confirm the list of charges she's holding against herself.

'I thought about how brave you were. You'd only met me once, but you came in here and talked about real things. You went for it.'

She looks at me sideways, wary as a cat.

'How do you know what's real? You're not psychic. You don't have some crystal ball,' she says, putting her hands round an imaginary one, her eyes all fuzzy, like she's on some terrible late-night cable show.

'You're right, I don't see dead people. But what you said felt pretty real to me. You let me see you, what's underneath.'

I wish we could pause here for a minute, the words reso-nating through her until they take hold, the sense that someone can see her secret self and not turn away – like her even more for it, perhaps. Instead she barely hears me, her words almost overlapping mine.

'You just want me to talk about Dad. You're like this.' She jerks her body forward, chin balanced on her knuckles, jaw clenched.

'I don't, actually,' I say, smiling at her cheeky impression. 'I'm interested in you. How you feel about things. How you're coping with all the . . .' I cock my head; I don't want to be all pompous and Brown Owl with her. 'All the shit you're having to deal with.'

Her face crumples for a second, the relief I suspect of someone honestly reflecting on what she's going through, but then I watch her tensing up, steeling herself. Vulnerability is weakness: I bet I know where that belief comes from.

'You were so horrible about him,' she says, almost spitting the words out. 'You don't even know him.' Her eyes blazing, she looks straight into mine. 'You were a total bitch.'

I pause a second, keep my face neutral. How must it feel, reading those things in the press? She's so confused – marooned between hating him and hating herself. Way easier to hate me.

'I certainly wasn't trying to be horrible about him. I'm sorry if that's how it sounded. I listened to what you said about him telling you about yourself, and how hard it makes you work to change yourself. Sounds pretty exhausting to me. I wanted you to know that you're always lovable. You don't have to spend your whole time trying to be perfect. It looks to me like your mum always loves you, even when you're fighting, and I bet your dad does too. Lots of people love you.'

'So stop making out he's some . . . some fucking abuser!' There are two feverish spots of colour on her cheeks, like a make-up artist's been at her with a brush. Her eyes are bright, her face more animated than I've ever seen it. That word, it's like a trip switch. 'Stop saying he's cruel to me. Tough love is love. All his love is love. My dad loves me more than anyone in the world.'

All love is created equal? I don't think so. I can feel that tension building up inside me again, memories clamouring. Maybe all love *is* created equal, it's just that sometimes what looks like love turns out to be nothing of the sort.

'So do you think he loves you more than your mum?' She looks at me, defiant, nodding that sharp little chin, carved directly from his face. 'And your brothers?'

'I'm his rock, Mia. That's what he calls me. I'm his little rock of Gibraltar.'

What is it about that statement that chills me so much? His rock, the thing he clings to – the only thing that stops him from drowning.

'What does it mean, being his little rock?'

'It means he can tell me anything and I'll keep it safe.'

There's something triumphant in the way she says it, the fire back in her eyes. She's baiting me, asking me to wonder what it is he whispers in her ear.

'Do you like keeping secrets?'

'I'm good at it, Mia. It's my superpower. What's your superpower?'

'People tell me secrets too. I don't know if I'd call it a superpower. You might have to tell me what the rules are.'

'Something you're better at than anyone else,' she says definitively. 'Something that makes you special.'

'OK. So what's it like if there isn't one thing you're better at than anyone else? If your superpower is just being you?'

It's funny, those moments when you dole out a piece of advice that you yourself need more than anyone else – I think of the Booker prize winners I've forced myself to the end of, even when I've been cross-eyed with boredom, the juice fasts, the endless exams I've crammed for.

'That's stupid. Spider-Man wouldn't have a superpower if he couldn't climb up buildings. He'd just be a burglar. He'd probably be in prison.'

A superhero, stripped of his powers and locked away.

'So if your superpower is keeping secrets, what's your dad's?'

'My dad IS a superpower. He's the best at loads of things. He went to Oxford, even though he wasn't posh like everyone else. He built up his business from nothing. He keeps Mum in the style to which she's accustomed.'

Not her phrase. Not her list. He's drilled her – no, he's brainwashed her – and then he's abandoned her. She's the one in prison, not him. If she is keeping his secrets, she'll never find the way out.

'Keeping secrets can be really hard. I've got Judith, my

boss, for when secrets feel too big for me to handle on my own.'

She looks up at me, her eyes big and round, the fight gone. She looks so small, her thin body framed by the plump sofa.

'It's easy to keep secrets. You just don't tell anyone. You zip up.'

'Like this?' I say, zipping my mouth. 'Does it make it hard to breathe?'

'I've got my nose,' she says, a half-smile playing across her face. 'You have to keep promises. A promise is a promise, Mia.'

Rage spurts upwards inside me, like a fountain. If he really has left her with a head full of secrets she's too scared to share, holding on to them the only way she knows how to prove her love to him . . . it's not even safe. The words are out of my mouth before I've given myself time to carefully pull the right ones down from the shelf.

'I understand it way more than you realize, Gemma, not just because I'm meant to be this big, wise therapist person. My dad would say things to me that would hurt me, and I'd swallow them. Or he'd disappear, and I wouldn't know where he was. But none of it was my fault, and none of this is your fault. You don't have to hurt yourself to prove to him you're a good daughter.'

She gazes at me, her eyes filling with tears. Then she flings her body across the arm of the sofa, sobs shaking the thin rack of her shoulders. I scoot out of my seat and sit next to her, waiting for her pain to subside.

'I know he loves me,' she says, her sobs making her breathing ragged. 'It's why he had to leave. I get it.'

Present tense.

'Because he tells you?'

She raises her tear-stained face, but doesn't answer the question.

'Are you someone's mum?' she asks, her eyes tracking me.

'I'm not going to tell you that, Gemma. Why do you think it is that you want to know?'

Children often want to find out if they're the special one in my life. It's never a question I answer, but hearing her ask it now makes my heart ball up tight. Have I blurred the lines too much? I don't want to be yet another adult who doesn't know what the job description is.

'Just tell me, Mia! I need to know.'

'It doesn't matter,' I say soothingly, my hand over hers. 'All that matters is that I'm here for you right now.'

And we sit there quietly for the last few minutes, her sobs gradually subsiding. That was either a brilliant session, me at my dazzling best, or the absolute opposite.

Chapter Six

I'm trying to decide between mozzarella and hummus – fat versus taste basically – when Marcus calls. I look at his name flashing on the screen, deliberate for a second about whether to pick up. My skin still feels taut, stretched thin like a drum, every moment of contact landing like a blow. My session with Gemma is looping round and round in my head, my carefully manicured hand shaking as I reach into the chiller cabinet.

'Hi, gorgeous,' he says, the words sticky with intent, and I junk the mozzarella.

'Hi.'

'Listen, bad news. I know you were longing to see me later . . .'

'I was,' I say, instantly comforted by the normality. 'I was howling at the sky, beating my breast.'

'Please don't talk about breasts,' he laughs. 'Not when the whole office can see me. But, darling, listen, I've got to go to Dubai.'

'Dubai?'

'Yeah, me and Juliet are flying out today. This deal's looking wobbly. Needs a charm offensive.'

'Oh, OK.' Friday night on my own. I'm almost disappointed, but it swiftly starts to mutate into something involving tracksuit bottoms, three episodes of *Girls* back to back, and a second glass of sauvignon blanc. 'Will you be back tomorrow?'

'Hope so. Listen, we need to move on this flat. The agent's chasing. Let's just get on and sign, shall we?'

'It's not as simple as—'

'OK, fine. Let's talk about it when we see each other,' he says, cutting straight across me. Did he hear the stop sign in my voice and ride roughshod over it, or did it not even register? 'Take care of yourself while I'm gone, sweetheart,' he adds, his voice softer now. The sound of the words stays with me even after he's hung up.

The whole afternoon it feels as though I'm hovering over my treatment room in a helicopter, painstakingly critiquing my own performance. I skilfully draw my clients towards subtle insights and major breakthroughs, my professionalism never faltering – I'm the Scarlet Pimpernel, deftly leaping between the Parisian rooftops. Even so, none of it quashes the nagging feeling that I pushed Gemma too far today. I do sometimes share carefully curated fragments of my life with my clients to help them feel less alone, but this was something different. It's not so much what I said, it was the emotion of it. It was a piece of raw meat slapped down on a butcher's block, bloody and livid. Gemma needs safety more than anything, to know that the adults in her life are *her* rocks, not the other way round. Have I – in my nuclear zeal to prove that fact to her – succeeded in doing the absolute opposite?

I need to call Annie, I need to speak to Judith – and yet I do neither. Instead, once I know Marcus has gone AWOL, I give Maria, one of my favourite clients, the precious after-work appointment that she's been begging me to find for her. She's going through a bereavement, hot on the heels of a torturous divorce, and I know how much she'll value it. The net result is that I'm the last one in the office, all set to lock up, when I hear footsteps ascending the stairs.

She's pink in the face, hair scraped back, make-up free. She looks like the child she sort of is.

'Hello, Doc,' she says, breathless.

I feel like a cheap magician, like I've conjured her up with the force of my fizzing thoughts.

'Gemma! You can't just turn up here, you know that. You need an appointment. You're lucky I hadn't already left.'

A sliver of ice traces its way down my spine. Was it luck or something more calculated?

'Yeah, I'm sorry,' she says, looking hurt. 'I just wanted to give you this.'

She reaches into her rucksack and pulls out a cellophane package, an extravagant pink bow tied around it. Two expensive bottles nestle together on a wooden stand, bubble bath and body cream, inviting and luxurious.

'Gemma,' I say, trying to order my thoughts. 'It's a very sweet thing to do, but you shouldn't be wasting your pocket money buying me presents.' It's more than a pocket-money present, even more so for a family who've had their assets frozen. She's still holding it out to me: I take it, then swiftly drop it onto the reception desk. I don't want to hold on to its shiny, slippery surface a minute longer than I have to. 'I'm just doing my job. You don't owe me anything.'

'No you're not,' she says, quick as a flash. 'My teachers are, the *police* are. You're different from them.'

She watches me, like she's flicked a stone into a pond and is waiting for the ripples.

'What we do here is different, you're right. But your teachers care about you too. We're all trying to take care of you. You don't have to give something back. You're entitled. It's yours to keep.'

'You're such a liar,' she says, hurt swiftly mutating into scorn. I know her now. 'You're seeing me cos you're paid to see me. If you weren't getting paid, I'd be out on the street.'

'You're right, your mum's paying me because she wants to support you too, but it doesn't mean I don't want to see you. I could say no. I could put my feet up and read *Grazia,* or see someone else. You're not my only client.' She smiles at me fleetingly. 'Does your mum even know you're here?'

'She won't mind. She *loves* you now,' she says with a roll of her eyes. She pauses, cocks her head. 'Was your mum nicer to you than your dad was, Mia?'

'OK, Gemma, time out,' I say, my unease mushrooming. She thinks she's found a secret passageway, a hidden route into the heart of my life. I shouldn't have lent her a flashlight, let alone snatched it back. I'll need to make this right, but not here in the deserted waiting room, the alarm beeping at me because the code's only half tapped in. 'That's why you can't just turn up. We talk in our sessions, not outside them. You need to get home.' I pick up the heavy package. 'Give this to your mum. I'm sure she'll love it.'

And then I hear the stairs creaking again, my heartbeat pounding in time with the heavy footfall.

'Hello?' I call, just as he comes through the door. He pauses a second, bright eyes roving around the room.

'Hello there,' he says, grinning. He looks at Gemma. 'And hello to you.'

I try and make my voice light and calm, whipped butter. 'Hello, Mr O'Leary. Gemma, I'll see you on Tuesday, same time.'

Gemma's rooted to the spot, her eyes sweeping over Patrick. She's such a chameleon, so young one minute and the next suffused with a knowingness that chills me. She lays the present down on the couch. Patrick stares back at her, sticks out a large hand.

'Gemma Vine, I presume?'

He's dressed more casually today: belted chinos with a pale

105

blue polo shirt, clumpy shoes that are a weird kind of trainer hybrid. What's the message supposed to be? Unthreatening, chummy.

'Yeah, that's right,' she says, still showing no sign of moving. 'I came to see Mia. I brought her a present.'

She looks at me, gives me a smile that's a test.

'Patrick works with the police,' I say. I wanted to spare her that knowledge, but she needs to know. I pause, thinking it through – it's the second unlikely coincidence of the last hour. 'Why don't you come to my office and tell me what it is you want?'

'I'd be delighted,' he says, all bonhomie.

Gemma grabs her rucksack, alert and watchful.

'Tuesday,' I say, squeezing her thin arm, hoping the touch will somehow anchor her. But how can anything anchor her?

'Don't forget your present,' she says, eyes sliding towards Patrick. She pulls her rucksack over her shoulder, finally heads for the door.

'Nice to meet you, Gemma,' Patrick says to her retreating form. She turns.

'Bye, Patrick,' she says, looking straight at him, no fear there. I almost admire the chutzpah of it, but it makes me wonder: has Christopher taught her that the Vines fly first-class, soaring above the law?

'Bye, Mia. We did good work today, didn't we?'

'We did.'

Patrick watches us, a look of faint amusement on his face,

not conceding any power. He turns back to me. 'Now, Mia. Where were we?'

Patrick O'Leary talks a good game. He perches on the arm of my sofa, long legs spilling out over the carpet, pouring out silver-tongued justifications.

'I went in too hard, I accept that,' he says. 'I just want the chance to explain why.'

'I don't *need* you to explain why,' I say, pointedly piling my files into my handbag. 'And you're apologizing for the exact crime you've just committed.'

'How so?'

'Ambushing me! Ambushing Gemma. There's something pretty sick about stalking a traumatized child, don't you think?'

'Stalking?! Oh what, you think I followed her here? I'm a lawyer, Mia, not Columbo.'

'I don't believe a word you say.'

'It's all a bit more complicated than you think. Let me buy you a coffee, give you a bit more background.'

'I don't need background either!' He looks at me, those dark brown eyes wide and hurt. I can't help but feel like I've kicked a puppy. 'It's Friday night, Mr O'Leary . . .'

'Come on, it's Patrick.'

'Patrick. Surely you've got better things to do than hang around strange women's offices pushing caffeine?'

'I know, it's sad, isn't it? Let's have a proper drink.'

'No!'

'Mia, joking aside, I think it's worth both our whiles us having a wee chat.'

There's something, something in the way he says it – before I know it I'm letting him clatter his way down the stairs behind me.

I try for Caffè Nero, I really do, but it's full of backpackers with overflowing rucksacks and harassed baristas screeching orders at each other over the hissing machines. Patrick rolls his eyes towards the musty wine bar next door, an empty table right there in the window, two green leather chairs either side. I haven't the fight for this fight – I have a feeling I might need it for later.

'I'll go to the bar,' he says. 'What'll you have?'

'Sparkling water.'

He stands there just looking at me, and I try to glare back but after a while it makes my eyes hurt. He lopes off, then comes back with his hands full of glasses. He sets the sparkling water down in front of me, swiftly followed by a glass of white.

'Seems rude to sit here with a drink, and you not have one. Especially on such a beautiful evening. If you don't want it, it'll save me making another trip.'

'This isn't a two-round scenario.'

'You clearly haven't seen how fast I drink,' he says, smiling.

I take a small, sanctimonious sip of sparkling water.

'So what is it that you think I so desperately need to know?'

I don't like myself for my sarcasm – not least because it makes me look like a naive idiot – but I like him less for snooping on a vulnerable child. It tugs at my heart, the way she thrust the present towards me, desperate for me to accept it. Accept her.

'I just wanted you to understand why I was putting pressure on you last week. With Christopher gone, there's a real chance that we're going to have to call Gemma to give evidence.'

'What does that even mean?'

'Playing back the video tapes of her interview. Cross examining her on the stand and looking for holes in her story. We're running out of options.'

I think about her pale smudge of a face, the way she can blank out until she's no more than a ghost. How far into the ether will she float away if they try to trap her? When their briefcases have slammed shut and their case notes have been shredded, there'll be no one left to bring her back down to earth.

'What's the point of that? If she doesn't know where her dad is, and there's no evidence that she does—'

'It's not just about that. From everything we've learnt, those two are uncommonly close. You know he took her to New York on a business trip? Just her?' I keep my face neutral, ignoring the way he's scrutinizing me for a reaction. He smiles, shrugs. 'Whether you do or you don't – these kind of scenarios. She may've overheard stuff that'd give us proof.'

'Proof of what, exactly?'

'That her dad knew that Stephen was corrupt. Information about deals, things that tell us where the bodies are buried, financially at least. Al Capone didn't go down for gangland killing, he went down for tax evasion. If we had access to all the accounts, could see all those dirty channels of money, I guarantee we could lock Stephen up and throw away the key.'

'Yeah well, even if Christopher Vine does know, from the sound of Stephen, I'm not surprised he doesn't want to hand over his calculator to you lot.'

Patrick's jaw clenches, his eyes cold.

'Them's the breaks,' he says. 'If you take the money, you take the risk. Have you seen their house?' I shake my head. 'Big white fucking pile in Wimbledon, looks like a wedding cake. He's enjoyed that gravy train long enough. Stephen's victims deserve better than him getting away with it because Christopher Vine's too much of a coward to pay his dues.'

'I'm sure it's completely irrelevant to you,' I say, icy, 'but, in my professional opinion, being forced to be part of a criminal trial — to testify about her dad — would be incredibly damaging for Gemma. She'd never forgive herself for betraying him.'

He goes to reply, then swallows his words back down. He takes a sip of his drink, looks at me.

'Not true. It's very relevant for me, Mia. She's a vulnerable witness. Emotionally vulnerable and, potentially, physically vulnerable.'

'Do you really think she is?'

'The kind of guys Stephen Wright has around him don't mess about.'

'I know, but she's a child!'

Patrick gives me a look that borders on pity, like the only real child is me. I look back at him, almost pleading with him to reassure me, to tell me that the world is not as dark as he's painting it, and he stares straight back at me, refusing to let me off the hook.

'Stephen's looking at a very lengthy sentence. He'll do whatever it takes to make sure that doesn't happen. It's better we know what she knows, and give her witness protection if she needs it. If she testifies, and he goes down, she's far safer than she is now.'

'If she even knows anything! You're making huge assumptions. If Christopher loves her so much, surely he'd protect her from this stuff. He's not stupid.' The words echo inside me, bouncing off the damp walls of my history, around the chambers of my heart. I know better than anyone that love doesn't work that way. Patrick's studying me, his gaze too penetrating. I pause a second, my voice less shrill. 'She's soft still. These – these traumas – they could shape her whole life.'

He smiles in a way that makes me self-conscious. I've shown him too much.

'And that's why it needs to be handled so sensitively. I can see how much she relies on you. We can support each other here.'

'You saw us together for two minutes!'

'You can sense a lot in two minutes.'

'So you're Mr Sensitive all of a sudden?'

That wounded look again, those kicked-puppy eyes. He pushes the second glass towards me.

'Have a sip. It won't kill you.'

I look at the cool dampness of the glass, the pale apple hue of the wine. It glides down my throat, taking a tiny bit of the heat with it.

'I don't know how you do your job,' I say.

'I love my job,' he says hotly. 'I don't know how you do yours.'

'I love *my* job. Just because you don't see the value of therapy—'

'How do you know that?'

'Oh come off it.'

'Went to a therapist after my dad died. Well, a "grief counsellor",' he says, doing inverted commas in the air with his daddy-long-legs fingers. 'Wept like a baby.'

'When did your dad die?' I say, before I can help myself. I wish I didn't have this compulsion to unpack people. He's not a lost suitcase, not something for me to rummage around inside of in search of a handy piece of ID.

'Couple of years ago. Lung cancer.' He looks down at his glass, then takes a gulp. 'It was kind of self-inflicted.'

'Some people smoke eighty a day and live till they're a hundred,' I say gently.

'I don't think he necessarily wanted to be here,' he says, his eyes meeting mine for a brief second. There are so many ways for a parent to abandon their child, and every single one cuts to the bone.

'I'm sorry.'

'How'd we get on to that?' he says with a half-smile. 'You're good, aren't you?'

'Devastatingly good,' I say, smiling back, despite myself. I take another sip of my wine, against my better judgement. It's pretty heinous on second tasting. Patrick's staring at me again, almost crackling with nervous energy. I steel myself.

'This entire case could collapse without Christopher's evidence. Or Gemma's, if that's what we end up needing. Quite apart from all those people's livelihoods and all that dirty money, we're talking about a cost of millions to the taxpayer. I can't stand by and watch that happen.'

I grab my jacket, my blood boiling now. It wasn't me opening him up, it was the exact reverse.

'Just stop it, OK? Stop using me to threaten her. You're shameless.'

Patrick's arm shoots out, bars my way.

'Mia, I'm sorry. OK?' His expression is deadly serious. 'I'm sorry. I'm obsessed, and it turns me into an insensitive dolt, but . . . It's not just you who's worried about her welfare. I shouldn't tell you this, but we think it's possible she's hiding evidence for him. Papers, documents.'

'Don't be ridiculous.' Gemma's face floats up before me, the way she fixes her gaze on the rushing cars when my questions get too real. She's holding on to something very tightly.

I sit back down again, my legs almost giving way. Patrick's voice is soft.

'You might be the one person who can stop her sacrificing herself for him.'

'He does love her,' I say, the words jagged, 'however screwed up their relationship is. Surely he wouldn't put her in that kind of danger . . .'

'Love can get twisted into some very strange shapes,' he says, half smiling again. 'Kind of like balloon animals.' We sit there for a minute, the information silently exploding like a pill dropped in a tall glass of water. Then he glances meaningfully at my wine, a clump of his floppy ginger hair falling across his milk-fed face. 'Well I, for one, am going to the bar. You've barely touched yours. Quite an unimpressive performance there, Mia.'

'I'm not much of a drinker.'

'Wasn't the best choice either, was it? I'm going to see how we fare with an upgrade.'

I should stop him, insist on going home to my slice of tracksuit-bottomed solitude, but somehow I don't manage to do that. The truth is, I'm not sure I can face being on my own right now. He comes back from the bar, puts another couple of glasses down and chinks his against mine, even though I'm not holding it up.

'Cheers. To second chances.'

'Who says I'm giving you a second chance?'

'You have to admit, we're having far more fun than we did last week. Go on, try your wine.'

I look at him, taking a deliberate, dubious sip. It's about a million times nicer. I take another one.

He raises a questioning eyebrow.

'You win.'

'Though to be fair, the first one was like horse piss.'

'You still drank it.'

'The thing you need to know about me, Mia, is that I've got very low standards.'

It's me who goes to the bar the next time, though I don't know why I do. Maybe it's self-protection. Patrick O'Leary isn't going away, and I need to know what it is that I'm dealing with. I put his glass down in front of him.

'Why serious fraud? Why not – I dunno – juicy divorces or megamillion City deals?'

He gives a big, theatrical yawn.

'No stakes. Did you watch *The A-Team* when you were a kid?'

'No.'

'No? What, you just watched girlie telly?'

'Mainly I read a book. My parents didn't like American television.'

Quite an understatement. A camera flash: me snuggled up to Lorcan on the sofa, watching a scratchy VHS of *A Matter of Life and Death*, too young to really understand anything much beyond the fact that he loved it. We spoke to each other in those clipped English tones for weeks – the more Mum begged us to stop, the more he'd egg me on.

'Right. Well I watched it – religiously – every Saturday. This is like *The A-Team* for me.'

'What, you're Mr Zee, triumphing over evil? Is that what you're saying?'

'Mr Zee? I can only hazard a guess you mean Mr T.'

'You're some kind of avenging angel?'

I can't quite keep the sarcasm out of my voice. He catches it.

'Don't really see what's wrong with that. You quite a fan of evil then, Mia?'

'Yeah, no, it's good. It's just, it's not always that simple, is it?' He looks at me, disappointment etched into his expression, three glasses of wine leaving his face wide open, like a door hanging off its hinges. I've sipped no more than a centimetre off the top of the last glass: it sits, undisturbed, in front of me, getting warm and soupy. 'Words like evil, they're reductive. I mean – in my work I see every possible side of things. Even when someone's behaviour seems inexcusable, there's always a whole network of drives and reasons underneath.'

'How'd you work that out with Hitler? Big fan of Pol Pot, are you? I'm sure he had a whole network of reasons—'

'Obviously Hitler was evil, but you don't get many Hitlers in the real world.' I look at him, thinking of the way he slunk up the stairs after Gemma like a fox hanging around the bins. 'And actually, I think his childhood *was* incredibly brutalizing.'

He snorts to himself, looking around the bar like he can't

116

quite bear to dignify the remark with a response. The crowd are older than us; suited businessmen buying Sancerre by the bottle for women who should know better, a group of Japanese tourists with enormous cameras, probably put to ample use on this afternoon's Sherlock Holmes tour. What am I doing here? What am I doing here with him?

'Do you know what, I don't see what's wrong with simple. I think we all make everything so fucking complicated—'

'I bet you're a Catholic.'

'Dr Cosgrove, you're a genius. Patrick O'Leary's a Catholic. Do you know what, if we had a time machine, I reckon you could probably get Hitler to see the error of his ways. Change the course of history with your noble counsel.'

'The way you talk about good and evil . . . I went to a convent school. I know what it's like, heaven and hell and fire and brimstone. Life just isn't like that. People aren't like that.'

'Oh I bet the nuns loved you.'

'They did, actually.' At least for a while. Then they really didn't. I hate the way the past keeps lapping at my toes like it's high tide. 'I should go.'

He downs the last of his wine, his eyes mock pleading.

'But it's your round.'

'I'm afraid I've reached my limit, Mr O'Leary.'

We look at each other, neither gaze wavering. Who are you? Who are you really? Is that what he's thinking too? I glance at my phone in my bag, a message silently flashing up at me like a flare. It must be Marcus, the thought an instant comfort. I stand up.

'Thanks for going one stage further than a latte,' he says, a lilt in his voice that I ignore.

'My pleasure.'

He stands up, touches my arm for a second.

'I know you think I'm a – I'm a fucking mosquito, buzzing in your ear when you're trying to sleep, but think about what I said. You could really make a difference.'

'That's what I'm trying to do.'

A vein pulses urgently in his neck, like the monster of his frustration might burst forth from his body, horror-movie style.

'OK,' he says, anger contained. 'But Mia, I'm not trying to scare you. They'll know who you are. We need to keep talking.'

My whole body clenches and tightens, my heart quickening in my chest.

'I get the feeling I don't have much choice,' I say, forcing a nonchalance I don't remotely feel.

He smiles at me, eyes softening in a way that looks real. I'm grateful for it, even if I won't admit it.

'Don't be like that,' he says.

'Like what?'

'Like I'm the enemy.'

If he is the enemy, then whose side am I on?

'I know you're not,' I say, giving him a fleeting kiss on the cheek like we're party guests at a glamorous soirée. And then I'm out of there, Cinderella as the clock strikes twelve.

July 1994 (fifteen years old)

Everything is Technicolor; the sky a bluer blue than I've ever seen, the sea sparkling like a handful of diamonds. I don't think I've ever been this happy. Happy slash anxious.

I haven't slept for a month, anticipating this holiday, the excitement churning my stomach and gripping my heart. Ten days in the same house – or gite, as I now know it's called – with Jim. I'd only seen him once since the party night, over the breakfast table the next day, but I didn't stop thinking about him for a second. I'd spilt my guts in green ink all over my diary, but that was the only place. There was a certain loneliness to it: I knew I couldn't tell Lysette, which meant we were no longer spit sisters in quite the way we were, but it was a small price to pay for being in love.

We flew out on Wednesday. I saw Jim before he saw me, slouching his way down the coffee queue at Gatwick, cool and handsome, a total contrast to the sweaty holidaymakers, passports clutched in clammy hands. His eyes were roving around like he was looking for something, and I couldn't help hoping it was me. He was dressed in an artfully faded pink T-shirt, those leather strings wound around his thin wrists, his fingers playing with a handful of change.

'There he is! Let's ask him to get us something,' said Lysette. I'd been thinking about this moment for the whole train journey, and now it was here I felt frozen, rooted to the spot. It's easy to treasure a fantasy – I couldn't imagine how much it would hurt if I had to chuck it aside and admit it was rubbish. Jim gave a slow smile when he saw us.

'Little sis,' he said, giving her a quick hug. 'And little sis sidekick,' he added, smiling at me.

'Mia,' I said, too quickly.

'I know. Mia.' His green eyes stayed on me. 'Do you want a double cappuccino? With extra froth?'

'That's exactly what I want,' I said. 'You read my mind.'

Lysette shot a quick glance between us.

'Me too,' she said.

'Then hand me some dollars,' he said, putting out his palm. With my eyes I traced the lines that criss-crossed it, then forced myself to look away. 'Cash money, ladies.'

We sat in a row once we got on the plane, Jim by the window and Lysette in the middle. He listened to his Discman most of the way, head resting against his rolled-up linen blazer, eyes closed.

'Please don't think me rude,' he said at one point, long eyelashes peeling up to look at us. 'Big night last night. I wanna be back on form by the time we land.'

'Lazybones,' said Lysette, digging him in the ribs.

'Slag,' he said, prodding her back, and they collapsed into giggles. I looked down at *Just Seventeen*. The whole problem page seemed to be about sex.

Jim is Gloria's son from her first marriage. His dad is French, and sometimes he goes to Paris to see him, but he acts like Lysette's dad, Gordon, is just as good. Lysette's mum and dad kiss each other all the time. She calls him 'honey', like they're in an American soap, and he looks at her deep, tanned cleavage unashamedly. 'It's gross,' says Lysette, but I like it. 'They're proper lovebirds,' I tell her – she doesn't know how lucky she is. Gloria never tells us off. In the morning we cycle down to the beach, Lilos and suncream crammed in our rucksacks, and we stay there all day, equipped with enough francs for an Orangina and a baguette at lunchtime.

Every morning is a sweet kind of torture, as I wait to find out if Jim is coming with us. Some days he just groans at us from his bed, ignoring Lysette's teasing entreaties. Other days he's up before us, fresh-faced at the breakfast table, telling us to 'hurry the fuck up'. Day four is one of those days. He cycles out ahead. 'Come on, losers,' he shouts, pedalling furiously, his calf muscles bulging out. Lysette and Jim laugh at me when I decide to invest a few francs in an umbrella. The sun feels relentless on my pale English skin, and I can see my shoulders have already developed an angry reddish tinge. When I show them both, Jim unexpectedly reaches out to feel it, and I pray he won't feel my body shiver at his touch.

I'm wearing my gold bikini, the cups roomier than I'd like. His fingers lightly graze the left strap, hooking underneath it to better see the burn.

'Sorry, loser, but she might be right,' he says.

'Pah,' says Lysette. Her routine is to rub greasy circles of tanning oil into her body, and then bake herself until she's as golden as an oven chip.

'Will you rub some cream on me?' he says from under his long eyelashes. 'If you can spare it.'

'Of course,' I say, too quickly again. He bounds over to me and kneels on the sand. I kneel behind him, trying to ignore the loud motor of my heart. I've got to stop being such a dork. A boy like Jim would never love a dork. 'How does sir like his cream?' I say in a silly voice.

'Shoulders, please, masseuse.' I squeeze a torrent of lotion onto my hand, and have to wipe some on my knees. I watch my white fingers progressing towards his skin, time slowing down to a crawl, and then they're there, splayed out on its hot surface. I start to gingerly move them, hoping it doesn't feel like I'm prodding and poking at him.

'That's nice,' he says, so low I'm not sure Lysette hears. 'Keep going.' I carry on for a minute or so more, before he suddenly springs up like a jack-in-a-box. 'Who's coming in the water?' he says, sprinting towards the sea.

Lysette and I are dragging round an entire library of dirty books. *Forever* seems tame now I've moved on to Jilly Cooper and Jackie Collins and *Flowers in the Attic*. Jim lies on his Lilo reading *The Great Gatsby*, and asking us to read out the most filthy bits we can find. I read him a relatively tame bit of *Riders*, something about someone 'entering' someone 'like an otter diving into a stream', and Lysette counters with a piece of filth from *Hollywood Wives* that makes my ears burn. I can't quite believe people are unashamed enough to do those things outside the tattered pages of these books.

'Enough!' says Jim. 'I'm enjoying a hearty dose of literature over here. You losers should try it some time.'

'I loved *Jane Eyre*,' I pipe up.

'You are *such* a loser,' says Lysette, an edge in her voice I don't remember ever hearing before.

'Takes one to know one, loser,' I reply, quick as a flash.

By the time we cycle home, I feel light-headed, like I've got sunstroke. Gloria's sunbathing by the swimming pool, her large breasts ('bosoms' as Lorcan would call them) spilling out, dark brown nipples like targets.

'Hello, my darlings,' she says, sitting up to talk to us, making no effort whatsoever to cover them. Jim and Lysette don't bat an eyelid, but I try desperately to keep my eyes focused on her face. An ex-model, she's deeply glamorous, her hair dyed a mellow honey colour, her green eyes feline, the lines on her face taking nothing away from her blatant sex appeal. 'We thought we'd toddle out for din-dins tonight. Get yourselves scrubbed up, and we'll leave in an hour.'

When we get back to our bedroom, I scrabble around in my purse, counting my dwindling notes.

'I don't want to be a loser, but I don't know if I can

come,' I say to Lysette. I'm such a fool: I spent all my babysitting money on holiday outfits, leaving myself vulnerable to Mum's parsimonious attitude to pocket money. I should've asked Lorcan, I think, even though part of me knows why I didn't. He might've thrust a bundle of notes at me, but he might just as well have got his disappointed look and told me what a spoilt baby I was. I don't want to think about it now.

'Don't be a loser. Mum and Dad'll pay,' says Lysette, spraying herself extravagantly with a can of Impulse.

'Choking!' I say, coughing just as extravagantly. Lysette giggles, spraying it right at me.

'Loser!' she says. This is literally the happiest day of my life.

The restaurant opens out onto the sea, the candlelit terrace punctuated by overflowing pots of bougainvillea. I can smell the salty freshness, hear the waves lapping up the beach. It's the most beautiful place I've ever been to. When we're shown to our table, Jim sits down quickly, green eyes meeting mine, and lightly cocks his head towards the chair next to his. I sit down, heart hammering. I'm wearing lipstick, mascara and eyeliner: I hope it's subtle, not clownish. I run my tongue discreetly over my teeth in case the lipstick's gone walkabout.

'Gordon darling, why don't you decide what we should eat?' says Gloria, signalling authoritatively for a waiter. 'Excuse me, can we have a round of Kir royals for the table?' she says, her ring-laden hand resting chummily on his arm.

The bubbles slip up my nose, the sweetness making it all too easy to sip like Ribena in a baby's cup. I'm giggly, chatty, loving the way Gloria and Gordon ask me things like they're genuinely interested. When the steak tartare appears, I prod at it with a tentative fork.

'Dig in, Mia,' says Gordon. 'Nothing to be afraid of.'

'To be fair, it *is* a bit like posh dog food,' says Jim, and I wonder if there'll be an explosion – a tirade about ingratitude – but Gloria and Gordon hoot with laughter.

'Cheeky monkey,' says Gloria, stroking his cheek affectionately from her side of the table.

Just for a second I wish they were my parents, then hate myself for being such a turncoat.

'You need some red wine to wash it down with,' says Gordon, going to pour me a glass from an ice bucket. It's chilled, a light Beaujolais. I've never even heard of chilled red wine before.

'Half a glass, Gordon. Honestly!' says Gloria, smiling at me.

The wine sloshes in and I take a sip. The unfamiliar coolness makes it taste like Ribena too.

'Cheers!' I say to Lysette, worried I haven't been paying her enough attention even though she's my best friend, the person who gave me this incredible gift. 'Cheers,' says Lysette, and then everyone joins in.

'Now, Jimbo, what's going on with that Natalie girl?' asks Gordon. 'Dangerous business, dallying with a girl in an adjoining dorm.'

'Yeah, no, she's nice. Didn't work out,' he says, and, in

the same second, reaches his hand under the table and plants it firmly on my leg. It's almost on my thigh, just above my knee. I try not to react, even though my body feels like it's been hit by a bolt of lightning. I can't tell if it's fear or excitement: I think they've been shaken up together into some kind of lethal cocktail. His fingers run up and down like he's playing a scale, getting higher and higher.

'You're a terror,' says Gloria. 'I thought you might bring her out here with us.'

'No chance,' says Jim, his fingers moving around to take in my inner thigh. I can feel my face flaming up. I push the chair back.

'I'm just, just going to the loo,' I say, walking swiftly across the decking.

I sit on the closed seat, waiting for my heart to slow. I wasn't imagining it: he felt it too! All this time. But now it's here, now my ship's come in, I have no idea how to proceed. I've kissed one person, once, at Julia Barratt's Christmas party, a spotty cousin of hers who seemed to want to scoop out my insides via my mouth and smelt like sour milk. I realize how little thought I've given to the reality of what Jim will want from me, what he'll have learned to expect from the limpid-eyed blondes who follow him around like he's the Pied Piper.

I can't wait any longer, for fear of Lysette coming to find me. I splash water on my flushed face, my eyes bright and wild, then open the bathroom door.

He's there, standing right outside. Before I have time to

speak he's pushing me against the wall, his mouth on mine. His tongue comes next, insistent and skilful, telling me that not all the kisses in my life will feel like a dirty protest.

'Jim,' I gasp, once I sense a pause. 'Someone will see.'

'I don't care,' he says, his breathing heavy. 'I had to kiss you. I've been thinking about this all week. You have too, haven't you?' Try months. Months that felt like years.

'Totally,' I say, winding my fingers into his silky brown hair as I stare up at him.

'I want you, Mia,' he says, into my ear. Does 'want you' mean what I think it means, or can it mean something gentler, less outside my comfort zone, I think, sobered by the realization of how pathetically small my comfort zone really is. Perhaps he sees the uncertainty in my face. 'I really like you. Like, really like you,' he says, stroking my cheek. 'You're ridiculously fuckable.'

'Me too,' I say, barely able to breathe. How can I be that, that thing? I want to be, I want to be worthy of the hardness of his body and the intensity of his gaze. He gives one of those lazy half-smiles.

'I think it's still your line.'

I smile back goofily. All I can think is: I love you. I love you, and I'm a virgin, and you're my best friend's brother. I don't say any of it of course.

'We need to go back,' I say, my eyes telling him too much truth.

'We do. But I want you to know,' he says, gripping my face under my chin, 'this isn't over. It's only just begun.'

127

Chapter Seven

Mum's digging up the back garden when I arrive, grey-streaked hair piled up in a messy bun, denim dungarees rolled up to her knees. She's attacking the ground with her spade, like the worms are her sworn enemy and they've reached their final standoff. She doesn't see me until I'm close by, so complete is her focus. She gathers me up in a hot, damp hug that feels fiercer than the situation demands. I try not to wriggle.

'Looking very boho there, Mum,' I tell her, the smell of manure already starting to overwhelm me. I haven't been out here for ages, the lush apple tree a trip switch for my guilt. It was bare in November, the skeleton of its branches stark against the grey sky. This is the house we moved to when I was ten, Lorcan's parents helping with the deposit, a gift that always felt like it came with strings very much attached. It's small and it's suburban, but the fact it had a proper garden, felt like an unimaginable luxury at the time.

'Potatoes,' she says, nodding at the soil she's turned over. '*You're* looking too thin. You've lost weight.'

'No I haven't.'

'A mother knows these things,' she says, brooking no argument. Is that how it feels, motherhood, a bedrock of instinct, of certainty, underpinning all the choppiness? I don't think it feels like that for Annie, even if it's what she chooses to project when she's trying to get one up on me. I wish the Vines weren't invading my everything. It's Sunday now: since my unwelcome Gemma/Patrick sandwich on Friday, I've barely thought of anything else. I force myself to stop with the mental time travel, looking instead at Mum's strong hands gripping the spade, age spots spreading across them like a map of the world. I don't see it so much in her face. Is it because I see those same familiar expressions I always have, regardless of her lines; the worry I can never quite steal away from her, however much I tell her I'm fine, the bafflement at how much I'm willing to spend on a pair of boots?

It's hot today, an unexpected blast of springtime sunshine. I'm wearing massive oval sunglasses that Marcus bought me in the Nice Duty Free, and a flowery dress that suddenly feels too short. I put it on in anticipation of our date later, but now I wish I'd rolled it up in my bag and worn a pair of jeans.

'Where's Nick?' I say, backing away from the stinky manure. The doors of the house are all wide open, but there's no sign of my stepfather. Sort of stepfather – they're not married, but they've been together twelve years. I don't know if

Lorcan's refusal to submit to such a bourgeois convention put her off for life – I suspect the doggedly loyal Nick would relish a real commitment. Nevertheless, I don't see her skipping out on him: their relationship is like a warm, shallow bath – something comforting she can submerge herself in without fear of drowning.

He was her first real foray into love after Lorcan. Day after day he'd come into the café where she worked and buy a coffee, gradually wearing her down. She was mistrustful, skittish – a foster kid who didn't want a new family. She agreed to have lunch with him, eventually dinner. It was when she invited him to hear her choir sing Handel's *Messiah* I knew she'd started to give in to his campaign of unbridled adoration. 'It'll sound like nails down a blackboard,' she said, self-conscious, but of course he loved it. He loved her, and for him that was something both simple and urgent.

'He's upstairs, working in his study.'

'On a Sunday?'

She gives a smile that doesn't reach her eyes.

'Lunch is in the oven. Let's go and give it a poke.'

The house is red-brick and square, the kind of shape you draw at primary school when you're asked to draw home – it's even got a chimney. The fixtures and fittings are all woefully dated – Mum's never been one for splashing cash on anything 'unnecessary', years of frugality ingrained in her. There's an aubergine parmigiana bubbling away in the oven, and some more of her potatoes baking around the sides.

She makes her voice gossamer light. 'I thought you might bring Marcus with you.'

'He's been in Dubai all weekend. He's got this huge deal going through.'

'Another huge deal?' she says, and I try not to hear judgement. Children are like dogs, the way they can hear a pitch in their parents' tone inaudible to other humans. 'Is it the money, or the thrill of it, do you think?'

'Bit of both.'

'Your time together must be . . .' She hesitates. 'Quite scant?'

It's true, I think, but then I remember how much time she spent sitting around waiting for Lorcan's key to turn in the lock. What's wrong with two alpha people living life full tilt and coming together when circumstances allow?

'It's not just big bad Marcus, Mum. I'm studying for an extra qualification. And I'm dealing with some pretty complex cases now. You'd be proud of me.' She looks at me, waiting for me to elaborate, and I start to scorch with self-doubt. It's still a couple of days until I see Gemma, I tell myself, time enough to confide in Judith about what's happened, but the truth is, there's been time enough already. My words about Lorcan keep echoing around my head, a soundtrack to the looping memory of the way her face scrunched up with hurt and anger as she realized I really wasn't going to take her hazardous present. I need to make it right. I need to put the pieces back in place. 'Client confidentiality, Mum. My lips are sealed.'

'And the flat hunting?'

'Yeah, I'm sure we'll find the right thing soon,' I say, slicing into the ripe flesh of the avocado she's given me for the salad, my eyes trained on the green mulch that's oozing out of the ruptured skin.

'That's good!' she says, watching me. 'But you're still planning to rent, not buy?' I nearly spell it out for her, save her from wrapping herself up in endless riddles. She wants to ask if I think Marcus is the one, even if he's not entirely to her taste – if she can make her heart vulnerable to the possibility of grandchildren or if that one lost moment was her only chance – but she's far too sensitive to plough straight in there. I appreciate that about her, I really do, but the less she tries to pressure me the more it feels like pressure.

'Yup, rented. I'll rent out mine. Keep your eyes on the road, Mum – there's nothing to see. Promise I'll tell you as soon as there's news.'

'Good,' she says, so much complicated love visible on her face that I feel it land in the centre of my chest, a grappling hook that lodges itself in my heart. 'Nick,' she shouts, 'lunch is ready!'

'Will you pull it out for me?' asks Mum, throwing an oven glove at him as soon as he appears in the kitchen doorway. She shakes dressing over the salad, leaving him to find the cutlery, and I chide myself for my slightly cool assessment of the state of their union. There's something seamless about their soft-shoe shuffle that's lovely to watch.

Once Nick's thumped the parmigiana down on a cork mat, he crosses the small kitchen to kiss me hello. 'It's terrific you could come,' he says, beaming at me. His relentless enthusiasm always reminds me of a local-radio DJ, forced to make the harvest festival sound like breaking news. His body is short and stocky, his hands big, capable paddles, constantly looking for something useful to do. Right now they're engaging me in a hug that's neither cold nor overfamiliar, a textbook step-parent embrace. He's bald, but even that reads like a clear decision, rather than an unfortunate side effect of late middle age. He's not handsome exactly, but the fact that he isn't almost makes him more attractive.

'So what's with you slaving away on the Sabbath?' I ask him, once lunch is dished out. 'How's that whole retirement thing working out for you?'

'You're one to talk!' laughs Nick. 'No, I'm – I've taken on some exam marking.'

Nick was a headmaster until a couple of years ago, a job I know he was born to do. Marking must pay peanuts. I look between the two of them, but their faces don't tell me much. Mum still cooks in a café a few days a week, but I hoped that money was an added bonus rather than a necessity. Nick deftly changes the subject, asking the same questions as Mum did about the flat hunting, minus the whispery subtext, and enquiring about Marcus's trip.

'Interesting place, Dubai,' he says. 'Extraordinary amounts of growth, but does he worry about the human rights side of things?'

Does he? Surely he must? I should know things like that. Is it me, self-importantly beavering away and never listening, or is it him never talking about anything tricky?

'Um, yeah. He does a lot of pro bono type stuff though. And it's a huge opportunity.'

'Undoubtedly,' says Nick, a *Guardian* reader to his very core.

'They're very ethical in the way they do business,' I say quickly, thinking of that grateful student from some godforsaken town who's now working his arse off for his architecture qualification.

Once we get to pudding, I can see that Mum's got something she wants to get off her chest. It's the way she's worrying at her spoon, like she's contemplating matchmaking it with her ice cream but she's lost her nerve.

'Mum?'

She gives a brief, snatched smile.

'We've got some news.'

'Don't tell me you haven't been using protection?'

She giggles, properly giggles like she needs the release, and I feel a sense of that lovely bubbly warmth we sometimes manage to find.

'Worse.'

'Charming!' says Nick, but when I look at his face it's scarily serious.

'We're getting married,' says Mum, the words out of step with the way that they sound, like a badly dubbed snatch of Euro-porn.

'Congratulations,' I say, looking at them both, waiting for the happy smiles. Nick's trying, but even his reliable mouth seems reluctant to comply. A trickle of dread slithers through me. I'm not ready to lose another parent, not yet. 'But why now? Mum?'

They shoot a quick, meaningful glance at one another. Mum looks at me, serious.

'Have you heard anything about this vile Stephen Wright character? I know how busy you are, but it's been all over the news.'

'Yes . . . no. I think so,' I say, aware that I'm stammering. That was the last thing I was expecting.

'I'm afraid I invested a chunk of my retirement savings in his organization,' says Nick. 'Fool that I am. It's gone – kaput. If we get married we'll at least improve our tax position.'

'I'm so sorry,' I say, my hand flying out to meet Mum's. 'That's awful.'

Mum's jaw is clenched, her eyes filling.

'Darling, please don't worry. No one's ill. We'll get through this. But . . . we're going to have to sell the house.'

I can feel the blood leaching from my face, my heart lurching. What a stupid irony: I spend so much time finding excuses not to come home, but when I find home may no longer exist it seems cataclysmic.

'Can I help?' I say, groping desperately for a solution. My hand is wrapped around the seat of the wooden kitchen chair, as if holding on tightly enough will stop it happening. 'I've got some savings.'

'No, of course not,' she says. The thought of losing the fairly modest nest egg I've accumulated terrifies me, but I'd do it in a heartbeat.

'I could sell my flat.'

'No you couldn't,' she says firmly. 'You need that security. You're not . . . in any position.'

She edits herself, but I hear the rest of the sentence. My lifestyle is built on sand – it's not actually my money.

'Let's not waste any more time talking about it,' says Nick. 'We'll do what we can. At least if they track down this accountant and get it to court there might be some kind of class action against the organization.'

'I really hope they find him,' I say, the words dry and chalky in my mouth. I wish Patrick's face would stop popping into my consciousness, all bright-eyed and righteous.

Marcus is in full James Bond mode tonight. He sent me coordinates – actual coordinates – for where we're meeting, which Nick helped me decipher on his ancient desktop. I should never have asked him: it's a bar at the top of a skyscraper in the City, yet another place where a glass of house wine will cost double figures. We watched a panorama of London roll out across the screen. 'Makes me queasy just looking at it,' Nick said drily, and I was filled with a surge of anger, an impotent longing to protect them.

Marcus is sitting by the window when I arrive, a half-drunk glass of red wine on the table. He springs up and encircles my waist, pulling me so tight against him that my organs feel like road kill. There's something pulsing here, a force field vibrating around him. I'm not sure if it's repelling or attracting me.

'I missed you,' he says, his voice low and guttural.

I'm too soft after the day I've had – soaked through with a tender sadness that's painful but also reassuring – sometimes it's good to feel something so completely, without any questions. I went up to my bedroom after lunch. It's full of junk now, the wardrobe stuffed with old coats and shoes that Mum refuses to throw away even though the soles are paper-thin, but my single bed's still there, covered in the old green bedspread I bought in Camden Lock when I was fourteen. I sat there, playing with the tassels, running them between my fingers like rosary beads, thinking about all the other times I'd done exactly that. It took a lot to stand up and leave.

'I'm surprised you had time. Sounds like you were flat out.'

'Doesn't mean I didn't think about you,' he says, a strong hand caressing my thigh. It feels like ownership. Why am I being so snarly? I snatch his hand and place it on the table, then stroke his fingers to soften the gesture. I should tell him about today, but I can't quite find the words. A small, proud part of me hates the idea he might think I'm asking for a loan.

'Did you do a good job?'

'What do you mean?'

'Did you save the deal?' I say, something jagged in my voice. Am I asking him a question I haven't been able to bear to ask myself? 'That would be doing a good job, wouldn't it?'

'Long story. We don't need to talk about it.'

'Well excuse *me* – have you got somewhere to be?'

'Let's get you a drink,' he says, pulling his hand away to signal for service.

Marcus says something discreet to the barman, who swiftly returns with an ice bucket and a couple of champagne flutes. He hands us each a glass. I hold it for a second, looking into its empty recesses.

'So,' says Marcus, signalling to the barman to pour. 'We celebrating?'

I watch some of my clients doing this, driving round and round the culs-de-sac of their own minds, waiting for the perfect moment to have a child or quit a hateful job or pop the question. Frankly it's boring. Boring and paralysing. I look into his eyes, flinty with concentration, a muscle in his jaw twitching. I should be grateful for his certainty. If there's one thing today has illuminated in neon lights, it's that there's no such thing. We should enjoy the moments when we can plausibly kid ourselves that there is.

'Yes. Yes!' I say, bumping my glass against his. 'Let's rent the fridge, damn it.'

He leans across the table, kisses me like we're naked. I try not to look around at who is close to us. I gently push him backwards, my hands spanning his broad chest.

'It's going to be good,' he says, eyes dancing.

'The agent did say she could give us a deal?' I ask. 'Because I can't remotely afford what they quoted.'

'Just don't worry about it,' he says, kissing my neck. 'You never have to worry about it. You know that really, don't you?'

'I'm not your geisha.'

'Did I say you were?'

'I didn't say you did,' I say, looking into his eyes. 'What about the kids? Juliet looked the polar opposite of pleased the other night. I don't want to be the wicked stepmother, Marcus.' I shouldn't have said the S word. Shouldn't have said the M word. They still feel too dangerous. I grab a salty almond, try for casual. 'Poisoned apples aren't my thing.'

'Listen, if you're worried, we can put something in writing.'

'What, like a prenup?'

'A prenup lite,' he says, smiling. 'And don't worry about the kids. Trust me, Juliet won't have time to think about it.'

'Why?'

'This job's going to cost a lot more than we first thought.'

'What, like thousands more?' Marcus raises his hands, palms upwards, almost as if he's offering it to the heavens: nothing to do with him. 'Millions?'

'Yup.'

'And did Juliet do the costing?'

He shrugs, his expression hard to read. He doesn't want to talk about it – I know that – but I can't stop myself from digging. It makes me think of Mum – all angry and hot and purposeful. 'But it sounds like you saved the day?' That cast-iron self-belief of his, it seduces me most of the time. I'm sure it seduces most people. 'It's sorted?'

'You have to get bloodied in this game,' he says. 'All part of the ride. She'll be fine.' His gaze is sliding sideways, his fingers worrying at the almonds, just like mine were. We're like a couple of shifty squirrels, out for a night on the tiles.

'What, so she took the rap?'

'We would've lost the job if she hadn't.'

'And it wasn't her fault?'

'They can't think I'm fallible. I'm the brand. I'm what they're buying. She knows that.'

'But Juliet loves her job. She'll feel about three inches tall.' He stares at me, his eyes cold. 'Like a Borrower,' I add, trying to lure him back from wherever it is he's retreated to, but he doesn't give me even a flicker of a smile.

'She took one for the team, she'll be fine. She doesn't have anything to worry about either.'

'Yeah, of course she knows you won't sack her, but it's about her reputation in the industry. She won't want to look like the only reason she's got a job is down to nepotism.'

I should back away from this. You should never tell a parent how to be a parent, especially when you're as under-qualified in that department as I am.

'Swings and roundabouts, darling. She just took a tumble on the slide: no harm done.'

'Do you not think that's kind of patronizing?'

Why am I picking a fight, tonight of all nights? I look at the smooth lines of his profile, which is all he's showing me right now. Here's the problem with chiselled features – they're made of stone. A snake of panic wraps itself around my gut but I force myself to ignore it. I've made a decision.

'I'm not asking you to understand,' he says, raising a hand for the waiter to top up our glasses.

'What, because you don't think I can?'

'That's not what I'm saying.'

'I did have a father,' I hiss, poking around in my handbag for something completely imaginary. My cheeks are hot, splashed red. I don't trust myself to look up. I can't carry on like this, the past a livid bruise that throbs at the slightest touch.

'Did I say otherwise?' he says. We look at each other for a long moment, neither of us speaking, and then, somewhere in the silent space that stretches between us, we decide to make up. 'Drink up, gorgeous. Let's go back to mine and celebrate properly.'

I think about it for a second, imagine spiralling down in the lift, sticking my arm out for a taxi and sailing back to my own bed.

I think about it, but I don't do it.

November 1994 (sixteen years old)

It's Jim's eighteenth birthday tomorrow and I'm in a total panic. It's not about what to get him – I've babysat around the clock to fund a moss-green Calvin Klein jumper from the first floor of Selfridges that he has to like, considering how beautifully it will match his eyes – it's that it's D-Day. Or should that be L-Day? I've finally convinced him that we have to tell Lysette, and we're going to do it on the afternoon of his birthday party. I can't stand deceiving her any longer. The longer we lie the bigger the lie will become, until it's big and black enough to eclipse our whole friendship. I want both: I want both forever. I hope that's not too greedy, because I would hate to have to choose.

Lorcan lopes down the stairs as my single slice of brown toast erupts from the toaster. I won't be having any butter on it, even though it means it tastes like cardboard. He looks exhausted and wide awake all at the same time. He's like a Mad March Hare at the moment: his album's about to come out, and, against the odds, it's getting a release in the US with a big publicity campaign.

'Morning, beautiful,' he says, grinning widely.

I do feel beautiful at the moment. It's a revelation – like the world is floodlit, bright and magical. I've had my sixteenth birthday, and my body's stood up to attention, my cleavage something real, the spots that plagued my early teens finally wiped away. Which came first, the chicken or the egg? It might just as well be having a gorgeous boy to kiss me and whisper unrepeatable suggestions into my ear.

August was like a dream, even if making endless excuses to Lysette was more like a nightmare. I would sneak off to meet him on Hampstead Heath or at the cinema, and we would kiss until my lips were chapped and my chin was red raw from his carefully cultivated stubble. 'I don't think I can wait much longer, baby,' he would murmur, his erection pressing hard against me through the knobbly seam of his jeans, and I would kiss him back more fervently, hoping it would be enough to keep him warm. Since my birthday his pleading has got more bullish. It's so much harder to see him now he's back at boarding school, and I'm terrified I won't be able to hold on to him with my clumsy pawing. The fact we've had to meet in public has been my secret blessing.

'Toast?' I say.

Lorcan waves me away, scooping a mound of coffee into his stovetop espresso pot. I grab my school books, ready to head for the bus.

'Eight o'clock,' he says. 'I need my little girl there, front row.'

He looks at me, fear etched into the Modigliani planes of his face. I nearly go and throw my arms round his bony shoulders, but I'll miss the bus.

'You got it.'

Lorcan's playing a showcase in a bar in Soho tonight. I'm sort of looking forward to it, I just wish there weren't so many things criss-crossing over the top. Mum's scurried off to see her best friend in Brighton, which seems pretty cruel to me.

'We're not in California any more, Toto,' he shouts after me. I'm so stupid. Too much Saturday-afternoon *Beverly Hills, 90210*. Sometimes I feel like I'm so many different people I can't remember who the right one is.

Lysette comes home with me after school, a stretchy tube of Lycra rolled up in her bag with a pair of clumpy high-heeled sandals. I've got better at putting make-up on these last few months. She watches my profile as I sit in front of the mirror, dabbing on red lipstick with a brush, then blotting it with a tissue to prepare for the second layer.

'Who's it for?'

'Who's what for?' I say, playing dumb.

'All of this,' she says. I've not yet put my top on, my new black bra cupping my almost cleavage. 'You haven't got a secret boyfriend stashed under the bed, have you?'

'It's nice to look nice,' I say, gazing into my own duplicitous eyes.

'You'd tell me?'

'Ob-viously. Anyway, you look nice too!' I say, forcing myself to turn towards her before the atmosphere congeals any more than it already has. 'Your legs look amazing in that dress.'

'Thanks,' she says, happier. 'Do you think I should wear it for the party?'

'Two days on the trot. Stinky!'

'Skanky!' says Lysette, laughing. 'Come round early and get ready, yeah?'

'Course I will,' I say, the words truer than she knows, my tummy turning over like a Ferris wheel.

We're actual VIPs, it says so on the list, which means we're waved right to the front of the longish queue. The club is deep in a basement, dark and atmospheric, the walls lined with posters from bands who are properly famous and have played here over the years. My heart swells up with pride like a balloon inflating: finally Lorcan's getting what he always deserved. We eye the bar nervously, too scared to try our luck. The crowd are filtering in now, and my fragile sense of sophistication is being sucked right out. We look like girls at best, adolescent and awkward. A blonde woman with eyeliner like Madonna had a few years ago approaches, and I wonder if this will be over before it began. My life seems to be like a computer game these days, a constant fight to make it to the next level.

'You must be Mia!' she says, her accent cut glass. 'You've got your dad's eyes.'

'Thanks,' I say. 'This is my best friend Lysette.'

'Your BF! I'm Bella. I've been told to get you naughty BFs a drink. If anyone asks you, say it's a softie. What would you like?'

'Malibu and Coke,' says Lysette, quick as a flash.

'Same,' I say.

'Coming right up,' says Bella, laughing at our speedy response.

It's an excellent choice, the Coke sweet enough to disguise the taste of the alcohol (does anyone really like the taste, or just the effect?). Bella stays with us for the first few sips, and I track her carefully to work out if she's me and Mum's enemy. I'm good at this.

'I like your earrings,' she says, her fingers fondling the interlocking gold hoops I'm wearing. I can't help blushing – they were my treasured birthday present from Jim – but it's too dark for anyone to see. I watch her smile, follow it until it reaches all the way to her kohl-smudged eyes. Perhaps I'll just relax, let the tide of Malibu lap its way through my system.

It seems to take forever for Lorcan to come on, but maybe it's just my nerves that make the time crawl past. Finally he appears, longish hair in a ponytail, his guitar under his arm. His backing band are minimal: he's the real attraction.

'Hello, London,' he says, and Lysette squeezes my hand tightly. 'Let's get specific. Hello, Soho.'

And then he's off. His songs are soulful and acoustic, a classy, timeless backlash against all the dance music that's taken hold. He performs each one like he's singing it directly to each of us, his voice caressing us. I mouth the words, loving how rapt the audience are. 'He's ama-zing!' says Lysette, and I know it's true. The audience scream for an encore and, eventually, when we've almost given up, he strides back out.

'This one's for someone very special,' he says, and I stand up tall, hoping he can see me over the sea of heads. 'My daughter's in the audience. Petal, I'm so glad you're here.'

I could actually burst. It's an older song, and I'm not sure if most of the audience remember it, but he played it all the time when I was a kid, the central riff lodged deep in my memory. It keeps catching on my heart, like a snag of wool on a favourite jumper. 'One more!' shout the audience. 'Encore!' and Lorcan sidles back towards the microphone.

'This really is your lot,' he says, giving that grin that even now destroys Mum's best intentions. He starts to strum, looking to the band behind him. It's the final song on the new album, a slow one which stretches out far longer than the rest. 'Bella, you've been an angel. Thanks for making tonight happen.'

Don't think. You don't know, so don't think. And then I'm singing it, belting it out, even though it's not that kind of song, my hand tight around Lysette's, forcing our sweaty palms up into the air like a flagpole. All I can hear in my head are the words. I can't hear the other voices that stalk me.

Bella comes and finds us afterwards. She looks at me a second too long before she speaks, unable to stop her eyes shining. What she doesn't realize is that my superpower is being two people at once: I can know and not know, the truth and the untruth nestled so tightly together that they're one piece, like the teeth of a zip. 'Your dad wants you to come backstage,' she says, and soon we're crammed into his tiny dressing room, his arms pulling me into a hug that's sweaty and real. Even now, when I feel the ladder of his ribs pressing against my cheek, something in me feels like I've come home.

'You were so brilliant!' I tell him.

'You totally were,' says Lysette, and he hugs her too.

'I had to be brilliant for my little girl,' he says, his face alight. 'We can relax now. It's time to take all you glamorous creatures to the after party.' He's looking at Bella when he says it, but he re-angles his gaze.

'Yay,' says Lysette, and I try and make my face go right. I know Mum would want me to go home now, get a good night's sleep so I can make a start on revising for the flurry of pre-Christmas mocks coming my way. A wave of anger sweeps over me: why isn't she here? She's only got herself to blame. We're hustled through to a back room in the club. It's already rammed with people, all making use of the waterfall of booze pouring from the free bar. A cheer erupts at the sight of Lorcan, swiftly followed by an orgy of back slapping from his producers and managers. Lysette turns to me, wide-eyed.

'Your dad is so cool!' she whispers, grabbing my hand and pulling me towards the bar. 'Mine's such a total plonker.'

I think of her father, calm and measured, but still twinkly of eye. He'd be putting us in a cab right now.

'Your dad's amazing too,' I say, meaning it, but she's not really listening. She's high with it all, revelling in making it to the next level.

'Come on, partner,' she says. 'Free booze!'

No one bats an eye as she orders more Malibu and Coke. I've gone off it now, it's started to taste like cough medicine: I order a Perrier alongside, and try not to make it obvious it's all I'm drinking. I'm watching Lorcan out of the corner of my eye, just like Bella is, from her sneaky vantage point at the far corner of the bar. He's ordering shots of tequila, but there's an abundance of champagne too. He sees me watching, raises his flute in a toast, and points at the bottle. I shake my head, try to smile, dragging Lysette to the packed square of dance floor, my heart pounding as loud as the bass line.

Lysette's a properly good mover – she somehow manages to lose herself in the music without looking like a pretentious idiot. I try and copy her, but my feet feel like flat irons. 'You OK?' she shouts, and I nearly drag her off to the loos and pour it all out, but I don't want to give Bella a clear shot. It's more than that: I don't feel like I deserve a best friend like her, not now I've been so two-faced. I wish I'd told her in France, but I was terrified of the spell being broken. Please let her understand, please let her not hate me after tomorrow.

I force myself to take another sip of my proper drink, then give her a spontaneous hug. Being no fun is way worse than being a liar. I make my feet start moving and my mouth start smiling, keeping my gaze tight on the square of sweaty bodies. Lysette catches the eye of a dark-haired man – he's old, thirty at least – and soon they're dancing together. I miss Jim so much it actually aches: I don't want to be a secret.

'Going to the bog,' shouts Lysette into my ear. 'You coming?'

'Do you like him?' I say when we're crammed into a smelly cubicle. He's been trying to touch her, even though it was proper dance music, not a Whitney Houston smooch.

'He's sexy.'

'He is OLD,' I say, and we collapse into the kind of giggles that seize hold of you and won't let go.

'Just because he hasn't got a mate!'

'What, like Terry Wogan?'

And we're off again, stumbling back to the dance floor in fits of giggles, gripping clammy palms to keep our balance. But now it's not safe. Now Lorcan's there, dancing like he's twenty years younger to music he hates. His whole leg kicks up, clearing a space around him, his eyes wild. Bella's there too, laughing and clapping, egging him on. He looks like a total fool. I stand there, frozen, wishing I could disappear. When he grabs a champagne bottle, starts spinning round and spraying it across the room, a bouncer rushes up to him.

'Is Lorcan OK?' says Lysette.

He's arguing with the bouncer now, shoving a finger in his face. I can't bear it. I push my way over there.

'He's just excited,' I say. 'He's being stupid because it's his big night. I'll look after him. I take full responsibility. He's my dad.'

Lorcan turns to me, his pupils tiny pinpricks. He doesn't even look like my dad: it's like someone's bodysnatched him.

'Don't you dare talk about me like that,' he says, his words slurring. 'You stupid bitch.' He turns to Bella. 'Get them out of here,' he says, then turns back to me. 'Go on, get out. You're a fucking child. I should never have had you here.'

'Lorcan, don't,' I say, trying not to let his words break my skin and burst inside me. 'You're drunk. Let's go home.'

He looks at me with an expression of cold contempt, then turns away. Now he's dancing again, his pipe-cleaner limbs flying in all directions, until the bouncer pins them to him and starts manhandling him towards the exit.

I don't know whether I should follow him. How is it possible to love someone this much and hate them just as much?

Chapter Eight

Gemma's iPad, wafer-thin and shiny, gleams with newness. Her eyes track across the fast-moving screen, her finger expertly swiping at it; she's totally oblivious to me watching her from the doorway. A hot gust of anger sweeps across me, but I swiftly rationalize it: if I can't rationalize it, I can't be here with her. It's not her fault that Mum and Nick are scrabbling around to try and keep a roof over their heads. And they're just a pinprick, one of a nameless mass of people battling impossible odds. I start to think of all the darker things that Patrick's implied, then slam the brakes on. None of it is Gemma's fault.

I look at her again, chapped bottom lip caught between teeth that protrude a little, her bony body swamped by a baggy grey T-shirt. **Pow!** it says, in big neon-yellow letters.

'I've come to prise you away from Facebook,' I say, smiling down at her.

There's a deliberate pause before she looks up, her eyes

slowly deigning to meet mine. They're slate: cold and flat.

'I'm not on Facebook. Facebook's lame.'

'I suppose it is a bit 2009,' I say, keeping the smile on my face. 'Come on, let's go through.'

Gemma sits on the sofa, places the iPad next to her reverentially, her bag discarded in the corner. Now I'm getting a closer look I can see it's literally brand new, a model that only dropped last week. Her ragged nails are unexpectedly red, the lacquer chipped and lumpy. It makes me think of Mum, how much of an impostor she was when she tried to enter the world of grooming. She's comfortable now, muddy and comfortable. At least she was. Gemma pulls and nibbles at them, avoiding my gaze. I wait it out.

'Don't you have your twenty questions prepared?' she snaps. '"Gemma, tell me about your fa-ther."'

'I don't prepare questions,' I say. 'We don't know how we're going to feel before we arrive in the session. I think it's better to let it unfold as we go.'

'How modern. Very 2018.'

'Oh I'm cutting edge,' I say, but she won't raise a smile. I wait a second, watch her. 'Do you *want* me to ask you about your father? We talked about him a lot last week, didn't we?'

'No. Why – do you want to talk about yours?'

We need to deal with this. I try not to get bogged down by the internal acid of self-judgement.

'Did it bother you that I talked about my dad?'

'No. I just thought it was a bit pathetic.'

'I wasn't asking for your sympathy, Gemma, I think it's

important you know that. I don't need you to look after me. I was just trying to let you know that I understand how complicated it can be with dads. And that sometimes we can end up feeling responsible for things that aren't our fault.'

'That's *your* dad,' she spits back. 'He's so obviously a loser. My dad takes responsibility for EVERYTHING. He runs the whole business and then he has to come back and run our house too. He looks after all of us.'

'That must make it extra hard, him not being here.'

She looks at me, unable to hide the hurt in her eyes.

'That police guy . . .'

'Patrick. Yes, we need to talk about that too. It shouldn't have happened.'

'I know the police are after us. I'm not a baby.'

'Of course. But you shouldn't have been here, and neither should he. This is your safe place, Gemma, and it must feel less safe once you've seen the police – invading it.' She shrugs, face set. I continue, trying to stay soft within the hard point that I must make to her. 'That's why we have appointments. We need boundaries – rules. It was sweet that you wanted to give me a present, but you can't just turn up on the doorstep when you fancy.'

'Tell you who really wants to give you a present. Patrick!'

'What do you mean?'

'He totally fancies you. It's so obvious.'

'Gemma—'

'He was checking out your arse! Like this.' She swivels her

head a hundred and eighty degrees, widening her eyes, jaw dropping open, then smirks at me. I laugh, I can't help it.

'How did it make you feel, coming face to face with the police here? It made me feel very protective of you. I don't want the outside to come in.'

'I'm not traumatized, if that's what you're asking. Sorry to disappoint you.'

'Is that what you think? That I *want* you to be traumatized?'

'Yeah. So you can fix it. That's your job. It's what gives you the raging horn, isn't it?'

I smile, pause to watch her. Is this what it's like between her and Annie – so much unsaid, communication played out via cleverly aimed poison darts? When I spoke to Annie, told her about the present, I wondered if it would set off alarm bells, but she affected the same world-weary acceptance she displays towards any revelation about her daughter's behaviour.

'What made you turn up unannounced? You're a clever girl, Gemma. You know what the rules are. I might not have even been here.'

'I wanted to give you your present, but you obviously don't like washing.'

'You don't need to waste your money giving me presents. I want to be here with you.'

'Er, correction: you're *paid* to be here with me.'

'We've already talked about that. I've got plenty of clients. If I didn't want to see you, I wouldn't.'

She draws herself up, a snooty look on her face.

'But that would be hay-ly unprofessional,' she says, in a la-di-da voice. She's a bit of a ham, I'm starting to realize, the posturing a way of deflecting anything that comes too close.

'Gemma, listen to what I just said. It's important. I *want* to be here with you.' I look her in the eyes as I say it. I watch as her shoulders collapse down like the starch has been washed out of her: something's hitting home.

'OK,' she says, voice small.

'Do you believe me? You don't have to just agree.'

'My dad wants to be with me all the time,' she says emphatically. 'That's why he takes me with him, even when he shouldn't.'

My senses switch up a gear, the atmosphere shifting and sharpening between us. It's one of those times when her mentioning his name almost conjures him up, a living ghost that's haunting the room. She looks at me, face twisted and defiant, waiting for my next move. I'm not the enemy, I silently intone, mind racing back over Patrick's words. Could he really drag her up onto the stand? Maybe it would be a softer landing if her secrets spilled out here.

'What, like when you went to New York?'

'He takes me everywhere, Mia. You think because he's gone, he doesn't want to have me there.' She reaches for the iPad as she says it. She's gripping it, fingers of one hand trailing languidly across the surface until it lights up. Where is 'everywhere'? 'But sometimes things are the complete opposite of how they look.'

'I don't think he doesn't want to spend time with you. I'm sure he loves you, and I know how much you love him.'

'Don't just say that!' she snarls, face flushed. 'You're so fucking horrible about him. He loves me more than anyone in the whole world, but you don't understand about that, because your dad is such a loser.'

I pause, try and give us a moment to breathe. The truth is, I deserve her anger. I shouldn't have handed her these weapons.

'I've been trying to reflect back to you what you've told me. And yes, like I said, I think it's tough for you if you end up feeling like you have to act a certain way to earn his love. And telling you that little bit about my dad – that was me trying to tell you I feel empathy, not just sympathy. I'm sitting beside you, metaphorically and in real life. But I'm very sorry if it made our relationship confusing. Like we said earlier, boundaries are a very important part of the process we're in together. They're what keep us both safe.'

I wish I still believed it was that simple. She watches me, eyes narrow. She's fingering the screen again, drawing my gaze to it. I deliberately look away from the green bubbles of messages that fill it. I won't let her lead us.

'That's the new one, isn't it?' I say, trying to work out if she's actually trying to show them to me.

'Yeah, no. I've had it a while.'

'You can't have done. They were only released last week.'

'Not in New York!'

I look at her, waiting for her to back down from this

obvious lie. New York. Is that where he is? Did he take her so she'd be able to imagine him there once he'd gone?

'I'm not sure why you're saying that. Is it because you don't want me to know your family's still spending money? It's not what I'm asking.'

'It was a present.'

'I guessed that. They're a lot of pocket money. I'm kind of jealous.'

'Why, can't you afford one?'

'I could, but it'd feel extravagant. Does it feel extravagant to you?'

She shrugs, her pert little nose wrinkling at the very question. Of course it won't be; I'm guessing possessions are the one thing she's never wanted for. I feel a chill: the way she's fondling it isn't about the machine; I'm sure it's about how it got to her.

'I could be wrong, but I feel like you want me to see those messages.'

She quickly turns it face down.

'God, Mia, you're so nosy! Dad says that's what you are. You're a professional nosy parker. Big sticky beak.'

She's miming a Pinocchio nose, grinning at me, but there's no warmth in her smile. It's more like contempt. *Dad says.* That chill starts to slither its way through me again. *They'll know who you are by now.* I take a breath. It's me who needs to keep control in here – not her, not Patrick. One place I can still guarantee our safety is between these four walls.

'I didn't know you and your dad had talked about therapy.'
She stares determinedly out of the window. 'Has he had it?'

'My dad does not need therapy! Stop being so spiteful
about him.' I wait it out, wanting to see where she'll go next.
'It was school,' she says eventually, voice low. 'They wanted
us to come.'

'Your teachers thought your family should come for
therapy?'

Why didn't Annie tell me this? Gemma nods, almost
imperceptibly, curling in on herself like she's protecting herself from the whole damn lot of us.

'Why do you think that was?' I ask as gently as I can.

'Dad knew I didn't need it. We've got each other to talk
to. I can tell him anything.'

'Can you?' I look back to the message-laden iPad, then at
her. She doesn't take the bait.

'Yeah, and him me. I knew about Janey for ages.'

'Who's Janey?'

'Him and Mum nearly broke up, but we got through it.
He really needed someone to talk to then.'

Anger whooshes up inside me like a pilot light igniting.
I look at the baggy swathes of fabric that fall around her
too-skinny frame, the breasts that are barely budding. It
feels like she's split in two; forced to fake an emotional
maturity she doesn't possess to win his toxic confidences, all
the time stifling her impending womanhood. It must be
terrifying to her, the thought of her body telling her that
her time is up. From the vantage point she's been forced to

see it from, adult life must look like a dark playground with no rules.

'What do you tell him, Gemma? I'm hearing what he tells you, but what about when it's your turn?'

'I can tell him anything.'

'Like what?'

She looks at me, styling it out.

'Clue's in the question. They're secrets.' I look back, wait. 'Anyway, him and Janey are just friends.'

'But it nearly broke him and your mum up?'

'FWB,' she says, almost rapping. 'Friends with benefits. We need different things from different people. You can't expect to get everything from one person. If you love someone, set them free, that's what Dad says. But Mum can't understand that. Doesn't have the nous.'

I cringe so much when she tongue-twists his middle-aged phrases. I look up at the clock, aware we've got only a few minutes left. She knew that too, I'm sure: she wouldn't have told me any of this without a get-out clause.

'I know you like being close to your dad, but it has to have been hard to hear those things. I wouldn't have had a clue what to say to him, if I'd been you. Knowing I couldn't share it with my mum without it hurting her.'

Gemma shrugs, leaning down to grab her rucksack, sliding the gleaming machine inside. It's halfway in, face up, when she looks to me again. I look, I can't help it. **Love you, babes**, says the top one. **13.24.** It's 13.45 now. 'Babes' – is that a girl thing? What if he really is using her to move evidence around for him? I realize I'm shaking. I want to bolt the door, stop her going back out there into a world more dangerous than she could, or should, even know.

'That's where you're wrong. Again. It wasn't hard at all!'

I can't hold it in.

'Gemma, it's not right for you to have to keep secrets for him. He's got adults he can talk to. You should be his daughter, not his best friend. He should be protecting you from his adult problems.'

Not his pseudo mistress is what I'm really thinking. That's how those creeping tendrils of adult need feel, even if there's nothing as stark or undeniable as physical touch.

'Janey loves films,' says Gemma, zipping up her rucksack. 'When I went to her apartment we watched *Pretty Woman*. Julia Roberts is a hooker, nothing like in *Eat, Pray, Love*.'

She stands up, gives me an empty smile.

'Why don't you sit back down? We can run over a few minutes. This doesn't feel like the right place to finish.'

'I can't. I've got to go and see someone now.'

'It's a school day.'

Can she hear the fear in my voice? I breathe deeply, internally lower my pitch.

'Yeah, *at* school. Take a chill pill, Mia!'

She's angry again; it's coming off her in waves. She's angry, and she's lying.

'What you just told me is a big deal. If you want to stay and talk more about how it felt to know that about your dad, we've got time.'

She was headed for the door, but she stops now, perches unexpectedly on the arm of the sofa. She's closer to me than she is when she sits on it properly. It feels oddly intimate.

'I just wanted to give you a present,' she says, real and vulnerable. 'That was all. I'm sorry if I shouldn't have come.'

'I know you did,' I say, smiling at her, keeping my eyes deliberately soft. 'But you don't need to give me presents.'

'You could have a new iPad if you wanted,' she says, her slyness creeping back. 'Even if you can't afford it, you could just get it on Amex.'

'I feel like there's something else you want to tell me. Is it about who gave it to you?'

'No one you know. Stop going on at me.' She gazes at me, eyes clear and steady. 'Did your dad give you presents? Is that why you don't like it when you get them now?'

That chill spreads through me again. She doesn't seem like a child when she steps into this place.

'We're not here to talk about my dad.'

'You don't like it when we talk about him, do we? You just like slagging off mine.'

Her proximity feels oppressive now, my decision to let the session run on yet another mistake. Boundaries are all we have. I keep my face neutral.

'Let's talk more about all of this next week.'

'Bye, Mia,' she says, standing up abruptly, hugging the rucksack against her like it's her baby. 'I'll see you then. Don't be a stranger.'

APRIL

Chapter Nine

When I peek round Judith's door she's on the phone. 'Two minutes,' she signals, her fingers swishing through the air, pushing me away. If there is such a thing as a past life, then Judith was a warrior – bare-breasted, spear aloft, charging into battle. I'm dreading this. She takes a good hard look at me when I come in.

'Sit down,' she says, motioning to her sofa. Today isn't like other days. Today I need permission. I perch on the marshmallow cushions, unsteady, waiting for her to speak. She sips her espresso, thinking it out. The cup clatters against the saucer, making the silence that surrounds it even more silent. 'You've been avoiding me,' she says.

'Do you really think that?'

She gives a dry smile. 'That's why I said it. It's Tuesday morning. It's over a week since we last spoke about Gemma, and that was a rushed conflab in the waiting room. I've had to ask you twice for this meeting.'

I look down, look up, a smile in place.

'OK, Miss Marple—'

'Don't pull that one, Mia,' she interrupts. 'Don't use being funny to get around the sides.' A wave of shame washes through me and I look back down at the carpet, wondering what fresh piece of idiocy might be queuing to come out of my mouth next. 'Let's be real with each other. We both know this case is a big one for you. Your story's either going to help you or hinder you. I'm here so we can make sure it's the first one.'

Truth is a funny old thing. Part of what my job's taught me is that there's rarely an incontrovertible truth, just our dogged belief in our own version of events. I spend my time listening for the gaps and contradictions in the stories people tell me, just like Judith's listening to me now, her eyes pin-sharp, tracking every movement in my face as I describe the last sessions. I stumble and fall in places, plagued by stage fright.

'I do realize I shouldn't have told her anything personal—'

'Sure, it may have been a slight misjudgement, and I certainly don't think you should share any more information about yourself, but I can absolutely understand why you did. Your reasons were good.' She looks out of the window for a second. 'It's not even the words, Mia, it's the fact that they caught light so easily. It's still flammable, isn't it, the whole story around your dad? And Gemma's seen that light – she's a moth to the flame. No wonder she's bringing you presents, trying to get closer to it.'

'I just wanted her to know she wasn't alone. I get the feeling she feels like a freak, and what's happening to her now' – I hear my voice rising and I try to push it down – 'she's lost the only person who she believes can really see her.'

'Is that how it felt with *your* father?'

'Sometimes.'

It's a non-answer, and we both know it. We sit there in silence.

'And do you still think she might know more than she's letting on? Could Patrick be right about that?'

'She certainly hasn't told me anything.'

Like I told you, the truth lies in the gaps in what we say, not in the words that actually come out. The same goes for Gemma. I can see the iPad, those green bubbles relentlessly popping up all the way through our hour together. Judith hasn't missed my swerving of the question. She tries a different way in.

'What do you think Little Mia would say if she was here? This case must be bringing up a lot of feelings for her.'

Judith's very big on the idea that our inner child stays with us throughout life, needing us to mother and take care of her. If we don't, there's a danger the child feels omnipotent, snatches the wheel and drives the car off the road. I understand it in principle, but in practice it makes me feel faintly silly. The week I tried having a cosy chat with her in the mornings like Judith had suggested, I felt like I was the worst ventriloquist ever, about to get booed off *Britain's Got Talent* in favour of a dancing schnauzer.

'I think she'd probably roll her eyes and ask you if she

could go and watch *Beverly Hills, 90210* in her hideous Aztec-print leggings she mistakenly thinks are trendy.'

'Only if she'd already finished all of her homework,' she says. Her face says *I know you, I know you so well I don't even have to tell you what it is you're doing.* 'I think Little Mia might want you to talk to her, and reassure her that this is Gemma's life, not hers.' Her tone hardens. 'That you know that you can't fix it.'

'I do know that! And you're right, of course it's touching on my stuff, but perhaps that's why she's opening up to me.'

'You need to be very careful that there's not some magical thinking going on. That you're not trying to heal your own past by going in all guns blazing to mend her present.'

Tears prickle at the back of my eyeballs, a lump not in my throat, but in my chest. Somewhere more fundamental, harder to spit out. I'm a cat with a fur ball, something choking me that's made out of the very stuff of me.

'I know I need to put clearer boundaries in place, but I really think she needs me.'

'Mia, you've only seen her a few times. How will you cope if she suddenly does blurt out some vital piece of information? I'm not sure how easy you'd find it to tell the police, knowing what she'd have to go through. You could really compromise yourself here.'

I haven't told Judith even half of what Patrick's told me, what he's implied. It'll give her too much ammunition. I kept my story simple – office bound, free of warm white wine and half confidences.

'I don't want to abandon her!'

'Why do you think you would be?'

'Her dad means everything to her!' I say, my voice rising. 'She's found somewhere safe to express it – anger, sadness, whatever it is she wants me to witness. Of course she'd feel abandoned!'

'She might experience it that way, but it doesn't mean you *would* be abandoning her. And anyway, it's pure speculation. We don't know how she'd feel. You're the only one talking about abandonment.'

I try not to look mutinous.

'I can do this, Judith. You might just need to trust me, at least for a bit longer.'

'You're an excellent therapist, Mia. I'm not questioning that.' I sit there, panic creeping up on me. It sounds like the first half of a sentence I don't want to complete. Dot, dot, dot, each dot more ominous than the last. 'Is it maternal instinct being triggered too? Moving into – what is it you keep calling it, the fridge? – must be making you think about that stuff.'

'We're not ready for kids. One step at a time. I – we – want to see how it goes first.'

'Why do you think you call it the fridge?'

'It's just a silly joke between us,' I say, realizing that Marcus hasn't called it that once. 'You know, it's big and flash, but it's a bit of a cold bachelor pad. It's definitely a Smeg.'

'It's an interesting image. Has it got a freezer, this fridge of yours?'

It's more like a trap than a question. Dot, dot, dot. I shrug, nod. No big deal.

'Does it feel like you'll be frozen? Like time will stand still when the door slams shut?'

'No, not at all,' I say too quickly. 'I've made a decision. I'm moving forward. We're getting the keys tonight! It's the opposite of frozen.'

'But it was your mum's news that really triggered the decision, wasn't it? The prospect of losing your childhood home . . . so many ghosts.'

'It's horrible. I wish I could do something to save them.'

'It could've made you feel, I don't know' – her creased, ring-laden hands swoop through the air, like birds in flight – 'fuck you about the Vine family. But it hasn't. If anything it's made you feel the opposite.'

It's only as she says it that I realize it's made me feel both.

'I've never had a case like this before,' I say stiffly. The truth might make her deem me overemotional, loop us back to where we've been. 'It's invaluable experience.'

Judith glances at the clock. Saved by the bell.

'Your story was messy and painful and hard.' She looks at me, her gaze penetrating. 'It gives you insights, but what we're seeing is that it doesn't give you distance. Take the session with her this week, and then we need to meet the very next day. I *will* put a stop to it if I feel it's dangerous for either of you.'

'Thank you,' I say, suddenly exhausted.

'I think you need to work on the material around your

own father in your personal therapy too.' I nod, not trusting myself to speak. I stopped going a couple of months ago. It felt like I was continuously reversing over the same patch of road. 'And I think it's vital we keep Patrick on side,' she says, watching for my reaction, a hint of mischief about her. 'He'll be less of a loose cannon if he thinks you're his pal.'

'Definitely.'

'If any information does need to be shared, you want to be in control of that process. You don't want them demanding access, interpreting your notes as they like.'

The phone on her desk buzzes, and I stand up.

'Thanks, Judith.'

I smile at her, try to keep my mouth turned upwards, when gravity's pulling all of me downwards. I want to curl up on the sofa, my feet tucked underneath me, grab a box of tissues, start again. I want to tell her everything, including every dark implication that's crossed Patrick's lips. I want to tell her I'm scared I might've waded into the sea, right up to my waist. I want to tell her that my instinct is my guiding light, my Star of Bethlehem, but now I don't know if I'm following a rogue flare. I don't say any of it. I smooth down the skirt of my green corduroy dress, keep my smile in place and walk back out into the unknown.

Patrick's sitting on a bench by the duck pond in Regent's Park, stringy body hunched over his phone. I scrutinize him as I make my approach, watching the way his attention is constantly being dragged away by their miniature dramas, however hard he tries to stay focused on the tiny screen. A minor skirmish leaves him rapt, two ducks with their wings spread, squawking wildly at each other, a troop of ducklings watching from the safety of their mother's side. He's a sentimentalist at heart.

'I didn't have you down for a twitcher,' I say, holding out a latte as I sit down.

'A twitcher?' he says, raising a quizzical eyebrow to check the coffee's for him and then taking it. He smiles gratefully, like I've handed him something far nicer than a cup of luke-warm foam from a dodgy van.

'Bird fancier.'

'So not a mentalist?'

'Jury's out on that one.' Bad phrase.

The temperature's been inching up the last few days: people are lying prostrate on the grass, with all the desperate neediness of humans who live most of their year swimming in grey soup. Patrick, dressed in a crumpled white business shirt, looks like he's been lightly steamed, his face pink and damp-looking, his ginger locks flopping around his face for a bit of extra insulation.

'Isn't it just?' he says drily, turning to me. 'Lovely surprise you calling me, Mia. Didn't have you down for a caller.'

'I just . . . I wouldn't want you to think I wasn't taking my responsibilities seriously. I do understand I have a legal obligation to the police investigation.'

'It did all get a bit heated, didn't it?' he says, holding my gaze.

'Did it?'

'I thought so.'

Conversation grinds to a halt. I watch a speckled brown duck kick up water, feathers ruffling with the sheer joy of it, and for one stupid second I want to swap places.

'I know I called you, but you were the one who was so keen to meet in person,' I point out. 'It's like some kind of Cold War assignation, third bench on the left, forty-five degrees north of the mallards.'

'It's a beautiful day, and it's equidistant from our offices,' he says. 'You're quite an overanalyser, aren't you? Guess it comes with the territory.'

'This isn't a session,' I say snappishly. 'I don't need a breakdown of my character.'

He gives me that half-smile I'm growing to hate, like he's enjoying a private joke.

'Just an observation. Are you thinking you've got a monopoly on the observations?'

'Not at all.'

'I wondered when you rang if you'd something to get off your chest,' he says.

'I've only seen Gemma once since we met. How about you?'

'You've lost me.'

'Oh come on. Turning up at my office just when she happened to be there . . .'

Patrick rolls his eyes, his hands bouncing on the slats of the bench.

'And she's off again with the rampant overanalysing.'

He swivels round, looks out across the water. I watch his profile, trying to work out whether this is act two of his performance – flirtatious and jocular haven't worked, so let's have a go with pensive and thoughtful. There's a tightness to his jaw, like he's swallowed something bitter and can barely hold it down, his palms grinding against the wooden surface of the seat. The easy charm might be an act, but this comes from somewhere more deeply felt.

'I really need your help now,' he says, brown eyes burning. 'We're running out of time. I know you'll just keep pushing back, making out I'm – I'm the *Chitty Chitty Bang Bang* child catcher . . .' I can't help laughing. In fact, I need to laugh. He eyes me, smiling for a brief second, then carrying on, urgent and intense. 'You're in pole position to find out what she knows. You could draw it out of her. She'd do anything for you right now. And if you don't – if we don't stop Stephen – people will die. It's serious organized crime, Mia. I know I keep saying it, but it's like you can't hear me.' He smiles again, eyes bright. 'Are you deaf, is that it?'

'I do know . . .' I say, my hand reaching for his forearm without me consciously sending it there. 'I understand it's real lives, not just case notes.' I've rung Mum every day this last week, and every day she's sounded more Stepford and cheery than the last. I know from years of close study in the field that the shinier she seems on the outside, the dingier she feels on the inside. 'But that's entrapment, pure and simple.

174

The reason she trusts me, if she does, is because she *can* trust me. I couldn't live with myself.'

'But if you led the conversation . . . it's just you and her. It's semantics. No one can prove that you set out to take her there.'

'No! That's not where I want to lead her.'

The word catches in my throat. Is Judith right – am I too bruised, too broken, to help her? Leading her is very different from supporting her, but it's so hard to fight my desperation to draw her away from the long shadow cast by her dad. Lysette's stupid card pops into my head; I'm feeling cracked all right, but it's not letting the light in. It's letting the shit in, if anything. I shrug out my shoulders, wonder how quickly I can extricate myself from this. I take a slug of bitter, lukewarm decaf, look out over the duck pond, trying to find some equilibrium.

'Do you have to be so bloody middle class about it?' snaps Patrick. 'I'm not some neurotic writer stopping by for a whinge and a sniff of your scented candles. You're so big on your grey areas: have you thought for one second that the moral thing to do might not be what you think it is?'

'Excuse me, Mr Hotshot Lawyer, it's hardly like you work down a bloody coal mine,' I say, sliding myself away from him down the bench. It's the least important part of what he's saying, but it's the cheapest shot I can line up.

'I'm not middle class,' he says, his voice a low growl. 'I've worked my arse off for this.'

'Oh what, and you think my qualifications got handed to me out of the back of an Ocado van?'

We glower at each other, the sun suddenly feeling relentlessly oppressive. I find my huge sunglasses in the recesses of my bag and jam them on my face, shielding myself from him. Why does it always end up like this: I started out so determined to pull off that cool, neutral professionalism Judith was steering me towards, and now I'm scrapping with him, two small children kicking a Coke can. I pretend to be trying to find something else. I should probably just leave, but leaving right at this moment feels like failing. Dangerous too, winding him up like a clockwork toy and leaving him to scoot away in whichever direction he's facing.

'Mia,' he says, his tone conciliatory now. 'I shouldn't be telling you this, but there are people who would love to see this case fall over.'

'What do you mean? Stephen's people?' He pauses again, then stares at me with an intensity that almost frightens me. He's assessing me, working out if he can trust me. 'Tell me.'

'People who should want the absolute opposite.'

'Like? What, police?'

He nods grimly .

'Really?' I search for anything in his face or body language that would tell me this is a tactic, a last-ditch attempt to turn the screws on me. 'Well surely you can just report them? You're all for fighting the good fight. Get them up on a charge.'

'It's not as simple as that. As you're so very fond of telling me,' he says, smiling for the first time in ages, his twinkle momentarily restored. There's something childlike about it that makes me warm to him, almost despite myself. 'It's why it's taken so many years to get this close to bringing Stephen down.'

'So you're saying he's got police in his pocket who've kept the investigators away from it? And what, they're so embedded, you can't dig them out?'

It makes me shudder. How hard must it be to believe your enemies are out there on the battlefield, a clear and certain target, and then find the fight is so much dirtier than that? No wonder he's looking for any tactic, any weapon he can lay hands on.

'Gross simplification,' he says, still smiling, 'but basically, yeah.'

I smile back at him, accept his invitation.

'I'm sorry I'm so gross and simple.'

'I know,' he says, the fight briefly leaving him. 'Crying shame.'

I grab some sunscreen from my bag, push my sunglasses onto the top of my head so I can smear it on. The circular movements, the pads of my fingers working it into my skin, feel soothing.

'But how are they so untouchable? It doesn't make any sense.'

'There was a guy, a detective, who felt just like you do. He pursued it, and pursued it, tried to get Stephen on a corrupt property deal where he'd been paying backhanders to council officials. Kept going until, guess what – he's the one up on a corruption charge. Lost his job, lost his pension, his reputation, got sick. It was like Alice in Wonderland, no way back.'

'Is he OK now?' His face. Mild disbelief at the question. Could I? Could I help him? As soon as I have the thought I slam it in a box. If I don't hold on to what I know is right, then everything is transformed to wrong.

'He'll be a lot more all right if he gets to see justice finally being done.'

Patrick turns away, looks back at the ducks. There's a little boy holding on to his stroller with one hand, his other clutching a bag of crusts. I'm sure bread's bad for them, but it's hard to imagine him not having the satisfaction of watching them flap their way towards him, waddling and quacking. He turns to his mum, delighted, chubby face no more than a grin. I hope nothing bad ever happens to you, I think. I hope if it does there's someone there to hold your hand.

'But there's still no definitive proof that Christopher knew about any of it,' I say, trying to yank the wheel back towards our well-worn argument – it's safer there. Patrick's eyes stay on the little boy, now bowling a piece of bread towards a fiercer-looking greenish-black customer.

'These gangsters, they keep it all above board by using people like him. A man as clever as Christopher doesn't miss a trick. It's in Stephen's interests for Christopher to look whiter than white, with his kids at the posh school and his big cars. Stephen's got all the same toys. It's all about the illusion.'

It's a dangerous business, illusion. We look at each other for a second, a silent standoff. An ice-cream van starts up, the tune jangling in my ears. Patrick jumps to his feet, the long length of him stretching upwards, light streaming behind him. He shades his eyes to look down at me, and I notice for the first time how his brown eyes are punctuated by little speckles of amber.

'Want one? I'm fancying myself a 99 with a flake.' He cocks his head. 'Maybe two.'

'Flakes?'

'I like to live dangerously. What'll you have?' He looks down at me – no, assesses me, and I feel suddenly self-conscious.

'I'll just have a bottle of water.'

'Come on. A Solero?'

'Sparkling – you're not the only one living on the edge. I'll come with you, anyway.'

I should leave altogether. Instead I follow his diagonal course across the grass, my heels wedging themselves into its spongy surface. Why doesn't he take the path like a normal person? He gets to the van, looks back at me. Come on, slow-coach, says his smile. He's already mid-order when I arrive. There's an oldish woman at the hatch, her hair dyed an implausible shade of black, big gold earrings glinting in the sun.

'. . . and a lemon ice for the lady.' He glances over. 'AND a sparkling water.'

'Honestly, I don't want ice cream,' I say, standing one-legged, trying to wipe the mud off my heels with a tissue. Patrick looks down at me, looks back to the lady: *Do you see what I have to deal with?* She beams at us, her smile reaching right through her – we're a happy couple enjoying the sunshine, a tiny, vital boost to her faith in life, the same way that little boy was for me. I don't want to snatch it away.

'It's good,' she says, her accent Italian, her colouring making sense. 'If not, you bring it back.'

'I believe you,' says Patrick. 'She won't be returning anything.'

I look at him – who's the real control freak here – but it's impossible to sustain my grump. She hands it to me, and I know on first lick that he had a point. I don't think about additives or calories; it's cold and slippery, its sharpness a welcome kick. It makes sense to me. Few things do right now. We walk away from the van saying cheerful goodbyes, Patrick cricking his neck to nibble at his flake like a giraffe zeroing in on a particularly delectable leaf.

'It's nice,' I say, the words expensive.

Patrick gives a look of gratitude to the heavens, grins. The sun's less fierce now, early evening stealthily creeping up on us. It's more than an hour we've been together, the time slipping past equally stealthily. I need to go.

'So how do you do it?' he asks, attention moving away from the flake. 'How do you climb inside people's heads?'

'Don't say that. You make me sound like some kind of evil genius.'

He gives an evil-genius cackle.

'If I was your patient, rather than a complete pain in the arse, what would you do? Where would we start?'

He stops a second, cocks his head expectantly, a thin stream of lemon ice melting its way down his bony wrist. Something's happened. I'm actually enjoying being with him – I only realize it now, a wave of guilt instantly boomeranging back. Commuters are starting to stream through the park, walking from the West End to Camden, back to their real lives, a hat perched on top of the head of the day. This mustn't be the hat. I think of Judith, draw some comfort from it. I'm keeping him on side so well that I've even fooled myself.

'You could be my patient AND a complete pain in the arse.' Patrick shrugs his acceptance. He's scrutinizing me now, like the answer really matters to him. 'OK, let's say you're a pain in the arse, you only half want to be here. Your wife's left you, and it's your only shot at persuading her you're trying to change—'

'The little fool!'

I realize with a jolt how many assumptions I've made. He doesn't wear a ring, but it doesn't mean he's not married. He's Irish enough, Catholic enough, to have got it out of the way early and got back to the serious business of winning cases. Is there some exasperated woman at home, knee deep in little Patricks, trying and failing to drag his nose out of a case file?

'You've had a sneaky look at *Guardian* "Soulmates". You

don't like the look of single life. As a last resort you come and see me.'

'I did that once – lasted one date. I swear the woman was in love with her horse. Talked about him all night like she was two-timing him and he'd be sobbing into his oats. Have you ever tried it?'

'No,' I say, shutting him right down. 'I might actually bring you somewhere like here. Watch how you operate, out in the big bad world.'

'So how does that work?'

'British Museum, that would be a good one. Why do you head straight for the Elgin Marbles, not the Roman bronzes?'

'Because the Elgin Marbles might not be here forever. They're always trying to nick them off us, aren't they?'

I called it right – so right he hasn't even questioned my assumption. I smile to myself, back in the zone.

'So are you going because it's the thing – the thing that's most tempting and interesting – or are you going in case it's something some cunning stranger is going to snatch away from you?'

'It's just a fact. It could be my only chance.'

'Nothing's just a fact. They'll give you plenty of warning if they're going. You could go then.'

'Of course some things are facts,' he counters, annoyed. 'Two plus two equals four. And anyway, I don't waft about, finishing at four and pressing a cold compress to my fevered brow to temper the stress of the day. I'm there, on site. Course I'm gonna go.' He looks like he's the one who could do with a cold compress, particularly now; but I don't say it. I nod sagely. Irritatingly. 'So come on, what's your diagnosis?'

I'd never be so pompous and judgemental with a client, but he doesn't need to know that.

'Competition runs through your veins, doesn't it? I bet you're a demon when you stand up in court.'

'You say it like it's a bad thing.'

'If you were my client, I'd certainly be interested to see how it plays out in other areas of your life.'

'Such as?' he says, voice dripping with sarcasm.

'Love.' Perhaps the light in his eyes slightly dims when I drop the L bomb. He isn't married, I'm sure of it now. 'Home. Friendships. I think our greatest strengths tend to be our greatest weaknesses too. They're our points of extremity.'

He's watching me intently, like he's waiting to see what comes out of my mouth next, but I've run out of words, caught by the spider's web of my diagnosis. I'm thinking of him sliding his way round the reception door, catching Gemma out, willing to stop at nothing to get his win. I think he must see it in my face.

'I don't need you fixing me,' he says, defensive.

'I'm not offering. You're the one asking the questions.'

We carry on walking, silent now, although it's a noisy kind of silence. We skirt the side of the rose garden, heading in the direction of the grand iron gates that open up onto the wheezing artery that is Marylebone Road.

'Right, I've got to go,' I say, making slightly too much of a show of looking at my watch.

'What's the rush?'

'I'm signing a contract on a flat. I've got to meet my . . .' 'Boyfriend' is a ridiculous word for Marcus. 'Man friend'? 'Lover'? All heinous, suggestive of a chest rug and a glowing cigar. 'Boyfriend at the estate agent's in like, fifteen minutes.'

'Where is it? Let me guess. Holland Park? Knightsbridge?'

'Is that who you think I am?'

'It's what I think *he* is,' he says, an edge to him. I feel a tremor of unease. Lucky guess, or something more considered?

'It's in Ladbroke Grove. I live in Balham, really.'

'South London. Total mystery to me.'

'Where do you hang out then?'

'Stoke Newington. I've moved roughly three miles in my entire thirty-two years on the planet.'

So that clears up one question. Thirty-two: he probably dates twenty-three-year-old PAs who fall hook, line and sinker for his Irish blarney and don't murmur a word of complaint when he doesn't call them for a fortnight.

'Are your family still there?'

'My mum,' he says, a look of slight exhaustion crossing his face as he says it. 'Are your parents in London?'

'My dad's not around any more,' I say, the words sounding high and discordant, a jumble of notes that crash inside my head. 'And my mum – well, barely. Hillingdon.'

I pick up pace. I can't keep existing in this weird bubble – ducks and ice cream, flirtation and attack – I need to step back into real life. I can hear the relentless stream of traffic, the fumes slyly infiltrating my nasal passages.

'Walk me back to the main road?' I say. I'm not looking at him, but I can feel his eyes surfing my profile.

'Sure thing.'

Our feet obediently track the tarmac, none of the wild zigzagging anarchy of his route across the grass. I'm rifling around my brain for a neutral bit of conversation to throw his way, like the synthetic white bread the toddler tossed to the ducks, but I can't find a scrap.

The wrought-iron gates loom up in front of us. I turn to him, give him a quick smile.

'This is goodbye, then.'

He pauses, looks at me. It occurs to me that I have no idea what it is he's thinking. I look down at my bag, the message light flashing on my phone.

'Mia . . .' I don't want to hear the rest of the sentence. 'Will you promise me you'll keep your wits about you? I get how smart you are, but don't assume . . .'

'I thought you said my degree was from the University of Ocado?'

He won't do it, he won't smile back at me. For a second I hate him for it, for the way it makes the dread start up inside me again, a cold and oily trickle.

'I do care about Gemma, whatever you might think, but I care about you too.'

I can't let those words enter my being and start to mean something. Trusting him is not to be trusted.

'Don't try and scare me into doing what it is you want.'

'Just because she's a child it doesn't mean she's an inno-cent. I wish for her sake she was. If you insist on thinking she's a sacrificial lamb, I'm worried that you're the one who'll get sacrificed.'

'Ooh, very iconoclastic. The priest would be so proud of you, Patrick O'Leary.' I say it too fast for my glibness to be convincing. I gather my cardigan around my body, the chill that's spreading through me about more than the rapid descent of the blood-orange sun. I need to go.

'I know I've said it before, but . . . They'll know who you are by now, Mia. Christopher doesn't ever take off her training reins. If she gets too close, too loose-lipped, and you don't have my back-up—'

'I've already said I'll tell you if she says anything relevant to your investigation. I get it. Wasn't that the whole point of the last two hours?'

Was it? say his brown eyes.

'I know you think it's me who sees the world in black and white, but I think it might be you,' he says. 'You think you can make it that way if you try hard enough.'

'You don't know how I see the world.'

Patrick shrugs in a way that doesn't concede anything.

'Just make sure she knows who's in charge.'

'I'm not some Dickensian headmaster.'

'I'll be here, Mia. You can call me any time.' His face sof-tens, the intensity draining away. 'Shame really, I reckon you could pull off a mortarboard. Jaunty angle,' he says, reaching up to his unruly mop of hair to adjust an imaginary one. 'You know.'

'Thanks for the fashion advice. Well, for all the advice.'

We stand there a second, looking at each other.

'Can I have a hug?' he says, his long arms, strings of spaghetti, already wrapping themselves around my shoulders. He smells nice in a way that's not about well-chosen aftershave. I stay inside the wrap of his arms a second too long, and then I jerk myself away, smooth down my dress.

'It seems like you can,' I say, prim. I'm quite unfair to him really. I remember Lorcan's parents taking in a rescue dog, a black mongrel with a white patch over his left eye, then shaming him every time a river of pee would slither across the kitchen floor, like he was maliciously staging a dirty protest. 'I'm sorry,' I say, the words escaping before I have time to pack them away.

'What are you sorry for, Mia?'

'I don't know,' I say. 'I just am.'

He steps towards me before I can protest, holding me against the thin damp fabric of his shirt.

'You don't have to be sorry,' he says. 'Like I said to you, we're on the same side.'

And I stay there a second longer, oddly soothed by the steady drum of his heart. Then I say a final hurried goodbye, rush away, my hand already stuck out into the traffic, searching for a cab.

December 1994 (sixteen years old)

We didn't tell Lysette. I couldn't face it after the gig, couldn't take the risk of losing someone else precious. A phoney war is better than an actual war, I've decided.

It's not that I've lost Lorcan, but I've lost my trust in my ability to read him. I was like a guide dog, attuned to his every movement, silently anticipating what he needed from me – what he needed from the world. Now I'm on the same lurching seesaw as Mum, grasping at what little of him he'll give me, all the time hating him for the fact he won't give more. Not that he's even noticed, as wrapped up as he is in his newfound success. He's been in America the last couple of weeks, sending us postcards of the kind of tourist traps (the Statue of Liberty, the Empire State Building) that I know he'd sneer at in real life. It's a double bluff: I'm thinking of you, sort of.

I holed up at Lysette's for that entire weekend, trying not to look at Jim in case my face gave me away. She didn't really know what to say about what had happened, although she gave me the kind of hugs that told me she knew how much it must've hurt.

'He really likes a drink,' she said, squeezing me hard.

'He doesn't mean to get like that,' I told her. 'He's just . . . he's an artist.'

'Big personality!' she agreed, and we left it at that. For me it was enough just to be with her, to be with her family, and not my own. The party was a blur of tequila shots and paranoia, the weekend one that's best forgotten.

I'm happy, actually happy. It feels like being spirited upwards in a hot-air balloon, higher and higher, the unhappy things shrinking until they're as small and insignificant as ants on the pavement. Jim wraps his hand tightly around my gloved one, and I fight the urge to pull my glove off, feel his skin against mine, but I worry I'll look like a total keeno. We're squeezing through the tightly packed stalls in Camden Market, sniggering at the way the nearest stallholder has artfully draped fairy lights over a bong in the hope it'll look like the perfect festive gift. It's freezing, a few days before Christmas, a sense of controlled panic in the air.

'Hot chocolate!' says Jim, yanking me towards a van. 'Mexican hot chocolate. Have you ever been there?'

'What, Mexico?' I say, trying not to sound incredulous at the question.

'It's really spicy,' he says, handing a fiver to the dark-skinned man behind the hatch. 'Ah, we can have rum in it. How great is that? You got any bucks?'

I scrabble in my purse, hand him another fiver. I love the way he makes everything such an awfully big adventure. He slurps his hot chocolate straight back, crumpling the cardboard cup ready to toss whilst I'm still gingerly sipping mine.

'Again!' he says, slapping down a tenner. 'The man's a wizard.'

We walk down the canal towards Primrose Hill afterwards, my head a little muzzy, our breath clouding up in the sharp blue cold.

'What do you want for Christmas?' he asks me.

'Duh. A bong! One of those ones with a neon peace sign painted on.'

'Oh no. No bong for you. I'm gonna get you some of those Tibetan slippers. The ones with the tassels and the mirrored bits for your little tootsies.' He turns to me, pinches my cold cheeks as he says it, grinning.

'I'm going to get *you* one of those incense-burner things so you can hang it above your bed at school and think of me. The boys'll think you're *sooo* cool.'

'Wind chimes! No, a dream-catcher.'

I'm laughing so much by now I can barely speak.

'Hemp doorstop,' I counter.

Jim swivels me towards him, slips his hand into my hair, kisses me like it's the climax of the best film I've ever seen. I wish I could tell him I love him, but he has to say it first and boys don't like saying soppy things.

'Let's go home,' he mutters. The rest of the family have gone to visit Gloria's mother in Devon, the house our playground. I've known about this weekend for weeks, the unspoken meaning writ large.

'I thought we were going to go to the cinema this afternoon?' I say, squeezing his hand.

'"And I-yee-I-yee-I will always LOVE yooo-oo,"' he croons, his arm wrapped tightly around my waist, dancing me into the rubbish-strewn undergrowth. He trips over a discarded can of Special Brew, kisses me, laughing. 'Let's make our own slushy movie, not see one.'

'I really wanted to go,' I say, my voice verging on whiny. I don't, not really, but I'd like to stay a virgin a few more hours. A few more months, truth be told, but I know my time is up. There's a lot riding on Jilly Cooper right now.

Jim's key turns in the lock, the sound magnifying in my head. Everything feels hyper-real to me, loaded with significance.

'Gordon's got some champers somewhere,' he says, heading for the kitchen. 'Let's put it on ice.'

'OK,' I say, standing in the doorway, watching him rootle through the kitchen cupboard. I'm twirling my hair around my finger like I used to when I was little. Jim pulls a bottle out of the dark recesses, sticks it in the freezer.

'Half an hour and we'll be good to go.'

Gordon and Gloria have a bath in the corner of their bedroom, a pinkish colour, deep and round, with jets for bubbles strategically placed. It seems wrong to be in here, Gloria's fat, shiny jacketed novels stacked on her bedside table, Gordon's reading glasses and half-drunk water on his, but Jim laughs away my objections.

'The cats are away . . .' he says, pouring a great stream of bubble bath into the water and taking a swig from the bottle of champagne. The bubbles whoosh up in the steaming water like a perfumed cloud. He crosses over to me, takes my face between his hands. 'Come on, little mouse. I think it's time you got undressed.'

He peels off my jumper, leaving me standing in front of him in my bra; it's a black one, new, the wire digging into the underside of my breasts. I'm wearing a denim skirt, thick woolly tights. Jilly Cooper heroines wear fishnet stockings, suspender belts, but they don't find themselves walking up canal towpaths in deepest winter, wind howling up their gussets.

Jim leans down, kisses my left breast, his hand slipping inside my bra to cup the other one. My nipple stiffens at the feel of his cold fingers. I kiss him, trying to peel off my tights at the same time, wobbling around on one unsteady leg like a crane. The bath's close to overflowing. I whip off my knickers and my skirt, diving under the water before he can get too close a look at my nakedness. I've never let him see all of me.

He strips off, utterly unselfconscious. I've never seen an erection either, his or anyone else's, all our fumbling having taken place in the dark or through clothes. I can only glance at it, my eyes flicking quickly to his beautiful face. He dives in, kisses me, his hands, slippery with bubbles, roving all over me. I try and lose myself to it, block out the fear and the anticipation. I love his kisses: there's something almost professional about how skilled they are. He makes soft noises, his fingers growing bolder, then stands up, his erection right there in my eyeline. He hauls me out, wraps me in a towel.

'I can't wait any longer,' he says, urgent, manoeuvring me towards the bed.

'We can't. Not here!'

'It's a king size. Lots of room to roll around,' he says, laughing, kissing me some more. I think I'm enjoying this.

We lie there afterwards, my head on Jim's caramel-coloured chest, a few straggly hairs around his nipples. I'm not a virgin any more. I'm sixteen years old and I've had sex. It felt sharp and painful at first, but then I started to get used to the feeling of it. I think I could start to like it, although I'm not quite sure what the fuss is about yet. I liked how close we were, although my fear didn't leave me. It was almost like he was a different version of himself, animalistic and hard to find. He muttered filth into my ear all the time, getting louder and louder, his groans reverberating round the room as he came, his eyes glazed and rolling.

'You need mopping up,' he says, reaching for a handful of tissues from the box on Gloria's side. I do; there's a puddle of his white stickiness on my stomach.

'Are you sure I won't get pregnant?' I'm an idiot. I should have made him wear a condom, but he swore to me that everyone does this. 'You're my girlfriend,' he said. 'I want to feel you properly. Don't you want us to be able to feel every inch?' I couldn't think of a good way to say no to that.

'Course you won't,' he says, soaking the cold mess off me, kissing me as he does it. 'Look at your gorgeous stomach.'

'My fat stomach.' I've not eaten breakfast all week, trying to make sure there wouldn't be an inch of podge when I exposed it.

'Shush,' says Jim, then crosses to the bath to get the champagne. He's so unabashed about his nakedness. He tops up our glasses, snuggles back up to me. 'Did you come?' he asks me, his voice low in my ear.

I don't really understand about girls coming. I've read about it, like I've read about everything, but how it would feel is another matter. I tried a little exploratory touching, but I felt too ridiculous and shame-filled, not turned on at all. I wait a few seconds, the silence starting to congeal like cold custard.

'I don't know,' I say. 'I think so.'

'You think so?' says Jim, peering down at me, nestled in the crease of his shoulder. 'How does that work?'

'I've never done it before.'

'Well we know that,' he says, an edge to his voice. One thing I'm very good at is hearing the edges. 'Don't you ever diddle yourself?'

I can feel myself blushing, which is ridiculous. He's my boyfriend. I should be able to find the words.

'Not really, no.'

'Wow, so you're like a *super*virgin.'

'Girls aren't like boys. They don't spend their whole time wanking,' I say, anger splashing my words, despite my best efforts.

'Trust me,' says Jim, swinging himself out of the bed, 'some of them do.'

He pulls on his boxer shorts, grabs Gordon's robe, leaves the room. The bed feels huge to me. I hug the pillow his head was lying on, try not to put every single sentence we uttered through the computer. I don't want to read the report.

When we do it again, later that night, I copy him. I learn his noises, learn how to gasp, claw at his back like I'm his fellow animal. Like we're properly mating. My eyes are fixed on the light fitting, my brain on a pair of Chinese pandas I saw on the news this week, forced to breed at London Zoo, the world's eyes trained on their performance.

'That was supercalifragilisticexpialidotious!' he says afterwards. He rolls towards me, his hands tangled up in my hair, his perfect mouth covering mine.

'Wasn't it just?' I say, kissing him back, making the weird, alien words a little breathy.

'There's hope for you yet,' he says, slapping my naked bum.

Don't think, just feel. Don't think, just feel.

Chapter Ten

I'm surrounded by cardboard. Box after box, the bookshelves bare and gaping, the cupboards half empty. When the buzzer goes, it sounds like something alien, shrill and dangerous. My heart lurches in my chest before my brain catches up. I know perfectly well it's just Lysette.

'Look at you!' she says, shoving a bottle of Prosecco in my direction as she walks in. 'This is actually messy! And it hasn't killed you stone dead.'

'Oh shut up,' I say, laughing. 'The bad news is I think I've packed the glasses. We might have to share my tooth mug.'

'Colgate Bellini doesn't sound so bad,' she says, crossing to the kitchen. It's open plan, my little flat, the living room giving way to a galley kitchen, a balcony opening off it where in summer I grow geraniums, red and cheery, in terracotta pots. The bedroom's up some precarious stairs, a raised platform in the eaves. The fridge has no outside space. I'll have to leave the pots behind for the tenants, even though the thought of doing it makes me feel like an unfit mother.

'Sorry, I'm still in hideous chaos. I thought we could go round to the pub for supper.'

Lysette takes it all in, looks at me. I'm covered in a layer of dust, my hair scraped back, my nails black. I'm suddenly so happy she's here that I could actually weep.

'It's your last weekend. End of an era. Let's just order a pizza and have it here. We can eat it off that awful Sade CD you bought to "make love" to.'

Sometimes, when she's so silly that I get a stitch from laughing, I can't help missing Jim. The fun of their family was so utterly infectious.

'I'm totally taking that with me. Marcus won't know what's hit him.'

The packing's both better and worse now that there's two of us. I love the company, but it makes the whole fact that I'm leaving my home behind seem more weighty and significant. I pull out a hideous brown-wool dress, an expensive potato sack, and try and put it on the Oxfam pile.

'Do it!' says Lysette, fingering the weird jewelled neckline as I cling on to the hem. 'The Millennium called. It wants its outfits back.'

'Do you remember David?' I say.

'David?'

'That artist. I was seeing him for about three months. I was wearing this the night I broke up with him.'

'Oh my God, you were crazy about him for a bit. He did those awful abstract things Saffron could make with maca-roni and he lived in a tunnel.'

'A shed. A posh shed in Chiswick. It was in his uncle's garden. We could hear the foxes making love,' I add, sniggering.

Lysette deftly manoeuvres it from me and drops it on the pile. We're in my bedroom, ghostly marks on the wall where my pictures hung until an hour ago. My antique gilt-framed mirror is still up, and I catch sight of the two of us in profile, same but different.

'What's your point, Mia?'

'I don't know. You know that thing people say, about how the only thing that's inevitable is change? I did really like him for a bit.'

'What, you're wishing you were back in his potting shed?'

'No! But – when you got married, you believed in it, didn't you?'

Lysette sits down on the bed, taking a thoughtful sip of the rapidly dwindling Prosecco.

'Yeah, but I hadn't met Ged. And if I hadn't married Ian I wouldn't have had Barney. I mean, it was grim when we broke up, but I learnt tons. I appreciate what I've got with Ged a lot more because of it, rather than getting hung up on the fact that he's a bit like a stoned tomcat.'

She's half smiling to herself as she says it, like she's uncon-sciously wrapping herself up in the thought of him. He would exasperate me. I'd exasperate him even more.

'So you don't mind that you got divorced?'

'I'm not saying that. It's passed, it happened. We've all had a clean bill of health, even Ian. Although that woman he's married has an arse like a sideboard.'

'I'm not being judgemental, I'm just—'

'We can't always get it right first time. Or second time. It's OK to fuck up a bit.'

'I know.'

I do know. In principle. I wonder how Marcus's packing is going? Something tells me he'll have paid his cleaner double time and washed his hands of the task. I wish I believed in fate. It sounds so comforting, a benign blue sky with puffy white clouds. When you've been holding on to the wheel this tightly, for this long, it's hard to stay alert. I start in on the chest of drawers, pulling out a handful of my knickers and chucking them into the big suitcase that's lying open. Lysette springs up.

'You need a system,' she says, grabbing a cloth shoe bag and putting them in. 'You of all people know that!' She reaches up and squeezes my hand. 'What's going on in there?'

I keep sorting through the drawers, untangling pairs of tights, knotted together like secret nylon lovers.

'I don't know. I . . . I don't feel entirely like myself at the moment.'

Understatement of the century. The one thing – the one place – I've always trusted myself is at work. I had another session with Gemma yesterday, one in which she barely spoke, her face twisted into a permanent sneer, her rudeness bordering on abuse. Maybe I have made her life worse, not better. Given her less certainties not more.

'It's a massive life change, moving in with someone.'

'Yeah.' I sit down, still untangling. I smooth the static-y fabric across my knee.

'Mia, are you having second thoughts about this? It's not compulsory, you know.'

'I don't know what's nerves and what's a tiny, stupid tremor of muffin love.'

'Hang on,' she says, grabbing me round the waist. 'Muffin love?'

'Pointless muffin – not love, a tiny muffin crumb – with someone who's out of the question. I'm just being a fuck-up,' I say, balling up some socks and aiming them into the cavernous suitcase. It's snuck up on me, the thinking about Patrick. He's texted a couple of times suggesting coffee but I've pleaded busyness, my brittle messages my best defence. I'm out of my depth, on so many fronts. The most stupid thing I could do is start to think that he's some kind of anchor.

'I hate it when you talk to yourself like that.'

'Even if I wasn't about to move in with my actual boyfriend, it would be completely unethical.'

'What, is he a client?'

I wish I could tell her absolutely everything. I grab the bottle, top us both up and sit back down. I love this bed linen, it's white and lacy without being twee. There's no way it's going to fit on Lila's perfectly constructed oak masterpiece. I can't believe I let Marcus talk me into letting him bring his marital bed, but I could hardly get emotional about it when neither of us has found the time to go furniture shopping. Our nest is not so much unfeathered as feathered by last year's jackdaws.

'As good as – he's connected to that girl I'm seeing. I actually can't talk about it.'

'Tell me some bits you can tell me – how's it going with her?' I shrug, stay silent. 'Tell you what, tell me in German. There's got to be some reason you insisted on taking it.'

'Guten tag mein liebling,' I say, laughing. I chink my glass against hers. 'She's being an absolute fucking nightmare, but that's probably my fault.'

'It probably is,' says Lysette, ironic. 'Most things are.'

'I feel like I'm screwing up everything, all at once. I'm like the world's most incompetent juggler.'

Lysette doesn't smile, she just watches my face. 'What?' I demand.

'I've never seen you like this over a client. Even that night you got me pissed on Martinis and stayed stone cold sober. I could see it then. It is only work. I mean – I know I'm not really qualified to tell anyone about work – but . . . You don't have to give it like - your bone marrow.'

'I just want to help her, but maybe the truth is that I can't.'

'I know *you* don't, but I like it when you're human.'

'Don't say that! I'm not a bloody cyborg.'

'I didn't mean that. But if you let yourself be a little bit less impeccable the rest of the time, it wouldn't be such a shock.'

'Trust me, I am the opposite of impeccable right now. I've been thinking about someone who isn't my boyfriend. I'm unprofessional. My nails are dirty. I'm drunk. Not to mention the state of my sock packing.'

'And you own a Sade CD, don't forget.'

'I let someone hold me, the very day I was signing up for the flat. What's wrong with me?'

Thanks to the fact I was wasting time with Patrick, I was half an hour late to the estate agents. I thought that Marcus would be angry: the fact that he wasn't made me feel like a con artist. 'Did your six o'clock crazy have a meltdown?' he said, kissing me in that uniquely Marcus way – like the people around us are a grateful audience. 'I'm so sorry,' I said too fervently, but by now a slimy man in a pinstriped suit was shoving paperwork across the desk. 'Just sign here, here and here,' he said, crosses already marking the spots, and I stood there, frozen, watching Marcus's fountain pen glide seamlessly across the contract. Suddenly I wanted to turn tail, hare across Ladbroke Grove, dodge the cars like I was in a video game. But even more than that, I didn't want to be Lorcan, blue eyes constantly checking the horizon. 'Give me the pen,' I demanded, and watched my hand like it was an alien object, the letters of my name trailing out after it like vapour from an aeroplane.

'You can't honestly think that counts?' says Lysette, incredulous, once I've described what happened. Two extended hugs does sound pretty tame, truth be told, but it was more the weird sense of intimacy that rattled me. 'I pretty much snogged our next-door neighbour the New Year before last. I blamed the absinthe, forgot about it.'

Lysette's always been a championship flirt: it's charming, not slutty, and, if you cured her of it, you'd lose something precious. I hope that I don't do that: neuter people's personalities, cure them of their most charming side effects.

'What if I just can't really do it? What if – for all this professional sanity – I'm basically a chip off the old block?'

'Mia,' says Lysette, serious now, 'you're not like Lorcan. You're just not. You're terrible at drinking, for starters.'

'I see it all the time with clients. They do everything in their power not to make the same mistakes as their parents, and then their subconscious takes over in the most sneaky ways. Suddenly they're divorcing at the exact same age or going bankrupt, just like Dad did.'

'Divorce – how shocking!' I smile, reassuring her it wasn't a sneaky sideswipe at her. 'Maybe you're just mourning being able to flirt about a bit.'

'Yeah, probably. He's a bit of a dick really,' I say, smiling. 'Muffin man I mean. He's a total child,' I add, thinking about how he described a woman as having a fatal attraction for her horse.

'How does muffin man's dickishness manifest? Or is that protected under therapist/dick privilege?'

'He can't be serious for more than five minutes – it's all Irish blarney. Not that I'm saying he's Irish. Welsh blarney.'

'What else is wrong with Daffyd, apart from the fact that he's highly amusing?'

'He's such a boy! It's so weird. He's the last person in the world I should feel comfortable with, but I spent two hours with him and it felt like two minutes.'

'Do you think Marcus has got wind of it?'

'Not remotely. He's been away so much,' I add, not sure if I'm letting him off the hook or accusing him of something.

Lysette knocks gently on my forehead.

'You're totally torturing yourself. I'm not dissing what you do, but it's not like everything that happens is a symptom, Mia. That's my point about muffin love. We can't analyse life to death. Because then it's dead.'

I hug her – there's no reply to that.

'Come on,' I say, 'the socks are in crisis.'

'Are you sure you should be taking your socks anywhere?' says Lysette, looking at me hard.

'I can always bring them home again. Their new pad's a rental. And they've paid the deposit.'

I walk Lysette to the tube about ten, giving her time to cross London and get her last train. I so rarely let myself get drunk, but tonight I'm enjoying the sense of the world being slightly out of focus. Focus hasn't been doing me much good recently. Even so, I still dart a couple of looks behind us as we walk down the backstreets. I'm glad she doesn't notice. It would be a hard one to explain away without freaking her out.

'It was so lovely to see you,' she says, hugging me. I hate saying goodbye to her.

'I feel like I talked about myself non-stop. I'm like one of those patients I secretly want to kill.'

'Do you really want to kill some of them?'

'Oh totally. I am so not a cyborg.'

'I didn't mean that,' she says.

'I know. But seriously, next time . . . tell me to shut up.'

We're being jostled by properly drunk people now.

'Don't be silly,' says Lysette, finding her Oyster card. We look at the metal barriers, neither of us moving. 'I'll see you at Saffron's birthday party?'

'Yeah . . .'

'You'd forgotten, hadn't you? You'd totally forgotten.'

I pull a face, sheepish.

'Wouldn't miss it. I won't now, anyway.'

Lysette rolls her eyes, holds out her Oyster card.

'Love you,' she says, quick and firm.

'Love you too,' I say, all of me in there. I grab her arm as she's starting to turn, the words out before I can stop them. 'Lys, does he ever ask about me?'

She stops, shock in her face.

'Jim? Yeah. Yeah he does.'

'OK,' I say, not sure if I believe her. 'I just wanted to know.'

Chapter Eleven

Annie's teaspoon surfs the top of her latte, skimming the froth and flicking it onto the saucer. She's playing for time. She didn't want this meeting, but I insisted on it, so here we are, in this hole in the wall around the corner from my office, jolly Australian baristas loudly dispensing takeaway cups of rocket fuel to the morning crowd. I thought meeting outside my treatment room might foster a bit more warmth, but instead it's just given her props. It took her a full five minutes to take her sunglasses off.

'Do you understand why I'm concerned?' I've got bored of waiting for her to answer, her spoon endlessly rotating its way round the stout glass that they serve their coffees in. We're squashed tight against a window, the table tiny. At least the fact it's so loud means no one's eavesdropping.

'Everyone's always concerned about my little girl. She makes sure of it.'

'Are you concerned?'

'I wouldn't have found a shrink for her if I wasn't!' she says. 'Sorry, I just—'

'No, I'm sorry. I wasn't questioning whether you care about her. I just wanted you to know that me sharing personal information with her might have been a mistake. Perhaps she needs to see a therapist who keeps the boundaries absolutely rigid.'

'Is this about that stupid present? That's just Gemma. She likes buying things.'

I look at Annie's large leather tote, ostentatious gold buckles holding it shut. She's not the only one. I feel a stab of pity for Gemma. Is that what love is for her? Twisted confidences and a credit card burnt to cinders around Selfridges? I don't want to abandon her, but, even more than that, I don't want to fail her.

'It's not about that, no, although I do think that's a symptom. She's obviously deeply confused about her dad. I don't know whether the fact she knows I had a confusing relationship with my father has made her relationship with me more confused. It feels like she's baiting me.'

'You can't cope with her?'

'No, I can cope with her, but I just wanted to be honest with you about how the work is going. It might be that we should do a limited amount of sessions together, like an introductory course, and then she should work with someone else if it's something she wants to keep doing.'

Annie looks at me, her eyes hard.

'You can't cope with her.'

'That's not what I'm saying.' I check in with myself. Maybe part of me is wondering if I can cope with *this*. With the darkness of it. With the shadows I can't chase away. I hate the way I've started compulsively looking behind me. Perhaps moving into the fridge will soothe the creeping unease I can't seem to shake. The iPad was back in session this week, the screen turned my way, nearly close enough for me to read the messages but not quite. I try and explain why it makes me so uneasy, but Annie doesn't so much as nibble on the idea.

'I know what you're thinking. How can she be spending that sort of money. Gemma's dyslexic. She needs it for her schoolwork.'

We can't keep spinning round in these dizzy-making circles.

'This isn't about money – your finances are none of my business. I want to make sure I'm helping to keep her safe, not doing the opposite.'

'You are.'

'I'm still deeply concerned about the self-harm too. She absolutely refuses to talk about it. The fact it was at school – to me, it links it straight back to Christopher.'

'She hasn't done it again!'

As far as we know.

'I'm glad about that, but it's not just about her cutting herself. It's about what it indicates, the level of pain she's in.' I pause, force Annie to look at me. 'Annie, are you sure she doesn't know more than she's told the police? I don't want to win her trust and then have to betray her by telling them what she's confided. The last thing she needs is another adult she believes in letting her down.' I think about it, think about Patrick's theory that the best thing that could happen to her is to have it flushed out. He'd hate to know I'm here, seriously contemplating withdrawal. 'Or at least seeming to let her down.' I pause a second. 'When she talks about Christopher she makes it sound like she's just seen him.'

Annie looks away, her eyes unseeing. It's not the caffein-ated commuters she's watching, it's something else, far from here.

'He was always obsessed with her, even when she was this tiny little blob in her carrycot. I know it's bad to say it, but I'm not a baby person. She didn't latch on, she was colicky. She was my first, and I didn't really have a clue.' She looks back at me properly, and I wonder if she's searching for signs of judgement. 'You don't have any, do you?'

Is it that obvious?

'No.'

'Our Christopher,' she says, vowels suddenly more Northern as she skims the surface of the past, 'he's an achievement junkie. He'd get up with her in the middle of the night, give her a bottle. They'd just sit there together, in the nursing chair, all tranquil, like they were a sculpture or something. Then he'd be up for work at six, like the Duracell Bunny, like he'd had eight hours. Made me feel like crap.'

'God, poor you. I bet that was hard. Was he like that with the other two?'

Annie shakes her head slowly, as though the weight of all those years is bearing down on her.

'She was his firstborn,' she says, her voice inflecting upwards, like she's heard him commandeer the phrase too many times to own it herself. 'He'd never had his own flesh and blood before. He's adopted.' It all starts to make even more sense, like a photograph developing, smudgy outlines coming into sharp relief. Poor Gemma, I think – no, not think, I *feel* it with my whole body, my heart sore and heavy. 'He'd look at her, her little nose, her eyes hardly open, searching for himself. Used to drive me a bit mad, if I'm honest.' There's guilt in her face, all these years later. It makes me suddenly furious; whichever way you cut it, motherhood's so often designed to make women feel like they're failing, and ducking out of the race altogether is deemed the biggest failure of them all. 'She was just – just a blob! She was our blob, and of course I loved her, but she wasn't this – this fucking heirloom!'

Anger animates her, burns through that simmering control that normally surrounds her like a heat haze.

'It's a huge change for any couple, first baby, even without that. I bet it was a big pressure on Gemma, too.'

Judith always says that babies are like wise Buddhas, more conscious than anyone realizes, and I think she's right. Gemma would've been steeped in that energy like a little pickled onion, no defences.

'Trust me, she rose to the challenge,' she says acidly.

I'm going to keep asking until she stops me – besides, I think she wants me to. She seems ragged around the edges, easier to touch than she's ever been previously.

'How did you two meet?'

'Sixth-form dance. Grammar school plus our girls' school. Quite the party.' She's smiling at the memory, but it's a smile that never quite reaches her eyes. 'I wore red. My mum was ho-rri-fied. Ruched at the top, tight on the skirt. Christopher said he couldn't keep his eyes off me.'

'How about you?'

'I was after Vincent Collins. To be fair, he was after me too. I wasn't chasing.'

'I'm guessing that died a death?'

'He didn't stand a chance. Wasn't like Chris was captain of the rugby team, or an amazing dancer. But he had this certainty. He always used to say he decided that night he'd met his soulmate. It was like he knew me better than *I* knew me – I know it sounds daft. He talked like an adult, and it made the rest of them seem like silly little boys.'

'Sounds incredibly seductive.'

'It was,' she says, the words like tombstones, past tense writ large. *Why didn't you leave him?* I can't ask her that. 'I followed him to university – he said he couldn't be apart from me – and that was that. I thought I was the only one who knew *him*. Adopted, never met his real mum. Seemed so tragic to me, made me wanna wrap him up in love.' I can just about see a softer Annie, far off in the distance, waving at me from a gentler past. 'But the truth is, no one really knows Chris. Not even my darling daughter, whatever he tells her when I'm not there.'

'She says the school suggested you go for family therapy.'

Her smile is crumpled, guilty.

'They did. Chris wasn't having it, of course.'

'Did you want to?'

'Bit of me did, bit of me didn't.' I can understand that. A tug on a single thread could have unravelled the whole tapestry. Poor Gemma – it's been cut to ribbons instead. 'I was so glad when we found you, though. He can't meddle now, can he?'

She looks up at me, blue eyes like rock pools, imploring me from their very depths. Is Judith right? Is the fact that every fibre of my being is telling me to help them exactly why I should walk away?

'Are you not worried by the fact she talks about him like she's seeing him?'

'No, cos I know what he's like. He gets in your head, colonizes it. Maybe now she's got a fighting chance of shifting him out.'

I look back at her, searching her face. She's attractive, Annie, not pretty. I think he probably took her prettiness from her, along with so much else.

'Do you think he'll come back?'

'I . . .' That single syllable sounds strangled, trapped in the back of her throat. She looks down, looks up, face neutral. 'I don't know, Mia.'

She nearly forgot herself. Not quite.

'Let's keep going for now, but you and I need to keep in regular contact. This situation isn't static. Gemma's welfare is what matters, but what's best for her could change at any time.'

'Thank you,' she says, already standing up, sunglasses heading for her suspiciously perfect nose. She only drank half her coffee, the saucer a soggy mass of cold foam. I stay a few minutes longer, twirling the spoon in the milky debris. I don't feel safe. Not even from myself.

'It's just a sandwich.'

'With us, there's no such thing as just a sandwich.' There's a pause. *Because of the case*, I tell him silently, defensively, aware it will sound even more so if I say the words out loud. I shouldn't have picked up, but I couldn't keep myself in check as strictly as I normally do. My conversation with Annie has been running around my head all morning, a shape-shifting animal, all claws and teeth, its form constantly changing. I know I could talk to Judith, but I don't necessarily want to hear what she has to say. When I saw her earlier in the week, she was visibly relieved I was contemplating making a grateful exit – the fact Annie's talked me round so easily is unlikely to impress her. Which leaves only one person I can discuss it with, however opaquely.

'I reckon you're crayfish and rocket.'

'I'm not, actually. I find crayfish distinctly rubbery.'

'Oh do you?' he says in a la-di-da voice. 'Well, m'lady, if

you tell me of a sandwich you find more delectable, I shall go in search of it.'

'Fine. I'll meet you by the little park with the swings behind my office. And, Sir Galahad? I've only got forty-five minutes.'

I'm a stickler for punctuality, but I'm running a few, unnecessary, minutes late. He's standing by the entrance, towering above the people streaming past him, a big paper bag swinging from his spidery fingers. He looks up and down the road more anxiously than I would expect, and I find myself almost scuttling towards him. His smile is pleased, open, warm: it pains me to admit it, but I can see why those doe-eyed PAs might fall for his chat.

'So I took a gamble,' he says, reaching into the bag as we walk through the gates. He holds out a polite palm, lets me go first. 'Looks like a vegetable Apocalypse to me, but I'm hoping you'll approve.'

It's a spelt-bread sandwich, oozing with avocado, an organic-looking tomato peeking out from the mess. It's rough-hewn, hacked from a loaf, the kind of thing you'd only find in a hemp-peddling kind of shop. There's a dark purple juice too, which I'll have to sip carefully to avoid frightening my afternoon clients with my beetroot moustache.

'Thank you!' He looks endearingly relieved, pulling another artisan production out of the bag.

'I asked for cheese salad – how badly could it go – but this is not what I understand to be cheese. Or indeed salad: it's vegetation.'

'I promise we can go to Subway if you feel undernourished.'

He looks at his watch.

'No time. By my estimation we've got thirty-seven minutes.' I look guiltily round the crowded little park. Not a bench in sight. 'If I lay my jacket over a metaphorical puddle, we could sit on the grass?'

So that's what we do. I tuck my feet beneath me, trying to stop my cotton dress from riding up, wishing I was wearing trousers. It's quite an operation, what with the Apocalyptic sandwich.

'So what was so urgent?' I say, taking a cautious nibble. Businesslike is a challenge under these circs.

Patrick's watching my struggle, amused, but his face shifts with my question like a car sliding into gear. It makes me wish I'd taken a couple more bites first, simply been here.

'I got a ripper.'

'What are you talking about? You arrested a serial killer?'

'RIPA. They're a big deal. You have to go cap in hand to the Home Secretary.'

'Go on.'

'It gives us the ability to listen in on calls. We can't use what we find as evidence in court, only to help us investigate.' He looks at me, brown eyes serious, weighing his words. 'What we've picked up on Gemma's phone gives me serious concern for her welfare.'

Why did I think I would find comfort here? Even the cunningly thoughtful sandwich is a ploy. I feel that familiar coldness spreading all the way into my bones, even with the sun beating down on us.

'No!' I say, no time for weighing and considering. 'Don't do this! Don't ask me again! If you want to question her, question her. It's not my job to manipulate her for you.'

'Mia . . .' Patrick puts his hand on my bare arm, but I throw it straight off me, furious. First Annie, now him. I'm sick of people trying to push me around the board like I'm too stupid to see their hand descend. 'This is serious. We're fairly sure she's talking to her dad. He's still in the country, complete with a pay-as-you-go. They're talking in code, but it sounds to me like he's asking her to destroy evidence for him.'

'Not my problem,' I say, swivelling myself away from him, trying to prevent his words from detonating inside my head. 'Above my pay-grade.'

'Mia . . .'

'Stop using my name. I'm not a bloody cocker spaniel.'

'She's not safe. If I call her in for questioning you know as well as I do she won't say a word.' It's true. Gemma has so many different versions of silence. Tears prickle as I think of her, a tiny, vulnerable piece of flotsam bobbing around in the vast, dark ocean. 'I might be wrong, I might be reading too much into what I saw between you, but I reckon she wants you to know what she's going through.'

I think about the iPad, the green bubbles she keeps shoving towards me like a tray of sweets. Could he be right?

'If she does, it has to come from her.'

'I'm not the psychologist, but even I know how much that's not gonna happen. You told me as much. She doesn't want to betray him.' He stares at me, willing me to admit he's right. 'She'd rather betray herself.'

I wish that wasn't true. Annie flits across my consciousness, the way she looked when she described how even as a callow teenager, Christopher knew how to take total possession.

'I'll tell you if she confides anything relevant. We've agreed.'

'Now's the time you need to do more than that,' he says, more an order than a request. 'What she doesn't realize is that the only way her darling dad is coming back is in a police van or a body bag. She could help us make sure it's the former.'

The brutality of it.

'Don't tell me what to do.'

It's his turn to look away, exasperation writ large, hands twisted around a clump of his coppery hair as though he's going to rip it out.

'I shouldn't even be telling you all this. If she does get involved in destroying evidence she'll be in way too deep. If Stephen's people find out, if she gets something wrong . . . you don't need me to spell it out.'

I don't want to hear him. I want to stick to the script.

'So protect her.'

'I can't. Not without your help. I'm taking a real risk trusting you with this. It's classified information. You can't be telling your boss. You certainly can't be telling Annie Vine. I'm telling you what you need to do to protect her.'

I take a sip of the pulpy juice, panic and confusion turning my thoughts to no more than white noise. I breathe in, breathe out.

'How do you do it, Patrick? I'm starting to think you're a little bit of a sociopath.'

'Oh yeah, how'd you work that one out?'

'How do you amble up here, full of chat about the vege-table Apocalypse, and then, once you've softened me up, swivel back round to the threats and insinuations?'

His jaw is rigid.

'It's a two-part question, that one. How do I do it? I do it because, if I lived my life permanently submerged in shit, I'd be . . . it wouldn't be a life. I have to walk on the sunny side of the street whenever there's a fighting chance. And con-trary to what you might think – contrary to what I might think right at this moment – I actually enjoy your company. I had something resembling fun finding your ridiculous rab-bit-food sandwich. And secondly, they're not threats and insinuations. I wish they were. I don't know how many times I have to tell you: we're on the same side.'

I watch him, his face flushed, his eyes bright. I almost reach out to touch him, try and quell the tremor I can see running through him like an electric current, but I stop myself.

'OK.'

'What, you'll do it?'

'I didn't say that."

'OK, I'm not a sociopath?'

'I don't think so. I could be wrong.' I stand up, brushing crumbs from my skirt. He looks vulnerable down there on the grass, limbs tangled up like string.

'Please Mia. I'm begging you. Just think about it.'

'Trust me, I won't be able to stop thinking about it.'

'I do trust you,' he says, eyes imploring me to give him some kind of reassurance.

'OK,' I say again, not risking anything more complex.

'I tell you what I've been thinking about, other than . . .' He flings a hand into the enormity of it as he stands up. 'What's your flippy coin? What's your strength that's your weakness? Cos I think you might've nailed mine, much as it kills me.'

We're standing next to each other now, quite close. I almost wonder if he'll be able to hear my heart, hammering out a bass line of fear. Words, normally my most beloved friends, seem to be wriggling away from me today.

'I try to do my best. I'm a perfectionist.'

'Hate to break it to you, but that doesn't sound like much of a fault.' I look away, look back up at him. 'No, I get it. It's a joy thief, isn't it? You can miss the sunny side of the street entirely if you're too scared you're gonna trip.'

Right at this moment I wonder if I'd prefer him to be a sociopath. Not the person who somehow seems able to see right the way through me.

February 1995 (sixteen years old)

I get it a bit now. I'm not saying I'm Linda Lovelace, but I've learnt how to do the basics – even if that makes it sound a bit like that cookery book for idiots with Delia Smith posing smugly with an egg. It's nearly Valentine's Day which means I've got almost two months of non-virginhood under my belt.

Valentine's Day is what's clinched it. I can't keep lying to Lysette, pretending I'm some kind of numbed-out nun-in-waiting, when the truth is the absolute opposite. She loves an excuse for a celebration: right now we're in the sixth-form common room looking through an anthology of love poems, trying to find something for her to send to Johnny Francis from the boys' college.

"'Shall I compare thee to a summer's day,'" she says, sounding like a radio announcer from the 1950s. "'Thou art more lovely and more temperate . . .'" I declaim along with her, before we give way to snorting giggles. Johnny's stubbly and stocky, with meaty hands that he uses to hammer at his drums – lovely and temperate doesn't really cover it.

'Mate, you're on a hiding to nothing,' I say. 'You should go for lyrics.'

'Push it,' sings Lysette, jumping up to do her best Salt-n-Pepa impression, her denim bum wiggling in my face. That's it, I'm convulsing now, earning a glare from Roberta Chalmers, who's sitting on the tatty green sofa on the other side of the room, her nose buried in a history textbook. The sight of her makes me feel guilty. They've set up extra classes for us Oxbridge hopefuls: I've been turning up, but I know I don't have the kind of dogged focus I used to have. I still want it, I still care about the French Revolution, but I find it hard to think about anything except Jim. When it's good I'm lost in fantasy Jim Land, but when there are days between phone calls my imagination goes into a darker kind of over-drive, imagining some skinny minx with designer jeans and tousled blonde hair dragging him into the woods and doing things to him that I haven't even heard of. The person who would normally douse out my paranoia is Lysette, but obvi-ously that's not an option. She's sitting down now, grinning, pink with her exertions. I don't think I could love her any more than I do. Maybe, just maybe, she'll be pleased, once she's got over the shock of the deception. After all, we could be family for real.

'Come on,' I say, standing up. 'We need to go and buy this famous card.'

'You can only help me pick it if you buy one too. There

must be *someone* who meets your exacting standards.' I busy myself collecting my books. 'Luke Farmer, you know you want to!'

Luke Farmer has enough acne to be the subject of his own medical trial.

'Shall I compare thee to a smallpox plague? It's a deal.'

Jim's approaching his A levels, whilst I'm still in the land of mocks, so it's not surprising he can't come home for Valentine's Day. I know it's silly, sentimental nonsense but I've never had a boyfriend before, and I want to live the dream. I'm sitting on the stairs talking to him whilst Mum busies herself in the kitchen, pretending not to eavesdrop.

'Do you want me to send you a dozen red roses?' he says.

'No!' I insist, even though I can't think of anything nicer. Actually I can. A dusty hardback book of love poems or something he's made himself, like that leather string he wears.

'I've already got my first card,' he says, and my heart plummets down a lift shaft. 'Got a couple actually. You got any yet?'

'One. But I think it might be from my dad.' A double lie: even Lorcan's postcards have petered out now. I can hear the heaviness in Mum's footfall as she makes our macaroni cheese, her sadness a cloak that she can't rip off. Part of me wishes she'd talk to me about it, credit me with the maturity to see through her Stepford good cheer, but a cowardly part of me's relieved she's letting me off the hook.

'Loser.'

'You're the loser,' I say, trying not to let paranoia seep its way into my pumping heart. 'I was thinking, if Mohammed can't come to the mountain—'

'Where do you get these weirdo phrases?'

'My dad says it,' I tell him, embarrassed. 'But . . . I could come to you. We could bunk off for the afternoon.'

Jim pauses, the only sound on the line his breath.

'That'd be wicked, but I've got a test paper on Thursday. It's the one day I can't do.'

'OK, don't worry!' I say, my Day-Glo words as bright and synthetic as Mum's have become. 'I'm still going to tell Lysette this week though.'

I'm testing him, if only he'd notice.

'Baby – everyone knows secrets are sexy. It's our sexy, sexy secret.'

'I can't do it any more,' I say simply, refusing to laugh. It feels good to tell the truth – I didn't realize how much I'd missed it.

I feel sick. I've felt sick all week, so much so that I've been wondering if I've got some gruesome lurgy that's not yet fully flourished. Or more likely it's nerves, the not knowing how she'll take it. Mum too. I feel cruel being so happy when she's the absolute opposite. I thought about getting her a card, but I'm not six years old: it might seem more patronizing than comforting.

'What do you think?' says Lysette, holding out her hand.

We've been trying out nail varnishes in Debenhams for a good half-hour without any sign of a purchase. It's not surprising the matronly sales assistant is glaring at us.

'Not sure pearly pink's your colour. Blue's better.' I'm sweating. It's like standing on the high diving board. There's nothing to do but jump. 'Lys—'

'Yup. Ooh, why is nail varnish so stinky?' The sales assistant is looking like she wants to kill us now.

'I'm seeing Jim.'

'Where'd you see him? He's not home until the weekend after next.'

'No,' I say, my hand on the puffy arm of her winter parka. 'We're going out together.' She tenses, her eyes staring straight ahead. I suddenly realize we've never had an argument; I don't know what the ground rules are. 'I'm sorry, Lys, I know I should've told you.'

'No. No, you shouldn't have told me, Mia. You should never have DONE it!'

'It just happened,' I say, aware how pathetic it sounds. 'I . . . we love each other.'

He has said it, at least when we've been having sex. I hate that phrase, it sounds so clinical, but 'fucking' (his favourite) sounds brutal, and 'making love' is obviously ridiculous. Lysette looks at me, all kinds of emotions playing across her elfin face. I wish we could fast-forward past this moment to a time when all of this is tied up in a bow.

'You really don't know what he's like, do you?'

'Maybe *you* don't know what he's like.' Her eyes widen.

'Sorry, I don't mean that like it sounded. It's just – a boy-friend's different from a brother.'

'I love him more than you do,' she says. 'I've known him all my life. You've known him like, five minutes. When did you come up with your brilliant plan, his birthday party?'

I look at her, all my noble truth-telling extinguished.

'Let's go and get a coffee,' I say, pulling at her rigid arm.

'No! When? Tell me. How long have you been lying to me?'

I think about white washing it – it's not like he'll set her straight – but I can't quite bear it.

'On holiday.'

'I took you to France! I've never invited anyone there before.' Her face is white, her eyes flashing with a rage that I've never seen in her. 'And that's how you thank me?'

'I loved it so much. It was the best week of my life.'

It's completely the wrong thing to say. What I meant was that I loved all of it, not just the Jim part, that I could never thank her enough, but I've already lost her. She turns on her heel and pushes her way through the gaggle of people at the counter. I try and follow her but she won't turn round.

'I love you,' I say, desperate. '*And* him. I just didn't know how to tell you.'

For a second I hate him for not being here with me helping to explain, but men aren't built that way. They don't like dealing with difficult things and there's no point making them. She's nearly at the door now. As she pushes it open, she twists back towards me, her face white and pinched.

'It's your funeral, Mia.'

It sort of will be too. I'm glad I don't know that yet.

Chapter Twelve

Red roses, their petals pillowy and full. It's not a dozen – of course not, too ordinary – it's twenty.

'They're gorgeous!' says Brendan.

'Mmm.' I've got two missed calls from Marcus, no message. I know where this is going. 'I can't have them in my room. Can you keep them on reception, or will we look like a funeral parlour?'

'You obviously haven't been to a funeral for a while,' says Brendan, bearing them off to the kitchen. 'More like a knocking shop.'

I barely slept last night, my mind whirring, the boxed-up flat filled with unfamiliar shadows. I've got half an hour before my appointment with Gemma – I want to get this out of the way so my focus is absolute. I'm trying to stay inside my own instincts, not get lured down a path carved out by Patrick. I head for the little park, refuse to think about him, plonk myself down on the bench where you can see the swings. Marcus picks up on the second ring, his hello a sheepish one.

'They're "I'm sorry" kind of roses, aren't they? I can smell it on them.'

'Do they smell bad? I told Wendy to send you the best ones they had.'

'Don't change the subject. Is it Dubai?'

'Chicago,' he says, exhaling.

'Chicago? So you'll be away all week? We're moving in together, Marcus! This was meant to be our first night—'

'I'll make it up to you, I promise.'

'How? By buying me stuff? This was – it was important. I don't want to feel like I'm four hundredth on your to-do list.'

He pauses, the atmosphere changing in the silence.

'I'm sorry, but I don't have a choice. You know who I am, Mia. You can't just pick the bits you like. You like feeling like Daddy's home, but there's a price. I can't leave a multimillion-pound client hanging.'

'"Daddy's home?"' I repeat, my voice soaring upwards. An old lady on the next bench turns her gimlet eye on me, and I gesture an apology, lowering my voice. 'Don't think I haven't noticed you using my history against me every time you feel threatened. You don't have the first idea how I feel about all of that. Not really.'

Or maybe he does, even if I don't say it. Maybe some part of him senses that the past doesn't feel far enough away any more.

'For fuck's sake, Mia, it's an expression. Don't be so literal. Is this what it's going to be like? My job's demanding enough without you giving me all manner of shit for doing it.'

'What, so you think it's a complete coincidence that you're having to fly to the other side of the planet the day, the actual day, we're moving in? You're an architect, not James fucking Bond.'

'Oh yeah, do please overanalyse me some more, Dr Freud. Do you think I'm stuck in the anal phase?'

'Yes,' I say, 'I do.'

And then I hang up, turning the phone off for extra protection. I look at its dead, blank screen as it shakes in my unsteady palm. I've got somewhere to be.

Gemma's early. She's got big white leather headphones on, the kind of noise-defying ones that cost a fortune and make you look like a rapper in waiting, and she's nodding her head to whatever's pumping through them. She looks up at me slowly, unpeeling the headphones and dropping them around her neck.

'Come on through,' I say, keeping my voice light. 'Let's get started.'

As she gets closer I start to hear the music that rises up out of the pillowy surface. I expected something tinny and bassy, but it's more old-fashioned — familiar, but too indistinct to name. I'm straining to identify it, my skin prickling. There are times right now where I really feel like I'm losing it.

Gemma sits down, pulling the iPad out of her bag, the cable attached.

'Sorry,' she says, turning the music off and unlooping the headphones. She's humming as she does it, her eyes darting around.

'What kind of music do you like, Mia?' she asks. 'I bet you're into really cheesy stuff.'

'What, like power ballads? It's true I do a mean *Total Eclipse Of The Heart* at karaoke. What are you humming, Gemma?'

'Was I humming?' she says, her face deliberately neutral.

'I thought you were humming. Don't worry.' I force the creeping anxiety downwards. 'What's been happening this week?'

I'm determined to simply let the conversation unfold, no agenda, see where it takes us.

'School. Home. School again. What's been happening to *you*, Mia?'

'We're not going to talk about me today. What's your favourite subject at school? What do you like most about it? Or what's the one you hate the least if that's too icky?'

Gemma's gazing out of the window like she might not even deign to answer. She turns to me.

'I like drama,' she says, 'and before you start, it's not because I like pretending to be someone else. Or escaping into another world.' She's sharp: that passive-aggression hides a brain far more perceptive than her so-so grades give her credit for. 'I like making the sets. I did anyway, till I got washed up in Shitsville Academy.'

'I didn't know that about you.'

'Yeah, like I made this forest for *A Midsummer Night's Dream*. I dyed this fake-fur coat green to make these mad leaves and the birds were made out of Mum's coat hangers.'

'Was the coat hers too?'

'She didn't even notice! It was manky, anyway. Dad got her a real one for Christmas.'

I look at her, thinking it through.

'So you *did* escape into another world. Or at least you brought things – well, stole things – from your world and transformed them into something for a made-up world.'

Gemma rolls her eyes extravagantly.

'Don't you ever get bored?'

'Of what?'

'Coming up with your made-up theories. It's like when people *analyse their dreams*,' she says, making angry quotation marks. 'How can anyone know what a dream means? It's just boring.'

'I do get bored,' I say, smiling at her. It's true: Isobel and Ben who still come every single Monday and whinge end-lessly about who takes the bin out and how to get the magic back into their sex life (Ben, a clue, stop wearing shapeless brown cords like you're a 1940s Oxford don) bore me stupid. If only they'd believe me when I tell them it's time for them to work it out for themselves. 'But our sessions never bore me.'

Gemma looks at me, alert.

'Don't lie.'

'Nope, never been bored. Sometimes I've been frustrated or impatient, but I've never been bored. You're officially the only one round here who is.'

It's only for a minute, but she positively glows. Then she shifts away from me down the sofa, reaching back into her bag for the machine she can't bear to be parted from.

'You seem to love that thing. It's like it's your familiar.'

'Um, hello, Harry Potter, you're the one who keeps going on about it.'

She's fiddling with it now, fingers running across the screen so it springs to life. My breath feels tight in my chest, my eyes tracking the screen.

'So was it a present for something specific? Hasn't been your birthday, has it?'

'No!' she says, lighting up again. 'But my dad gives amazing presents when it is. Way better than this, Mia.'

Are we walking into the woods now, the path finally emerging in front of us?

'Like what? Give me the rundown from last year.'

'Thirteen: he said it was a big one. He threw me this lush party at this hotel in the country where film stars go when they want some R and R.'

'Wow. Is that what you wanted – rest and relaxation? Were you very stressed?'

'No! I took loads of the girls in my class, and we went in the jacuzzi and had facials and stuff.'

What must the bill have been like? If Christopher really is corrupt, would he really want to be seen to be splashing his cash so ostentatiously? I'm trying to imagine how it was: I don't get the feeling Gemma has many friends. Or at least, not unless he buys them for her.

'Did your mum come along?'

'Yeah, for a bit. We had this big dinner, and Dad let us have champagne and then he got in trouble for it.'

Poor Annie, constantly relegated to a no fun footnote.

'Dad, not Mum? Had she gone by then?'

Gemma nods briefly, her fingers slipping back towards the screen. Was it a cover, an elaborate way to score a dirty weekend with his mistress? There'd have been so many easier ways – unless he wanted to rub Annie's nose in it, make Gemma complicit.

'The year before he got me a pony, but I wasn't good at riding so we had to sell it.'

'Tell me more about the party. Why didn't your mum stay for dinner?'

'She didn't like my present.'

'Was there a present as well as the party?'

'Not that present.' We sit there, the silence a pressure cooker – this is too important to draw back from. 'Stephen's present,' she adds eventually.

'So Stephen – Stephen who your dad works with – got you a birthday present?'

'Yes!' she says, snapping at me. 'It was a Marc Jacobs handbag, Marc by Marc Jacobs actually.' I glance at that tatty

233

rucksack – any fool would know that designer bling is something that's not yet on Gemma's wish list. 'But Mum didn't think he should've come and given it to me.'

'So Stephen Wright came to your birthday party?'

'Yeah, I told you that! To give me my present.' Tread carefully. 'Mum was really angry. She says Dad works all the time. But Dad just wanted some grown-up company from someone who doesn't chew his ear off.' She's flushed red, her voice high, like she's right there in the midst of it. If Christopher knew what kind of man Stephen was, why would he let him pollute his beloved daughter's birthday party? No wonder Annie lost it.

'I'm a bit sad that your birthday party got spoiled by your parents having a row.'

Gemma shrugs, face set.

'Dad let me have champagne. He said Mum would get over it, and that we could stay up as late as we wanted now she wasn't there, swinging her keys.'

'Swinging her keys?'

'He says she's like a prison guard. And Stephen stayed for dinner, even though it was just a load of us girls. It was the best fun.'

I sit there for a second, letting it percolate.

'Do you understand why your mum was angry? Maybe she was trying to protect you – make sure that everything about your birthday was for you, and not about your dad's work.'

'You're doing it again! You're so sneaky. I tell you something, and you twist it and TWIST it till you can make out my dad's done something evil. That's the evil thing, not him.'

'I'm not trying to twist what you're saying, I'm just reflecting back to you what I'm hearing. I'm wondering if you thought about it from your mum's point of view.'

'Oh and I know you talked to her, by the way. Sneaking around behind my back. Telling tales.'

Her eyes dart back down to the iPad, like it's the other patient. She couldn't be recording this, could she? I can't go on like this – I can't work properly when every move I make is blighted by my own paranoia.

'I wasn't telling tales, Gemma. I didn't tell her anything secret that you've told me.'

'You said you might not see me any more. You said you'd had enough of me.'

'It's true we discussed how long you should come for, but I certainly didn't say I'd had enough of you. And if you're not sick of me, we're just going to carry on for now.'

'Maybe I am. Maybe I am sick of you.'

'You don't have to come and see me, Gemma. I want to help you, but if these sessions don't feel supportive . . .' Her eyes are darting around the room, her face pale and pinched. Something's making her deeply agitated. What if Patrick's right? What if I sit here being gentle and non-confrontational and middle class and she walks out of the room and gets herself killed? 'I can tell you're really angry today. If your anger was going to be a prop, if you were going to make it into something, what would it be?'

'I'd make it into a bird,' she says, animated, 'but like, a really big one. An eagle or something. They can just swoop down and eat stupid, crappy things like mice.'

'So would you like to be the eagle? Be a big predator that swoops in and takes little animals away?'

We stare at each other now, our gazes locked. My heart's hammering in my chest. I don't want that to happen to you.

'This is just another one of your stupid riddles,' she says, head jerking away. 'You're just waiting to get back to my dad, start slagging him off. I'm on to you Mia.'

She rips open her bag, the sound of the zip loud in the silence. She drops her iPad in, fiddling with it as she does so. This time there's no mistaking it: Lorcan's voice fills the room, swooping over the familiar chords, every line soaked through with emotion. Tears spring to my eyes before I can stop them.

'Gemma—'

'I like this one. It's definitely my favourite.'

Mine too.

'You *little* bi—' I stop myself, horrified by my reaction. 'You should *not* have done this,' I say, injecting myself with a syringe of fake calm. I watch her, that maddening half-smile playing across her blanched face: just for one awful unprofessional second, I would do anything to be able to reach across the room and slap her without being struck off. 'You had no right to go poking around in my life.'

'Ditto,' she says, triumph in her eyes. Right now this second I hate her.

'Gemma, I'm your therapist. We've been exploring your life together. This is very different. It's . . .' I want to say abusive, but I stop myself. 'It's totally unacceptable.' Maybe it's me who's been abusive. I should never have given this mixed-up child enough rope to weave us a double noose.

'I just wanted to know who I was dealing with,' she says, standing up. 'I'm sorry if I upset you. See you next week.'

'I'll need to think very seriously about that,' I say, my voice shaking. Gemma looks at me, stricken. 'Gemma, I'm not sure we can continue. The boundaries have got very confused. I don't know if I can help you any more.'

Now it's her eyes that fill with tears.

'I'm coming back,' she says. 'You can't just get rid of me. Don't think you can.'

And then she's out of the door. I think I'd have preferred her to slam it. The smooth click feels more sinister to me now.

March 1995 (sixteen years old)

I'd hoped that it was a temporary break in service, like when the BBC puts up that picture of the chubby-faced girl with the blackboard as a reassuring reminder that there's nothing much to worry about. Surely Lysette would go away and think about it, her anger burning itself out as harmlessly as brandy round a Christmas pudding, and then realize that this really could be a good thing? Her upsets were normally transitory, clouds scudding across a blue sky, but it seemed that now I'd brought down a thunderstorm.

'Please will you talk to her properly,' I begged Jim, my hand gripping the receiver, wishing he'd hurry up and come home for the weekend. We loved each other, we were spit sisters, and yet now, when Lysette saw me at school, she'd turn on her heel theatrically, her hazel eyes as narrow as a cat's. I'd taken to sitting with the geeky girls from my Oxbridge classes, but their dry conversations about how to balance out the prestige of the college against the likelihood of getting in made me want to scream. I wanted to laugh like we laughed – stupid private jokes which would make my stomach heave and my breath escape me like air from a whoopee cushion. I'd tried approaching her, but she'd just stalked off, and my letter – logical and pleading in equal measure – elicited nothing but more stony silence.

'Stop your fretting, little mouse,' said Jim. 'She'll be right as rain before you know it. She's probably on the blob or something.'

But if she was going to get over it, surely she'd have got over it by now? It had been over a fortnight. School was torture – I felt like a spurned lover, but one who deserved the rejection, denied the luxury of a warm bath of self-pity. The mention of periods, however crude, had sent up a warning flare. I didn't want to read the flash. Couldn't face it, not yet.

'But have you really tried to talk to her?' I pleaded.

'She doesn't want to talk about it,' he said, exasperation mounting, his engraved silver Zippo, his eighteenth birthday present from his louche-sounding Parisian father, flicking open down the phone line. 'I really don't need this aggro. I dunno why you went on such a spastic truth-telling crusade, Mia. Sis-ter Mia,' he added in a holy voice.

'If you keep lying to people, everything rots,' I said, my voice low: the last thing I wanted was a row. Lorcan kept telling Mum he was coming home, and now she was convinced he really was, would be walking through the door in a fortnight. I wanted to wrap her in cotton wool, cushion her from the almost inevitable disappointment of a no-show, but instead I was being extra specially snide and secretive. I couldn't work out how to make my insides match the outside, however hard I tried.

'Thanks for the tip,' he said, snarky, but then his voice softened. 'I'll be home this weekend. We'll sort it out, promise.'

I melted, like I always did.

'But you can't promise,' I said, even though I loved that he had.

'You don't have a big brother. Big brothers rule. I'll sort it.' He took a drag on his fag. 'Now I've gotta go. Keep your chin up, little mouse.'

Miss Dicker, newly hatched from teaching training college, was obsessed with *The Waste Land*. Gingery-blonde and geeky, a lover of twee cashmere cardigans and, Lysette and I suspected, Mr Harlow our chemistry teacher, she would well up at almost every line, intoning it as if she was on stage and beseeching us to reflect on what it 'truly meant'. I looked over to Lysette, smirking, as she trilled 'cruel-est month' through her pale pout. I knew she felt my gaze on her, but she looked straight ahead, her mouth a grim line, as if she was taking Miss Dicker deadly seriously.

That was when I felt it, a heaving monster deep in my belly. I'd been feeling intermittently queasy for a while, but I'd ignored it at first, then blamed it on the row. This was bigger and fiercer. I stood up, my hands covering my mouth, but it was too late: I threw up right there and then, the vomit forming a watery pool around my feet.

'Mia!' squeaked Miss Dicker. I sat back down, light-headed. I wanted to stay that way: the truth was becoming almost impossible to dodge. 'Lysette, I think you should take Mia to the nurse. Anna, you get some paper towels from the lavatories.'

Just for a second, Lysette forgot she was meant to hate me. She was looking straight at me, concern and kindness writ large, and I allowed myself a spurt of hope. Then she hardened, crossing the room on taut legs and slipping her hand under my elbow.

'Come on,' she said, the kindness still there despite her best efforts, and I stood up, leaning on her more heavily than I maybe needed to.

'Thanks,' I said, hoping she could hear how much the single syllable contained, and she squeezed my arm in reply, her fingers clam-tight around my grateful flesh.

I sat on the thin mattress, the curtains drawn around the cubicle. The privacy was a nonsense: I knew Lysette would be able to hear every word. The nurse turned her owlish gaze on me, disapproval etched deep into her features. I'd already admitted that my period was weeks late, that I'd put it down to stress. It was true that I didn't eat much, and sometimes my periods would stubbornly refuse to play ball.

'Are you sexually active?' she asked.

My cheeks flamed, my heart racing like an engine.

'Yes,' I said, my voice barely a whisper.

Her springy hair was a grey artillery helmet, a wedding ring jammed firmly on her meaty left hand. I reckoned she hadn't had sex since the Falklands War was won.

'And are you using contraception?'

'Sort of.'

'Sort of?' she said, voice rising in disbelief.

'He withdraws,' I muttered, wishing I was a slimy snail, wishing I could wind in on myself and hide somewhere dark and inaccessible.

She exhaled with self-satisfied exasperation.

'If you girls are going to insist on starting these relationships – behaving like you're grown women – the least you can do is employ a modicum of womanly wisdom. I assume you've *heard* of the pill?'

I looked down at the linoleum floor, shame spreading through me like a lethal injection. I suppose the convent setting gave her carte blanche to humiliate us at will, but I wanted to fight back. I was no fool, I had an A in GCSE biology, and in January I'd taken myself off to an over-stretched clinic behind Tottenham Court Road where they'd scribbled me a hasty prescription for the pill whilst lecturing me about the importance of using condoms (fat chance). I'd been waiting for my period – my longed-for period – so I could pop the first one, the packet lodged under my mattress where I hoped Mum wouldn't find it. I'd lied to her of course, pretended I was still a virgin when she'd clumsily tried to ask if it was 'getting serious', and luckily, or unluckily, she was too distracted and sad to call my bluff.

'Yes, I've got some. I just haven't started taking them yet.'

Nurse Brown's beetle brows shot skywards.

'Too little knowledge, far too late – I rather suspect the horse has bolted. You'll need to take a pregnancy test. I'll go and find you one.' She flounced through the green curtains, spotting Lysette. 'Are you still hanging around? You should have gone straight back to lessons.'

'I'm here for my friend,' said Lysette stoutly, and a sob immediately rose up in my throat.

'Very admirable,' said Nurse Brown acidly, but at least she didn't forcibly eject her.

There was no real suspense: of course I was pregnant. We managed to persuade the evil nurse to let me take the test at home, and I perched on the loo seat, Lysette poised by the sink, waiting for the white plastic stick to confirm the inevitable.

'Shit,' she said, her hand covering her mouth as the blue line appeared. I couldn't speak, I just sat there, the ridged plastic digging into my knotted palm. I thought of the kitschy Swedish snow globe Lorcan had brought back from a long-ago tour and left, pride of place, on our mantelpiece: the way you could shake it as hard as you liked, knowing with absolute certainty that the flaky chaos inside would return to perfect order within a few short seconds. It used to obsess me when I was little. This was the polar opposite:

whatever I did, whatever happened, there was no going back. I was indelibly changed, one life left behind.

'What are you going to do?' said Lysette, white with shock.

'I don't know!' I snapped. 'Sorry,' I said quickly, 'it's just – it's too soon.' The last thing I wanted to do was alienate her again. Why did it have to be her brother? I felt tender, defensive: I didn't want her disapproval to start rolling over me, her cast-iron conviction that she knew him best. 'Let's go to my room.'

We struggled to find words, put on The Cure's *Disintegration* and let Robert Smith's gloomy vocals fill the space instead.

'My cousin had to, you know . . . get rid of a baby, and she's fine now. She's at Manchester doing theatre studies.' Normally I loved Lysette's relentless buoyancy, her absolute commitment to living life sunny side up, but today I couldn't take it. This was too big, too dark, to be tucked neatly into a box and tied up with a pink ribbon. Or maybe – just for a second I let myself imagine it – a giggly baby, as plump and easy to cherish as some of the ones I'd looked after, Jim smiling down at us both, unable to resist her charms.

'I need to talk to him,' I muttered, aware what a minefield I was walking into. I did need to talk to him, but a part of me wanted to put it off for as long as I possibly could.

'Yeah, course you do, but . . .' She looked at me, eyes wide, her pity visible. 'Mia, he's not gonna want to be a dad!'

I didn't say anything, just mechanically ran my fingers across the raised diamonds of my green satin bedspread. It was my

Christmas present from Mum a few years ago, even though it was me who actually bought it. She always wanted to get me the right present, but didn't trust herself to meet my exacting standards. I couldn't bear the idea of heaping more pain on her, but, now the school knew, there was no escaping it.

She laughed when I told her, a high-pitched hyena shriek which I knew came from shock and disbelief. 'I'm so sorry,' I said, tears rolling down my cheeks. 'I know how stupid I've been.' I couldn't quite get over my own stupidity: I kept tracking backwards, ever more furious with myself. It never once occurred to me to hold Jim even partially responsible: I think it was a strange kind of self-protection, a half-knowledge that if I wanted to hold on to him I'd have to treat him like a skittish animal who needed careful handling.

Mum had no such timidity. She raged at me, raged at him, then hugged me, her tears raining down over us both. 'You're such a clever clogs, Mia, you can't just throw that away.' We looked at each other, both us still too squeamish to use the A word. She and I were fairly feeble Catholics – I was baptized because Lorcan's Anglo-Irish family were Catholic, his parents religious enough to stump up the fees for my convent school – but despite our lack of religious conviction, we both shrank away from what seemed like the obvious solution. 'I should be more sorry than you,' she said. 'I've been a hopeless, unfit mother. We've both been hopeless. I'm going to call your dad.'

'No, don't!' I said, panicky, but she was determined. The

phone in his apartment rang out — it was mid-afternoon in New York — and I wondered if I should steel myself and call Jim.

'Not yet,' said Mum, as protective as a lioness. I secretly liked it. 'Let's work out what you want to do before he gets to stick his tuppence' worth in.'

We stayed up until midnight, Mum drinking red wine, me endless cups of tea, talking like we hadn't talked in years. I'd somehow forgotten how much she loved me, how much I loved her, this crisis stripping everything as bare as winter branches. Could this be me in sixteen years, being wise and responsible for my own child? The idea was ridiculous.

'You don't have to decide overnight,' said Mum, but I could see relief as well as sadness in her expression as we finally faced up to the idea of me having an abortion.

'I know,' I said, yawning, bed calling to me. Now the adrenalin was wearing off I could feel my deep exhaustion.

It was three in the morning when he rang: Mum had left a message on his answering machine and he must've heard something in her tone that told him he should heed this particular call. I stumbled down the passage, hearing her voice, low and insistent. Once I was downstairs, she held out the phone, her eyes brimming.

'Dad?' I hadn't risked calling him that for years, but normal service had not yet been resumed.

'Hello, petal,' he said, his voice soft and soothing, not at all what I'd expected.

'I'm sorry I've been so stupid,' I said. Tears were starting again, but they weren't just about my ridiculous condition. I wanted to believe in the version of himself he was transmitting to me. I needed him.

'Sweetheart, you were an accident and you're the best thing that ever happened to me.' I tried to track the words before they entered my heart, listen for any slurring. 'The best thing. I think it's meant to be. You can have the baby, and we'll all move to Oxford. It'll be an adventure. I'll be your Mary Poppins, don't you worry.'

'Do you really think that?' I unconsciously put my hand on my belly. I was the only protection this tiny smudge of life had right now.

'One hundred per cent. No, one thousand per cent! Don't let anyone judge you, Mia – you're like me, you're a free spirit. I'll get on a plane tomorrow. You'll feel like a different person once your daddy's home.'

Chapter Thirteen

I'm sitting on the floor of my office, my back leant against the sofa, my fingers tangled up in the white fringe of Lysette's rug. My eyes are chasing the circles, desperately searching for some kind of order. I can't leave the room, can't face joking about funeral parlours with Brendan or subjecting myself to Judith's all-seeing eye. I'm a mess.

I'm trying Lysette for the third time (her perky voicemail, 'This is Lysette' when it so blatantly isn't, is making me boil with frustration) when the phone rings in my hand. I watch his name flashing up. Flash, flash, flash. On the third ring I give in.

I make my voice steady. 'Hi.'

'What happened?' he says, sounding worried.

'Nothing. I'm fine.' The sound of his steady breathing sets me off again, tears threatening. 'Bad day, that's all.'

'I'll take you for a glass of wine.'

'We can't do that. It's inappropriate.'

'You're right, I'm the world's worst sommelier. Come for a pint of Guinness.'

I laugh, despite myself, my body starting to unclench itself, my heartbeat slowing. I unravel my fingers from the fringes of the rug.

'It's still inappropriate.'

'What, and the two of us talking when you're so stressed you can barely breathe *is* appropriate? Let's go out and discuss your dictionary, I think you should bin it.'

'No.'

'Coffee? Come on, Mia, I know how much you like a frothy coffee.'

The thought of going to the fridge – where I'll be imprisoned between its Farrow & Ball walls like I've been committed to an upmarket mental asylum – is making me shudder. No, it's not that. The truth is I want to see him.

'I only drink decaf after lunchtime.'

'You are one wild date, my friend.'

A hotel bar seems like a decent compromise: I can start with a professional seeming mint tea and then move on to a glass of wine without losing face. I choose the one near King's Cross Station where I met Lysette last month, but as soon as I arrive, I regret it. What's happened to me in the space of a few short weeks? I sat there that night, perched on my stool, coolly judging strangers and sipping a single drink whilst she downed three. I feel like a ragged, broken version of that Mia. The song keeps playing around my head like Chinese water torture. How many lives can I live in this one little life? I feel like a cat, well into my ninth, time running out.

Patrick's frantically waving at me from the crush at the bar, pulling me out of my looping thoughts. I push my way towards him, and he hugs me roughly, kissing the side of my face. It feels shocking somehow, his lips against my skin, even for that brief second.

'I've finally got this fine man's attention. You need to tell me right this instant what it is you're drinking. And make it worth our while.'

'Mint . . .' I look at him, then at the barman. He's young and Eastern European-looking, olive skin rendered pale by the stress of dealing with hordes of commuters waving cash and barking demands like he's a voice-activated vending machine. Even so, he can't help but grin at Patrick, the other punters an irrelevance for this tiny moment. 'Glass of Prosecco,' I say.

'*Two* glasses of Prosecco,' says Patrick, his face lighting up: Marcus would've given me a look of amused disbelief and ordered a bottle of Veuve. Guilt pokes me hard, but I push it back. I can only deal with life one moment at a time.

'Have you had your hair cut?' I ask, playing for time. We're sitting down now, shoved on a small, cramped table which looks over the platforms. It's not just avoidance, he does look different tonight, more grown-up somehow. I thought he'd be wearing one of his flammable-looking suits, but instead he's dressed in jeans, a well-cut black shirt thrown over the top, paired with shoes that actually aren't hideous. If I'd been asked to imagine his bare arms I would've guessed they'd be like white drinking straws, but they're not, they even suggest he might've seen the inside of a gym.

'I have,' he says, visibly pleased I've noticed. 'Do you approve?'

'At least your face is visible now.'

'I know. Lucky, lucky you.' I shake my head at him, smiling, then look away. 'Can I say "Cheers", or is that listed under "inappropriate" in the dictionary?'

'Cheers,' I say, raising my glass, and bumping it softly against his.

'Come on, we can do better than that,' he says, going in again. 'Cheers!'

I clink harder, feeling a lump rise up in my throat. Patrick studies my face, concern etched on his.

'Sorry . . .'

'Don't be sorry,' he says, his hand clamping over mine with surprising gentleness. Tears prickle my eyes like the bubbles in my glass.

'No, I am sorry,' I say, snatching up the thin paper napkin they've given us with the silver bowl of nuts and trying to catch the tears before they send my mascara south. 'I'm being such a fucking idiot at the moment . . .'

'Hey,' he says, taking my hand again, discarding the damp, sooty clump of paper. 'You're one of the least idiotic people I know.'

'Now *there's* a compliment,' I say, pushing my fingers

between his and letting our hands rest on the table between us. I look up at him, our eyes locking together. 'I really don't know why I'm here.'

'No, me neither,' he says, squeezing my fingers. 'How about you tell me about your day and we take it from there?'

I pause, groping around in the darkness for the right thing to pick up.

'Right now this instant, I really wish I wasn't Gemma's therapist.' I shouldn't have said that. I expect him to seize on it like a dog chasing a ball, but he stays looking at me, his brown eyes soft smudges.

'That's hard. I know you really care about her.'

'Yeah, it is.'

And I breathe, feeling the relief of telling the truth. Of him hearing it. I scissor my fingers together, squeezing his, and he squeezes back harder.

'Did you see her today?'

I nod.

'Don't get excited,' I snap. 'There were no revelations. This isn't about her,' I say, pointing at my face. A wave of embarrassment hits me, and I lever my hand away, digging around in my bag for a mirror. It's not a pretty sight: my skin is streaked and blotchy, my eyes like raisins, all puffy and swollen.

'You look lovely,' he says, which weirdly makes me feel even more embarrassed. I should go to the loos and tidy myself up – I'd hot-foot it if I was here with Marcus – but I can't find the wherewithal to fight my way through the scrum.

'I don't,' I say, too sharply, but he simply smiles, then lets his hand hover over mine like a helicopter on a rescue mission. I give a tiny nod, feeling my whole body relax as the warmth of him radiates through me.

'I beg to differ.'

The relaxation is starting to give way to something else. I'm in a public place, holding hands with a man who isn't the man I'm meant to be starting a new life with tonight. I'm Lorcan's spawn all right – nature and nurture perfectly fused. I should take my hand away, but instead I move the parcel we make downwards, rest it on the rough denim of his knee.

'You're a terrible liar,' I say, but when I look at his face there's no lie to be found.

'So if it's not just about Gemma . . .'

Is he playing the long game, lulling me into a false sense of security with his big brown eyes, almost cow-like in their gentleness, or is he really here for me?

'What's it like being a man?'

'Sorry?' he says, laughter in his eyes. 'You might need to get more specific. Or, I dunno, maybe not.'

'I don't mean what's it like having a dick.'

'Now that's a relief.'

'Of course I *do* kind of wonder that,' I say. 'But – can you just cut off from work? Do you ever come away feeling like this?'

'I haven't left the office before 2 a.m. for a fortnight. I'll probably have to go back there later.' He smiles. 'I hope you're feeling suitably blessed.'

'What, your presence is my present?' He nods, smiles at my ravaged face. 'Scrub that, I don't usually come away feeling like this either. I don't know what this case has done to me. I feel like it's – I don't know if I'll ever be the same now. I'll be holding on to the side, not swimming, always frightened I'll get sucked down again. This isn't me, Patrick.'

It sounds so ridiculous, so pompous, as it reaches my ears. The idea that there's a 'me' – a solid bronze that's been cast – is absurd. My work would be redundant if there was. And yet perhaps I thought I was different.

'The Vines are a poisonous bunch,' he says, and I try not to react to the unsaid 'I told you so'.

'This isn't just about Gemma.' Saying her name out loud brings her close again, fury and pity curdling inside me. Was I a fool to ever think I could make a difference? 'But I'm seeing my boss in the morning. I'm going to tell her I'm going to stop seeing Gemma.'

Again, he stays quiet. I watch his face, daring him to start wheedling. I want somewhere to put this anger. Maybe he senses it, dodges the bullet. Or maybe – maybe he's less single-minded than I thought.

'So which bit isn't about Gemma?'

'Dads should protect their daughters,' I say, my voice staccato, carrying too much. 'When you're a little girl, your dad's everything. It's like that awful song at primary school. You know – "He's got the whole world in his hands."' I sing it softly, tunelessly. Even singing makes me think of her crazy-making humming.

'When did you lose him?' asks Patrick softly.

'Ages ago. Your dad died a couple of years ago?'

'Two years' – he looks upwards – 'four months, nine days.'

'Were you close?'

'Ish. He wasn't big on heart to hearts. And I set up camp under my desk after I qualified.'

'Do you think about it much? Do you wish it'd been different?' I'm asking him to match me, to expose the soft underbelly of his story. 'Tell me to piss off if you think I'm being a nosy bitch,' I add, self-conscious.

He reaches out, very gently stroking my nose with his long index finger. I don't look away, even though I should, and he leans in and kisses me, his lips light and fleeting on mine.

'I don't see much point in dwelling on it. I try and see my mum every few days, even if it's just a cuppa on the way to work.' That exhaustion again. Is there a river of guilt running through, measured out in an infinite line of steaming mugs? 'Seems a better way to approach it. Now can I kiss you again?'

I want it too much. I kiss him this time, leaning in and crushing my mouth against his before I can overthink it. I shouldn't be doing this. I shouldn't be dancing on the rubble.

'You know I've got a boyfriend,' I say, pulling away. I force my hands to my sides, even though all I want to do is hold him.

'I do. Just not convinced by him. You're half-hearted.'

'I'm moving in with him.'

'Still don't believe you.' Perhaps, now I've sinned, there's no point in stopping. Not until the ride slows down, comes to a halt, disgorges us back into normal life. Besides, I'm off the case. It's over. 'You're a moral person,' he continues, his eyes not leaving my face. 'You're more than that, you're anguished. Sometimes you're even a tiny bit' – he makes a little gesture with his hand that makes me giggle – 'I dunno, sanctimonious.'

'Oh piss off.'

'Come on, you were Miss, sorry, Ms, Hoity Toity when I first met you. Couldn't for the life of me work out why I wanted to shag you so much. Anyway, my point being, if you really, really liked him there's no way you'd be kissing me the way you just kissed me in a bar. Or anywhere else for that matter.'

'How did I just kiss you?'

This time it's Patrick who leans in. He slips his hand around my face, his thumb resting gently on my neck, tilting me towards him with strong fingers. His mouth reaches mine as his other hand slips around my waist, pulling me tightly against him. When he finally kisses me, the blood pounds through my head, knocking out any kind of rational thought. Eventually we pull a few centimetres apart.

'You shouldn't be kissing me like that,' I say, kissing him again, my lips trailing the soft pink surface of his. His mouth is full, easy to melt into. 'Even if I didn't have a boyfriend, we're the last two people in London who should be kissing each other.'

'I told you last time, we're on the same side.' I go to reply, but he bats me away. 'Let's not talk about it. Boring. You do realize we've got a full-scale Prosecco emergency on our hands, Mia?'

I don't want him to leave my side – it'll give real life a chance to bundle me up and kidnap me. He builds a fort from his newspaper, the glasses placed at menacing angles, and grips my hand tightly as we cross to the bar. I feel drunk just from that one glass, the lights brighter than they really are, the bass a thumping heartbeat.

The truth is that I'm not very good with booze – my tolerance is pathetic. When I sit there all high and mighty it's because I know how easily I could topple, and no part of me will let that happen. But tonight my desire to escape real life is outrunning my self-control, and I let Patrick keep filling my glass from the bottle he insisted on buying. Soon the edges start to blur, our kisses one long kiss, our conversation no longer a fiercely fought tennis match.

'Surely you've got a girlfriend?' I tease, squeezed in so close I can smell him. I remember how much I like the way he smells. It's unabashed maleness – no sweat, no cologne. 'Just tell me the truth. I don't want to feel like the only sinner.'

I am a sinner. Where's Marcus right now? Sitting round some dimly lit restaurant table, his artist's hands digging into the expensive dim sum as he simultaneously charms and fleeces his latest client. I shouldn't be here, and yet I can't leave. As soon as I do, the song will start up again. And that's only the beginning.

'I won't lie, I'm no priest. Father Patrick O'Leary,' he declaims, his arm flung out dramatically.

'So you do?' I wish I hadn't asked. It's giving real life an open invitation to join our circle of two.

'Sometimes.'

'You've got an on-off lady friend?' God, I'm out of practice. 'A friend with benefits?' Gemma's obviously lodged that horrible, crass expression in my consciousness. How could she have had to associate that with her own father?

'No,' he says, sounding vaguely annoyed. 'They come and go. Not really my priority.'

'Sounds lonely. Or are you a bit of a player?'

I don't want the snarky tennis match to start up again. Are we protecting ourselves from each other? The thought makes me sad.

'Mmm, and it sounds like a real barrel of laughs with King Midas.'

'Have you been spying on me, Patrick?'

'First of all, I haven't been spying on Gemma. I've been doing my job. And second,' he says, anger spitting up, 'you're not signing up for some West London shag pad with a bin man.'

'That's not why I'm with him. It's bullshit. The Vines are your proof. All those expensive birthday parties and ponies – Gemma's pretty much the unhappiest, angriest child I've ever laid eyes on.'

'What, when he took her to The Grove?'

'Yes.'

'With Stephen.'

'Yes.' I could be wrong, but I feel like something clunks into place. 'Patrick, we agreed not to talk about this.'

'That's how he does it,' he says, the cogs visibly whirring. 'Stephen goes and finds Christopher in places where he knows he won't be bugged. Perfect cover, lounging round the jacuzzi in their trunks. Fat, middle-aged bellies spilling out.'

It consumes him, this case. As soon as it intrudes, he can't see or feel anything except his own righteous quest.

'I shouldn't have said that,' I say, furious with both of us. 'This is exactly why—'

'I thought as much when I found out about that party. The timing of it. It had to be a cover, a way to see Stephen. He was just using Gemma, like you said.'

'You tricked me . . . you're the user.'

'I didn't trick you. I knew. You confirmed my suspicions.'

The legalese is the final straw. I stand up, grabbing my bag.

'I am SUCH a fool, an incompetent fool, for letting you manipulate me like this. Leave me alone. And leave Gemma alone – she's just a kid. She doesn't need another man abusing her.'

He stands up, tries to come after me, but I shove my hand against his chest, push him away, tears blurring my vision.

★   ★   ★

It's humid and drizzly, traffic choking up the busy highway. The taxi queue snakes around the side of the station, inching forward so slowly I could scream with frustration. Everyone seems to have a houseful of luggage, an incomprehensible address to mutter in broken English. My heart is racing, anger – with Patrick, with myself – thrumming through my veins. I can't face the fridge. There's nothing much left in my flat but my bed and a few boxes, but with three more days before the tenants arrive, it's still there as a refuge.

The shame I'm feeling – so old, so familiar – is even more toxic than the anger. How could I have been so stupid? How is it, that, even now, Lorcan can leave me so vulnerable? Tears roll down my cheeks, and I scrub at them with the sleeve of my trench coat, hating them for their refusal to obey my will. Self-pity is the last thing I deserve. I'm nearly there, just two harried commuters and a Japanese tourist to go, when he appears.

'Please don't tell me to fuck off. You've got every right, but let me speak for' – he looks at his horrible gold-plated digital watch, fiddles with it – 'ninety seconds, and then you never have to see me again.'

'Well I do, don't I? That's just another lie. You can subpoena me . . .'

He holds a hand up, puppy-dog eyes pleading. I want to kick him.

'You get to me. I'm the one who feels like a fucking idiot, chasing after some glamorous creature who's going to go straight back to her perfect life, with her George Clooney lookalike boyfriend, once she's had a sneaky nibble on a bit of rough.'

'You're not a bit of rough . . .'

He waves an angry hand at me.

'Hush. You're stealing my seconds. You asking me about girlfriends – I'm shit at this stuff, at least I'm shit with the ones I might actually want to be with. You'd never look at me in real life – you're just having some kind of meltdown. This case can do that to people. It's a nasty, disgusting business. And I'm sorry if I dragged us back there, but I've got a job to do. And you making me think about my dad, and about you – I can't do that right now. There's no time.' He looks at me, his gaze so direct I can feel it reaching right inside me and grabbing hold. 'But the truth is I can't stop thinking about you. It's not an option.'

'Excuse me, are you planning to avail yourself of this cab?' It's a grey-haired man, his voice cut glass, his wooden-handled umbrella like something from another era.

'Yes, I'm taking it,' I say, trying to drag my gaze from Patrick's face.

'No you're not.'

'Yes I am! This isn't me.'

'Be not you then. Just for now. I'll take any version I can get.'

Patrick holds out his hand and I step towards him, letting him envelop me in his arms. The man looks between us, flummoxed.

'I think I'll just hop in,' he says, and I grin at him, whilst tears run down my cheeks.

'I'm sorry if I make you think about things,' I say, my face buried in Patrick's bony clavicle. 'I can't stop thinking about the things I don't want to think about either.'

'What like?' he says, hooking a piece of my damp hair away and kissing my ear with supreme gentleness.

I look up at him, wondering why it is I'm about to tell him what I'm about to tell him.

'I did lose my dad, but not because he died. I just lost him, Patrick. I lost him.'

Chapter Fourteen

Patrick's arm is flung around my shoulders, my face pressed flat against the warm expanse of his chest. We're quiet right now, but it's a soft kind of quiet. We're about to cross Waterloo Bridge, my favourite bit of the journey, the lit-up London skyline splayed out like a winning hand of cards. Tonight it feels like crossing the Rubicon, the point of no return.

'So there's literally NOTHING there?'

'Nope. No milk. No wine—'

'Hang on,' he says, throwing himself forward. 'Driver!'

I've missed laughing the way he makes me laugh. I grab his arm, yank him back towards me.

'It's a good thing. I can't drink another drop. I'll die. Time to get excited about some delicious, nutritious hot water.'

'Oh, so you've got a kettle?'

I cock my head, pull a face.

'I couldn't swear to it.'

★　　★　　★

My key scrapes loudly in the lock, another Rubicon about to be crossed. Patrick steps straight inside, his big brown eyes quickly scoping out the space. My sofa's still here, a bog-standard Ikea number bought with one of my first pay packets, and I've accidentally left a print hanging up, a Modigliani of a woman in a green bonnet.

'It's pretty swish,' he says, stroking the painted wooden frame of the big sash window that looks out over the narrow road. I liked how hidden away it was when I bought it, quiet and cosy.

'Thank you,' I say, pleased and self-conscious all at once. Marcus never seemed to come here: for him, Balham's the equivalent of Antarctica.

'So we've got some art work to gaze at,' says Patrick, tilting his face and stroking his chin extravagantly, 'but no kettle?'

'You are SO uncultured,' I tell him, grabbing his hand and leading him towards the sofa, marooned in the centre of the bare room.

'Uh uh. I know your game. I'm going to get myself some of that delicious hot water before I let you ravish me.' Patrick spots everything, even the tiny moment where I lose my game face. He puts his arms around me. 'Hey, Mia, I'm joking. We don't have to do anything. You know that, right?'

'You're lovely,' I say, reaching up to stroke his face. It's soft, his skin, its pale milkiness giving it a smoothness that I wouldn't have appreciated all those times I snootily dismissed him as a callow youth. I try not to think about how different it feels from the stubbly landscape of Marcus's face. This isn't me. This is another Mia who I most likely won't be on speaking terms with this time tomorrow. 'I mean, you're obviously a doofus, but you're a lovely one.'

And then he kisses me again.

It's me who suggests we go upstairs, me who pulls him down onto the bed, me who ignores the text beep from my phone, even though I know in my bones it's from a newly landed Marcus, all ready to kiss and make up.

'Are you sure about this?' says Patrick, his fingers starting to undo the buttons that run down the front of my black cotton dress. I look at them weaving into the gaps in the fabric, grazing my naked skin, and think about stopping him.

'I'm sure,' I say, leaning upwards to kiss him, my hand slipping tighter around him, pulling us closer. I unbutton his shirt, push it off his shoulders with an urgency that comes from somewhere I can't quite own. He looks at me – no, gazes at me – naked but for my black bra and knickers. I feel my hand unconsciously reaching to cover my stomach, but he gently puts it back by my side, continues to look. He smiles. 'You're even more beautiful than your imaginary incarnation.'

'Have you hung out with her a lot?'

He makes an embarrassed face, shrugs, makes me giggle. I reach towards him and unbutton his jeans. He awkwardly shrugs himself out of them, looks back at me.

'Socks on, right?'

Now he's exposed too. He's more lithe than skinny; his long legs have a racehorse quality to them, his chest punctuated by unexpected ridges of muscle, dusted with more hair than I'd have predicted. I run my finger down it, feel his heartbeat speed to my touch. I pull him back towards me, craving his lips on mine – right now, his kisses are my oxygen. I lose any sense of time, but as the wanting builds up inside me I roll on top of him, look down at the face that looks beautiful to me now. He stares back up at me, his long fingers pushing my hair away from my face. His eyes burn dark, suddenly hard to read.

'What?' I demand.

'We shouldn't do this.'

'I'm sorry?'

He groans, slapping his palms hard against the mattress.

'I can't believe I'm saying this. I am going to hate myself tomorrow. But I'd rather hate me than have you hate me.'

I roll off him, turn my back, hot humiliation scorching through me like a forest fire.

'Fine.'

'Mia . . .' He tries to roll me, but I make my body as heavy as lead. He leans in, his lips brushing my ear. 'Listen to me. This is too important to trash.'

'What, this is trash to you?' I say, the words spitting out at him.

'I'm not saying that. Jesus, you're the therapist.' I don't feel like a therapist tonight. I feel like the vulnerable, stupid girl who got knocked up by a man who saw her coming. 'I don't want to take advantage of you. You're in a state.'

'What, I'm too much of a bunny-boiling loony to shag?'

He grabs my shoulder now, turns me over, forces me to look at him. I want to reach up to him, but I force myself not to, keep my eyes cold. Could this all be just another move? Pawn two steps forward, checkmate?

'OK, stop it. You're the one with a boyfriend.' The shame I've been damming up torrents through me. How is it that he's the one affording Marcus proper respect? What is wrong with me? 'How about if I don't want to get hurt?'

I look into his brown eyes properly now, so soft they could almost be velvet. I feel my own eyes filling, my heart too.

'I don't want to hurt you,' I tell him.

'Come here,' he says, opening his arms. I snuggle against him, let him stroke my hair. He adjusts our position, pulls me back in. 'Sorry, my head and my nether regions are having a serious disagreement.'

'It's pathetic how gratifying that news is.'

I don't want to go to sleep – it's stupid, but I don't want to leave him. Tomorrow is another day, and there's only so long I can keep real life chained up. It feels unsaid, neither of us articulating it, a thought bubble floating above us in the bare bedroom.

'Do you want to tell me about it properly?' he says, his body snaking itself around my exposed flesh like a creeping vine.

'Oh Dr O'Leary, I feel like I could tell you anything.' He doesn't snap back with a smart reply, he waits it out. I told him a little bit when we were standing in the King's Cross drizzle: that Lorcan and I are so terminally estranged that I don't even know where he is any more, that I like to think it's for the best, the only way I can protect myself, but that on a day like today I come face to face with how it makes my heart feel like a bloody steak, raw and tender.

'I don't mean to be a nosy parker,' he says, stroking my nose like he did earlier. 'I just . . . I hope you don't end up with unfinished business. They do go,' he adds, his voice low.

'I know. I know he's not immortal, but he could contact me. He's the parent.'

'I get that . . .' says Patrick, still stroking me.

'Anyway, I thought you said you didn't have regrets?'

'Er, hello, year one, Mia. We don't always say exactly what we mean. Or maybe it's that we think that if we say it with enough conviction it'll start to be true.'

'I know.' It's too uncomfortable. I can't open up this creaking treasure chest of memories with him beside me, then say goodbye. I've had too many abrupt exits in life to go wilfully courting another one. I've got to get it all out, whilst we're together.

'Patrick, I've been thinking a lot about what you said. About the corruption. I can't stand the idea that the people who should be on your side aren't on your side.'

He sits bolt upright in bed like a meerkat, and I

immediately regret letting the case puncture our fragile, precious bubble.

'There's a lot of people snuffling in the trough, chasing the
kickbacks. People who think the system screws them and
want payback.' I can feel as much as hear the scorn that soaks
his words.

'Why don't they get thrown out on their corrupt, sorry
arses?'

Patrick shrugs, face like granite.

'Goes too far up, some of this stuff.'

I stroke his fingers, searching for him.

'Are you in danger, Patrick? You would tell me if you
were?'

'Don't worry about me,' he says, pushing me flat, his
hands tangled in my messed-up hair. 'I'm made of stern stuff.
But, Mia? If you can help me, you won't just be helping me.
You know that, don't you?'

The alarm on my phone shrills out at 6.30, a relentless ban-
shee. It's downstairs in my handbag, and I stumble off in
search of it, rudely awakened in every sense. There's not one
but three messages from Marcus, increasingly demanding.
I've landed, baby, says the first. **You snuggled up in our
bed? Call you when I'm past customs.** Typical Marcus:
his bad mood's evaporated so he assumes the world he surveys will reflect his shiny new reality. The next text is at least
a bit less cocky: it makes me aware of how rare it is that I
challenge him and let him get to a point of contrition. I can

hear Patrick starting to stir upstairs, my shame stirring with him. What have I done? **You sulking? Didn't mean to abandon you, Mia. I'd do anything to be in that bed with you right now. xx.** There's one final text, probably sent around the time Patrick and I finally, reluctantly, went to sleep. **Not going to ring in case I wake you. I love you, darling. You know that though, don't you? xx.** I stand there, Patrick's shirt – the nearest thing I could lay hands on in my empty bedroom – hanging off me. I'm a horrible person: I've given myself a cancerous secret I can never tell Marcus, all for a man I can't be with. I'm winded by another stab of shame as I remember the Stephen Wright conversation. How could I have been so careless with Gemma's confidences? I love Marcus, I know he loves me.

And here's Patrick, clad only in his boxer shorts, giving me a sleepy smile from beneath his messy ginger mop. He looks like he's been assaulted by a tomcat.

'Well, don't you look a picture?' he says, taking in the barely buttoned shirt. The thought of constructing a reply to Marcus, of meeting Judith, of going to that sterile, empty flat – I can't do this. I can't do it, and yet I have no choice. I feel like my evil twin stepped into my body, wreaked havoc and stepped straight back out again. It would be a horror movie if it wasn't my actual life.

'I've really got to get going,' I say, avoiding eye contact. 'I'm sorry, I don't even have a towel to give you.'

'Mia . . .' As Patrick steps towards me, my whole body stiffens. He stops, thinking better of it, the light in his eyes dimming. I want to cross to him, wrap myself up in his spidery limbs, never let go, but what good would it do? *I don't want to get hurt.* That's what he said. It seems to be my speciality, just like it was Lorcan's. I summoned Lorcan up, like the genie from the lamp, and look what happened. 'It's OK, I was a Boy Scout, I'll improvise. Do you want to go first?'

'No,' I say, gesturing to the bathroom door, eyes sliding away. 'Feel free.'

We're both dressed now. I found a few stray things from the chucking-out pile that my cleaner had stuck in the cubby hole under the stairs. I'm unfashionable, but tidy. Patrick, meanwhile, looks a state, his shirt (clearly doubling as a towel) damp and crumpled, his hair refusing to submit to gravity.

'Are you going straight to work?' I ask, putting on a swift, efficient coat of lipstick in the mirror by the front door.

'What, you mean looking like this?' There's an edge to his voice. 'No, I'm gonna have to make a pit stop at home.'

'That's miles away.'

'I know.'

His voice is hard and cold, a boulder rolled straight at me. I deserve it, but it still feels unbearable. I turn to him, pleading.

'Patrick . . .'

'Just to warn you, I really might have to call Gemma as a hostile witness.'

'Don't do this. Don't use her to get at me. I don't mean to

271

be cold, it's just if I start feeling any of this, I don't know if I'll be able to put one foot in front of the other. I'm seeing Judith in an hour, my tenant's moving in . . .'

'You're quite the narcissist, aren't you?' he says, eyes narrowing. 'I was giving everything I had to this case long before you came sashaying into my life.'

Anger whooshes up inside me.

'Is it because of The Grove, is that why you're going to call her? Is it because you somehow managed to wheedle that information out of me?'

Pain washes across his face, but then he hardens himself. Or maybe it doesn't: maybe he's used that narcissism he's spotted and played me for a fool.

'I knew about it anyway.'

'You didn't *know* know, you suspected.'

'We haven't got Christopher. We're almost out of time. This was always gonna happen.'

'How convenient. Convenient and coincidental.'

He looks at me, his eyes softening.

'Mia, come on. Come back. This is us . . .'

But I'm throwing my files in my bag by now, my mind racing a million miles a second. If I've really done this to Gemma – become the person who's forcing her to get up on the stand and betray the person she loves most in the world – I don't deserve a shred of mercy. I promised I'd protect her. At least Patrick believes he's doing what he promised – I've got no defence.

'There is no *us*, Patrick. There's one sordid almost shag

that should never have happened.' I hate this – the bile's as much for me as it is for him – but I won't let him see it. 'You won. Congratulations.'

'It wasn't that way for me. It was never something sordid. I wanted you. In every sense.'

'Mmm. Not that much.'

He cocks his head, eyes deep dark pools. I don't want to leave him. I want to barricade the door, lead him back upstairs, forget the world outside exists.

'You have no idea how much I wanted you,' he says.

Past tense. It's all I hear.

Chapter Fifteen

I stop off at the Australians' and load up with coffee and croissants, a flimsy and desperate attempt to make nice with Judith. I stare at the booth where I sat with Annie, wishing that the force of my longing could somehow be enough to teleport me back there, give me another chance to listen to the soft knowing inside myself. The rest of that day threatens to unfurl out too, the memory of us sitting on the grass, the way I watched his big hands wrapped around his puny wholewheat sandwich, virtually destroyed by one large mouthful, and secretly loved him for bothering to indulge my whims. Now I don't know what any of it means, least of all what my part means.

Judith beams at the sight of the steaming coffee, reaches out an eager hand. I wonder if I should just launch in, but she beats me to it, blowing on her coffee as she speaks.

'Delicious! Mia, I've had Annie Vine on the phone twice . . .'

I should've come and thrown myself on Judith's mercy last night. There are so many things I should've done differently last night.

'*Mea culpa*. I've fucked this up – I'm not going to pretend I haven't—'

'That's not what the Vines think,' says Judith. 'Annie says Gemma cried all night, kept saying how amazing you were, and that she'd pushed you away. She begged me to persuade you to keep seeing her. What actually happened here, Mia?'

I look at Judith, trying to find the words, willing my voice to stay steady.

'She found out who my father actually was . . . is.'

'Mia,' says Judith, laying a wise and crinkled hand, the skin like scrunched-up greaseproof paper, over mine. 'The perils of practising in the internet age.'

'It's my own fault,' I say, insistent. I won't duck this. 'I told her too much. She hasn't let up since I said what I said.' Judith regards me, the make-up I've painstakingly applied no match for her penetrating gaze. She can sense I'm close to my breaking point. 'I've failed her.' I think of her angry little face, that vacant triumph. 'And I've failed *you*.'

Judith regards me thoughtfully.

'It's a fine line, isn't it? You could say you've failed her, or you could say you've gone the extra mile. But where you are right is that you should've limited the amount of sessions. And I should've insisted on it.'

And then I tell her about Gemma playing the song, how

deep it cut, the humiliating way I lost my professional poise. She's still so calm, a point of stillness in the chaos.

'She brought your dad right into the room, didn't she? I'm not surprised you reacted. But, Mia – what does that tell you?'

A sob rises up in me. She doesn't know the half of it yet. I went through a very holy stage when I started at convent school: I think I loved the sense of order, rules to be obeyed, virtue its own reward. I remember being fascinated by that story of Jonah and the Whale, Jonah swallowed up whole by the might of God's will. Maybe I thought I could become the whale – become God even – grow so strong and wise with all my qualifications and distinctions that I'd swallow up the past and make it a harmless little digested piece of detritus.

'I know. I'm still a mess around that stuff.'

'You definitely need to properly engage with your own therapy. These supervision sessions aren't enough. And as for Gemma . . .' She stops to think, dark eyes burning with concentration. 'I do think a final session, a chance for you both to get some kind of closure, could be the best solution.'

A sick feeling spreads through me at the thought of it. But then I feel into the gap, the void of never seeing Gemma again. It feels even worse, but is that just me trying to atone for something I can never atone for?

I take a deep breath.

'I think she really might know where Christopher is.'

I tell her about the iPad, the bubbles of messages she waved in my direction, the dark secrets she kept alluding to. It doesn't sound so compelling when I lay it out. *This is classified*, that's what Patrick said, quietly forbidding me from telling anyone about the bugged phone. It feels like a string of barbed wire pulled tight around my solar plexus. There's a different section of truth for each situation, but a section of truth is very different from truth itself.

'I still think there's every chance that it's nothing,' says Judith. 'The fantasies of a mixed-up kid, desperate to prove to you her precious dad isn't the man he's being painted as. I don't think it's anything you need to tell the police about.' I look down, my face heating. 'Mia . . .'

'I talked to Patrick last night,' I say. 'I didn't out and out tell him anything, but I let him lead me into confirming one of his suspicions, and now he says he's going to call her as a hostile witness.'

'Last night?'

Something shifts in her face now. Her sympathy is being sucked away, like water swirling down a drain.

'Yes.'

'So your reaction to this hugely emotional session was to – let me get this straight. Did you seek him out?' I give a tiny nod. 'To expose yourself – expose Gemma – to the lawyer working with the police investigation?'

'There's no excuse,' I say, my voice a disembodied noise inside my head. 'I know that.' Will explaining more make it better or worse? 'He met me for lunch the day before, told me some more information about the investigation – information that made me really worry for her!' Judith looks at me, gaze cool and flat. 'He rang me last night, I didn't ring him.'

'What are your feelings for this man? What on earth would possess you to do this?'

Here it is: I've finally reached the outer limits of my truth-telling zeal. *Sister Mia*, said Jim, all those years ago, disgusted by my piety.

'I've been trying to keep him on side. And I do totally understand his obsession with bringing Stephen Wright down. The man's a monster. But I know that breaking confidentiality is the worst thing I could've done.'

'Just tell me exactly what was said,' says Judith, her hands clenched white on the arms of her chair. I give her the edited highlights, resetting that first, extended meeting in Caffè Nero where we tried and failed to have a Frapuccino a few short weeks ago, and cutting out the fact that I said my last angry goodbye to him less than an hour ago. When I've finished she sinks back into thought, refusing to lay eyes on me, anger like a heat haze.

'Your behaviour was extremely unethical – not something I'd ever have expected from you, Mia, and there will be consequences. But you haven't actually spelled out new information to him, and this is something he could've gleaned if he'd chosen to seize your notes.'

'I'm so sorry.'

She doesn't even look at me, pauses for what feels like forever.

'I'm afraid I'm going to have to suspend you. Not immediately, it's too disruptive, but, after a week, time for us to warn your regular clients, I'm going to enforce a month.

During that time I and the other partners will decide if you still have a job here. The ABA position is out of the question. I'm going to have to share some of this with Annie, and if she chooses to make an official complaint, which she may well do, your position could become significantly worse.'

'I could lose my licence?' I say, the enormity really hitting home now. What have I done?

'I'll try and couch things in such a way that that doesn't happen. I do understand that you've been having a full-blown personal crisis, but that's why you have the safety net of supervision!' Her voice rises. 'None of us can do this incredibly responsible job properly unless we obey the rules. You know that.'

I'm crying properly now, fat tears rolling down my cheeks, laying my carefully applied make-up to waste.

'I deserve every word. I've been arrogant and irresponsible. I don't deserve to do this job.'

Judith waits, observes me.

'You're an excellent therapist, Mia, really excellent.' She looks out of the window, then looks back at me, her gaze properly landing. 'But you're haunted.'

Judith gave me the option of going home, but I was determined to work. The prospect of my suspension, of having nothing to occupy me but my thoughts, is almost too much to bear. My first session starts a little shakily, like I'm a colt learning how to walk, not sure my legs will hold me up, but then I find my stride. I don't want to think about anything beyond this room, and I pour all my energy into being the best therapist I can.

Angela's my last client of the morning, a one-time bulimic who's gradually learnt she doesn't need to binge, to stuff the outside inside her, to feel whole. She'd had a messy break-up recently, and she's still managed to resist the urge – I feel ridiculously proud of her. She cries during the session, but there's strength running through those tears. As we hit the last ten minutes, I broach the fact I won't be here for the next little while.

'Why?' she says, her distress palpable. I always give my clients weeks of notice if I'm going to be off – for many of them the regularity of contact gives them a safety they never experienced in their chaotic early lives. Seeing her face brings on a whole new wave of self-flagellation. I've not just let Gemma down, I've let all my clients down. What if I can never come back?

'It should just be a few weeks,' I tell her. 'Something personal's come up that I have to deal with.'

'OK,' she says, fear in her eyes. Angela's mother died suddenly when she was six, and she was sent to live with her grandparents, not even allowed to go to the funeral. Whether or not she knows it, I suspect that little girl, Little Angela, is being triggered.

'I'm not ill,' I say gently. 'I'll . . .' No more lies and half-truths. 'Hopefully I'll be back.'

I sit there for a few minutes when she's gone, sadness engulfing me. Where are my certainties? Where is home?

I've texted Marcus back, guiltily saccharine, but it's still early there. He'll be home in two days: is honesty really the best policy, or has today proved it's the absolute opposite? If I tell him the truth two things are guaranteed: I'll devastate him, and I'll destroy our relationship. But when I think about holding on to that secret painting over the black mark, I know I'll always see its outline through the whitewash.

I'm shaken from my thoughts by a smart rap on the door. I'd think it was Brendan, except I know he'd just barge in.

'Hello?'

Juliet pokes her head round the door, all glossy blonde blow-dry and wide grin.

'Juliet, what are you doing here?' I recover my manners. 'Hi!'

Her eyes are darting round my room, taking in what they can. Is she thwarted by how intentionally neutral it is, nothing here for her to report back on to her mum? I chide myself for my negativity.

'Sorry to ambush you!' she says, bustling over to kiss me. She smells so clean and polished, salon-fresh hair and expensive perfume. 'I was in the area for a meeting, and I thought I'd call your office on the off chance. Brendan – it is Brendan, isn't it? He's gorge, isn't he? – said you were about to break for lunch.'

This is a nightmare. I admire the concept in principle, but today is the last day I want to have to try and find my inner stepmother – step-monster is the best either of us can hope for.

'I am!' I say, feigning as much *joie de vivre* as I can muster. 'Do you want to go and grab a sandwich?'

'Yeah!' she says, her voice as tinny as my own. 'And I wanted to give you this. Dad asked me to.'

Oh God, please, let it not be another elaborate, extravagant gift: guilt prowls around my insides like a big cat left to languish in a tiny cage. I try and prepare my face as she reaches into her huge, beautiful handbag, but all that comes out is a manilla envelope.

'What's this?'

'Um, he said it's . . .' She at least has the good grace to look a bit squeamish. 'What did he call it – a prenup lite? Said you'd know all about it.'

A sharp burst of shame spreads through me. I didn't think for one minute he really meant it. Does he really think I'm lulling him into a false sense of security before I fleece him for every penny? Perhaps he was both right and wrong: did he sense on some animal level that I wasn't to be trusted?

'I don't know what to say . . .'

'I'm sorry if I've – he said you knew!'

'He sent you to do his dirty work?' Her pretty peaches-and-cream face rearranges itself into a bland mask. 'I understand if he wants to do this, but he should've talked to me himself.'

'Mia, I think you're overreacting.' I shoot daggers at her. 'He was called away. Sending me was the last thing he planned to do. Of course he'd want to be here.'

I should leave well alone, but I can't.

'Do you honestly believe that, or are you just parroting what he told you to come out with?'

'I'm not *parroting* anything,' she says, suddenly haughty. She's got a strange sandwich of a personality: the outside as confident and articulate as her top-class education and life of privilege guarantees, the filling – the thin slice of Juliet that's lying inside – weak and uncertain. She only dares see herself in the mirror that Marcus or her adoring fiancé holds up for her. 'My dad has an incredibly responsible job. It's not his fault if you can't appreciate the kind of pressure a person at his level has to deal with, day in, day out. He protects you from it.'

I snort unattractively, like an angry warthog.

'Just leave his stupid, insulting contract on my desk.'

She casts a wary look at me, trying to work how to angle her next shot.

'He asked me to make sure you sign it, so I can take it back for our lawyer.'

I bet he did. I'd wager a guess there's some legal requirement that the ink's on the page before we formally begin cohabiting. Is this work trip an elaborate ploy to get it done and dusted without our having to deal with a messy bit of business?

'Well, you can tell Daddy that you tried to, but I was completely unreasonable. Tell him that, for some reason, I refused to submit to his commands. Luckily he'll still have you.'

There's a coldness to Marcus, a way he has of cutting off.

Just for a second it makes me long for last night to have been different, for Patrick's entreaties in the rain to have added up to something real, but I shove the feeling away.

'You're lucky to have him,' she says, two rosy spots of colour splashing her elegant cheekbones. 'You should be a bit more grateful.'

'Thanks for the advice,' I say acidly. This is horrible, the day nothing but a series of pitched battles. 'Juliet, I'm sorry for what I just said – about you, I mean. Your relationship with him is none of my business.'

'Dad says you're like this. Always acting like you're the oracle.' I can just imagine him saying it too. I should've listened to my instinct, instead of driving myself forward like I was an old car in need of a sharp stamp on the accelerator.

'Yup. I'm sorry. I really would like you to leave now.'

Juliet grabs her enviable leather bag in her diamond-encrusted hand, and flounces out. So many compromises, so many contradictions. Goodbye, Juliet.

When my last client leaves, I can barely prise myself from my sofa. After Angela's reaction, I've dreaded telling them I won't be here, silently transmitting there's more to it, however much I pour out reassurance. Our goodbyes have taken on the feeling of real goodbyes.

I'm sitting there, frozen, looking out into the streaming traffic with the same blank, hypnotized gaze that Gemma often had. A wave of regret rolls across me as I think of her.

There's a soft tap on the door, and then Judith appears. Her smile is muted, but not without kindness.

'Mia, I don't know how you're going to feel about this . . .'

'Tell me,' I say, shivery suddenly.

'I've spoken to Annie Vine, and been as honest as I needed to be. She was furious, understandably, but she's just rung back. Gemma's still begging to have one last session with you. How do you feel about doing it?'

March 1995 (sixteen years old)

Lorcan was as good as his word, bursting through the door the very next night. This state of affairs was almost unimaginable – belief in him sprang up inside me, like bright purple crocuses bursting through winter soil. Normally I'd have stifled it, but nothing was normal. Not now.

'My precious girl,' he said, hugging me fiercely. I could smell whisky, in fact I could see it in the slight wateriness of his gaze, but I pushed the thought aside, and concentrated on how it felt to be enclosed in the tight cage of his arms. He beckoned to Mum, and I wondered if she'd step forward. I could see wariness in her eyes, a choice being made. But then we were three, a tight huddle, my DNA muddling up around me, another tiny bundle of it inside me. The thought made my eyes fill with tears, as almost everything had since I'd found out.

Mum laid out the chicken she'd roasted, and Lorcan got stuck into carving whilst I rooted out some plates. Why couldn't this just *be*? I pretended it was for a few short minutes, but then Mum soberly reminded us that we needed to talk.

'She hasn't told Jim yet,' she said. 'He'll be back from school tomorrow.'

Lorcan swooped his fork down, stabbing a roast potato with a showman's flourish.

'He should be pleased!' he said, waving it around. 'You can tell him that from me.'

I swept my eyes over him, a quick forensic analysis. His jeans were new, dark blue denim and straight-legged, more expensive, I'd bet, than Mum's whole outfit. His hands moved through the space with a new kind of self-belief: even the nails on his long fingers had lost their raggedness, looking almost manicured. He wore an effortlessly cool checked flannel shirt, which hugged a chest that had developed a newfound masculinity. At first glance his stubble looked messy, but it was no more than an artful pretence. Coldness gripped me: somebody, somewhere was moulding him in a whole new image and he was revelling in it. How could Mum be so blind?

'He won't be pleased!' I said. I hadn't gone to school that day, had stayed on the sofa watching mindless crap whilst my mind whirred at a million miles a second. Would this be the reality, the intellectual highpoint of my day a snatched episode of *Neighbours*? But then my feelings would swing around a hundred and eighty degrees: this baby was conceived in love – of course it would be hard, but how could I throw that away, submit to some nameless doctor sucking the life out of me? Lysette had left an awkward message on the answering machine, but I didn't want to expose myself to her relentless practicality just yet.

'*I* wasn't pleased!' he said, as if that clinched it. 'I was a fool. He might be an even bigger fool, but this baby's a Cosgrove. We'll make it work. Won't we, Granny?' he said, raising his wine glass to Mum.

Her smile was equal parts love and exasperation. She'd barely eaten anything, just pushed it round her plate, like I often did. Poor Mum.

'Mia needs a chance to really work out what she wants,' she insisted. 'This is her whole life we're talking about. If you want to have the baby, of course we'll do everything we can to help, but you've got years ahead to have a family. It's hard doing it on your own.' Lorcan sent her a quick, dark glance at the 'on your own' but she pretended not to notice. It stung me too, the assumption that I'd be a single parent. She hadn't even met Jim, and she was assuming the worst.

'Thanks,' I said, reaching across the table to give her hand a squeeze. I knew she meant well. The skin felt dry and flaky to my touch. I'd buy her some posh hand cream with my babysitting money, I thought, then imagined a whole new life where any spare pounds had to be spent on dull necessities like nappies and baby wipes. I don't want to have you and resent you, I said silently. You don't deserve that. I'd found myself talking to it with worrying frequency these last twenty-four hours.

'What's wrong with you, woman?' said Lorcan, his blue eyes flashing, his hand hitting the table. 'This is our grand-child! Our flesh and blood.'

My hand swooped unconsciously to my still flat tummy. I was less than three months gone: when I was trying to be hard-headed, I forced myself to think of it as a bundle of cells, but hearing Lorcan say that made me wince. Mum stood up, crossed to the sink.

'Newsflash, Lorcan,' she hissed. 'It's not all about you.'

It wasn't exactly an advert for family life. But Jim and I were different – we loved each other. Perhaps I could start again, build a family from scratch in my own image? After all, Jim's family was everything I'd ever wanted – we could be an unexpected branch that sprang off their mighty oak. I caught Lorcan's eye as I lost myself in the fantasy, and he smiled at me with something that looked a bit like pride. I smiled back. I couldn't help it.

Jim met me at Hampstead tube station. I was late, unusually for me, delayed by the pile of discarded clothes on my bed. I wanted my outfit to be perfect for this momentous occa-sion, but I didn't want it to look thought out: I was aiming for that flung-together insouciance that the tousled-haired girls always pulled off. I watched him as I hurried up the hill from the bus stop. He was smoking a fag, fidgety, head-phones in his ears. This was his before moment, but he had no idea.

'Er, loser! Late,' he said, smacking hard lips against mine.

'Sorry, sorry!' I said, grabbing his hand. 'Let's get hot chocolates at the Dome.'

'Yeah, and you're paying.'

The Dome was a pseudo-French bistro a few feet back down the hill, the jewel in the social crown for North London youth. The staff were hot and so were the crowd: no one cared that the croque-monsieur tasted like an old slipper. Jim's bad mood evaporated once our drinks were in front of us. He lit up another fag and I tried not to breathe in the smoke. Would he stop smoking if he was a dad? It was so much a part of his shtick, the fag always loosely held in the left-hand corner of his mouth, the silver Zippo a beloved pet.

'I need to talk to you,' I said.

He reached out a hand, stroked my cold cheek.

'Sorry I didn't ring this week, but you don't want some thicko who fails his exams. I got an offer from Durham.'

Three hours on the train at least.

'Course you did. They know quality when they see it.'

'Too right. I'm not just a pretty face.' His eyes were roving the room, checking out the scene. I took his beautiful chin between my fingertips and turned his face back towards me.

'Earth to Jim. I *need* to talk to you.' His eyes darkened as he heard the catch in my voice, and I almost backed away from the edge. I suddenly craved a few more drops of the before, but the truth was that the before was already over. 'I'm pregnant.'

The colour drained from his face. I waited for something to register there.

'You can't be.'

'I am. I've taken three tests.'

We sat there for an agonizing minute as he tried to absorb it.

'Fuck's sake.' I reminded myself of how shocked I was when I first found out. This was shock, pure and simple. 'Listen, I'll help, of course I'll help.' I started to breathe again, relief flooding through me. 'Mum and Dad'll pay for it if your mum and dad can't.'

'They don't have to completely support us!'

His expression was one of pure disbelief.

'I meant . . . Mia, you can't have a baby!' He saw my stricken face. 'I mean, we're not old enough to be parents.'

I cried, yet again, and Jim signalled quickly and efficiently for the bill, dropping a crumpled fiver on the silver platter and leading me out.

We spent hours criss-crossing the Heath, Jim pleading with me to see sense. I knew he was right – that the part of me that wanted to keep the baby was entirely illogical. The problem was it was stubborn too.

'Your mum's got it sussed,' he said eventually. 'There's plenty of time. We can have a baby when we've got jobs and a mortgage and money for some flash pram we don't even know how to put up.'

It was a master stroke. It didn't make me want to have an abortion, of course it didn't, but I didn't really and truly want to be a mum either, particularly now I'd seen his face. There were so many areas where I was riddled with self-doubt, but academic achievement wasn't one of them. I loved the simplicity of it: what I put in I got out. I didn't want to be like Mum, all thwarted ambition and broken dreams. I was going to be a top-flight human rights lawyer, noble and accomplished with great suits like they wore in *LA Law*. There was no perfect solution, but I knew in my heart that this was the least imperfect one. We sat on a bench, my damp face on his shoulder, one of his hands stroking my hair whilst the other manoeuvred a fag. I still avoided the smoke.

'Shsh,' he kept saying, his touch hypnotic. 'It's all going to be fine now. Hunky-dory.'

He didn't seem to understand about before and after – it might've been his baby, but it wasn't his body. Still, he was here beside me, and in that moment it was all that mattered. The next time I sprang this momentous news, I vowed, it would be a very different story.

When I told Mum, I could tell she was relieved, even though she hated the fact that she was. It made me hate myself in turn for exposing her to a situation where every solution felt like a miniature tragedy.

'I know how hard this is,' she said, enveloping me in yet another hug, 'but there'll be time for you. A better time. I'm sorry if I failed you.'

'You didn't fail me!' I said, hugging her back harder.

'Of course I'll come with you.'

'No, Jim's coming,' I said, ignoring the look of utter contempt that crossed her face. 'But thank you. That's what he said,' I added defensively. 'That we'd have plenty of time for kids.'

'Did he?' she said, her eyes like chips of ice.

We didn't mention Lorcan – safely out of the way with some of his muso mates – although his presence loomed large. Mum admitted she'd already looked into options, and thought it was best to do it privately and quickly. We made some phone calls right there and then, an initial appointment booked for Monday. Mum hung up the receiver, looked with pure maternal love at my pale face. I couldn't promise to be able to give that, not yet.

'And if you change your mind, you know I'll support you every step of the way.'

She didn't say 'we'. She was right not to – we just didn't know how right.

Chapter Sixteen

When Brendan buzzes to say that Gemma's arrived for her session, I close my eyes and take three deep gulps of air. So much of me wants to creep away from the mess I'd made, convince myself that the most responsible thing is to never see her again, but she's asked for this. I owe it to her.

I find my poise – she deserves poise, not cringing – and walk confidently into the waiting room. I was expecting a scowl, or another self-satisfied smile of triumph, but instead her eyes widen with pleasure, her smile more genuine than I've ever known it to be.

'Mia!' she says, like it's a glorious reunion.

I feel something in that moment that's almost love. I'm glad she's here, despite everything.

'Hi, Gemma,' I say, smiling back. 'Let's go through, shall we?'

She throws herself down on the couch like it's her own personal resting place.

'I thought you wouldn't see me. I thought you meant it!'

'I did mean it, Gemma, but with everything that's happened I think we all thought – you, me, your mum, my boss – it would be good for us to have a chance to . . .' It's unexpectedly hard to finish the sentence. 'Say goodbye.'

She goes to speak, but then shrinks in on herself. Her eyes dart up to mine, and she gives a brief nod. It's stupid, but I want to put my arms round her thin shoulders and hug her, promise her that everything's going to be all right. However bad it feels now, you can get through this: if you wait it out, eventually time will decide it for you, make you mistress of your own destiny. But how can I make her any promises?

'What if I don't want to say goodbye to you?' she says, her voice cracking. Her grey–blue eyes fill with tears, her face puffy with emotion.

It twists on my heart, the way she gives herself to me now. I've become a mirror for the parent who treats her badly, and now she wants me more than ever.

'Gemma, I'll miss you too, but I think it's for the best. We've blurred the lines. I blurred them because I care about you, but it wasn't my finest hour. You deserve better.'

'I don't want better, I want you!' Her hands fly up to her face. 'You get me, Mia. No one gets me. They all think I'm weird.'

'Who thinks you're weird? You're not weird, you're you. Remember what I said? There's only one Gemma Vine.'

'Everyone does,' she says, her voice a painful quaver. 'Everyone at school. They even think the props I make are weird. My teachers – but they have to make listening faces, like this.' She twists her mouth into an exaggerated moue, her eyebrows arching up. I can't help laughing at her, which makes her preen. 'My waste-of-space family,' she continues. 'The only people who don't think I'm weird are you and my dad.' She pauses. 'And you probably do think I'm weird, but you've had, like, years of training to make *your* listening face.'

'Gemma, look at me.' She does, her gaze naked. 'I don't think you're weird, I promise, and nor does your mum. She loves you. More than I think you sometimes realize.'

'Yeah, no. I know she loves me,' she says, sarcastic in a way that tells me she knows it's true.

'I think you're dealing with an awful lot of things that a person your age shouldn't have to deal with. And actually, you're doing pretty well.' I have to look away as I say it, the thought of the potential hidden evidence blindsiding me. I can't protect her. I thought I could, but I can't. All I can hope is that it was nothing more than a tactic on Patrick's part, but the way his face looked when he told me said otherwise. 'And I'm really sorry that I let you playing my dad's song get to me. You shouldn't have done it, but I'm the adult, and I should've stayed calm.'

'I'm sorry!' she says, a sob rising up. She buries her blonde head in her arms. She looks so thin and vulnerable, no more than a wispy pencil sketch.

'You don't need to apologize,' I say, keeping my voice soft. 'I should never have told you so much about me. It was confusing. If I hadn't, you wouldn't have . . .', I was going to say 'had the ammunition', but it would have sounded too raw, too emotional – too like a break-up. 'Known what to find.'

'I do like his songs!' she says, raising her gaze.

It breaks my heart, the way she's clutching at straws, looking for ways to please me. I don't take the bait, I simply smile at her.

'Listen, Gemma, we're here to talk about you. Not me. I'm boring, irrelevant!' I say, holding her gaze, hoping she'll come back with a smart reply. She doesn't.

'Don't leave me, Mia!'

I'm choking up now, but I swallow it down: I owe her total professionalism, even if it feels like a muzzle. It's funny, I've always worked from gut instinct within these four walls, and yet, outside them, I've struggled so much to listen to anything but the deluded diktats of my thoughts. I can't imagine how it's going to feel next week, not having this amazing playground. So much of what makes me me, at least in my eyes, is here in this room.

'There are other therapists, Gemma . . . you can still have support. I think what we need to do, in the time we've got left, is make sure there's nothing left unsaid between us.' She nods, big eyes asking me to carry on. 'I know your mum's talked to you about Patrick, the lawyer.' It feels odd calling him 'the lawyer'. It's been six days, and there's been no contact. He doesn't know that I'm homeless, single and – the hat trick – potentially unemployed. Would he even care? Much as I'm still raging with him, I can't help believing he would, despite all the evidence to the contrary. Maybe I need to believe in something, a life raft to save me from the existential bleakness of my and Marcus's bloodless severing of ties. He ranted at me when I called him, but it felt like it was his titanic ego that was hurting more than his heart, and the truth was that I didn't hurt enough either. Perhaps there's too much else going on for me to feel it just yet. 'I want you to know that I didn't tell him any of the secrets you told me about your dad. But I can understand if you're angry I talked to him at all. They've asked to interview you again, right?'

'I'm not angry,' she says, insistent.

'It's OK to be angry, Gemma. You won't hurt me.' I wish she'd break, smirk at me in the infuriating way she usually does – like I'm an incompetent fool, and she's the one who should be firing the questions. It's so Alice in Wonderland. She's been furious with me, week after week, and now, when anger would be entirely justified, she can't lay claim to it. 'And it's OK if you're not, too. Or if it comes later.'

'Can you talk to them with me?' She looks up, finally cheeky. 'Can you come and talk to your boyfriend?'

I smile at her, shaking my head.

'He's *not* my boyfriend.'

'I know he likes you! And I reckon you like him . . .' I don't reply. 'You think I'm just being a pain in the bum like Mum says, but I'm not thick, Mia. Dad always says I've got nous. Your face does something funny when you say his name, like you're having a row inside you.'

She's sharp, this one – I wish I could tell her that. Then I start thinking it through, watching the knowing smile that tugs her mouth upwards. So far there's been no formal complaint about me, but I can't help wondering if the axe will fall after the session they begged me for has been delivered. If her erratic mood pings towards anger, if she tells Annie what she suspects about me and Patrick, there's no way I'll escape a formal investigation. I'm a cowardly fool for not telling Judith the whole sorry tale when I had the chance. I quickly recover myself. This is Gemma's time.

'Gemma, we're talking about me again, and I want to keep talking about you. I can't come with you to your interview, but I can try and help you prepare.' I pull back, Patrick's dire warnings flooding back. 'Emotionally, I mean. Are you nervous?'

'No.'

'Really?'

She's silent, her gaze fleeing out of the window. I look for that familiar blankness, but her face is a picture of fierce concentration.

'If I tell you . . .' she says. 'Mia, if I tell you what I know about my dad, could you tell your boy— tell the police for me, so I don't have to go?' I look at her, my heart beating hard in my chest, trying to work out how to respond. 'If you care about me, if you really *are* sorry for going behind my back,' she adds, the sharp little manipulator back in the room, 'then you'll do it for me.'

Chapter Seventeen

I sit there looking at her, my mind whirring. She has extraordinary power for one so young; I don't want to be a horse, kicked hard in the flank, clearing a fence neither of us should ever have attempted.

'That's the rule, isn't it? If I tell you something that's' – she makes quote marks in the air, an affectation I hate – '*relevant to the police investigation*, you're meant to tell him. That's what I want to do. Simples,' she adds in that annoying voice from that annoying advert.

'Gemma, I'm not sure if that's appropriate at this stage—'

'You always say it's my session, to use how I want. This is how I want to use it.'

Perhaps this has always been where we were heading, the natural conclusion to our work together. God knows I didn't dodge it, nudging her to tell me about those messages, asking her all about her dad.

'So what *do* you want to tell me? And, Gemma, I'm going

to coach you here. Go very slowly. Stop any time. This is our last session, and I don't want you to be left with your guts hanging out because you shared too much.'

She looks at me, vulnerable again.

'If I don't finish telling you, can I come back?'

Is this what this is all about? I think of Annie recalling her seduction, how powerless she was to resist. Gemma's learnt at the feet of a master. If Patrick could see us now, he'd be punching the air.

'No. We've agreed this is the last session and we're going to stick to it.' Would I have been so adamant if I was the only person who could extract the truth? The thing is, for her own safety, she can't be allowed to feel like she's omnipotent, running the show. It's imperative I hold the boundary, at least for now. She looks at me for a long minute, her jaw rigid. 'You don't have to talk at all, Gemma, remember that. We could just sit here together.'

'No! Mia . . .' She pauses again, her chewed fingers wrapping tightly around themselves in her lap. I need to be ready to stop her if it becomes too much, whatever Patrick might want.'The thing about my dad is – I'm his little rock. His rock of Gibraltar.'

'I remember you said that.' I hated it then, and I hate it now – it's no more than an emotional chokehold. I can't help noticing, yet again, how young she looks in her shapeless clothes. He's subtly telling her that if she ever grows up – kicks against his control, like any normal teenager must – he won't survive the betrayal. It takes all my strength not to muscle in, but I stay silent. I did my best to make her question his demands – hopefully some of it lodged in her consciousness.

'But it means I'm his Achilles heel. You know what that is, right?'

'I do.'

She looks straight into my eyes.

'He isn't gone.'

'What do you mean?'

'He's here, in London.' Her gaze travels across me like a minesweeper. 'I told him all about you.'

I take a breath. I need to make sure, for both our sakes, that it's me holding the reins.

'So you've seen him?'

'Yeah. Stephen's looking after him.' 'Looking after' – it sounds so benign, so caring. 'They want him to go abroad but . . .' Her face tightens, tears springing to her eyes. 'He can't leave me, Mia! He can't just up sticks and leave me.'

I think about what Judith so wisely said – this really could be no more than the fucked-up fantasy of an abandoned Daddy's girl. Her instinct could be better than Patrick's intelligence. But now there's that phrase – his Achilles heel. It sounds like it's come straight from the horse's mouth.

'So where do you see him, Gemma?' She studies me, like she's working out all over again whether I deserve her trust. 'Remember you can stop any time.'

'My piano lessons. He comes and meets me there. We have a McDonald's.'

'I didn't know you liked McDonald's. You're so slim, you don't look like a hamburger's ever passed your lips.'

I'm pulling on the reins here, seeing what happens if I jerk us off the course she's set.

'I don't,' she says, grinning, 'but Dad loves it! We go to the drive-in one . . .'

Is she playing a blinder here, merging fantasy and truth to create something that's impossible to call?

'So, Gemma, I don't understand. Are you saying that your piano teacher smuggles your dad into her house?' She nods solemnly. 'And . . .' Should I even ask this? 'Does your mum know?'

'Course not,' she says, her eyes dropping, then flicking back to my face. 'Stephen's people can make anything happen.'

The horrible thing is – even if everything else she's claiming is absolute rubbish – she's right about that. I feel a strangely satisfying surge of Patrick's righteous anger. If there's even a small chance this is true, I need to glean everything I can. *We are on the same side.* The thought makes my heart contract. Does he feel it? Is he here with me, on some parallel plane?

'So let me get this straight. You're saying that every week you trot off to piano, and there's your dad? And then what, he goes back to a safe house?'

'Yeah, for now!' she says, her voice rising, colour flushing her pale face. 'But he can't . . . he can't stay much longer, Mia. It's not safe for him.'

I bleed for the depth of pain that flashes across her face. I engage the brakes, determined not to feel pressured by the clock which ticks ever closer to the end of our session. This is Gemma, the girl I've grown to care about, the girl I know desperately needs the adults in her life to behave like adults. I don't want to accidentally become as bad as Christopher, treating her like she's some kind of human slot machine, feeding in coins and demanding she pays up.

'I think we should stop here, Gemma. I can tell Patrick what you've told me, if that's really what you want, but I want to leave us some time to properly say goodbye.'

'I think Stephen's gonna make him!' says Gemma, almost as though she doesn't hear me. 'He can make anything happen. What if he makes him disappear?'

'Are you worried he's going to . . .' I don't want to plant that thought in her head, if she's not there yet.

'He could just put him on a plane, just like that,' she says, voice rising even higher, her eyes wild. Or worse: *a body bag or a police van.*

'Gemma, look at me.' She does. 'You shouldn't be having to carry all this around with you, these secrets.' If they're real: I study her pale face, her look of desperation and fear never faltering. It's hard to believe that's fake. 'It's better the police know.' I wish I could swear that was true. Honestly, I feel like my version of the police was roughly akin to *Trumpton* before Patrick told me the grim reality. He can do this, surely?

'He said . . .' She's sobbing, properly sobbing now. 'He

said this could be the last week.' A cynical part of me sits up at the phrase. This is meant to be her last week here. Coincidence or projection? She looks at me, her body opening towards me. I cross to the sofa, put my arm round those spindly shoulders, and let her cry into my chest.

'You've told me now,' I say as sobs rack her body. 'I heard you. I know how hard it is.' Can I really leave her, after this? I'm flattering myself. It's not my choice, I'm suspended. I talk a little more, keeping my voice soft and calm, hoping that some of the words will filter through her distress. I tell her how much I've valued the sessions we've done together, how hard she's worked, how much I hope she knows her own value.

And then, once Brendan's buzzed for the second time, reminding me my next client's been waiting fifteen long minutes, we say goodbye.

March 1995 (sixteen years old)

Mum wanted me to wait a couple of weeks, leave time for me to change my mind if that was what was meant to happen, but I didn't want to risk it. An odd, arctic calm had descended on me, a permafrost of self-preservation. Doctors were seen, forms were signed and now I was a day away from my body being vacant again. It sounds cold, but the truth was it had started to feel like an alien continent. I was nibbling food without tasting it, walking to school like I was walking on the moon, air-sprung feet barely landing on the pavement. Lorcan had raged and shouted, told us he'd go straight back to New York, and then slumped into a disconsolate silence. He wouldn't look at me, would stay in bed until I'd left the house, and then disappear in the evenings.

But Jim made up for it. He was so utterly lovely to me, coming home the next weekend and taking me to a proper Italian restaurant in Primrose Hill, his hand never leaving mine throughout the meal. He even fed me a forkful of spaghetti. 'You're being so brave,' he kept saying. 'We've just got to hang in there.' On the Monday, he sent me roses and I tried not to think about Valentine's Day. Mum took delivery of them, hiding the vase in my room so Lorcan wouldn't see it. **Love you, Jim xx**, said the card, and I Pritt-Sticked it into my diary, reading the sparse, precious words again and again. Logically, this didn't have to be a disaster. I would survive it, and life would go on – there would be other babies, babies we could parent properly. I just had to protect myself from the volcano of Lorcan's rage erupting again.

Lysette was loyal but tongue-tied. We were inseparable at school again, apart from when I went to my Oxbridge classes. I'd had a surge of motivation, aware of how much I'd been taking for granted. I wasn't going to be a problem-page cliché, my future ruined by a stupid mistake. My teachers stared a little too hard at me, but I ignored them. We'd had to tell the head of year, who had been suitably, Catholicly, horrified, but they'd decided not to suspend me. For now, I was a purposeful robot. How odd that that never struck me as dangerous.

English was our last class of the day on the eve of my abortion. I was back in the desk where it began, but at least now Lysette was smiling at me. I could see the worry in her eyes, and I gave a brittle, uncertain smile back. She linked her arm through mine as we left the classroom.

'Do you wanna go to the Coffee Cup,' she asked, 'or do you want to go straight home?'

'I'm meeting Jim in Camden,' I said, and a look swept across her face. What was it? Pity, disapproval? I was so weary of getting that look from her and Mum. It was none of their business. 'Did I tell you he sent me roses?' I said, my voice tight and haughty. 'Ten of them. Big, fat pink ones.'

'That's . . . that's nice.'

Now it was Lysette's turn to go robotic, her words clipped and sterile.

'Why do you have to be so negative about us?' I said, anger surging up. 'Fuck's sake, is it so bad that we love each other? What have we actually done wrong? We made a stupid mistake, but . . .'

Lysette's face was white, her jaw clenched.

'You don't want this baby, do you?' she said, her voice a strangled whisper. 'It's not because he's persuaded you . . .'

I couldn't look backwards, revisit moments that I'd burnt through. I'd overcome the useless sentimentality that had dogged those first few days.

'We've made a decision.'

'As long as it's *your* decision. It's your body! You know I don't think you should have it, but I don't want him manipulating you.'

'Manipulating me?' I said, puffing up with righteous indignation. 'He's your brother, Lysette. Why are you always so shitty about him?'

'I'm not!' she said, almost desperate. Lysette was always such an open book, but right now she was fighting to keep the pages tightly closed. Our eyes locked – she broke. 'He's

not faithful. He can't be. All the things that make him fun –
he's spoilt. He doesn't mean to be a bastard.' She saw my
stricken face, tried to hug me. 'I'm sorry, I shouldn't have
said it. Not today. But I had to, in case . . .'

I was as stiff and straight as a pencil. I felt as though I might
topple clean over, the blood rushing to all the wrong places,
but I forced myself to regain control.

'I'm going now,' I said, shaking her arm off me. 'I know
you're only trying to help,' I added mechanically, guarding
against us falling out again.

He lied of course: he lied and lied. And I lied too. I pretended
to him, and to me, that I believed him. I used my favourite
trick, the one where you can choose not to know something
that will be too ruinous to your happiness. He dropped me
home and I kissed him goodnight obediently, like a puppy
who has finally learnt how to get a treat. But I was cleverer
than him, I always had been, I now realized. I was cleverer
than most people. I'd decide when to defrost myself.

Mum insisted I ate breakfast, a soft-boiled egg that made
me want to gag. She made me soldiers, like I was a little girl
again, and watched me anxiously as I nibbled at them. I loved
her so much in that moment, and I nearly broke, asked her
to take me, but I couldn't risk going off course. Lorcan
wouldn't come downstairs, his heavy footfall making the
house reverberate with anger. Jim was early, a state of affairs
that was unheard of. My God, he wanted to make sure this
was in the bag.

'Hello, Mrs Cosgrove. We finally meet,' he said, putting out a polite hand. Mum made the briefest contact with it.

'We do,' she said, her eyes like slate, 'and it's Claire.' She turned her back on him, hugging me close. It was so warm there, her heartbeat so unexpectedly comforting. I lived inside that body once. 'Darling, are you sure you don't want me to come with you?'

I shook my head, not trusting myself to speak. I stayed where I was.

'We should go,' said Jim eventually, and I could feel Mum's glare, even though I couldn't see her face from my vantage point in her arms.

'You're right,' I said, pulling away. He put out his hand for mine, and I looked at it. It was like a dead fish. I opened the front door.

'I'll be here when you get home,' Mum said, and I smiled gratefully, then walked down the path towards Jim's car.

Lorcan came out of nowhere. He must've gone out the back door and lain in wait. He barrelled into Jim, taking him completely by surprise, pushing him down on the pavement.

'Who the fuck do you think you are?' he shouted. 'That's my grandchild!' He was gripping him, pinning him to the ground, Jim still too shocked to fight back.

'Get off him,' I screeched. Yet again, I felt like I was having an out-of-body experience. We were trapped in a cliffhanger from a bad soap opera. 'Mum!'

Lorcan turned his face towards me, his eyes wild and staring.

'You're no child of mine,' he said.

Mum came running out, and started trying to pull Lorcan off him, but it was like Lorcan was possessed. I hated it when he got like that, unreachable and terrifying. He could do anything in this state.

'Lorcan, stop. Stop!' I pleaded. Jim was trying to push him off, but Lorcan's skinny body seemed to have supernatural strength. Jim was slight too, a lover, not a fighter.

'You trying to get away from me?' Lorcan screamed. 'Don't you fucking dare. You're a murderer!'

I looked down the suburban street, desperate for help. Curtains were twitching by now, but no one had come out to help us. Mum was pulling at Lorcan, as Jim aimed punches.

'Get the fuck off me!' he shouted. 'You fucking lunatic!'

I felt a deep wave of dread. I could see Lorcan's face, his rage reaching boiling point.

'Don't you fucking dare,' he said again, grabbing Jim's head. As the police car screeched to a halt, he was hitting it against the pavement. Jim screamed, then stopped screaming, blood pooling around him. I was screaming too, but I didn't even know it.

By the time the ambulance pulled up, Lorcan was already in handcuffs. I was on the ground, kneeling next to Jim, but he couldn't hear me. 'I love you,' I said, again and again, the last twenty-four hours an irrelevance. And then, as they put him on the stretcher, I felt a deep pain inside my belly that was more than shock.

Chapter Eighteen

My car's an ancient Polo, totally incongruous amongst the sleek Mercedes and BMWs that line the road the fridge is on. The stupid nickname grates on me now: Judith was right, there was something so obviously awry for me to be undermining our first home together so slyly. I sit there, looking up at it, the sadness I've been holding at bay suddenly overwhelming. I've stifled it, swinging between whipping myself for my night with Patrick and whipping Marcus for being so callous and cut-off. Now, sitting here, I just think that we're both a bit hopeless. We did have happy times, but somehow we couldn't convert a handful of shiny beads into an heirloom-worthy necklace.

I feel sick with myself for what happened with Patrick, but there's a reason it did. Ringing him yesterday – the first contact since he strode out of my bare flat without looking back – was savage.

'Mia,' he said, picking up on the first ring, his voice thick with something. Guilt? Regret? What was real and what was manipulation? I've obsessively tracked back over all our time together, trying to juice the truth from it, but I've lost too much faith in myself to make a diagnosis. I can only trust in empirical facts, one of which is that he's made absolutely no contact with me since he got the information he so desperately sought.

'This is a professional call,' I said, my voice clipped. I had to keep the two things separate, my feelings vacuum-sealed. I couldn't fail Gemma again. Couldn't fail myself.

'OK, fine,' he said, his voice already hardening.

And I outlined what Gemma had told me, promising to scan my notes and email them over. Patrick took it all in, long fingers tapping furiously at his keyboard like a woodpecker, his quick, tense breaths audible down the phone.

'Thanks a million for this.'

'Yeah, seems like all your hard work finally paid off,' I said, childish hurt finally getting the better of me.

'It wasn't—'

'You don't need to say anything else,' I said, as icily as I could.

'Mia?' The way he said my name, it punctured me. 'Firstly, I meant every word I said to you, and,' he added, before I could jump in, 'what do you think? Did you believe her?'

I paused. I hadn't really and truly had time to think it through. Saying goodbye to her had felt so jagged – a goodbye amidst a chorus of other goodbyes – and then I'd distracted myself with the immediate aftermath. I'd spoken to Judith, got her blessing to make this call, then picked up the phone.

'There was definitely truth in it,' I said, then realized how airy-fairy that was, unhelpful to a police investigation. Like Patrick had said by the duck pond, he wasn't after a sniff of my scented candles. 'Yes. You know what, it sounds unlikely, and she can be a manipulative little . . .' I stopped myself. Poor Gemma: the enormity of what she was going through felled me again. It was suddenly hard to speak. 'But I do think it's true.'

'Thanks,' he said, voice sombre. 'Because I know how – how amazing you are at what you do. If you think it's true, then—'

'Yeah, Patrick, I am pretty amazing,' I said, suddenly furious at everything I'd lost. Surely Annie would report me now – the person her daughter had chosen to confide in? And Patrick had turned the screws. 'I've got to go. Good luck with it all.'

I've told the estate agent I'll make sure all my boxes are stacked in the hall so the removals people can pick them up in one fell swoop tomorrow. I'm going to grab some clothes whilst I'm here, take them back to Mum's, stop looking like the girl fashion forgot.

The door swings open into cavernous emptiness, the polished wooden floors gleaming. It's a blank canvas, ready to be drawn on. Tears come now, a whole life I was about to step into abandoned. I can't go back. I don't want to go back. And yet . . . I need to grieve. I step into the living room, the walls punctuated by an enormous cinema screen of a TV that Marcus insisted on, and sink down onto one of my packing boxes. I sob, sob for all of it, wiping my runny nose and wet face on my sleeve, like a woeful toddler.

I don't even hear the key in the lock, but I do hear that familiar tread. It's funny, all the things you get to know about a person, which you don't even know you know. There he is, framed in the doorway, bulky and definite.

'Thought champagne would be a cliché,' he says, holding up a bottle of white. I look up at him, my face wet and snotty, and he pulls a big cotton handkerchief from somewhere. He's classy, Marcus: it was one of the things that first made me fancy him. He crouches down next to me, puts his arms around me. 'Don't cry,' he says. He can't stand seeing me cry, but trying not to always makes me cry harder. I lean into his suited chest, even though I don't deserve the comfort.

'Did the agent tell you I'd be here?'

'Yeah. I thought it'd be better than a summit.'

I smile up at him, remembering that I love him. I love him, and yet it's not enough somehow.

'I'm sorry,' I say, the meaning bigger than the three little syllables. We look at each other, sober and quiet, and I nearly tell him everything. 'I'm sorry I went off at the deep end. But you shouldn't . . .'

He puts up a hand. It drives me crazy, the way he always dampens me down. I feel like an opera singer constantly denied her aria.

'I know. I should've talked to you. But you're always so bloody defensive. Whacking out your card all the time. What did you say? "I'm not your geisha"? I'd like to be able to look after you sometimes.'

'It's not about that though, is it?' I say, jumping in. Then I pause a second, think about it. 'It is a bit,' I concede. 'But it's also because we can't talk about anything hard or uncomfortable. You shut me down, and tell me not to cry. Or you get on a plane somewhere . . .' He shrugs. Mea culpa. 'Sometimes I feel like we don't really know each other. Not properly.'

'I like the way you keep something back. You've got a bit of mystery about you.'

Am I a palate cleanser, an antidote to the drudgery of decades of marriage, complete with the dirty nappies and conversations had so many times they're like grooves in a vinyl record? I look round the bare, polished room, sadness bubbling up again. This was where it was meant to begin, our own version of normal.

'Don't you want us to see all the crappy, unattractive bits of each other too? Isn't it lonely otherwise?'

Marcus looks at me, his smile laced with something I can't quite name.

'It's the way I am, Mia. Real men don't eat quiche? I don't eat quiche.'

I smile at him, stroke his stubbly cheek, guilt torrenting through me as soon as my fingers graze it. It's too late. I opened the door, and now I can't shut it again.

'I think you're underestimating yourself,' I say.

'Maybe,' he concedes.

'The divorce too. You're bruised. I never wanted to think about how soon after it was . . .'

'It's hard for you to understand all that. You haven't gone there. I gave you all the certainty cos I knew you needed it, but when it came down to it, I knew how bad it could turn.'

'So why didn't you talk to me about that, rather than sending your progeny round with a legally binding contract?'

He shrugs, smiles down at me.

'I'm going to open the wine,' he says, 'and you're going to drink some, even if this is one of your sodding three days off.'

It used to drive him mad when we went to dinner on a Sunday, and I'd only managed two. I stick out a glass, smile back at him.

'Fill her up.'

He looks back at me, sex in his eyes, always so gratifyingly quick to flare up, but I gently shake my head. He pulls out the cork with a satisfying pop, washes wine into my glass. It's delicious, naturally.

'Cheers,' he says, and we knock glasses. Everything, every little thing, reverberates with my duplicity. I look down for a second, suddenly overwhelmingly grateful to Patrick for slamming on the brakes when he did. Marcus pulls up a packing case, sits down on it, turns to me; we're two gnomes chewing the fat on our cardboard toadstools. I smile at the thought, almost kiss him. Instead I take his large, powerful hand, trace the palm with my fingers. I'm going to miss his hands.

'Talk to me,' I say.

'I should've talked to you, you're right. But you're actually quite hard to reach, despite your fancy qualifications—'

'So are you,' I say, too fast.

He holds up his other hand.

'I know. But also, I might just not talk the way you want me to talk. I don't talk quiche . . . And, you've been different recently, Mia. You're not really here. I know you're stressed about your mum, but it's more than that, isn't it?'

And then I start to cry again, tears streaming down my raw face. He pulls me close, dries them with his hankie, listens as I tell him about my suspension, about the bare bones of Gemma, about how hard it's been to surf the waves of a set of circumstances so far outside my comfort zone. And of course, as soon as I get close to the case, I start to hate myself for the fact I'm leaning into his broad chest, soaking up his murmured words of kindness and reassurance.

'There's so much I can't tell you, but there's something I really should . . .'

He holds up his hand again.

'Don't, Mia.' His voice is fierce. 'I don't need this bit.'

His eyes are dark and flat, a slammed metal door. He means it.

'OK,' I say, my voice small.

His gaze softens as he looks at me.

'You don't want this. I could fight for you, but I'm not going to do that.'

'Do you want it?'

'It's enough for me. It's not enough for you.'

So simple. So true. We don't always need quiche. I hold his face without letting guilt poison my touch, look into his eyes to signal he's right and avoid a tortured explanation. He leans in, kisses me, and I lose myself in it, this last and final kiss.

'I don't want to lose you from my life,' I tell him as we stand up, holding hands.

'Give it some time,' he says with a rueful grin. 'Man's got his pride.'

'I mean it. It's not some stupid platitude.'

'I know. So do I.' He looks down at me. 'You're lovely. Fucking exasperating, but you're lovely. I always knew it'd be hard to keep you.'

'Marcus, women hurl their knickers at you all the time—'

'Don't,' he says, a note of warning in his voice. 'Besides, it's not a numbers game.'

'I know.'

We pause for a minute, surrounded by bareness and boxes, a strange sort of wasteland.

'You want me to help put a couple of these in the car?'

'That'd be great.'

He lugs mine into a neatly arranged cube, ever the architect, then hauls a couple down the stairs for me. I watch his retreating back, his broad shoulders, his confident stride. Am I crazy to let him keep walking? For some inexplicable reason I can't do anything else.

I don't know why I'm here. I might as well have boiled his pet rabbit and had done with it. I'm parked up outside the police station, in view of the door, Radio 3 playing through the tinny car speakers in an effort to calm my thumping heart. I want to thank him, to apologize, to wish him God speed for tomorrow. What I should do is pick up the phone like a grown-up, instead of lurking in the shadows, but I'm too frightened of how his voice might sound. At least if I could see him . . . He's probably not even here. He's probably in some sticky-floored pub, a coquettish twenty-something with a lawyer fetish laughing a bit too hard at his jokes.

It must be an hour I wait, my heart leaping every time the door swings open. Then I give up, turn the rusty key in the ignition and head for home.

Chapter Nineteen

I'm so glad I stuck to my word, although it makes me feel viscerally guilty for the litany of broken promises that have gone before. It's not that I don't love Lysette's children – I really, really do – it's just that I see so little of her that I can't help revelling in an uninterrupted stretch of time with her, devoid of sticky hands and slamming doors. But when I see Saffron's chubby, cake-mixture-splattered face light up at the very sight of me, I remember, deep in my chest, why I have to make the journey out here on a far more regular basis.

'Thank God you're here!' says Lysette, dressed in a vinyl apron, hair messily pulled back, face similarly splattered with goo. The annoying thing is that she still looks fabulous.

'I brought Prosecco,' I say, pulling it out. I probably shouldn't drink any, not when I'm feeling this wobbly, but it seems churlish to cast Lysette as the lush. I knew exactly what she'd do – chuck orange juice in it and recast it as a brunch-time Buck's Fizz – and within minutes it's in my hand.

'You're my heroine,' she says, taking a swig. 'We've borrowed this cupcake machine. Car-nage.'

It's true. Every surface in the tiny kitchen is piled high with paper cupcake cases, plastic bowls, cereal packets and – a hammer.

'Ged!' shouts Lysette, seeing me eyeing it. 'Move your tools!'

'Who are you calling a tool?' he says good-naturedly, kissing me hello. Saffron's crawled up onto my knee by now, and guards me jealously from his attentions, her arms wrapped around my neck, cake mixture lodging itself in my hair. Carnage indeed. It's perfect. I don't think it would necessarily be my perfect, but it's perfect nevertheless.

'So have you spoken to him?' says Lysette above the noise of the whirling cupcake machine. Saffron's standing on a chair, watching the machine with eagle-eyed fascination, while her older brothers sit at the kitchen table making her a birthday banner out of pink crêpe paper.

'Marcus? I haven't told you about last night—'

She cuts across me.

'No. Muffin man.'

'Yes,' I say, and her eyes light up instantaneously. 'But only about the case.'

'At least you're talking,' says Lysette, ever the optimist.

'Trust me, we're not talking.'

She looks at me, not saying a word, but I can read it off her as clearly as if she had a cartoon thought bubble floating above her head. She's thinking how judgemental I can be, how I can end up cutting off my nose to spite my face with such zeal that I'm left bleeding out. I feel a surge of irritation. I'm going to argue the toss, tell her that, for all his warm and fuzzy compliments, he's obviously found forgetting about me a breeze, all the time dying a little inside at the thought of how long I spent parked up outside the police station, but she still hasn't said it out loud, and now Saffron's grabbing my arm, round little body wobbling like a jelly as she teeters on the chair.

'Mia, listen to me, we're going to put MINSTRELS on top!' she says, as if it's the most outrageous stroke of genius.

'Fantastic!' I say. 'Can I have a go?'

I hug her extra tight, drawing her warm parcel of a body as close to mine as I possibly can. Where's Gemma right now? Wherever she is – even if surrounded by a screaming mob – she'll be utterly alone. *I'm thinking of you*, I silently tell her, *I'm hoping today brings some kind of deliverance.*

Soon there's a steady stream of mothers dropping off present-wielding little girls in uniformly pink party frocks (no purple, no green). I smile politely – I hope not coldly – hanging back as Lysette hugs her tribe hello and catches up on gossip. This is emphatically her life, not mine: I feel a little twinge of shame at not having my own pink-frocked treasure to steer and cajole. Saffron is hysterical with excitement, the floor littered with torn-up wrapping paper and ribbon, no neat stack of presents kept for later. Would I be a total control freak of a mum? I don't think I ever really believed Marcus's half-hearted promises about 'being open' to more children, a phrase that gives a big fat V sign to 'wanting'. Maybe that suited me. I'm not sure it would any more.

Little kids are loud. They start with a round of pass the parcel, which obviously ends in hysterical tears, and then Lysette sits them in a circle so that Ged, dressed in a pointy hat and cloak, can perform some highly dubious 'magic tricks'. Saffron's entranced – it's her dad after all – but the other ten or so kids seem more engaged in picking their noses and stuffing Rice Krispie cakes in their dribbly faces.

'Let's leave them to it,' says Lysette, grabbing my arm and pulling me towards the kitchen. For now the older boys have got it covered. It's sweet how they want to help out, determined to make their sister's birthday special. I bet Gemma's brothers love her far more than she ever notices: we hardly got to talk about them. I almost text Patrick to find out what's happening, but I stop myself: it's no good building a wall and then constantly peeking over the top. My part in the trial is, hopefully, over. If I'm very lucky, I'll be allowed to go back to listening to Ben and Isobel droning on about whether porn would spice things up or demean her. This much I know – I'll never risk going near another criminal case.

'Oh, my mum gave me this for you,' I say, scrabbling around in my handbag for a plant cutting that she thrust on me as I left. 'She said to send you loads of love.'

'Bless her for that,' says Lysette, filling a glass and popping the cutting in. Lysette's garden is beautiful, a perk of living out of London, and she and the kids get a real satisfaction from growing fat, misshapen tomatoes and muddy carrots. 'How the hell is it? I kind of want to come round and sit on your bed while there's still time.'

'No need for that. I mean, obviously I feel like the world's biggest loser.'

'Don't feel like that!'

'Er, no job come Monday,' I say, ticking off menu items on my fingers. 'No boyfriend, let alone husband slash children, and now the *pièce de résistance*, I'm back in my teenage bedroom.' As I say it, I feel my shoulders hunch inwards like a bird curling in its wings. It's the strangest thing, even though my Matisse prints and piano grade certificates are long gone, it feels like stepping through the looking-glass. 'It's nice to be with Mum though.'

It is. She can't keep up the Stepford act now I'm there to stare her out, and she's at least started to talk to me truthfully about how difficult it is to have had so many of her certainties swept away. Perhaps the one positive to come out of my personal tsunami is that Mum can actually believe I understand. It makes me realize how much time I've spent breezing through, gaze welded to my iPhone, airily saying 'My treat' at some fancy place that probably made her toes curl inside her sensible shoes.

'And they've got a buyer?'

'Yeah, I think it's going to go through this month. Then I really might be on your camp bed.'

'Hurrah! So no chance you can get your flat back?'

'Nope.' The primary school teacher 'adores' it, and definitely wants her full six months (thank God I only agreed to six, although what does it say about my attitude to commitment?). Until the consequences of my suspension become clearer, going home feels like the most sensible stopgap. So hello, Loserville. 'Don't worry, I'm not serious about the camp bed.'

'You could, you know.'

'I know,' I say, grateful. 'I'd pay rent though.' I get the Prosecco out of the fridge, top Lysette up. 'Seriously, I'm bored of listening to myself moaning. And I've got a plan.' I open up my iPad, show Lysette the links I've downloaded for her. 'Garden design, you can do most of the course online. You'd be amazing at it!'

Her finger swoops across the screen, her attention totally focused.

'I don't know if we could afford it . . .' she says, but I can tell she's considering it.

'Look, I've got more time at the moment. It might not be this, but there's loads of stuff you're brilliant at. What are they called — transferable skills?'

Just then, a child appears at her elbow. She's slightly bigger than the others, her dress — whilst pink — slightly less puffy of sleeve and balloon-skirted. I can't put my finger on it, but even her entrance into the kitchen suggests a certain self-possession.

'Auntie Lys, Saffron dropped Ribena all over Peppa and

now she won't stop crying. I told her Peppa could go in the washing machine but' – she shrugs nonchalantly – 'she doesn't get it cos she's only four. Today.'

I look at her, shock filtering through me; those sea–green eyes, her full pink lips. 'Auntie Lys' is more than an affectation. Lysette darts a look at me.

'I'll be right there. Sorry,' she says to me, as she hurries through. 'I was gonna warn you, but I thought you didn't need anything else to think about. He's not coming, I promise.'

That child. Jim's child. Jim's child and not my child. I try not to think how old she'd be (why do I always think she'd have been a she?) but I can't help it. Twenty – I could be the mother of a twenty-year-old.

I think back to what must have been Jim's wife, a har-assed–looking woman with frizzy hair and nondescript jeans, slurping loudly from a Starbucks bucket of something. In fact, her volume setting seemed high for everything. Her laugh was loud, and when she said goodbye to – Violet? – her voice boomed from the back door like a ferry tannoy. It's not how I'd pictured her at all: I thought the woman who'd finally succeeded in taming Jim would be some ethereal, unknowable beauty who had effortlessly popped out their three children like petits pois from an organic pod. I chide myself for being such a judgemental bitch, my point-scoring far more unattractive than her untamed hair.

I look at my bag hanging on the back of the door, seri-ously tempted to make a run for it. But maybe that's what

I've been doing all my life. I'll go before going-home time – I'm not a total masochist – but I can get through this.

Saffron's tears are drying by the time I go next door. She's safe in Lysette's arms, a sausage roll half hanging out of her mouth like Jim's fags used to hang out of his, crumbs spraying everywhere.

'Auntie Mia's here!' says Lysette, throwing me a concerned smile. I smile back properly. 'Which means it's time to cut the cake!'

Saffron automatically – chokingly – holds out her arms, and I swing her up, leaving Lysette free to light the four candles on Peppa Pig's sponge incarnation. We sing our hearts out, cut the cake, and then I say my hurried goodbyes, give in to my desire to disappear.

I thought the danger lay there. It didn't.

December 1995 (seventeen years old)

The tube judders down the line, wheezy and uncertain, almost as if it's colluding with my jelly of a heart. Rampant egotism of course – London's blanketed in three inches of snow, has ground, hysterically, to a halt as if we've accidentally house-swapped with Antarctica. I count my breaths as I count down the stops, forcing myself not to spring through the doors, run over the bridge and high tail it for home.

The building springs up before I'm ready for it, a brick monster, ready to gobble up anything in its path. Again, I nearly falter. It's consumed Lorcan, but there's still time for me to dodge it, to keep myself intact. As soon as I've stepped through those dark metal gates I'm a prisoner's daughter. There's nothing noble about it: it's not like he's a freedom fighter or a government whistle blower. If you look at the charge sheet, he's no better than a football hooligan or a mugger. I don't want to feel ashamed, but shame feels like it's my blood, pulsing through every last crevice of my body. I can feel it, or I can not feel.

I'm late. The queue for the visitors' centre already snakes halfway across the front yard, people stamping their feet and blowing on their hands in a vain attempt to keep warm. A small brother and sister are having a snowball fight, their mum smoking fag after fag, forced to grind one out under her heel when the little girl wails with fury as she suffers a direct hit, right in the middle of her chubby face. An elderly couple stand in front of me, clad in matching beige anoraks that look like they're from the back page of the *Telegraph*, their gloved hands tightly entwined, their gaze never venturing beyond each other. I can see what they're doing: they're trying to exist on a different plane, where 'the thing' never happened. I'm sure my grandparents will have made an appalled visit by now, done their duty. They're not speaking to us now Mum's thrown him out – I get the feeling they blame us for the whole sorry mess – but they're still scribbling angry cheques to cover my school fees. A couple of off-duty prison officers, callow and spotty, snort with laughter and shove snow in each other's hoods as they head for the exit.

Eventually I'm inside the visitors' centre. I give them my passport, with its scant stamps, sign the form and wait to be called, like I'm going to take off on the world's worst holiday. I'm stretched thin between wanting the wait to go on forever, and wanting this all to be over, to be gulping the clean air of a life lived outside these grim walls. We've been told that, if he keeps his unpredictable temper tightly buttoned, he'll only serve six months, and he's already done three. Perhaps this could be my one and only visit? I agonized about it, but I couldn't quite stand the idea of him spending Christmas locked in a prison cell, wings not clipped but sawn clean off, deprived of everything that gives his life meaning.

'Are you sure?' Mum kept saying. Mum, the patient priest who'd always give Lorcan two Hail Marys and her forgiveness, has well and truly cast him out into the wilderness. He didn't live with us whilst he was out on bail, and she point blank refused to attend his sentencing. I went because he rang up and begged me to, but the sight of him in the dock, pale and spaced out, Gordon and Gloria glowering at him from the other side of the public gallery, was almost too much to endure.

I saw them in the lobby afterwards: for one crazy moment I wanted to run up and hug them, erase the last few months with the force of my longing, throw myself on their mercy and tell them that our holiday had been the best two weeks of my uneventful little life. I'd loved Jim, no question, but in a funny way I'd loved them – what they represented – just as much. They were a foreign language, passionate and vivid, I was desperate to learn and one I'd have never stopped speaking if I'd been given the chance. I attempted a smile, hoping they'd see in my face how terrible I still felt about what Lorcan had done. I'd written to them to say as much, a letter that the prosecution had bandied around in court to try and increase his sentence.

Jim had recovered well, mercifully, off now on a gap year that was starting in a Bondi Beach bar: I wasn't expecting a postcard. We hadn't seen each other since that gruesome day. Lysette was kind enough to keep me posted on his progress, but made it absolutely clear I wasn't to come near the hospital. Poor Lysette, the faithful messenger, always taking the risk of getting shot for the sake of what was right. She'd been the one to tell them that the baby was lost. I couldn't help obsessing about how that had made Jim feel, secretly hoping that his reaction had contained a trace of something sweeter than relief.

He was never going to tell me, I knew that now. Thank God my love for him had evaporated, replaced by a deep shame at my puppy-dog naivety. I was cleverer than that. I didn't plan to put down the shield it provided any time soon.

The little girl throws out her arms for the stout female warden, a big grin on her face at the adventure of it all. 'You're a very good aeroplane,' the warden tells her, gently putting her down and reaching into her pocket for a mini Mars Bar. I almost wish I could be an aeroplane too, but instead I keep my face neutral as she checks me for contraband, then waves me through to the barren visitors' room. Why am I doing this? I don't know.

I see Lorcan before he sees me, a pale comma curving over the Formica table, skinnier than I've ever known him to be. He's still got that glazed look in his eyes that he wore in the courtroom, like he's dumped real life in left luggage and sped off on a train somewhere far more exotic. It fills me with an unexpected surge of righteous determination. I'm going to bring him back, restore some kind of normal so we can all move on with our lives. He'll come out of prison, bloodied but unbroken, his recent success still there for the taking. Mum will begin enjoying her life, no longer dragging around the dead weight of their broken relationship, and I'll go to Oxford, push myself so hard that a First is an inevitability. I'll debate things fiercely and row boats and star in plays and none of this will matter one jot.

'Hello, Lorcan!' I say, sailing up to him, the energy still pulsing through me.

Lorcan's rheumy blue eyes rise slowly, drinking me in. The other visitors all seem to be hugging their loved ones – crying and clinging – although if they hold on too long the wardens tell them off or prise them apart, like prudish teachers at a sixth-form disco. My flame starts to dim. I'm slightly repulsed by it all. I don't want to hug him, the anger I've been suppressing suddenly rising upwards like a grizzly bear that's been poked with a stick, and yet I desperately wish I did. I look around the room, envy and judgement shaking themselves up into a toxic cocktail, and then slide myself into the uncomfortable plastic chair.

'You came then,' he says, voice drained of enthusiasm.

'Yes. Here I am.' My voice sounds high and staccato, like a children's TV presenter's on a piece of crackly archive footage. 'How are you?' I remember a play that me and a friend wrote at primary school, the 'dialogue' as we learnt it was called so bad it was almost impossible to say, however many times we tried to make it read like two people talking. That's how I feel right now.

'All right.' Those two syllables make me shiver. Lorcan hates plainness in all things. I'd expected some scorching put-down at the ludicrousness of my question, or an impassioned rant about his plight, but not this. I feel a flash of anger towards Mum. Whatever he's done, we should never have left him to get into this state: we know how fragile he is. His artistic temperament – it makes him feel things more deeply than other people. I'm blindsided by the sense that I'm all he's got, the realization making it almost impossible to suck the fetid air of the visitors' room into my crumpled lungs.

'You're not, though, are you, really?' I say, putting a hand out and then pulling it back, like a mouse after the kitchen crumbs spying a stalking cat. I'm way out of my depth, the blinding clarity of a few minutes ago nothing but a joke.

'Mustn't grumble,' he says, flashing an awful, unexpected smile at me, his teeth protruding, fang-like, from his thin face.

'It must be so horrible in here. Not being able to play your guitar, or watch films . . .' The look he throws me, through narrowed eyes, is a targeted missile, designed to precisely convey the utter stupidity of my observation. It's a look he's given me so many times in my life, and it echoes and reverberates through all those jagged bits of our shared past like a gust of air hitting a wind chime. Anger whooshes up inside of me – I'm all ready to roar at him, to tell him that he wouldn't be in here if it wasn't for his own self-destructive death wish, to remind him that he's not the only one who's paying the price. But as soon as the words start to rise up in my throat, they skitter straight back down again, just like they always have. 'At least you're halfway through. You'll be out by Easter.'

'I've missed you,' he says, his eyes softening, and I fight to keep myself safely walled up behind the anger. His gaze is a seducer's gaze, tempting me into feeling guilty for abandoning him. This is *us*, it says. We understand things no one else understands.

'You shouldn't have done it,' I say, my voice low and measured. 'You do know you shouldn't have done it?'

Mum has these old-fashioned green metal tins she's always kept on the kitchen shelf above the counter – salt, flour, sugar, tea, coffee. When I was little I would hate it when they got out of alphabetical order, would beg her to restore them to their rightful places. Maybe we can get through this if we can at least agree on the order of things. Lorcan stares at me, his eyes colder now.

'Yes, Mia, I do know that,' he says, looking around the room a trifle theatrically, and then down at his sorry self stuck on the orange plastic chair.

'Not just for you, Lorcan! You could have left him with serious brain injuries. It's a miracle he's all right.' And me, I think, but I can't get that part of the story out. It's almost like, because I was going to have an abortion anyway, I've got no right to feel sad. And yet I do feel sad. What does that mean? When the sadness creeps up, I need to tell it firmly that the net result was the same. It needn't lurk around.

'And I'm sorry for that. But there was a child involved.' His eyes are intense again. 'A baby.'

'Not now,' I say more quietly, not trusting myself. Not trusting him. I need to go, and yet my legs won't obey me.

'I only wanted to protect you.'

'Protect me? How the hell was that protecting me?'

'I'm telling you what the core of it was, Mia. I'm not defending what I did. It was primal. You won't understand until you're a mum.' He stares at me. 'If you're ever unselfish enough to live up to the job.'

A wave of nausea surges up inside me, my anger so huge, so blinding, that I can barely see him.

'Don't you dare tell me about being a parent. The way you've treated me and Mum—'

'You've always known, from the day I first held you in my arms, that you're the most precious thing in the world to me. I'm in *prison* thanks to . . . the blindness of my love for you. My American career's finished, do you realize that?'

A fierce-looking warden, his hair cut in a blunt grey bowl, turns towards our raised voices. I hiss out my next words, low and violent.

'Don't twist things to pretend you attacked Jim for me. You just can't control yourself. You can't grow up! You're not a partner or a father – you're just a horrible selfish brat of a child.'

Lorcan's even paler, his long hands trembling, his eyes

dark. My words have hit home: I can see them burning their way into him like I've thrown acid. I want this to stop, oh God, I want this to stop: I wish Bowl Cut would throw me out.

Lorcan's calm now, his meticulous precision reasserting itself.

'You were willing to murder your *own child* for the sake of your precious ascent to the dreaming spires. I don't know what happened to you, Mia, how we bred such a cold little ice cube of a girl, but somehow we did.'

I shove my chair backwards, the legs making a gruesome screeching sound as they scrape the floor, and stand up.

'You won't need to give it any more thought. As far as I'm concerned, I don't have a dad any more. You're not worthy of the name. You never were.'

Lorcan gives a slow, superior smile.

'I'm dead to you? Don't make a habit of it, Mia. You'll have a very unhappy life. Try and defrost that heart of yours before it's too late.'

'Trust me, you won't be around to see it.'

And with that, I turned on my heels, and left a whole chapter, a whole book, of my life behind.

At least that's what I thought I'd done.

Chapter Twenty

It looks at first like the new normal. Mum's on her ancient desktop when I get back, the streaks of silver more visible than ever as she distractedly pushes her hair out of her face, her bottom lip pinned by the jut of her front teeth. I know what she's doing without even seeing the screen: trawling endlessly through estate-agent websites, hoping that her very own Manderley will have somehow have come on the market at a knock-down price. I hug her hello and go to the kitchen to make us both a cup of tea, ignoring the doorbell when it peals out. She's nearer, I reason. Besides, it might break the unhealthy spell. I hear the door open.

'What is this?' she says, her voice rising like smoke from a blaze.

'What's happened?' I say, racing through, nearly spilling boiling water on myself in my haste.

'Mia . . .' she says, a shaking hand thrust towards me like a stop sign, her face blanched white. A bulky, uniformed man is framed in the doorway, his van parked on the kerb, hazards flashing.

'Madam, can you try to . . .' His voice is no more than noise. I can't breathe now, so faint I'm surprised I'm still upright. It's odd how calm I feel, all at the same time, almost as if I'm soaring overhead, observing what's going on. I scan the three letters, the flowers they've so skilfully woven together. There are chrysanthemums in there, roses and tulips too. MIA, it says, each letter large and ostentatious, pink and purple and white.

'Just go, OK?' says Mum, trying to push the door shut, the man still immovable, struggling to compute.

'So you don't want me to leave it then?'

'That's Mia,' she says, gripping my arm too tightly. 'My daughter, the one you've just delivered a funeral wreath for. Just get out.'

I hate the smell that hospitals have, that mingled stench of industrial disinfectant and sweaty bodies. It hits the back of my nostrils as soon as I get through the big revolving door of the monolithic white building and almost makes me gag. The reception area is thronged with people; apologizing profusely, I dodge my way past an old lady who's being pushed in a wheelchair, my eyes trained on the front desk.

'I'm looking for a Patrick O'Leary,' I say, breathless. 'He's on Carroll Ward.'

I sprint for the lifts, then race down a maze of corridors, sticky with panic. Finally – finally – I find the door.

'You know visiting hours are over in less than a quarter of an hour?' says the battle-weary Ward Sister, clocking my flushed face.

'So I need to see him immediately,' I say. But as I set off behind her officious, uniformed backside, I suddenly long for nothing more than to gobble up her excuse whole. It's all got too real. Even when Patrick's been vulnerable he hasn't been vulnerable – he's felt complete in his Patrick-ness. If he's broken, I'm not sure I'll be able to make it back.

I called him before I'd had any time to calm down, my words a gibbering stream of anger and terror. 'Slow down, Mia, slow down,' he said, and then, as he grasped what had happened, he started to swear. 'I'm so sorry,' he said, his voice breaking. 'I took you too close.' That's when I heard it: it was more than distress, his words were a dull croak.

The night before, he'd been grabbed from behind as he put his keys in the lock, beaten so badly that he was delivered here in an ambulance. The raid itself was a dead loss, revealing no more than a twisted little manipulator drilling through her scales, and a few short hours later, the wreath pitched up at our door, underlining the point. Stephen Wright is taking no prisoners, and he won't be kept a prisoner either.

'I'm coming now,' I gabbled, yanking my coat on. Mum was staring up at me from the sofa, her eyes wide and glassy, the manic energy she'd had on the doorstep drained away.

'Listen to me, Mia,' he'd said, a stern-sounding nurse in

the background telling him to hang up. 'You have to stay where you are.'

He rushed around a team of detectives from the investigation, and they sprang into action, bagging up and photographing the wreath, dispatching more officers to question the florist. He had nothing for them: the flowers were paid for in cash by a man with a baseball cap tipped low over his face; there was no CCTV in the shop. Mum and I weren't much better. Most of what I could tell them had already been diligently logged by Patrick over the preceding weeks. 'I've stopped seeing her.' I trotted the phrase out again and again, like a mantra, like it would ward off the evil spirits. I wanted to keep them from Mum most of all, couldn't bear the way the shock had made a mask of her face, even though Nick had come back and held her tight against the solid wall of his chest.

I watched them together, shock still telescoping me in and out of that icy detachment. At least I would see Patrick. I would see him in a matter of hours, and then the scattered pieces would cohere into some kind of whole. *I* would feel whole again.

But now I'm here, I realize that the looping thought was no more than a dummy popped in the mouth of a screaming baby. Things might be about to get a whole lot worse.

And there he is, purple bruises like squashed blackberries decorating his face. His lip is split, a bandage around his head, and his right arm is in a cast.

'Patrick!' I say, rushing to him. He attempts to lift his bandaged arm, then winces. 'Don't move.'

He tries to smile, but that too is agonizing. I want to lie down next to him, to somehow suck the pain away and melt his bruises – but instead I stand there, useless, hoping the horror in my expression won't add to his distress. '*Mean Girls* doesn't cover it,' he croaks. 'We really pissed her off. No, actually . . .' He pauses, gathers strength. '*You* really pissed her off. Jeez, Mia, are you like, the world's worst therapist?'

And there he is, utterly Patrick under the bloody blanket of savagery. I don't care any more. I rush forward, put my head against his chest, my tears soaking his horrible green hospital gown.

'I was so terrified of what they might have done to you.'

He tucks my hair behind my ear with his free hand, his split lip brushing against it for a second.

'And another thing, you're rubbish at playing hard to get.' I look up at him, my face a freeze frame of everything that's flooding into me, nothing held back. I don't want to be anywhere but here: I can't imagine when I'll ever start wanting to be anywhere but here. And I haven't felt that since – since then. Muffin love! says Lysette loudly in my head, and I try to hug him without causing more injury. I feel him tremble with pain, but he doesn't make a sound. I loosen my grip, but he pushes his bruised ribs back against me. 'Looks worse than it is,' he says, mouth still close to my ear. 'They're probably gonna let me out tomorrow or the next day. Give me your news.'

'I've ended it with Marcus.'

'Now you tell me,' he says, something that sounds a little like delight in his froggy voice. 'Course I'm in hospital.'

'And I'm probably going to have to get a job in McDonald's.'

'Stop whingeing. You'll rock that uniform.'

I take his bruised, clawed hand in mine. As if any of that stuff matters right now.

'It's my fault for trusting her.'

'Come on,' he says, smiling his disagreement. 'They're not messing around, these guys, and I took my chances with Gemma's information. *Information*,' he repeats, rolling his eyes. 'I should've stopped you seeing her, not encouraged you to try and get more.'

Now my anger's flooding back. I think of her sly little upward glance as she told me that I could redeem myself by becoming her mouthpiece.

'She seemed so – so *real* – when she told me.'

'She was weeping like a baby, apparently, but she totally denied she'd seen him. So did the teacher, and she's got absolutely no criminal connections as far as we can work out.'

'I just couldn't help myself.' Shame trickles through me – as if I need any more reminders of my shortcomings. 'She reeled me in every time.'

'Come on, Mia, enough of that chat. Stop whipping your-self. You know what you're doing.' He looks thoughtful. 'It's just possible that, despite my unparalleled genius, I'm the one who's missing something.'

I shake my head at him, teasing him with my eyes. I remember what he said the day of the vegetable Apocalypse, how judgemental I was. I get it now: I get the fact that you have to grab every split second you can find on the sunny side of the street.

'Patrick. For the love of God, leave it, at least for today!'

'Fair point.'

We sit there for a moment in silence, his good hand intertwined with mine, our fingers criss-crossing. He gently strokes the wells between mine, then reaches up to stroke my cheek. How can quiet feel this full? I'm the one who breaks it.

'Do you think she's the reason you got beaten up, or is it . . . do you think there are people on your team sending information back to Wright?'

I feel a shudder run through me as the words leave my lips. I can't give way to the fear. I have to believe it's no more than a warning, trust that the cheerful policeman stationed outside our house for the next forty-eight hours is no more than a precaution. None of the lead detective's calm, profes-sional patter reassured Mum: she's given in to the fear wholesale. I need to go back soon. The fact I came here in a police car only gave her a crumb of comfort.

'Hard to say. Don't worry about the guys taking care of

344

you. No one's gonna come after you, I'm sure of that, but they'll look after you.' He looks at me, rueful. 'I'm so sorry. We shouldn't have got here, but we had to try it. Last bullet.'

'Don't say that. You can't let them scare you off now.'

Patrick raises the hand that's not in a sling and draws a shaky circle around his mashed-up features. Both of us start laughing, and once I do I actually can't stop, the release of tension so unexpectedly delicious. 'I'm sorry . . .' I say, but he just smiles back, eyes soft.

'Look, I'll be there for Gemma's questioning next week and, trust me, it won't be easy for her. But we're running out of time and there's no sign of Daddy Dearest. It's costing hundreds of thousands of pounds. We'll probably have to accept the trial's doomed to collapse and start investigating again.' He shrugs. 'If they'll even let me.'

In that second I feel a surge of hatred for Christopher Vine that's so pure, so molten, it frightens me.

'You can't just let him win this.'

'Sweetheart, you of all people should not be saying that.' He shakes his head, his look dark. 'You say you feel guilty. How do you think I feel about them threatening you? That's on me.'

'But, Patrick, you're right! If you didn't have them on the rack they wouldn't be . . .' I can't think too hard about what they're doing. What they're – what he – is thinking. 'You've got to follow it through, whatever it takes.'

'You've changed your tune.'

'Yeah, well. It turns out I was tone deaf.'

Patrick tries to pull himself upwards. He hooks his feeble arm around my neck, and pulls me into him.

'Kiss me properly,' he mutters.

'I'll hurt you. And in case you haven't noticed, that nurse has got a touch of the Nurse Ratcheds about her.'

'Kiss me,' he insists, and I do.

I know I don't have long. I sit next to him, clutching his hand, hoping Nurse Ratched never comes back. Joy keeps creeping up on me, before fear gets it in a headlock. Did I really misjudge Gemma so badly? Was my sense that I understood her, that I was the one person who could scale the castle walls, nothing more than a self-serving cocktail of arrogance and projection?

'I don't want to go back out there,' I say, my voice low. 'I screwed this up so badly. I can't see the wood for the trees any more. I feel like I AM a tree.'

'In which case you're a very elegant willow,' he says, gently stroking my cheek.

'I mean it . . .' I say, very gently pressing myself towards his touch.

'You're an amazing therapist,' he says, his voice low. 'I've always got that about you. And I've seen you with her. It's real, she trusts you. But think about the soil SHE'S grown up in. What kind of tree are you going to be? A pretty warped, rotten one.'

'We're more than that, aren't we?' I say. It's too loaded. 'We're not equations. We're not just the sum of our past.'

Patrick gives me a long look. He hasn't forgotten.

'Of course not.'

I sit there without speaking, listening to the hum of medical equipment and the ranged voices of the other visitors, whole families crowded close around their loved ones' beds. I'd barely been aware of the sounds, squashed inside this tiny cubicle, my focus pin-tight on Patrick.

'There he is!' someone says in a loud Irish brogue. 'I know I've only five minutes, but, trust me, I'll make them count.' The cubicle curtains open with a loud whoosh, revealing a stout woman with a determined expression on her red-veined face, a large Tupperware box in her hand. 'Pat! The bus took an age.' Her gaze swivels to me, and I move backwards in my plastic chair, my hands coiling back into my lap. 'Are you a friend of my son's?'

'I am,' I say, standing up and extending a hand. No shrinking. 'I'm Mia.'

'A work friend, I'm imagining.' She grips my hand firmly, her smile tight. She's looking at my outfit: a pleated silk skirt, above the knee, with a scoop-necked T-shirt and a pair of pink Converse. She doesn't approve, this much is clear. She's wearing a plain, dark cotton dress, Catholicly cut to mid-calf, with a modest V of red flesh visible at the top and a gold cross suspended over her impressive mountain range of a bosom. Her hands, gnarled and swollen, grip the Tupperware box like it's a treasure chest. I look to Patrick. His dark eyes have got that woodland-creature quality to them, darting rapidly between the two of us.

'Yes, sort of,' I say.

He smiles at me, expression still nervy, and I grin back.

'Mum, Mia's more than a work friend.'

'Oh?'

He looks at me, and my smile stretches wider.

'She's my girlfriend.'

A rush of fear jumps out of my chest, *Alien* style, but then it springs back in on itself with equal force. God, when I think of the Cold War between Marcus and me when we first started dating – neither of wanting to lose face and be the one to declare it a relationship. I look at him. *We haven't even . . .* and he valiantly tries to smile back, mostly with his eyes.

'I am,' I say impetuously. 'It's lovely to finally meet you.'

'Likewise,' she says, voice clipped, narrowed eyes trained on me with the precision of a sniper's rifle.

'But I should leave you to it.' I look at Patrick. 'Call me later, if you're up to it.' He nods, gaze soft. 'Or text me.'

I do an odd little Mexican wave of a goodbye with my fingers, far too intimidated to risk breaching the gap between me and the bed. Mrs O'Leary's taken charge of the territory, a tank planted squarely on the battlefield.

'Bye, Mia,' he says.

I freeze for a long second, unable to force myself through the blue plastic curtain. I don't want to go back out there without him, into a real world that doesn't feel real any more. The loud chime from my phone startles all of us. I look down at it.

I didn't lie to you, Mia. It's the truth!! I need your help. Gemma xxx

That swaying, wobbling feeling, my legs barely holding me up. I peel my eyes away from the glowing screen.

'What is it?' he asks.

'Nothing. It's nothing for you to worry about.' I give him a flash of a smile. 'Just my mum.'

Delete. Delete, delete, delete.

Chapter Twenty-One

I sit in the Starbucks downstairs for a while, nursing a latte until it's lukewarm, waiting for the aftershock of Gemma's text to stop vibrating through me. I shouldn't have deleted it of course, should have forwarded it to the police, but it was instinctive. Who am I to hector him, tell him he has to plunge back into the woods, when every bit of me wants to run in the opposite direction, chop it – chop her – from my memory?

I fiddle around with my phone, Googling things that don't matter, aware of how big and gaping a hole work's left in my life. My life was big and noisy, but it was big and noisy like a circus tent, primed for a sudden disappearance. Eventually I give up, accept my curfew. I ring Mum from the back of the car. She snatches it up on the first ring.

'Mum, don't panic, I'm on my way.'

'Are you all right?' It's not the words, it's the sound of the words. She hasn't climbed back inside herself yet.

'I'm fine,' I lie. When is it that we start lying to protect them? I'm not sure I can remember a time when I didn't know how to do this, like I sucked it in when I first drew breath. It was Lorcan's gift to me, my own special Spidey skill.

'Mia, there's something . . .' She pauses, her breathing hoarse. 'Just come home.'

'That's what I'm doing, Mum!'

Let me be normal, and then I'll feel safe. Perhaps.

'OK, darling. I'll see you soon. Soon soon.'

'Soon soon.'

The lights are blazing when the car draws up. I thank the boyish PC a little too effusively, hoping he doesn't think I'm stuck up. I couldn't chat during the drive, didn't have it in me.

It takes a second before I believe my eyes. He's there in the hallway, almost as if he'd always been there and we'd somehow been blind to his presence. He's still tall and bony, but his outline has softened. He's stooped, his shoulders pushing forwards like an upside-down ladle. His hair is streaked with slivers of silver like Mum's, but they seem shocking to me, robbed of the chance to watch them creep into being.

'Why are you here?' I say, the words almost wedged in my throat. I turn to Mum, raging. 'Why did you do this?'

She's crying, hands held out in supplication.

'What if something happens? What if something had happened? If one of you was gone – he's your father, Mia.'

Then I see it, the burnished gold around his long, skinny wedding finger. The thing he never gave us.

'No. Get out. I don't want you in my life. I meant it.' I whip back towards Mum. 'Don't you think I've had enough – enough shit rain down on me, without you ambushing me with him?'

Lorcan steps towards me, and my hands fly up, pushing him backwards through the air between us.

'Mia, please, can't we all sit down and talk about it? As a family?'

'Are you mad? You are mad, I know that. Do you honestly think you can just walk back in here after twenty years and use a phrase like that?'

Little ice cube – that phrase haunted me for years. It would jump out at me at the most unexpected moments – job interviews, blind dates, my finals. Sometimes it would spur me on – righteous fury like rocket fuel – and sometimes it would paralyse me. Freeze me, just like it was designed to do.

'I'm sorry, Mia, you've every right to say that . . .' His voice, it's so long since I've heard his voice. Tears fill my eyes and I jerk my face away. I don't want him to see them, to think he's got any kind of purchase on me. 'What I did was unforgivable. But please will you at least let me speak to you?'

'No.' I look at Mum, making sure she knows she's got blood on her hands, bringing him here. 'My baby died because of you. I might never . . .' I stop, the stream of words running dry. 'No. I won't speak to you. Not now, not ever.

You lost the job.' Those blue eyes, so familiar to me, now surrounded by a deep network of lines. They're landing, my missiles, they're reaching their target. 'You never even wanted the job. Don't try and pretend now, when it's all got a bit exciting.'

'That's not true,' he says, his voice breaking. 'It's not true, Mia.' But by now my hand's on the latch. 'I understand why you're leaving, but please – you think I didn't get in touch because I didn't love you? It was the opposite. I was a coward. I couldn't face it, knowing there was no way back.' His voice is almost a whisper now. 'I'm so sorry.'

I turn towards him, the movement almost involuntary, something inside those broken syllables that punctures me. The 'sorry's back then were different, like a figure skater gliding across ice, the move perfectly executed and utterly superficial. No. Don't get sucked in, don't hear what some lost part of you longs to hear. I push against the door.

'Mia, don't go,' says Mum, yanking at my arm. 'He always knew, I always made sure he knew you were all right.'

I shake her off, my body bucking; I'm revolted by her touch in a way I've never been in my life.

I plaster a smile on my face as I pass the policeman, hating the feeling of being under house arrest. I'm not, I've got every right to get into my car, and I pull off quickly before he's got time to dart down the drive and start asking me questions.

I'm blinded by tears, no idea where I'm headed. I pull up

outside a rundown strip of shops to put my phone on silent – anything to stem Mum's incessant calling. As soon as I've parked my head whips round, my heart racing. No one's following me. I bash my hands on the steering wheel so hard they'll bruise, fury boiling over. How did I get here? I'm no better than the man who made me, all those smug little signifiers of a successful life swept away in one fell swoop. **Patrick**. His name flashes once, twice, three times before I pick up.

'Hi.'

'Mia, hey. Has something happened?'

He can read me. One syllable and he knew there was something wrong. Just for a second it feels like a straitjacket.

'What, other than the obvious?'

Why am I being like this? It all seems so pointless suddenly, this afternoon no more than a bubble formed by those ugly blue plastic curtains. *You little ice cube.* I look into the lit-up mouth of the convenience shop outside the car, watch a woman buying a packet of ten. Is she kidding herself she won't eventually smoke twenty, or is it all she can stretch to?

'I was fretting about how you seemed when you left. Though to be fair my mum can have that effect on women. She's not the sex police, despite first impressions.' I don't laugh. 'I mean when your mum called.'

'I thought your mum seemed nice.'

It's got one step worse than obsessing about Gemma: now I'm behaving like her too.

'Well . . . that's good,' he says, a note of hesitation creeping into his voice.

I wish I could find the strength to pour out the contents of the last hour, purge myself of it, but I'm too frightened – frightened that I'm worse than cracked, that I'm broken. It's too much of a risk, to both of us.

'Are you OK?' I ask him, deliberately softening my voice. 'How're you feeling?'

'Getting better by the second. I'll be out of here tomorrow, no problem. In fact – and this is your fault for getting me riled up about Christopher, so don't start giving me gyp for working – I've had a bit of a breakthrough. Well, maybe.'

'What?'

'The piano teacher. She's got the same name as a cot-death baby from the '70s. Might be a coincidence, but could be something way darker than that.'

'What, so she's not who she says she is?'

'Don't know for sure, but that's the theory I'm working on.'

'So Gemma was telling the truth.'

'Maybe.' I sit there in silence, my heart aching in my chest. No words come.

'You still there . . .?'

'I should go. Well done.'

'Thanks,' he says, his voice matching mine for flatness. 'I don't want to hurt you' – that's what I want to tell him, but that particular handful of words could mean so many different things.

'I mean it,' I say, my voice catching in my throat. 'Well done. I know you can do this.'

'I appreciate the vote of confidence.' It's his turn to pause. 'Mia . . .'

'I really have to go. Just need to get my head round it all. Let's talk properly tomorrow.'

I hang up, stare at the phone, almost willing her to call me. Nothing.

I shouldn't do this. I can't not. Annie answers on the first ring.

'Is she with you?' she asks, breathless.

'Sorry?'

'Gemma,' she snaps. 'Is she with you?'

'No. It's nine o'clock at night. Why would you think . . . is Gemma missing?'

That pause, that click – that sharp intake of breath like she's sucking in oxygen, not a toxin.

'She's not here . . .' she says.

I need your help. Why did I do that – just erase her with a swift, panicky tap of my finger?

'Could she be with a friend?'

'Whatever she might've made out to you, she doesn't really *do* friends,' says Annie, barbed. 'Not friends she keeps hold of any length of time. Certainly hasn't made any in the new school. I've tried anyone I could think of. *Nada.*'

'In that case I think you need to call the police. They could trace her phone.'

'Her phone's switched off.'

'Is it? She texted me a couple of hours ago saying she needed my help.' And I deleted it – I don't add the post-script. 'That's what I was calling to tell you. Annie, with the text too – don't you think it's time to call the police?'

Annie doesn't reply; all I can hear is her breathing, the smoke curling its way down into her tired lungs. I want to scream at her, shake her so hard she wakes up from her trance. 'It's *your* help she needs, Annie,' I say, forcing myself to keep going. I struggle for the next words, weighed down by the burden of what Patrick's just told me. Does she know that Gemma's story could be true? Even if she does, I can't betray the fact that the investigation is on to them. 'Do you think she's with her dad? Could he have taken her?'

That's when she starts to cry. They're odd things, her sobs – sharp and staccato, like she's fighting them tooth and nail. Or maybe they're entirely under her control, a convenient distraction from the question.

'Can you just come over here? Her room's like the *Mary Celeste*, TV blaring, iPad on the bed . . . you might see something I've missed. I don't want to push the panic button if we don't have to.'

The irony: Gemma was pushing the panic button on day one, those scars as shocking as any indecent exposure. My eyes flick involuntarily to the rear-view mirror, slide swiftly across it. I check the doors are locked for about the hundredth time. Her iPad's like her fifth limb: if she was going voluntarily, why wouldn't she take it?

'It would be completely inappropriate, you know that . . . let me send the police to help you.'

Patrick. I think of him lying there, all bandaged up and hurting. He doesn't need to be trying to negotiate this from his hospital bed. That was the reason for not calling him I sold myself anyway.

'No!' she says, voice shaking. 'Listen to me, it's not just Gemma. I've got the boys to think of. You don't know . . .' She picks out her words, enunciates each syllable like she's teaching me a foreign language I'm too dense to pick up. 'You don't know what they're capable of.'

MIA – those flowers, so elegantly woven together, pink and purple and white. I do know. If Gemma's worth so much to Christopher, if he's willing to risk so much to keep seeing her, then she's worth almost as much to them. *I'm his Achilles heel, Mia.*

'I get how frightened you are . . .' I cringe as the words reach my ears. My session voice has crept in, like I'm trying to squash the situation into something I can control, a mosquito lying dead under the flat of my palm. If I lose Annie, if I fatally alienate her, I'll lose Gemma too. I turn the key in the ignition. 'I'm coming now.'

Chapter Twenty-Two

I pull up outside the big white house, kill the engine. The lights are blazing at the tall windows, a gleaming 4 x 4 parked in the drive. No wonder Patrick's so infuriated that their life of luxury is proving so hard to take away.

I forced myself to text Mum before I drove here, told her not to worry about me, that I needed some time to myself. I nearly switch off my phone – every time her number flashes up I start to feel the jagged waves of aftershock – but I know that I mustn't leave myself that vulnerable. I look back up at the imposing house, fear starting to thrum through me. I can't give way to it, not now I've come this far.

Annie flings open the door before I get a chance to ring, her face pale and pinched. She's always been so well armoured, but not today. She's in velour sweatpants, her blonde hair twisted up tight on the top of her head, dark roots insistent.

'Thanks for doing this,' she says, standing aside to let me into the wide hallway. 'Do you want anything? Water?'

'That'd be great.'

The kitchen is vast, a big tiled island in the centre, top-of-the range appliances either side. My eyes lock on a wall of photographs as Annie busies herself with a complicated chrome dispenser, built into the fridge. School pictures: Gemma and her brothers, her standing behind them, slightly apart. A wedding: Gemma as a bridesmaid, the frilly dress looking like a bad choice of fancy dress, her smile more a judicious baring of teeth. And then, a holiday shot, the whole family together. Christopher, tanned and relaxed, has an arm flung around Gemma's shoulders, her beaming smile a total contrast to the poor imitation in the other shots. It's Annie's smile that looks forced now, her gaze pulling towards the two little boys in the front of the frame. It's badly composed, blurry even, and yet someone's decided it's wall-worthy. There are a couple of Christopher and Annie at formal events. She's ball-gowned, professionally made up, her smile never wavering. Their eyes are trained straight ahead: they're so disconnected from one another they could've been Photoshopped.

There's silence now, the water no longer ostentatiously jetting into my glass. I turn round. Annie's watching me, her eyes narrowed.

'I've got some white open.'

'Water's great, thanks,' I say too quickly.

'Let's go upstairs, shall we?'

I almost say no, almost turn on my heels, refuse to step further in, but something compels me onwards. **I need your help**. I heard you this time, Gemma.

I'd have expected Annie to have tidied up, to have tried to assert some control over her wayward daughter, but Gemma's bitten-into sandwich is still lying there, the TV playing some chaotic reality show I don't even recognize. Annie hits mute, both of us looking at the iPad lying discarded in the middle of her unmade double bed. The bedding is black, even the sheets, in total contrast to the sprigs of pink roses that decorate the wallpaper: I bet she's begged to have the room rescued from her tweenie taste. There's a shelf above her desk that groans with objects, the place where you can see her desperately trying to assert her real-time personality. There's a plaster of Paris monster mask, painstakingly painted in greens and blacks, fur stuck to it, and a couple of other eccentric home-made props – she's proud of what she does in that workshop. There's a vinyl copy of Radiohead's *The Bends* propped up on a stand like it's a precious artefact, and a pristine hardback of *Mr Nice* along with a couple of dog-eared paperbacks. The autobiography of a middle-aged, male drug dealer? It's not exactly required reading for thirteen-year-old girls. 'Me too,' screams the shelf. 'I'm still your little rock, even when another part of me is carving out monsters.'

'Have you tried getting into it?' I ask Annie.

'Yeah, I don't have the password.'

I sit down gingerly on the bed, suddenly feeling like an intruder. I think of Judith for a second, cringe inwardly. If I had any chance of saving my career, it's being sucked straight down the plughole now.

'I know this is a bit Judy Blume, but do you think she keeps a diary?'

Annie looks at me like I'm an Amish, and I've just trotted over here on a pony. You can see exactly where Gemma honed her ability to wither.

'I told you, she's dyslexic. It's all texts and keyboards.'

Her eyes keep jumping around the room, as if Gemma might suddenly materialize in a puff of smoke. I need to start hammering home the fact that it's not going to happen, that now is the time to get over her antipathy to the police and start accepting that they're the lesser evil.

'Annie, do you think Christopher's taken her?'

Patrick told me that, when they carried out the raid, she completely denied any knowledge of Christopher ever having been there, dismissed it as nothing more than police harassment, but if Gemma was telling the truth, she must surely have known all along?

'"Taken her . . ."' she says, the words dripping with sarcasm. 'Not sure that's strictly necessary. I want to hear your professional opinion. Do you think my daughter worships her dad so much that she'd rather live her life on the run than suffer living here with us?'

The TV momentarily hooks my gaze. Two girls in vest tops are having a pantomime row, their French-manicured fingers jabbing viciously at one another. It's surreal sitting here, the tension so palpable I can taste it in the back of my throat.

'She's dangerously loyal, no question. Part of the reason I understand it—' I look to her, apology in my eyes. 'Part of the reason I went too far is because I was like that myself when I was her age.' I can't go there, however hard it pulls on me right now. 'But she does love you, Annie. She's got the luxury of taking you for granted. You're the safe one.'

'You just saying that?'

I pause, check. The last thing this situation needs is more lies.

'No, she does. But it gets buried. It gets twisted.' My eyes have found another one of her props, a metallic skull fashioned out of wire and coat hangers. 'We've been working on it. Taking Christopher off his big, fat pedestal and valuing all of you.' I look at her, a shred of hope visible in her expression. She's a tough cookie – I'm sure she's not one for soppy cuddles and declarations – but I'm certain her love for Gemma runs deep. 'Her anger lands in the wrong places.'

She doesn't speak for what seems like ages, her gaze still roving the room, tracking all the scattered pieces of Gemma. I look around the room too, fear needling my flesh. Why doesn't she feel the urgency? My eyes land on that flabby white-bread sandwich, the edges curling unappetizingly, a pinkish tongue of ham lolling out. Should I say this?

'Annie, if she wanted to go with him, why would she

leave her room like this? And the iPad – it's surgically attached to her.' We look at each other, the seconds stretching out till they feel like days. I keep inching forward, like a rookie soldier in no man's land. 'That teacher – it turns out she was a Stephen plant after all.'

I watch her face, catching the look that lands before the one she pulls off the peg and tries on for size. She did know. A wave of disgust torrents through me: how could she do that to Gemma? Not just to Gemma, to any other Gemma who is some mother's precious thing. I mustn't say it – I've come too far to lose her now. Her eyes flick up to me briefly, then she reaches for the iPad.

'Just try,' she says. 'You might know her better than you think.'

I take it from her, grateful for anything that can provide a momentary distraction. I start to fiddle with the screen, wrestling with my feelings. I try not to judge my patients, whatever they bring to me: I need to do the same thing here – walk a mile in her nude Jimmy Choos. I bet she started out turning a blind eye – most likely the only thing she could do to protect her family from imminent destruction – then found there was so much to ignore that it became a permanent disability. And who am I – the Mia that's trapped between the walls of Christopher Vine's palatial home – to judge? I know more than anyone that, once you've crossed the line, it can swiftly become impossible to cross back. So why do I say it?

'You knew, didn't you?'

The words fall from my mouth against my will. Her blue eyes are blazing.

'No, not always. Not at the beginning. It all looks so sodding easy from where you're sitting, doesn't it?'

I make my voice soft. 'Not at all.'

'I started to *suspect*, I didn't know. Piano lessons were Chris's idea, before he left, not that I told the police that. Get her a proper hobby, he said, like they're something you buy.' She looks at the ranged objects on the shelf, looks back to me. 'If I hadn't let her go, let him see her, this would've happened weeks ago. I hoped her sessions with you would stop her wanting to go. I tell you what I did know – he was always gonna come back for her.'

Her eyes brim with tears.

'That's hard,' I say, the words so tiny and inadequate. I've been randomly tapping in four-number codes as we're talking, more as a distraction than with any expectation of success. The date and day of my birthday – all I was doing was giving my monkey mind something to play with, but suddenly the screen opens up. Relief, swiftly followed by fear so acute it makes me nauseous. I never told Gemma my birthday. How much do these people know about me?

'What did you do?'

'It was my birthday. I never told her my birthday.'

'Typical Gem. She'll have pulled it from somewhere.'

My skin feels clammy, my hands are shaking: I watch them from above, my pale fingers tightly gripping on to the gleaming rectangle. I need to get us through this, find out enough to track her down and get out. I don't even ask Annie if she wants me to be the one to look, I just start jabbing at the screen.

It's strangely bare – a few lonely games she's downloaded, some music (I don't look to see if Lorcan still merits a playlist), no email account. I don't trust it: she's cleaned it up, pared it back. I click on the green messages icon, spinning the screen so we can both see it. I thought there'd be bubble after bubble, like there was when she slyly angled it towards me, but there's barely anything here either.

Need my little rock, says an unknown number, sent this afternoon at 5 p.m. Annie snorts angrily as she reads it.

I know you do. *xxx*, comes Gemma's reply.

For real. It's time to get your skates on. No kisses, no 'Dad'. There's something so brutal about his stark diktats.

Love you, Daddy. Mum's gone to Westfield, even though we don't have any £$£!! xxx.

Meet me for dinner. Be there or be square. Tell Mum you're with a mate.

The next message is from Christopher too, half an hour later. It's almost the most chilling.

No more games. xx.

Annie's face: pain and fury duking it out. I reach my hand out, cover hers, even though it feels corpse stiff to my touch. She's got to stay with me.

'She's left this for you!'

'Yeah I know,' she says, a hardness in her tone that I don't buy.

'Annie, she's not just left a trail of breadcrumbs, this is a full-scale ordnance survey map! Even if she has gone with him, she wants you to find her.'

'Don't!' she says, pulling her hand away. 'Don't, OK? Despite all the evidence to the contrary, you don't know my daughter better than I do. If she wants to say fuck you . . .' Her voice starts to wobble. 'If she wants to say fuck you this much, then maybe it's time to let her.'

She sobs, a big, jagged sob that possesses her. I can't wait for her grief to subside; it could take forever.

'Annie, you've had years of her sticking two fingers up at you, I get how – how utterly impossible it must be to see the wood for the trees. I'm not saying this because I think I know her better than you, I'm just looking at the facts. Why leave the iPad behind, with only those messages, if she didn't want to be rescued? Why not spin you a line like he told her to, so you're not looking for her?'

She looks at me, eyes burning like a trapped fox's.

'To make damn bloody sure I've heard her?'

'No!' I shout, frustration boiling over. 'Gemma might be the most confused child I've ever treated. She thinks she loves Christopher more than anyone, but part of her absolutely bloody hates him. She's bright, Annie. She knows enough to be frightened of him.' I brandish the iPad, shoving the screen towards her face. 'You're right here, look: that message is all about you. She's holding you up to protect herself against him.'

'How can you know that?' she says, almost pleading.

'You know – we all know – how it feels to love someone and hate them too.' I hope she doesn't hear the tremor in my voice. Her eyes meet mine, the years pressing down on her like some kind of medieval torture instrument. I stare back at her, silently imploring her to find the strength for this final lap. 'She doesn't know where she starts and he ends. It's too scary to stand up to him. This is the best she's got.'

Annie pauses for the longest time.

'I think you should call her.'

'I thought you said her phone was off?'

She shrugs, half smiles. She was lying. The lies just keep stacking up, a bottomless pit. No, there will be a bottom – I just hope I don't reach it.

'We've fought a battle over her from the day she was born. If she picks up the phone to you she won't be choosing sides.'

I can't think, I can only act. I grab my phone from my bag, find her number. There's a missed call from Patrick – suddenly I wish with all my heart he was here. What made me think I could handle this? It rings, once, twice, three times. Just as I'm expecting the voicemail to kick in, preparing to plead with Annie to finally let me call the police, she answers.

'I knew you'd ring!'

'Gemma!' Annie's face collapses with relief as she hears her name. 'Where are you?'

'You can't help it, can you?'

'Can't help what?'

'You keep coming back to me,' Gemma says smugly.

'Gemma, please just tell me where you are. This isn't a game. I've seen the messages.' I desperately need to break through to her. I soften my voice, almost like I'm trying to hypnotize her, remind her what we've shared. 'Your dad telling you you're his little rock.' *He's manipulating you.* 'Are you with him now?'

She can't be, surely: she'd never have picked up. My eyes meet Annie's, her face now white and rigid. Gemma doesn't speak.

'Can you come and get me?' she says eventually, voice drained of bravado. 'I need you to come and get me.' She sounds like a little girl now. 'That's why I texted you.'

I smile at Annie, try to give her hope.

'You're not with your dad?'

'He was meant to be here, but he's not. I was late. I went to Westfield.'

'You went to Westfield?' Was she looking for Annie? 'Is that where you are now?'

'No. He told me to get a cab out here. It's further than Twickenham even.'

'What do you mean? What, a service station?'

'Yeah. I'll text you where it is. Just come and get me, Mia. I'm not lying to you. Wasn't lying last time either.'

'I know,' I say, my voice gentle. I look at Annie and decide it's safer not to mention her to Gemma. 'I'm coming now.'

'OK. I've got to go now, Mia. My phone's nearly out of juice. Come quick.'

Chapter Twenty-Three

It's like an alien city, a biosphere from some time in the future when we've forgotten how to have a soul. Harsh strip lighting bathes it yellow-grey; a half-empty Costa Coffee – bleary-eyed lorry drivers getting their late night fix – sits next to a burger joint, the rancid, fatty smell competing with the synthetic lemon disinfectant from the nearby toilets. This is no time to be composing some pretentious ode to modern Britain – the second set of toilets is exactly where I'm heading for. That's where Gemma texted to say she'd be waiting, and Annie and I decided not to waste time questioning her decision: at least she'd be hidden away. I tried, yet again, to convince Annie that the police should be the ones to pick Gemma up, but she begged me not to call them, and the truth is, I didn't take too much persuading. Gemma's been through enough today without being shoved in the back of a squad car and thrown into an interview room, questions firing at her from all directions. She sounded so vulnerable on the phone, ready to give up the fight and tell me what Patrick and his team need to learn. I know Gemma well enough to know that official channels will make her silent and mutinous. Not that any of it matters right now: I'm not Patrick's source, nor Gemma's therapist, I'm just a person who cares deeply – too deeply – about making sure she's OK.

I feel a deep shiver of unease as I cut through the belly of the place. Annie asked that I do this solo, save Gemma from being ripped in two by choosing between them, yet again. But now that I'm here, alone and unprotected, I'm starting to remember how many lies and half truths she's scattered these last few weeks, a trail of breadcrumbs that I've dog-gedly followed. When my phone flashes up at me with Patrick's name it takes all my strength not to answer. I just need to get through this, then I can call him. I pause a second, send him a single kiss, then push my way through the random stragglers who are milling around.

I push open the heavy door, my heart thumping hard in my chest.

There she is, framed by the pockmarked mirror, standing alone in the empty toilet. Our eyes meet in the dingy glass, her face pale and set, a tube of cheap-looking cherry lip balm held up to her mouth like she's readying herself for a night out. How is it that she looks older and younger all at the same time?

'Found you!' I say, relief flooding my body.

'You took a-ges.'

'I'm here now.' I step towards her, and she turns to face me, her vulnerability almost palpable. 'Do you need a hug?' I say, choking up. She nods, her sharp chin jutting downwards, and I open my arms wide. She kicks aside the tatty old rucksack that she's got at her feet, steps into them, her heart hammering as hard as mine. She feels jerky, a frightened jack rabbit. 'You're safe,' I murmur, my hand stroking her hair. I want to envelop her, keep her cocooned. 'Your mum's in the car. We're going home.'

I pull away now, the sense of urgency flooding back, but Gemma seems almost rooted to the spot.

'Thing is, Mia, my dad will always come and find me,' she says, her voice little more than a whisper. The same words can be sculpted into so many different shapes: there's no triumph in that statement now.

'And you've got a voice,' I say. 'You know what you want. You didn't want to go with him, and you haven't – it was so brave of you. But Gemma, please, let's go and find your mum now. We can talk about all of it when we're in the car.'

Gemma looks back at me, blank and impassive. I feel helpless suddenly, held hostage by my own arrogant belief I could pull this off. How can I sustain an emotional connection in this bleak wasteland, the two of us stranded between a dripping tap and a scratched-up tampon dispenser? We've strayed so far from the safety of the four walls of my room. Her eyes pull back towards the smudgy mirror, far away from me.

'He's taking me to America again.'

'Gemma, come on—'

'He thinks I like Disneyland, but I'm too old really. Jake would still like it.'

Two more minutes and then I'm calling Annie. No, not Annie. Patrick. I'm going to give this one last try.

'Jake's seven, isn't he?'

I keep my voice light, unthreatening, all the time tracking her reflection. Her eyes are cloudy, her grip shaky as she forces the pinkish sheen onto her dry, pale lips.

'How do you know that?'

'Everything I could find out about you, I found out. I care about you.'

'Yeah and I found out everything I could about you,' she says triumphantly. 'Not cos I cared. Knowledge is power, Mia, everyone knows that. Anyway,' she adds, voice so soft I can barely hear her, 'you didn't care about me, you cared about your job. And your dick boyfriend. *His* job.'

She knows it in her bones – she knew about me and Patrick long before I did. Poor Gemma: her curse is to always know too much.

'That's not true. Do you think I'd be here – risking my career, risking pretty much everything . . .' My voice is rising now, fear and exhaustion getting the better of me. 'If I didn't care about you?'

Gemma stares at me, face deliberately blank, eyes stripping me down. The moment seems to stretch forever. She leans down, unzips the bulging rucksack.

'I can't go with you, Mia. I have to give him these.'

Papers. Reams and reams of papers, numbers closely typed. Patrick was right all along.

'Gemma . . .' I say, the words hard to liberate, fear closing my throat, 'do you know how important these are?'

Of course she does. She shrugs with that infuriating fake nonchalance.

'He told me to keep them at school. It was the safest place.'

'The day he left? When he dropped you off?'

She looks away.

'My locker was a state anyway. Bit more crap in there. No one knew.' She looks back at me, defiant. 'They never cleared it out when I left.'

We need to get out of here. She needs to want to get out of here. If she doesn't, he'll always be swooping overhead like that eagle she imagined, waiting to spirit her away.

'Gemma, I know how much you love him, I really do. It's not wrong for you to love him.' I force her to look at me. 'But I want you to love you too! Like your mum loves you, and your brothers. Everything you've done today tells me you don't want to go with him. You want a normal life. You deserve a normal life. You can love him without giving him everything, Gemma.' The truth of it fells me, tears streaming down my face. 'You're not his life support. You don't have to keep him safe from harm.'

That's when she collapses onto me, her slight frame racked with sobs, her foot viciously kicking out at the rucksack, papers flying across the sticky floor. Maybe it's the force of my wanting it for her, but it feels as though his hold on her is draining out of her.

'I love you, Mia,' she says, her face buried in my chest.

'I love you too,' I say.

'Don't leave me again. Promise you won't leave me.'

Can I promise that? I wish I could. She doesn't deserve any more lies.

'You'll always be part of my heart. Always.'

'Is Mum really angry with me?'

'No. She just wants you home. It's time we went and found her.'

We pull apart, finally ready to go, but before we reach the door it starts to swing open. It's a miracle really that it's taken so long for anyone to come in here. A miracle or a nightmare? Because there, right in front of me, stands Christopher Vine.

Chapter Twenty-Four

Blood swirls and rushes around my body, my legs like jelly. I surreptitiously hold on to the wet sink unit, keeping myself steady. Gemma's face lights up, instinctive, but her legs don't carry her towards him.

'Daddy!'

He stops in his tracks, surveys the scene. It's his eyes that get to me. They're a deep blue – ice blue – alive with rampant calculation. He misses nothing, and yet he refuses to look at me. He takes in the scattered papers, looks back at Gemma, his jaw tight and clenched.

'What you playing at, Gem?' I can hear that same Northern-lite lilt that Annie has, his tone deliberately, chillingly, calm. Despite everything he looks freshly laundered: dark jeans and a blazer, a pristine white shirt underneath. He really is the display model: there's no heartbeat there. 'I'm watching you,' he says, not turning his head towards me. 'Don't try any GI Jane bullshit. We're done.

You can go back to asking overpaid cunts what they dreamed last night.'

I recoil at the word, the violence of it. It's a calculated move: he's grinding us both under his hand-stitched leather heel and telling us who's boss. I force myself not to react.

'I'm not playing, Daddy.'

'Then what've you been doing all day – fannying around buying lipstick?' There's something so icky about the insult, the way he's hacking at her barely budding sexuality.

'Maybe she was frightened,' I say, unable to stop myself.

'Maybe no one asked you for your opinion. Maybe my daughter would have been a lot better off if you hadn't come marching into her life telling her what to think. Special branch of the thought police, are you?'

It's the first time he's looked straight at me, eyes glittering with dark power.

'She didn't do that, Daddy,' says Gemma, voice childlike and shaky. 'She took care of me.'

'No. *I* took care of you. I always take care of you even when I'm not here. I'm the one who looks after you. You know that.'

'No you didn't!' I say, the foolish words tumbling out of me before I can stop myself. 'You made her lie for you. You put her in terrible danger. What kind of father does that?'

I regret it the second I've said it. Gemma sobs, the sound strangled and broken, and my hand reaches out uselessly into the space between us. Christopher steps towards me, visibly enjoying the way I instinctively press myself backwards against the sink. He draws out a knife, the blade gleaming and winking in the yellowy light, then steps back again, his point made.

I silently curse myself: how is it that even a wreath woven into my own name wasn't enough to make me admit my limitations? I don't want to die here. Now, finally, I understand what Mum was trying to make me understand on the doorstep. Their tired, lined faces as I slammed out of the house, self-righteous fury writ large. Please don't let it be the last time I lay eyes on them.

Gemma's frightened eyes dart towards me – a warning – then swivel obediently back towards him.

'It's time to go, sweetheart. Car's out the back. We've got a route out. Got to be quick now.' He's holding her thin arms, something between an embrace and an assault. She looks at him, those big, expressive eyes full of competing emotions. He cocks his head. 'Daddy knows best,' he says, his semi-ironic twang telling me it's a lifelong phrase. He probably whispered it in her pink conch shell of an ear when she was a baby – an intoxicating lie of a lullaby. Gemma tilts forward with her head bowed, leaning into him so he can trap her in his arms. He's won.

Then she looks up, face plaintive.

'I want to stay with Mum,' she says, her voice a thin whisper.

My heart leaps up into my throat.

'No you don't,' he says, utterly calm. 'They've been

turning you against me, I get it. But it's you and me now.'
He grins at her. 'Lone Ranger and Tonto.'

'Oscar and Felix,' she says softly.

'Bonnie and Clyde,' says Christopher, quick as a flash. It's
another well-worn routine this one. I force myself to stay
silent. He links his arm through hers. 'Chop chop.'

'I don't want to go!' she says, voice rising. 'I'm sorry,
Daddy. I'm sorry. I love you. I love you so much.'

She's sobbing, her face a wet mass of snot and tears. I
direct a small smile in her direction, willing her to stay strong.
Christopher's face spins towards me, his strong jaw pulsing,
eyes almost black now.

'Enough!' he says, grabbing her roughly. 'I thought you
were sharper than that, Gemma. Thought you'd inherited a
bit of nous from your dad.' She's shaking her head, eyes full
of desperation. 'They've brainwashed you, sweetheart. We'll
get it all straightened out.'

He lets go of her, stuffing the mess of papers in the rucksack and thrusting it towards her like a battering ram. He
can't resist even the slightest opportunity to assert
control.

'Gemma,' I say, gabbling, 'if you start screaming, someone
will come and help you. There are loads of people out there!'

'She's not going to pull anything like that,' says Christopher,
dismissive. 'She knows enough about her dad to behave
herself.'

Gemma's eyes are wide, even though her mouth is firmly
shut, her twig-thin body no longer resisting his powerful

grip. There's nothing more I can do until he's out of my sightline. I hold her gaze. 'I love you,' I mouth. So stupid. Christopher catches it, his eyes flashing with rage.

'I'm not finished with you,' he says, stepping towards me.

'Don't you think you've given her enough nightmares for one lifetime?' For some reason it catches on something, stops his progress. He looks back at Gemma, her frightened face, her body shrunk small, something shifting in him as he takes it in.

'Gem . . .' he says, almost vulnerable. But before he can say more, the door blasts open. It's not a hallucination. It really is Patrick, battered but determined, a phalanx of police behind him.

'Found you,' he says, glancing at me before his eyes fix on Christopher. 'Do the honours.'

A detective claps handcuffs on Christopher. 'I'm arresting you . . .' The words run on, no more than background noise, as I allow myself to collapse into Patrick, every fibre of my being still alert to Gemma. 'Found you too,' he says, holding me close with his good arm. 'Traced your phone. You don't get to dump me that easily.'

'Thank you,' I say. 'Thank you for not giving up.'

Christopher is quiet now, the knife meekly handed over. Gemma's crying, watching it all unfold. I stay near, but not too close – I want to spare her another tug of love.

'Can I go with him?' she says, her cheeks red raw with

tears. 'Let me go with him. Just as far as the car.' She looks at the police team and then at me, her face a naked appeal. 'I just want to say goodbye to my dad.' She looks at him. 'I want to say goodbye.'

Christopher looks back at her, all bravado sucked away. His face is as soft as melting wax, blue eyes brimming with tears. She's right – he does love her. The tragedy is, that for a man like him, love is always first and foremost a weapon. 'If I come with her . . .' I say. Patrick and the lead detective exchange glances, nod.

'No long speeches,' says the detective, his gruffness a cover. I know it's got to him too. 'You just see him into the car.'

'It's not like you won't see him again,' I tell her quietly. She looks at me, something unreadable in her eyes. I've lost her for now. 'Your mum's out there too. She's waiting to go with you in the other police car.'

The rucksack's already been bagged up, the papers safely stowed. We make our way across the car park, Gemma walking close to the policeman leading Christopher. He's talking to her, but I can't make out the words. Patrick loops his good arm through mine, the feel of it all that's keeping my knees from giving way.

He must've spotted the car first, heard the wheels squealing – living so long on the run, he had become perfectly attuned to danger. He broke from the policeman who was leading him. Still in his handcuffs, he shoved Gemma so hard she fell to the ground, out of harm's way. There was no time left for him to save himself. Or maybe he felt he was beyond saving.

It was a single bullet. A single shot from a gun that would never be found. A few brief seconds to extinguish Christopher Vine forever.

JUNE

Chapter Twenty-Five

I'm sitting on Mum's bed in my pyjamas, my knees drawn up under my chin, a mug of tea warming my hands. The room's punctuated by open cardboard boxes, little bits of her life poking out like moles burrowing up from the soil.

'Mum, it's a month away,' I say. 'You haven't even exchanged.'

'We'll exchange by Wednesday, the solicitor says. I'd rather get a head start.'

What she's really saying is that she'd like to at least have the illusion of control. I get that. I stroke her arm, the skin looser than it once was, but still smooth. She's a very elegant woman, my mum, even if she downplays it. She's wearing a white chemise over some tartan pyjama bottoms, her hair pinned up in a bun. After everything that's happened, I'm perversely grateful for my homeless state, my watertight excuse to spend this time with her.

'I hate that you have to do this.'

'I know,' she agrees, her knees pulling up to mirror mine, 'but it's happening. We can't wait for the whole sorry situation to be unravelled.'

'Patrick's doing his best!'

I'm still at that infatuated stage where I jump on any excuse to say his name out loud. It's funny: the world seems so black and white right now, either wonderful or horrible.

'It does sound like Wright will get his day in court, doesn't it?' She's right: the cache of papers is what's really clinched it for the prosecution. Her sense of triumph starts to fade almost immediately. 'I can't stop thinking about that poor child,' she says, encasing my hand with hers. I nod, not trusting myself to speak.

'I should get going,' I say, jumping down from the bed, skittish as a cat. She looks at me, guilt shining in her ink-flecked eyes. 'I'll be OK.'

I've just got an address, a house in a lane somewhere outside Cambridge. I thought about Googling it, giving myself an early warning about the kind of life he's living, but I decided to fly blind. It's a shock, rolling up to the wrought-iron gates, a long drive leading up to a large, imposing brick house. Could you even call it a mansion? It's modern – ugly-beautiful, with a complicated water feature that runs down its tall grey façade. My brain's trying to kick in, control the situation with its relentless observations and judgements. I breathe in, breathe out, my hands gripping the wheel, the knuckles white and jumpy. I hit reverse, scoot backwards into the lane, stick the hazards on. They tick loudly, irritatingly, like a metronome. Patrick answers on the first ring.

'Tell me why I'm doing this,' I snap, no spare capacity for pleasantries.

'Seems from where I'm sitting you're doing it cos you can't not,' he says. 'I'm not Mystic Meg, so I can't give you a definitive answer, but that's my guess.'

It's true. When I close my eyes, it's not Christopher's crumpled, bloody body that I see, it's Gemma's face.

'Where *are* you sitting?' I ask, gentle now, the wind blown out of my sails.

'On my mum's sofa. She's doing a roast.'

'Can she hear us?'

'Mum, can you hear us?' he shouts.

'Not a word, Pat,' she shouts, suspiciously quickly.

'Don't worry. She's a fan.'

'Of yours.'

'Yours too,' he says more quietly. 'She's not got your natural charm, is all.'

He sounds so Irish in that moment, his voice dipping and curving around the phrase like a roller-coaster zooming round a track. Every new piece of him I uncover feels like a nugget of treasure – something to covet, admire, hold up to the light.

'I'll see you tonight,' I say, determined to do this, then find myself incapable of cutting him off. 'I . . .'

Silence hangs.

'Yeah?'

'I'll see you tonight,' I say again, hanging up quickly before I can find more excuses.

He's framed by the doorway, his lanky form stooping forward, not a comma but a question mark. I stare at him, both of us frozen, and then he breaks the spell, striding down the driveway towards me on long, denim-clad legs.

'Mia,' he says quietly, his pale eyes watery with emotion. 'Come here, petal.' His shoulders drop a little as I stay still. 'Only if you want to.'

Something that I can't quite name drives me forward into his arms. A lump rises in my throat. He smells the same; it's the scent he always had when I snuggled up to him, still rising up from beneath the layers of washing powder and expensive shower gel that his new life has painted over the top.

'Welcome,' he says, his eyes never leaving my face.

'Impressive,' I say, pulling away sharply, a stab of anger assailing me as I think of Mum piling her modest life into cardboard boxes from the corner shop.

'Long story,' he says. 'Caroline's disappeared herself.' I give him a questioning look. 'She's your stepmother.'

'She's not,' I snap, my eyes burning as I look at his left hand, the gold ring encasing his skinny finger. 'She's your wife.'

He shrugs the jutting wings of his bony shoulders, *mea culpa*. He married someone. He never married Mum, never made us the Enid Blyton version of a family that I longed for, then tossed his so-called principles to the wind once the big house was part of the equation. Why did I even come here?

'I've booked a table for lunch at the pub.' He must see something in my face. 'It's not a pub pub. I wasn't trying to palm you off with a ploughman's.' I still don't smile. 'And I've been teetotal for six years' – he looks up into the soupy grey sky – 'five months and three days.'

'Congratulations,' I say, my voice pancake flat. It's another blessing he failed to bestow on us. I feel a hot starburst of that old, familiar shame: did he not love us enough to step up and give us what we so desperately needed from him?

'Mia, I meant what I said. I'm so sorry.' He examines me in the aftermath of the word, looking for a sign it's landed. 'I'm honestly so sorry for not . . . not being better. For not being what you deserved.' I stare at him, no words coming, my eyes fixed on his face, so familiar and so other all at the same time. Silent tears roll down my face. 'Darling, come inside. I'll make us some tea.'

I blindly follow him into a well-appointed kitchen, perching on a worn green-velvet sofa that's more shabby chic than second hand. He brings me a mug, leans over me to hand it to me, something in his face that looks a bit like terror.

'Sit down,' I say, like it's my house, not his. He folds his long body onto the sofa, the zigzag of his posture still utterly familiar to me. It's how I feel about Patrick in perfect reverse. With Patrick I'm still seeking out all the fragments that coalesce and make him so utterly him: with Lorcan they're assailing me, a million tiny reminders – a whole life I thought I'd lost forever, like an ancient winter coat that you chance upon in the darkest recesses of the wardrobe.

'I'm so . . .' He pauses, the energy quivering between us. 'I'm so glad you got in touch.'

'Yeah, well . . .' I'm fighting an internal battle here, and I'm fighting it hard. 'Is Caroline some kind of hedge fund power bitch then?'

I look around the cream kitchen, searching for the personal touches. There's a neon installation above our heads, a heart with an arrow through that I'm guessing glows red when it lights up. There are some photographs on a chrome table in the opposite corner, but I can't make out the images from here, and I'm grateful for that. When we cut someone out, some magical part of us imagines they're preserved in that moment, like a sardine lying flat in a tin. I know I've been like that with exes – moving on, never casting so much as a glance behind me. But the truth is, we're not responsible for animating the world. When we shut our eyes, it carries on regardless.

'Why do you say that?'

'All this,' I say, my stiff hand slicing into the air around me like a karate chop.

Lorcan smiles, the lines around his eyes crumpling like wrapping paper.

'You don't have much faith in your dad, do you?' My face. 'Understandably. No, this is all me. Once I'd adjusted my expectations . . .' He smiles again. 'Unless you're Mick

Jagger, rocking into your dotage is not a good look – I found I could make a pretty good living.'

'How?'

'I've written some pretty major hits for other artists. Not under my own name. I wanted to keep the two things separate . . .' His expression speaks to something complicated. Another stab of anger: did he not want us to know, in case we came after him for his hard-earned cash? 'I've done quite a bit of commercial composition too. Have you seen that silly advert with the cows slow dancing in the buttercups?' He hums the tune, even his humming melodious, and I can suddenly hear it's his – that amazing ability to stitch a tune together in such a way that it lodges itself in your heart. I've heard that song time and time again, and yet I never heard it.

'Well done,' I say. I hope he knows I mean it.

He looks sheepish.

'I knew . . . I knew my parents were still paying your school fees, and then helping out when you went up to Oxford – they were very proud. Trust me, Mia, I didn't have much for the first few years.'

'So how did it change?'

I check myself. My therapist voice has crept in.

'I guess I got over my rock star pretensions. I couldn't go back to the States, not with a criminal record, and I never set the charts alight here. But if you're composing, you can do it from anywhere.'

'It sounds like it's all worked out rather marvellously,' I say, anger seizing me again, a tornado depositing me a million miles away from him. *Little ice cube* – it wasn't just him who got thrown into jail.

'Mia . . .'

'I don't know if I can do this,' I say, voice high and reedy. It's too late now, surely? If we try and put something back together all we'll see is how broken it is, a makeshift monument to what's been irrefutably lost. As I start to stand, Lorcan's arm shoots out, barring my way.

'Mia, don't leave.' His voice cracks. 'Not when I've only just found you.'

'You *didn't* find me,' I say, hot tears springing up. 'And there was no finding to be done. I was there. I was always your daughter.'

'Were you?'

'You don't stop being someone's child . . .'

'I thought that's what you wanted. Never to lay eyes on me again.'

'Don't you dare try and make it my fault.'

'I'm not,' he says, impassioned. 'Darling, I'm not. This isn't an excuse, or an explanation. I was ashamed.'

'You should've been,' I say, looking down at the tiled floor, the words guttural, dredged from the depths.

'Yes, I should've been,' he agrees. 'But I was too far gone.'

'What do you mean?'

'I always felt like a fraud.' His gaze is far away now, lost in the past.

'How were you a fraud? With us' – *us*, it catches in my throat – 'or with your career?'

'All of it, Mia. Your grandparents disapproved of the way I lived my life, but they always bailed me out. I was playing. I always knew that.'

'Play' is not a word I'd ever have associated with them. They're Anglo-Irish, old money, high Catholic – everything is strictly rationed, even love. Lorcan was an only too, squeezed out of their joyless marriage. He was abruptly dispatched to boarding school when he was seven, tightly clutching hold of Mr Trunk, his toy elephant. Mr Trunk came to a bad end, flushed down the loo in week one, a story which always gave me nightmares when I was small. No wonder he learnt to cut himself off with such brutal efficiency.

'But you made it.'

'Yeah, and look what happened as soon as I did,' he says with a rueful shrug. 'I'm sorry I was such a grade A fuck-up.'

'What finally made you stop?' And why didn't you come back when you did is what I really want to ask. Not ask – plead, demand. Does he hear the second half of the sentence? I feel like I'm howling it into the silence.

'I split up with a girlfriend. Actually she left me. I was feeling totally sorry for myself, drinking a bottle of whisky a night, renting a room in a house stuffed with twenty-some-things.' He looks straight at me. 'Now *that* made me miss you. I had this fantasy you'd come home one night with one of those girls. Reappear from nowhere . . .' He smiles, blue eyes twinkling. 'The Abominable Snowman.'

'In that case, why didn't you just ring?'

I'm saying it for show – the weird thing is, I understand perfectly. The fantasy would've been so much easier to indulge: the mundane and painful reality of making reparation, if it were even possible, would have been too hard for him.

'I borrowed a car from one of them. Borrowed – I nicked his keys. Crashed it into the front of Peckham Budgens.' And I laugh. God, it feels good: I can breathe again. 'I'd been late with my rent enough times that he was feeling vindictive. I spent a night in the cells, staring at the walls, inhaling the stench of it. Do you remember the smell?' I nod, the memory of that fetid air rotten in my nostrils. 'Thank you for coming then,' he says, taking my hand, both of our eyes filling with tears.

'Go on,' I say eventually.

'It was rock bottom. I couldn't fake it any more.' He smiles. 'I got on with it.'

'Not all of it . . .' I say, my voice little more than a whisper. I scrub at my eyes. I don't want this. Anger's better than this.

No, no it isn't. I think of Patrick – sense him – make a vow to myself that's more a feeling than a dry stack of words. Lorcan's watery eyes rake my face.

'I haven't got the answer, petal, I wish I did. I should've sought you out, begged you to forgive me. Don't think I didn't lie awake at night thinking about it, but something always stopped me.' He pauses. 'What I tried to say to you on your mum's doorstep was true. It was because I loved you, not because I didn't. I was always proud of you, even from afar.'

Mum wrote to him every Christmas, it turns out. It felt like a betrayal when she first admitted it, but it doesn't any more. I reach my hand out, my fingers spidering across his palm as if they've got a life of their own.

'OK.'

He looks at our hands with a sheepish kind of delight, then looks back up at me.

'I had this other fantasy, that I'd be dying and we'd be reunited. And we wouldn't be able to believe we'd lost all that time when we loved each other so much.'

I stand up abruptly.

'But that's so stupid! When you had it in your gift to pick up the phone and give us that time . . .' I sit back down heavily, take a gulp of freezing tea. 'That's disgusting. The tea.'

'Let's start again, shall we?' he says, crossing the kitchen and putting the kettle on.

He was right about the pub, there's not a ploughman's in sight. It's a beautiful old inn, with a cosy, dark-wood interior. Even though it's early summer, it's pouring with rain, and there's a fire blazing in the grate. The ruddy-faced manager comes rushing over when he spots us.

'Hello there, mate,' he says, pumping Lorcan's hand. 'No Caroline today? Who's this then?'

Lorcan's eyes rest on me for a few seconds.

'My daughter,' he says, the words a little broken. 'Mia.' I'm so glad he said it that way round, so it didn't sound like an afterthought.

'Your daughter?' He looks between us. 'Yeah, no, I can see it. Come and get yourselves settled in,' he says, leading us towards a corner table near the fire. 'Heard your song on the telly the other night.'

I can see Lorcan quietly preening.

'Really?'

'Yeah, some kid with frosted tips was belting it out on *The Voice*.'

'It was a massacre!' says Lorcan dramatically.

'Most certainly was. Good tune though.'

'You're too kind. Darling, what do you want to drink? I'll have a lime and soda, and – tell you what, Gavin, get the bar staff a round on frosted tips.'

He's still Lorcan – still the Pied Piper, even with blood, not whisky, flowing through his veins. He looks over the menu, insists I have steak. 'You're pale,' he says. 'You need feeding up.' I don't argue, decide to simply enjoy letting him parent me, even if it's only for this one, strange day. He met Caroline in AA, he tells me. I've seen photos, so I've already rid myself of the nightmare that she's a Russian twenty-something with a pneumatic body and a five-year plan. She sounds like a kind, stable woman who's had her own dragons to slay. He asks me about Nick, teasing me for details. He met him briefly that night, but it was hardly the time for small talk.

'Just didn't see your mum with a baldie. She's a very beautiful woman.'

'His baldness is not the point of him, Lorcan.' Will there ever be a time when I reclaim 'Dad'?

'Mmm.' I can tell that on some crazy level he's jealous. Would Mum be a little bit pleased, or would it just infuriate her?

'He really looks after her,' I say pointedly. 'He worships the ground she walks on.'

'So she's the star?'

'Does someone *always* have to be the star?' I ask, waspish. Surely what we want is balance? I think about what Patrick said to me when we were being rained on in King's Cross. I don't want him to make me a star, and then lose interest when he finds I'm just another civilian.

'Trust me, Mia, someone's always the star.'

'So, what, you're the star with Caroline?'

'In a way,' he says, smiling to himself. I guess it's a relief on some level that he's not had a complete personality transplant. There's a part of him that will always be a child, always be that little boy who watched Mr Trunk get flushed down the bog and vowed he'd never be made so vulnerable again. I feel a little internal shudder, a reminder that the things we hate the most in other people are the things we secretly know to be our own demons.

'Yeah, I don't think that's ever been carved into a stone tablet. Mum loves Nick just as much as he loves her.' Thinking about them – their earnest struggles to protect their small, precious life – makes me feel overwhelmingly sad. 'They're having a really hard time right now.'

Lorcan's alert, worry immediately blossoming in his face. I'm shocked by how much relief there is in seeing that he still cares about her: it makes me feel whole, not lopsided.

'She's not ill, is she?'

'No, God, not that. But she's going to lose the house . . .'
I tell him about it, trying my hardest not to sound judgemental or accusatory. How Mum never quite managed to
pay off the mortgage, remortgaging instead, always scraping
by on just enough. Nick's divorce settlement was a blood-
bath, so he's not had much to put in the pot, and the lack of
contingency has left them with nowhere to go now he's lost
his money to Stephen Wright. Lorcan sits there, absorbing
my words, his eyes mournful. By the time I've finished he
looks like he might cry.

'Should I ring her?'

'And say what?'

He sits there, pensive, then takes a thoughtful sip of his
lime and soda, like he's playing for time.

'Say I'll lend her the money. No, I'll *give* her the money!'

'You can't do that!'

'Who says?' he asks, his face ablaze.

'It's loads. What, you'd buy the house and sign it over to
her?'

He waves an airy hand.

'However it has to be. Don't care, my accountant can
make a plan.'

All the times I risked believing him, before I finally learnt
it was too dangerous. The birthdays, the Christmases. The
parents' evenings – oddly, they stung the most.

'Don't just chuck out these grand promises! You don't

know how much it'll cost. You haven't asked your wife—'

'My cows,' he says, putting his glass down heavily, and staring at me, 'dance all over America. They dance in Texas, in Chicago, in bum fuck nowhere Indiana. If I want to make amends for my appalling decisions, I've got the right to do it.'

'Well Nick might have something to say about it,' I say. He can't just buy his way off the hook – it's not the way hooks work.

'Baldie might well have something to say, but I'm going to give it a good go. You getting in contact when you did . . .' He's still got that infectious excitability: the truth is, it would be amazing if he could save Mum the indignity of losing her beloved home. If she could see it as her rightful compensation for what's gone before then perhaps she'd be able to convince Nick? 'There's no such thing as a coincidence, Mia.'

'God, has AA made you all weirdy-woo? Of course there's such a thing as a coincidence.'

''Fraid not,' he says, steepling his long fingers under his chin. He looks surprisingly unravaged, considering the years of hard drinking. He's lined, but the lines work with the angular planes of his face, and his light dusting of grey stubble looks distinguished on him.

'Well thanks for clearing that up.'

He hugs me like he might never let me go.

'Am I allowed to call you?'

We're standing by my car, rain drizzling down.

'Yes.'

What if he doesn't? What if he says that, and then doesn't? The fear quivers through me, and yet – I think I'll survive. I think I'll still be glad I took the risk. He tips my face upwards.

'I will. I'll come and see you. I'll introduce you to Caroline. You have to let me know as soon as you know you're free to practise again.' He looks into my eyes, smiling. 'I'm . . . I'm so proud.'

I shake my head, ready to shake off the compliment like a dog shakes off water, but then I force myself to breathe it in instead.

'Thanks.' I squeeze his hand. 'Thanks for today.' I realize I'll have to just climb into the car. I give him a short, sharp hug. 'Bye, Dad,' I say, quick and low, jumping into the driver's seat, not looking back.

Chapter Twenty-Six

'Murr-lot,' declares Patrick, pouring an extravagant splash into a dingy-looking wine glass and swilling it around. Everything in this flat feels a bit bachelor-tastic. 'Ruby red, from the foot-hills of Tuscany, the grapes squeezed dry by fit peasants.'

He looks at me – a questioning sort of smile on his sweet face – and I sink more deeply into the broken-springed embrace of his velour sofa. It's the most uncomfortable thing in the world and the most comfortable thing in the world, all at the same time.

'Are you reading that off the back of the bottle?' He hands me the first glass and gingerly pours one for himself. 'Have a beer if you want a beer.'

'I'm keeping you company,' he says, chinking his glass against mine, and dropping his long limbs down onto the sofa. 'You look like a girl who needs company.'

I hook my feet over his lap, lean backwards against a cushion. I feel like I could sleep forever.

'*Your* company. Not any old rozzer's.'

'Think that's the nicest thing you've ever said to me,' he says.

'Don't say that!' I bat him with my cushion, and he pulls me close.

'Are you going to tell me about it?' Am I? Am I really? I look away, try to work out where I would start. He reaches for my face, turning it gently towards him. 'You look different, you know.'

'I look like a crone who hasn't slept since we last declared war on Germany.' I put some lipstick on in my rear-view mirror, tried to rescue my mascara: nothing worked. I nearly gave up on this evening and went to take refuge at Mum's, but I realized in the nick of time I was being ridiculous.

It's funny the way time concertinas with Patrick. Sometimes I feel like I've known him for months, years – light years even – whilst at other moments it feels like the slim sliver of weeks that it really is. Will I sound like damaged goods, remaindered stock that's been sold off cheap, if I tell him the whole sorry truth?

'No you don't. Can't explain it. But you look different.'

I unconsciously run my fingers over the contours of my face. That was one of the bizarre things about today, remembering the pieces of me that come directly from him. The angular triangles of my cheekbones, the expanse of forehead that I used to hate – a great big spam – my hairline lodged too far back on my head. Now I wonder if the reason I hated it was for the quiet reminder it gave me every time I looked in the mirror.

'I wasn't fishing for compliments,' I tell him. 'Are you really going to order a pizza?'

'Just say if you don't wanna talk about it. I'll see straight through you if you give me an hour-long defence of pepperoni.'

'I HATE pepperoni. It's made from dead dogs, surely?'

Patrick gives me a long look, then unfurls himself from the sofa. Bruises, an almost pretty greenish colour, are still visible on the left side of his face; every time I see them they shock me anew. How could anyone set out to do that to him? I resist the urge to reach out and stroke them, rage at their existence.

'I'll go and find my phone. Luigi,' he says, reaching for it, 'thirty-four-incher with extra pepperoni and a pepperoni salad.'

'Ask him if he can make me a pepperoni trilby.'

'Jaunty!'

Pizza is by no means my death-row dinner. It's greasy, fattening, all the things I hate, but I don't want to be a princess. I stack my crusts neatly on the side of my plate, roll off the leathery olives like I'm staging a miniature bowls tournament. Patrick's watching: I guiltily pick up a crust and nibble on it.

'I don't know where to start.'

'Let's start at the very beginning,' he says, sing-song, like Maria.

'*Now* you tell me you're a fan of musicals!'

He reaches for my hand, gluing us together with pizza grease. I look at him, too scared, too overwhelmed to start.

'Edited highlights then. *Match of the Day* style.' He stares back at me. 'Sorry, I didn't mean . . . I just want to try and understand, at least a bit.'

'You *do*.' It's funny, I feel like he gets it, the vibration of it, even if he doesn't know the cold, hard facts. 'He was everything to me . . .' I say eventually. 'He was James Bond and Peter Pan and Mr Benn.'

I lie back, put a cushion in his lap and look at the ceiling, twin streams of tears running down my cheeks as I start to unravel it for him. Of course you can never properly convey the past to a person who wasn't there. As I'm telling him, his arm wrapped around my body like the warmest scarf in the world, I find myself longing for a parallel universe in which he had been. Why did I make it so hard for myself? It always felt like it was all on me.

I stumble over bits – the Jim bits mainly – not wanting him to feel that he's competing with my ghosts. Jim and Lorcan: twin spectres. But, as I describe it, I realize how much Jim was a piece of Lorcan broken off and transformed – another man who couldn't be captured in the butterfly net of my wanting. It takes all my strength to tell him about the baby – the baby that was, but never was – and yet I somehow eke the words out from somewhere deep within myself. I haven't got much puff after that. I don't tell him the details of that prison visit, the words still too blistering, too emotionally incendiary, to fling into the atmosphere. Besides, this isn't an exam. It turns out that life isn't an exam. I look up at him when I've run out of words, shocked by the expression I find on his face.

'Hey! You don't need to cry.'

He doesn't say anything for a second.

'I'm not. I'm just . . . I'm just taking it in.' He gives me a half-smile, his eyes dark, almost bruised. 'Thinking about who I want to hit first.'

'Let's not have any more hitting,' I say, reaching up and touching the sea-green traces of the violence with the softest pads of my fingers. I'm cringing a bit, my insides crumpled and small like holiday washing at the bottom of a suitcase, but I know it's old shame that I don't need to lay claim to any more. I never did.

'I'm sorry,' he says gruffly, but softly, like he doesn't trust himself to say more.

'Thank you,' I say, my heart suddenly racing. 'I promise it's not going to be all about me. I want to hear about the dodgy priests and the communion wine and the sixth-form discos . . . and your dad. I want to know everything.'

'There's time,' he says, unexpectedly solemn.

'There is!' I say, knowing now why my heart was racing. I can do this. I can. 'I love you,' I mutter, my face turned away, my hair a curtain I'm hiding behind. I force myself to look at him: his face is hard to read. 'I love you,' I say, declamatory now. Fuck it. 'I love you. I don't care if you're not ready to say it' – that's a lie, I care loads – 'but still . . . I love you.' He's grinning now, his face split in two, his eyes shining. 'I love you, Patrick O'Leary.'

Chapter Twenty-Seven

Brendan's lovely face lights up like it's Christmas morning when I come through the door.

'How was the deodorant audition?' I ask, hugging him almost too hard.

My eyes flick around the waiting room as we pull apart. I can't risk indulging the sense I have of coming home.

'I think I fell into that dangerous middle ground of looking neither pongy enough nor squeaky-clean enough to convince real men to sign over their armpits.'

'Honestly – no imagination!'

'I know.' He's inspecting me from beneath those long eyelashes, looking for signs of trauma. There are no bruises, Christopher never laid a finger on me, but I think that Patrick was right when he said that something in my face has shifted with all of this.

'Do you know when you're properly coming back?'

I shake my head, not trusting myself to speak, look to

Judith's firmly closed door. I don't know if I'm coming back at all, but I don't tell Brendan that, simply accept the cup of hot pink tea he gives me and settle down to wait on the couch, just like a nervous patient anticipating their first session. Gemma didn't risk it, made sure I was the one doing the waiting. I give the sofa a useless sort of pat: her presence is so strong for me now that I'm sitting here.

Here's Judith now, clad in a pair of black-leather trousers which she carries off with aplomb, saying a warm goodbye to a couple I don't recognize. 'See you next week,' she says, and I feel a sharp pang beneath my ribcage. I'd be lying if I pretended I wasn't aching to come back. I've spent far too much of my life trying to outsmart disappointment by not admitting to myself I want things. Judith finally turns to me, giving me a cool smile.

'Come on through, Mia.'

I perch on the sofa, trying not to feel twelve years old. Judith and I look at each other, neither of us speaking.

'I'm really nervous,' I say, immediately feeling better for naming it instead of choking on it.

She finally smiles.

'Don't be. How are you?'

I look out of the window at that familiar view of the park, not quite trusting myself to speak.

'Amazing, terrible, happy, sad. If I had to do a psycho-metric test they'd definitely mark me down as a sociopath.'

Judith's smile reaches right through her this time.

'Not if they came to me for a second opinion. You look well, you know.'

'Thanks.'

'Love suits you,' she says drily.

'Judith, I'm sorry,' I say, my hands reaching towards her and landing in my lap. 'I know I let you down. I know I was dishonest and . . . and arrogant, but it wasn't because I'd lost respect for you. I just couldn't get off the train.'

And I'm not sure I'd even want to, if I had the last three months to live again, but I don't say that. She looks at me, reflective, gives a slow nod.

'When we banish parts of ourselves, they tend to come back to haunt us. I did try to get you to see that.'

'I know you did.' I try not to feel ashamed of how stubborn I was, how sure that I knew the way out of the forest. Scrub that — I was pretending they'd paved over the forest and put up a parking lot, to paraphrase Joni.

'Annie obviously won't be pursuing a complaint now.' She looks at me, serious. 'It sounds like you were incredibly brave.'

'I still couldn't save her—'

'No, you couldn't.'

Touché. Her smile is kind though.

'Seeing her dad die like that, on the tarmac . . .' I feel cold, shuddery, almost as if we're still in the dark car park. 'It was just . . . I can't even describe it.'

Judith covers my hand with hers, warmth flooding through me at her welcome touch.

'At least she's not trapped any more. Her life was utterly impossible. You're a big part of that. I'm still not entirely clear what his plan was?'

'Patrick reckons he held on to the papers – well, got Gemma to – so he'd have something over Stephen Wright's lot. He thought getting out of the way until the trial collapsed would be enough, but it was never going to be. I don't think it was America he was heading for either. No point running to somewhere with an extradition treaty.'

'Where would he have taken her?'

'Somewhere she'd never have come back from. Mexico, maybe . . . He was so determined not to leave her that he screwed the whole thing up, left them with no choice but to get some faceless hit man to wipe him out. They didn't know the police already had their hands on the documents.'

The rest of the family are back home now, the trial pending. Patrick's promised me he'll try to avoid calling Gemma as a witness, let the paper trail she gave him stand in for her, and I know he means it. I've kept in regular touch with Annie, but I'm in no position to be Gemma's therapist. I think about her every single day. I'm comforted by the fact that Annie says that, although Gemma is very quiet, she's talking to her about her feelings in a way she never did before.

'Like I said, you were incredibly brave.'

'It was just instinct in the end.'

Judith smiles.

'I've always wanted that for you, Mia. More heart, less head. You could do that for your patients, never for yourself.'

A tear escapes, despite my best efforts.

'Heart doesn't seem like such a problem now.'

'That's a good thing.'

I told her about Patrick in the email I sent her last week, deeply grateful for the fact he didn't let me fatally compromise myself that night in my flat, however much it stung my fragile ego. At least I could honestly say the relationship proper started once I was, at least nominally, off the case.

'I'd know when to keep it in check!' I say, my voice rising. I sound like Gemma, that wheedling desperation. 'I wouldn't go off piste. I promise you I'd treat supervision with the respect it deserves. Anything you want to impose on me . . .'

'I'm not here to punish you, Mia.' She steps back into silence, leaving me to chase my own tail for a minute or so. 'I think you should come back,' she says, smiling at me. 'It's not appropriate for you to go for the ACA board position, but, now I've seen you, I feel even more sure I'd like you back here.'

I almost can't get a breath into my lungs, the relief winding me.

'That's OK, I just want to concentrate on patients for a while. And – I don't want to take too much on.' God, those words still sound like Russian to an achievement junkie like me. I run them through my head, check I can claim them. Yes, they're mine to take home.

'You've got a lot to think about, what with everything that's happened. Have you seen Lorcan again?'

'Not yet, but I will. My mum's cooking him dinner to say thank you!' Judith giggles, her eyes wide.

'It all sounds rather marvellous!' she says, rubbing her hands. She pauses, thoughtful. 'I do think you should take a couple more weeks though. Personal therapy is also going to be very important.'

'I know.'

'I think you do.' We sit there for a few seconds, this silence the healing kind. 'The thing is, the ghosts can help us once we've made friends with them.'

'Once they've stopped howling and pushing us down the stairs, you mean?'

'Quite.'

'The bits where we break and heal are where we're strongest?'

'That's exactly what I mean, Mia.'

I pull my knees up so my feet are beneath me on the sofa, look out of the window at that familiar view of the park. I'm home.

Patrick's parked at a jaunty angle on a single yellow, his hazards flashing like disco lights. I slide into the passenger seat.

'I was hoping for a Panda,' I say, kissing him hello. 'You know; flashing blue sirens, go-faster stripes, the works.'

'Jeez, you're a hard woman to please. Have you not had enough excitement for one lifetime?'

We smile at each other, and I subtly inspect the bruises. Nearly gone, thank God – he's starting to look like he's just very, very bad at applying eyeliner.

'Seriously, do you mind driving? The train doesn't take long.'

'I only drank all that wine cos I was trying to get into your knickers. I'm fine to pace myself.'

'Thank you.'

It's the little things I'm discovering.

We park up outside Lysette's, but Patrick seems in no hurry to get out.

'So is he really tall, this Jim fella? You know, rippling muscles, manly chest?'

'Patrick, I haven't seen him for going on twenty years. Hopefully I won't see him for another twenty.'

He turns to look at me, face serious.

'You thought about him though, didn't you?'

I can hear it in his voice, the vulnerability: there was a time not so long ago when it would've made my flesh crawl. Not now. I look at the lighted windows of Lysette's little house, then turn back towards him, take his hand.

'I did, yeah, but it wasn't about him. It was my shit.' I hold his gaze, my own vulnerability surging upwards. 'He was a just a stand-in. Another man I couldn't really have.'

Patrick smiles, his body softening. *You can have me*, say his eyes. I trace his palm with my finger, and he reaches under the seat with his free hand.

'I got a bottle of that Merlot you liked. You know, the one the peasants trampled the grapes for, with their sweaty peasant feet.'

'I love a sweaty peasant,' I say, leaning across to kiss him.

Lysette hugs me tightly, then stands on tiptoes to embrace Patrick. He thrusts the bottle at her a little too hard. I love the fact that it's me alone who can detect his nerves, read his tiny tells. As he heads down the hall in front of us, Lysette mouths, 'He's HOT!' her sparkly eyes wide enough for me to know she's not just saying it.

The kitchen is full of children, Saffron in a pair of pyjamas with fluffy attached feet. She throws her arms around my legs, casting a suspicious scowl at Patrick, and begs me to tell her a bedtime story.

'Oh God, PLEASE will you go and read to her,' says Lysette. 'It's about an hour past bedtime but she wouldn't go up till you came. She's a nightmare when she's this overtired – she's like Lindsay Lohan after a three-day bender.'

I scoop her up, lifting her high enough so that she's in Patrick's eyeline.

'Before I tuck you in, I want you to meet my friend Patrick. He's lovely. I like him even more than you like Peppa Pig.' I look at Patrick. 'And that, my friend, is a compliment.'

'I'm honoured,' he says, then gives her chubby hand a respectful shake.

I drink more than I intend to, Lysette's right hand inching towards my glass with dangerous frequency. 'I'm just so glad you're all right,' she keeps saying, the words getting thicker with feeling as she gets tipsier. Ged and Patrick slip into an easy rhythm, going out for the odd fag on the patio (I didn't know Patrick was a social smoker – I decide not to mind) and ferrying the plates to and from the kitchen so me and Lysette don't have to raise a finger.

'He *is* lovely,' says Lysette in a stage whisper.

'I know,' I say, my eyes mapping her face, suddenly emotional. It's a face I've known so long, watched shift and transform; she's no less beautiful now, it's just a different breed of beautiful.

'I shouldn't tell you this, I'm sure you don't care, but I've been worrying about it since Saffron's party. He's much, much hotter than Jim. He looks a bit like a rattlesnake who's swallowed a turnip.' She mimes a straight line, and then a massive hump. 'He's as vain as ever, so he's determined to stay skinny, but he's got dad tum. He HATES it.'

I take a swig of Merlot, snorting with laughter that won't seem to stop. Lysette clutches my knee, choking with giggles. Soon we're both weeping with tears of laughter that are totally disproportionate to the joke, wine starting to trickle down the inside of my nose.

'What's the joke?' asks Patrick.

I look at him, trying not to seem like too much of a sap.

'Who's the joke,' I correct him. 'No one you need to worry about.'

ONE YEAR LATER

'Look at you!' I say, unable to keep the depth of feeling out of my voice. There she is on the couch, dead on time, her hair shorter, less straggly, a pair of black cords skimming her newfound curves. She's nearly fifteen now: womanliness suits her.

'OK, calm down. I'm not ten years old, Mia.'

'Sorry,' I say, standing before her. She smiles at me, tentative now, then gets up. We pause a second, and then we hug. It's sharp, intense – brief. Brendan's pretending not to track us, but his eyes keep darting upwards from his computer screen. He's seen me duck out of my room about one hundred times to see if she's arrived early.

Gemma throws a careful gaze around the room before she sits down, reorientating herself. I wonder if it seems almost insulting; nothing's changed, and yet everything's changed.

'This isn't a session,' I say, partly to acknowledge that fact.

'I'm really glad that you wanted to come and see me though.'
I pause, let us both settle. 'I've thought about you so much.'

She looks down at the rug.

'Have you?'

'I've always told you the truth, Gemma. I meant what I
said that night about keeping you in my heart.'

She looks up at me, her grey-blue eyes like lasers, searching
my face for truth in the way they always did. I'd forgotten
that gaze, so peculiar to her. The gaze that sees so much.

'That guy you told my mum about – the other therapist.
He's got a beard.'

'Michael Fassbender's got a beard. David Beckham has a
beard. Nothing wrong with beards.' She gives a little eye-
roll, a friendly one. 'Has it helped, having him to talk to?'

'Yeah, a bit.'

'I'm glad. I know nothing can take it away.' Her body
hunches in on itself, and I remind myself to stay the right side
of the line. I'm not her therapist. I'll have to say goodbye to
her in less than an hour: I don't want to open a trap door,
then leave her in the dark. 'I'm so sorry you had to go
through that, Gemma.'

She clamps her lower lip between her teeth, her eyes
cloudy and damp. She doesn't cry.

'He'd hate my school,' she says. 'And I'm doing drama for
GCSE, not maths.'

'Are you? I thought all those props you'd made were so
cool. I'm glad you're doing a subject you really like.'

'Yeah, when you were snooping,' she says, a big grin on

her face. The fact I went over there, the fact I tracked her down – she loves the proof it gave her. A win.

'I'm just glad we got you back,' I say, but she's not listening. She's staring at my left hand.

I splay it outwards so she can get a better look at my twinkly little diamond. It's so new that I can't stop staring at it. An unexpected surprise on our first anniversary, which, according to Patrick, dates back to the night of the 'horse piss wine'. I thought about taking the ring off for today's meeting, but I decided that the truth might set us free.

'I knew it!'

'You did. You're no fool, Gemma, but it wasn't true when you first said it. And I never, ever put him before my care for you.'

'Was true for him,' she says, smirking. 'At least he doesn't have a beard.'

'It's true. He's a beard-free zone.'

'Mum's got a boyfriend too,' she says, a flicker of pain in her face. 'She keeps saying' – she affects a grumpy voice – '"He's just a friend, Gemma," but I can totally tell.'

'Does it feel weird?'

Poor Annie. For all the lies and collusion, I still can't help thinking she deserves a chance of romantic happiness. They've moved out of the big house, rented a small flat in Wandsworth. Maybe escaping the gilded cage has had some unexpected benefits.

'Yeah, well. I've got one too.'

'You've got a boyfriend?' She nods, grinning. 'I hope he's

worthy of you,' I add, a little too fast. I feel a squeeze in my heart, a sense memory of how very long it took me to learn the difference. I have to trust that beardy therapist – a man whose credentials I checked with the zeal of Homeland Security recruiting an operative – can guide her through that minefield.

'Jeez, Mia, you talk like it's the eighteenth century sometimes.' She pretends to doff what I'm sure is a three-cornered hat. 'Forsooth!'

'Forsooth indeed!' I say. 'It's only because I care about you.'

'We're doing *Top Girls*,' she says, seemingly ignoring me, her eyes telling me she's taken it in. 'At school. Me and Caitlin and Leyla.' She smiles as she says it – a real smile, that says real friends, before reaching into her bag. The rucksack's long been consigned to an evidence log, Stephen's life sentence under way. This new bag is black leather with gold studs, two smart pockets on the front. 'I brought you a present. Is that allowed under the rules of our Ann-ual Vis-it?'

I cock my head.

'Er. Depends how much I like it.'

It's wrapped in pink tissue paper, a wonky green bow tied on top, like one of Saffron's more outlandish up-dos. I open it gingerly, instantly regretting my joke. What if I don't like it? She'll know: she always does.

It's a fine wool scarf, large enough to wrap right round me, a grey-blue colour that matches her eyes.

'I thought you looked cold sometimes,' she says softly. 'In your big fat chair.'

'Thank you,' I say, my voice cracking now. 'I love it.'

'Thing about me is, I've got excellent taste,' she says, her eyes never wavering from mine.

'I'm glad to hear it.'

'Bye, Mia. See you next year. Better start thinking about my present.'

And with that, she stands up and gathers her coat, shutting the door behind her with a quiet click.

Acknowledgements

Thank you to my editor Jo Dickinson, for continuing on the journey with me! This book wouldn't be here without you. Thank you to the Simon and Schuster team for welcoming me into the fold. Huge thanks to Mary Tomlinson for a thoughtful, helpful copy edit.

A huge thank you to my incomparable agent Sheila Crowley, and the wider team at Curtis Brown. Rebecca Ritchie, Alice Lutyens and the foreign rights team – you're all amazing. A big thank you to Lucinda Prain for both excellent additional agenting and excellent gossip (and to the rest of the Casarotto team).

Thank you to Anne Mensah for legendary plot wrangling, above and beyond the call of duty, as always. I literally couldn't have done it (and many other things) without you. Thank you to Caroline Henry for reading about a million drafts and cheerleading all the way. Thank you to Sophia Parsons for a therapist's perspective (and for the ongoing

Ron Swanson love in). Thank you to Matthew Read for stating the obvious, which was somehow not obvious. Thank you to Ben McPherson for a late stage waffle trim. Thank you to legal eagle extraordinaire Caroline Haughey for brilliant suggestions and fact checking – I'm so lucky to have met you. Thank you also to Jenny Parrott for her fantastic help. Thanks too to Kitty – for everything. Thank you to the Brighton Massive – (cousin) Damian Barr, cousin Mike, Alex Heminsley and the irreplaceable and lovely Carol Biss.

Thank you too to my family cheerleaders for always being excited enough to read a new book when there are still commas in the most curious places – Mutt, Caitlin, Leyla.

Thank you lastly to the amazing women I'm blessed to call my best friends. My blue earrings make my lobes ache, but they're always the first ones I choose. You're all in here and in my heart.